The B↑ZARRO

STARTER KIT

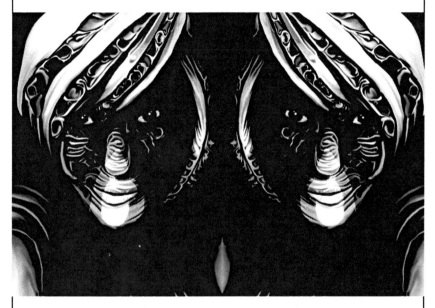

AN INTRODUCTION TO THE BIZARRO GENRE

BIZARRO BOOKS

Portland * Seattle * Baltimore

A BIZARRO BOOK
www.bizarrocentral.com

BIZARRO BOOKS
205 NE BRYANT
PORTLAND, OR 97211

IN COOPERATION WITH:

ERASERHEAD PRESS
SWALLOWDOWN BOOKS
LAZY FASCIST PRESS
AFTERBIRTH BOOKS
RAW DOG SCREAMING PRESS

ISBN: 1-936383-20-9

Cover design by Carlton Mellick III

Edited by: Team Bizarro

Printed in the USA.

TABLE OF CONTENTS

DEFINING BIZARRO

1. Bizarro, simply put, is the genre of the weird.

2. Bizarro is the literary equivalent to the cult section at the video store.

3. Like cult movies, Bizarro is sometimes surreal, sometimes goofy, sometimes bloody, and sometimes borderline pornographic.

4. Bizarro often contains a certain cartoon logic that, when applied to the real world, creates an unstable universe where the bizarre becomes the norm and absurdities are made flesh.

5. Bizarro strives not only to be strange, but fascinating, thought-provoking, and, above all, fun to read.

6. Bizarro was created by a group of small press publishers in response to the increasing demand for (good) weird fiction and the increasing number of authors who specialize in it.

7. Bizarro is:

Franz Kafka meets Joe Bob Briggs

Dr. Seuss of the post-apocalypse

Alice in Wonderland for adults

Japanese animation directed by David Lynch

8. For more information on the bizarro genre, visit Bizarro Central at:

www.bizarrocentral.com

RUSSELL EDSON

LOCATION:
Connecticut

STYLE OF BIZARRO:
Surrealistic Prose Poetry

BOOKS BY EDSON:
Ceremonies in Bachelor Space
A Stone is Nobody's
The Very Thing That Happens
The Brain Kitchen
What a Man Can See
The Childhood Of An Equestrian
The Clam Theater
The Intuitive Journey and Other Works
With Sincerest Regrets
The Falling Sickness (plays)
The Wounded Breakfast
The Reason Why the Closet-Man Is Never Sad
Gulping's Recital
Tick Tock (short stories)
The Song of Percival Peacock: a novel
The Tunnel: Selected Poems
The Tormented Mirror
The Rooster's Wife
See Jack

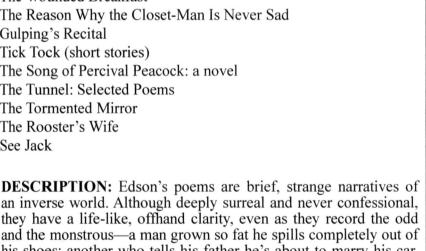

DESCRIPTION: Edson's poems are brief, strange narratives of an inverse world. Although deeply surreal and never confessional, they have a life-like, offhand clarity, even as they record the odd and the monstrous—a man grown so fat he spills completely out of his shoes; another who tells his father he's about to marry his car. Edson writes fables, some grim, some hopelessly funny, rich with non-sequiturs and transforming, mysterious connections. The work is original, a lyric mix of Dante and Warner Brothers.

—Marianne Boruch

ERASING AMYLOO

A father with a huge eraser erases his daughter.

When he finishes there's only a red smudge on the wall.

His wife says, where is Amyloo?

She's a mistake, I erased her.

What about all her lovely things? asks his wife.

I'll erase them too.

All her pretty clothes? . . .

I'll erase her closet, her dresser —shut up about Amyloo! Bring your head over here and I'll erase Amyloo out of it.

The husband rubs his eraser on his wife's forehead, and as she begins to forget she says, hummm, I wonder whatever happened to Amyloo? . . .

Never heard of her, says her husband.

And you, she says, who are you? You're not Amyloo, are you? I don't remember your being Amyloo. Are you my Amyloo, whom I don't remember anymore? . . .

Of course not, Amyloo was a girl. Do I look like a girl?

. . . I don't know, I don't know what anything looks like anymore . . .

OH MY GOD, I'LL NEVER GET HOME

A piece of a man had broken off in a road. He picked it up and put it in his pocket.

As he stooped to pick up another piece he came apart at the waist.

His bottom half was still standing. He walked over on his elbows and grabbed the seat of his pants and said, legs go home.

But as they were going along his head fell off. His head yelled, legs stop.

And then one of his knees came apart. But meanwhile his heart had dropped out of his trunk.

As his head screamed, legs turn around, his tongue fell out.

Oh my God, he thought, I'll never get home.

BABY PIANOS

THE LARGE THING

A piano had made a huge manure. Its handler hoped the lady of the house wouldn't notice.

But the lady of the house said, what is that huge darkness?

The piano just had a baby, said the handler.

But I don't see any keys, said the lady of the house.

They come later, like baby teeth, said the handler.

Meanwhile the piano had dropped another huge manure.

What's that, cried the lady of the house, surely not another baby?

Twins, said the handler.

They look more like cannon balls than baby pianos, said the lady of the house.

The piano dropped another huge manure.

Triplets, smiled the handler . . .

A large things comes in.

Go out, Large Thing, says someone.

The Large Thing goes out, and comes in again.

Go out, Large Thing, and stay out, says someone.

The Large Thing goes out, and stays out.

Then that same someone who has been ordering the Large Thing out begins to be lonely, and says, come in, Large Thing.

But when the Large Thing is in, that same someone decides it would be better if the Large Thing would go out.

Go out, Large Thing, says this same someone.

The Large Thing goes out.

Oh, why did I say that? says the someone, who begins to be lonely again.

But meanwhile the Large Thing has come back in anyway.

Good, I was just about to call you back, says the same someone to the Large Thing.

THE ADVENTURES OF A TURTLE

THE WOUNDED BREAKFAST

The turtle carries his house on his back. He is both the house and the person of that house.

But actually, under the shell is a little room where the true turtle, wearing long underwear, sits at a little table. At one end of the room a series of levers sticks out of slots in the floor, like the controls of a steam shovel. It is with these that the turtle controls the legs of his house.

Most of the time the turtle sits under the sloping ceiling of his turtle room reading catalogues at the little table where a candle burns. He leans on one elbow, and then the other. He crosses one leg, and then the other. Finally he yawns and buries his head in his arms and sleeps.

If he feels a child picking up his house he quickly douses the candle and runs to the control levers and activates the legs of his house and tries to escape.

If he cannot escape he retracts the legs and withdraws the so-called head and waits. He knows that children are careless, and that there will come a time when he will be free to move his house to some secluded place, where he will relight his candle, take out his catalogues and read until at last he yawns. Then he'll bury his head in his arms and sleep . . . That is, until another child picks up his house . . .

A huge shoe mounts up from the horizon, squealing and grinding forward on small wheels, even as a man sitting to breakfast on his veranda is suddenly engulfed in a great shadow, almost the size of the night . . .

He looks up and sees a huge shoe ponderously mounting out of the earth.

Up in the unlaced ankle-part an old woman stands at a helm behind the great tongue curled forward; the thick laces dragging like ships' rope on the ground as the huge thing squeals and grinds forward; children everywhere, they look from the shoelace holes, they crowd about the old woman, even as she pilots this huge shoe over the earth . . .

Soon the huge shoe is descending the opposite horizon, a monstrous snail squealing and grinding into the earth . . .

The man turns to his breakfast again, but sees it's been wounded, the yolk of one of his eggs is bleeding . . .

BRINGING A DEAD MAN BACK INTO LIFE

The dead man is introduced back into life. They take him to a country fair, to a French restaurant, a round of late night parties . . . He's beginning to smell.

They give him a few days off in bed.

He's taken to a country fair again; a second engagement at the French restaurant; another round of late night parties . . . No response . . .

They brush the maggots away . . . That terrible smell! . . . No use . . .

What's wrong with you?

. . . No use . . .

They slap his face. His cheek comes off; bone underneath, jaws and teeth . . .

Another round of late night parties . . . Dropping his fingers . . . An ear falls off . . . Loses a foot in a taxi

. . . No use . . . The smell . . . Maggots everywhere!

Another round of late night parties. His head comes off, rolls on the floor. A woman stumbles on it, an eye rolls out. She screams.

No use . . . Under his jacket nothing but maggots and ribs . . .

No use . . .

APE

You haven't finished your ape, said mother to father, who had monkey hair and blood on his whiskers.

I've had enough monkey, cried father.

You didn't eat the hands, and I went to all the trouble to make onion rings for its fingers, said mother.

I'll just nibble on its forehead, and then I've had enough, said father.

I stuffed its nose with garlic, just like you like it, said mother.

Why don't you have the butcher cut these apes up? You lay the whole thing on the table every night; the same fractured skull, the same singed fur; like someone who died horribly. These aren't dinners, these are post-mortem dissections.

Try a piece of its gum, I've stuffed its mouth with bread, said mother.

Ugh, it looks like a mouth full of vomit. How can I bite into its cheek with bread spilling out of its mouth? cried father.

Break one of the ears off, they're so crispy, said mother.

I wish to hell you'd put underpants on these apes; even a jockstrap, screamed father.

Father, how dare you insinuate that I see the ape as anything more thn simple meat, screamed mother.

Well what's with this ribbon tied in a bow on its privates? screamed father.

Are you saying that I am in love with this vicious creature?

That I would submit my female opening to this brute? That after we had love on the kitchen floor I would put him in the oven, after breaking his head with a frying pan; and then serve him to my husband, that my husband might eat the evidence of my infidelity . . . ?

I'm just saying that I'm damn sick of ape every night, cried father.

THE REASON WHY THE CLOSET MAN IS NEVER SAD

COUNTING SHEEP

A scientist has a test tube full of sheep. He wonders if he should try to shrink a pasture for them.

They are like grains of rice.

He wonders if it is possible to shrink something out of existence.

He wonders if the sheep are aware of their tininess, if they have any sense of scale. Perhaps they just think the test tube is a glass barn . . .

He wonders what he should do with them; they certainly have less meat and wool than ordinary sheep. Has he reduced their commercial value?

He wonders if they could be used as a substitute for rice, a sort of woolly rice . . .

He wonders if he just shouldn't rub them into a red paste between his fingers.

He wonders if they're breeding, or if any of them have died.

He puts them under a microscope and falls asleep counting them . . .

This is the house of the closet-man. There are no rooms, just hallways and closets.

Things happen in rooms. He does not like things to happen . . . Closets, you take things out of closets, you put things into closets, and nothing happens . . .

Why do you have such a strange house?

I am the closet-man, I am either going or coming, and I am never sad.

But why do you have such a strange house?

I am never sad . . .

ATHENA VILLAVERDE

LOCATION:
Toronto

STYLE OF BIZARRO:
Cute Punk

BOOKS BY VILLAVERDE:
Starfish Girl
Godzilla Girl
Clockwork Girl & Other Stories
Squid Girl
Plague Girl
Cthulhu Girl

DESCRIPTION: Athena Villaverde writes sexy and weird bizarro fantasy tales, often set in wastelands populated by colorful and magical characters. Part cyber-punk, part urban fantasy. Cute and disturbing.

INTERESTS: Tarot, knitting, fetish fashion, kawaii noir, chaos magick, hair dye, drawing and painting, dancing, Japanese anime, cult films, genetic mutations, parasites, survivalism, cosplay, steam-punk, gothic lolita, mythology, burlesque, body modification, new wave, ska, punk rock.

INFLUENCES: David Bowie, Hayao Miyazaki, Francesca Lia Block, Anais Nin, Jim Henson, Don Hertzfeldt, Salvador Dali, Vivienne Westwood, H.R. Giger, Edward Gorey, Robert Smith, Rube Goldberg, Alejandro Jodorowsky, Neil Gaiman, Tim Burton, Terry Gilliam, Guillermo Del Toro, Bjork.

WEBSITE:
www.athenavillaverde.com

CLOCKWORK GIRL

CHAPTER ONE

The clockwork girl felt the box scratch the top of her head and the bottom of her toes as the cardboard shifted around her. Even in the light of her breast's glowing filament, all she could see was the cardboard in front of her nose. She imagined faces staring back at her in the swirl-patterned paper. Zipties bound her ankles and wrists to the box. She couldn't move but she could still imagine. She had lost all concept of time. The faces she imagined scared her.

"Open this one next," said a woman's voice.

"Be careful with that, it's fragile," said another, deeper voice.

The box started to shake.

"Don't shake it. I said, it's fragile."

Scratching noises near her stomach. The clockwork girl blinked, adjusting her lenses to the brightly lit room as the box was torn apart. Beams of colored light glittered against her metal skin. Lying on her back, strapped into the box, all she could see was the high ceiling, its warm orange paint and dark wooden beams, the tip of a Christmas tree, a corn-husk angel on top. Then a girl's face. It was the first real face she had ever known. She instantly loved that face, jet black hair, big brown eyes.

"What is it?" said the girl, turning to her parents.

"A companion for you. A clockwork girl," said the mother.

"Holy shit! You got a tick-tock," said her brother.

The girl stroked her silver painted fingernails slowly across the etched brass skin of the clockwork girl, her light bulb breasts, her oval belly. The clockwork girl felt an electric pulse through her body as she was touched. The black-haired girl looked at her tenderly. It was as if she knew what was going through the clockwork girl's mind, how afraid and alone she felt locked inside the box. The young girl took out a pocket knife and slashed the zipties.

"This is a big responsibility," said the mother, "but your father and I feel you're ready. Don't let us down."

"She's a slave. You can make her do whatever you want," said the brother.

"She's a person?" said the girl.

"She is a toy, like your doggie," said the father.

"That means, inside, she's a real girl . . ."

"No, not anymore. Only her brain is human. They remove the brains from less fortunate girls and put them into mechanical bodies, transforming them into very special toys for nice privileged girls such as yourself. It's very sophisticated technology, and very expensive."

"This is wrong . . ." said the girl.

"Marisol, be grateful to your father. If it were not for him you would not have all of the wonderful toys that you have," said the mother.

"But I don't want a human toy, it's not right. She's a person."

The father gave Marisol a stern look and she knew better than to keep talking. The girl's brother snickered.

"Would anyone like some buñuelos de viento?" said the mother. She lifted her hand slowly and waved with one finger to the maid standing in the corner of the room holding a tray of Christmas cookies. Her finger drooped under the weight of a giant amber scarab ring.

The room was warm and festive. Christmas lights hung in the arched doorways. The smell of fresh tamales and arroz con pollo filled the air. Poinsettia flowers as big as patio umbrellas lined the walls. Servants stood in the wings holding platters of champagne and ready to assist if anything was needed. In the center of the room was a large tree with gifts clustered around the base. None of the boxes were as big as the one that the clockwork girl had emerged from.

Marisol took one of the cookies that her mother offered. It was shaped like a snowflake and just as delicate. She held it out to the clockwork girl. Marisol's brown eyes told the clockwork girl she should take it, but before she could move the mother snatched it from her hands.

"Ah! No food. She doesn't need that, she just needs winding," said the mother.

"Yes, it is very important that you wind her each day," said the father.

"She doesn't eat or sleep, the clockwork keeps her alive. But you must be certain to wind her each day or she will die," said the mother. She placed the cookie back on the tray where it crumbled into powdered sugar dust and she waved the maid away. "But never mind that right now. Come, open some more of your presents."

The girl glanced over at the stack of brightly wrapped boxes under the tree and her brother climbing amongst them, shaking each one next to his ear.

Then Marisol looked back at the clockwork girl. She had a large key on her back like fairy wings. Marisol reached out and took the clockwork girl's hand in her own, and the doll smiled at her.

"We have to take her back to the factory. I can't believe that you thought that turning a human girl into a toy for me was a good idea. It is sick and wrong."

"Marisol Yvonne Reyes-Jimenez, don't talk to your father that way," said her mother.

"We are not taking her back," said the father.

"Why not?"

"Because I said so. Do you know how many children are begging their parents for toys like this? Don't you understand how good you have it? Stop being an ungrateful brat and open the rest of your gifts," said the father.

"You aren't listening to me. I am telling you that we have to help this poor girl. What you've done to her isn't right and there's no way I am keeping a girl as a toy."

"She's not a girl anymore, she's clockwork. This is a very special model, one of a kind. Not just anyone can get one of these. Once you show her off to all your friends you'll be thanking me that you have such a generous father who gives you nice things."

Marisol opened her mouth to say something but the mother gripped her by the knee and whispered, "If you want to help her then you will take care of her. This is what I mean by responsibility. If we take her back to the factory she will be disassembled. She will die."

Ignoring her mother, Marisol led the clockwork girl out of the room by tugging on her arm. The toy girl's hip joints squeaked quietly as she walked, the clockwork gears in her chest ticked a little faster.

CHAPTER TWO

The toy room was two levels high. The first floor was a labyrinth of hallways leading into smaller chambers, each decorated with unique themes. The upper level had a glass floor so Marisol could peer down into each of the rooms below like a giant doll house.

There was a Japanese animation room decorated pink, filled with dolls with big eyes and funny cute stuffed animals; a pony room with toy ponies of every size and color; an aquatic room where the walls on all four sides were aquariums filled with tropical fish; a tea party room straight out of Alice in Wonderland; a dress-up room filled with costumes; a book room; and many others. The ceiling of the second level was a large dome upon which danced an image of the night sky like a planetarium.

The clockwork girl followed Marisol up to the second level, her brass feet clicking along the glass floor.

"What is your name?" Marisol asked the clockwork girl.

The doll stared back at her blankly, her eyes spun like bicycle wheels.

"What were you called before you were turned into a doll?"

"I don't know," said the clockwork girl, her voice sounded like a theramin, "I don't remember anything before the toy shop. In the toy shop, I wasn't called anything."

"Well, you need a name. How about I call you Lucilla?"

The clockwork girl frowned.

"Okay, how about Marcella?"

The clockwork girl tilted her head to the left with a squeak and said, "Definitely not."

"So what should I call you?" asked Marisol.

The clockwork girl looked down, she was standing above the aquatic room and she could see baby sharks circling in the tank below her feet.

"Pichi," she said.

Marisol laughed, "Okay, Pichi."

Pichi clapped her hands together and smiled, the sound of her hands clapping like cymbals. Then she was suddenly knocked off of her feet, something slamming into her from behind, and she toppled face-first into the glass. The baby sharks scattered beneath her.

"Maki!" Marisol yelled.

Pichi rolled over and came face to face with a giant drooling dog. Marisol ran over behind the dog and pulled it back by one of the spring links in its neck. The dog had gray fluffy fur covering its face and eyes. Its neck was a giant coiled spring. The dog's body was a patchwork amalgam of different types of fur, some long and some short, all different colors. From its body four more springs extended, acting as legs, and its tail was a wagging antenna. Pichi was scared for a moment but encouraged by the way the dog submitted under Marisol's strength.

"Don't mind Maki," Marisol said, "he's super friendly once he gets to know people."

Pichi got to her feet and carefully approached the dog. He sniffed her fingers and the sensation of his whiskers made the tiny lights on her knuckles flicker.

Marisol took Pichi to an empty room in the labyrinth. She told the clockwork girl that it would be her room and she would help her decorate it however she wanted.

"No sharks," said Pichi.

"Okay, you got it," said Marisol. She smiled, "We are going to be best friends."

"Time for bed," Marisol's mother said from the doorway to the toy room.

Marisol hooked her arm through Pichi's and the two girls walked out to meet the mother.

"Pichi is coming to bed with me," said Marisol.

"Toys must stay in the toy room," said the mother, "you know that."

"But she'll get lonely," said Marisol.

"She's just a toy, she doesn't get lonely," said the mother. She took Marisol's arm and carefully pulled it away from the clockwork girl.

"Goodnight Pichi," Marisol called after her, as the mother dragged the daughter down the hallway. "Maki will keep you company."

Pichi walked back to her empty room and lay on the floor, staring up at the blue twinkling night sky through her glass ceiling, until Maki came across the second level and sat on top of the room, blocking her view.

CHAPTER THREE

"Keep your eyes closed," Marisol said. The clockwork girl sat still while Marisol wound her up. "I'm almost done."

Pichi could feel the springs inside herself tightening like a corset as Marisol turned her key. The turning slowed and the clockwork girl felt Marisol brace her feet against something on the floor in order to gain the leverage nec-

essary to complete the final few turns.

This was the game that they played each morning. Marisol would come to the toy room after breakfast to wind Pichi up. She had to keep her eyes closed until she felt the final click of her key. Then Marisol would spin her around and scramble out through the labyrinth of the play rooms, playing hide and seek. Pichi was always fastest when first wound up so it was fun for Marisol to see if she could outrun her and hide before she got caught.

Pichi sped through the rooms, on little wheels that she could pop out of the bottom of her feet like roller skates. It was easy for Marisol to tell where Pichi was because of the whirring of her skates and the clatter of things she carelessly knocked over in her wake. Marisol held back her giggles and crept on tip toes through the rooms managing to avoid Pichi at every turn. Sometimes when they played this game, Marisol would climb to the glass level and watch Pichi spin through the labyrinth for a long time, unable to find her. Pichi never liked it when Marisol played that way.

Marisol crawled on all fours through a tiny door in the tea party room into the butterfly room. The butterfly room was filled with butterflies. There were monarchs and blue lilas and nymphflies and when Marisol entered the room they alighted on her arms and head and shoulders. That's when Pichi caught up with her, rolled too fast through the corridor and accidentally crashed right into Marisol.

Marisol fell over and Pichi landed on top of her. Butterflies scattered everywhere, filling the room with their rainbow colored wings.

"It's so beautiful," said Marisol, lying on her back looking up at the dancing wings.

"You're beautiful," replied Pichi, still lying on top of Marisol, staring at her pink heart-shaped lips.

CHAPTER FOUR

The first time that Pichi realized she was in love with Marisol was the time that Marisol told her about magic.

"Do you believe in magic?" asked Marisol.

"I don't know," said Pichi.

"I once met an old gypsy woman on the street in Oaxaca," said Marisol.

Marisol took a sugar cube out of her pocket.

"She told me if you write your wish on the sugar cube and put it in water it will come true."

Marisol handed a pencil to Pichi and instructed her to write on top of the sugar cube. Pichi had to write very small to fit the words on top of the cube. When she was done she handed the cube to Marisol who held it tightly between her fingers as she muttered some magical words. Then she dropped the cube into the cup of water and told Pichi to hold her hand over the cup.

When Pichi lifted her hand away from the cup after the sugar had dissolved, the words that she had written appeared in the palm of her hand: *I wish I were a real girl again.*

Marisol leaned over and saw the writing on Pichi's hand and gave her a hug. "You're still a real girl," Marisol whispered into her clockwork ear.

All the lights the on Pichi's body glowed. She could feel Marisol's heart beating against the ticking gears in her own chest, Marisol's small breasts squishing against her own hard glass lightbulbs, the empty space between their flat bellies. Pichi knew that she would love Marisol forever.

CHAPTER FIVE

In the middle of the night, Pichi snuck out of the toy room and into Marisol's bedroom. She hadn't been out of the toy room since the first night she arrived and was worried that she really didn't know where Marisol's room was. The house was dark and the ceilings were high, the hallways seemed cavernous. In the dim light, she crept past each door and took care not to make any noise and she peeked inside each one, nervous that her squeaking joints would give her away.

The first room she found was filled with tropical birds. All the furniture was covered in feathers. The birds heard her open the door and stirred from their sleep. Some of them started to sing and a few of them flapped their wings loudly. She quickly closed the door and ran softly to the next door. It was locked. She kept going down a wrought iron spiral staircase and past a giant stuffed tiger whose eyes shone like it was alive.

When she finally discovered Marisol's room, the girl was asleep inside. Pichi crept to the edge of the bed and stared at the sleeping girl. Her face looked so gentle in her sleep. The toy girl reached out and rubbed her metal finger along the sleeping girl's arm. Pichi liked the way her skin was soft and flexible.

Then Marisol's eyes popped open.

"Pichi?" Marisol said rubbing her eyes.

"Hi."

"What are you doing out of the toy room?"

"I missed you."

Mariol sat up in her bed and stretched her arms out and yawned. "I missed you too," she said slowly through her yawn.

Pichi watched Marisol stare off into space for a few minutes looking like she was going to fall back asleep.

"So what do you want to do?" asked Marisol.

"I don't know."

"Want to play dragon?"

"What's that?"

"Climb under the covers, I'll get the flashlights. We pretend like we are fighting dragons."

"I don't need a flashlight. I have lights on my fingers."

The two girls played late into the night laughing and whispering. It was a happy secret, and no one ever found out about their rendezvous. Each night after that first time, Pichi would sneak out after midnight and Marisol would wait for her. Sometimes Marisol would fall asleep with her arms around Pichi, her dark hair tickling her metal skin and making her lights flicker.

It was hard for Pichi to leave the bed before the parents woke up in the morning, because the girl's warm sleeping body wrapped around her brass skin made her feel more alive. It was as if she could feel the blood pulsing through her own wires and gears, like they had merged into one creature. She wanted to stay that way forever but she knew that the mother wouldn't like it if she ever found out about Pichi sneaking out of the toy room.

CHAPTER SIX

"I know a game we can play," said Marisol's brother, Miguel.

"We don't want to play with you Miguel," said Marisol.

"But it's a lot of fun, I used to do it with all my tick-tocks," said Miguel.

"Okay, what is it?"

"You have to trust me okay?"

"Okay."

"First, you have to tie her up."

"Tie her up?"

"Yes, otherwise the game won't work."

"Is it okay if I tie you up?" Marisol asked Pichi.

Pichi was distracted. She hadn't heard anything that they had said because she was too busy admiring what Marisol had chosen to wear today. Her dress looked like it was made out of giant flower petals and it twirled as she walked. Marisol wrapped the rope around her hands tightening them in place.

Miguel stood behind Pichi and after Marisol had bound Pichi's arms he held her key in place so that it couldn't turn for a couple of seconds. When he released it, her body jerked around wildly.

Pichi was disoriented. She wasn't sure what they were doing.

"You're hurting her," said Marisol.

"She can't feel it," he said, "trust me, I've done this hundreds of times with tick-tocks."

"No. You have to stop."

Miguel grabbed Pichi's key to do it again, but Marisol slapped his hand away.

"Fine. Have it your way," Miguel

said, "You never were any fun anyway."

"Come on Pichi, I'm sorry he is such a jerk," said Marisol taking Pichi by the hand. Pichi still wasn't sure what just happened to her.

CHAPTER SEVEN

One morning Marisol didn't come to the toy room after breakfast. Pichi waited. She climbed up to the second level and looked into every chamber in the toy room to make sure that Marisol wasn't hiding. Eventually, she couldn't search anymore because her clockwork had wound down so much she was running out of energy.

When Marisol finally showed up, Pichi glared, "Where were you?"

"What do you mean?"

"You didn't come at the normal time."

"What's the big deal? I come when I want to."

"But I need winding."

"I wound you up. You're fine."

Pichi wondered what was wrong with Marisol. She had never treated her that way before. She figured it was probably just her parents getting after her about something again.

CHAPTER EIGHT

The night of the full moon, Pichi and Marisol snuck outside in the middle of the night and went to the garden. They ran around naked under the stars. They climbed trees. Marisol bruised her knees and scraped her elbows. Pichi wasn't at all good at climbing, her mechanical body was not very agile.

"Did you see that?" Marisol asked.

"See what?"

"Fairies,"

"I don't see anything . . ."

"Hello, Queen Mab, Queen of the Fairies," Marisol said to a rose. "We are honored that you are in our presence."

Pichi remained quiet. She wasn't sure who Marisol was talking to.

"Please visit us in our sleep and grant our wishes."

"But I don't sleep," said Pichi.

"Shhh, you'll scare her away," Marisol said and she gently held her hand palm up in front of the rose.

Pichi switched her lenses and leaned in closer, but still didn't see anything.

"Queen Mab wants us to dance for her," said Marisol, taking off her nightgown.

Marisol's skin was pale and gleamed in the light. Her dark hair fell past her waist covering her like a shawl. Pichi couldn't imagine there was anyone more beautiful than Marisol. Marisol did cartwheels down the garden path and started swinging her arms about, jumping over small plants and swinging from low tree branches. Then it started to rain. Marisol danced in the rain. Pichi stood there feeling the water seep through her brass skin and drip through her gears which ticked steadily. Marisol danced faster, her chest heaving in and out, a puff of her breath clouding the cool night air.

Marisol grabbed Pichi's hands and started to spin. She spun faster and faster until they both got dizzy, lost their footing and fell on the ground. Sitting on the ground it looked like only Pichi and Marisol were sitting still and everything else was still spinning around them. Pichi felt like they were the only two people in the world.

She saw Marisol's face turned toward the sky, her mouth open, rain drops bouncing off her teeth. And Pichi leaned over and kissed Marisol on the cheek. Marisol snapped her head to the side and stared straight into Pichi's bicycle wheel eyes. Pichi felt a tightness in her stomach. She thought she might throw up. She wasn't sure what Marisol's stare meant. She looked away, looked down at her hands. She suddenly felt naked even though she never wore any clothes.

"We should go back inside," Marisol said, her voice was flat and distant.

Pichi didn't say anything, she just stood up and offered Marisol her hand to help her stand up. Marisol pushed Pichi's hand aside and jumped to her feet.

"I'll race you there," she said, and grabbing her nightgown with one hand she took off running, her pale bottom glowing in the moonlight.

CHAPTER NINE

Pichi sat in the toy room waiting for Marisol to arrive. It felt like she had waited an eternity for Marisol. She was extra excited this morning because she had a surprise for Marisol.

While Marisol slept, Pichi came up with the idea to make Marisol a special toy. She collected bits of Maki's fur and some metal parts from toys that are never used and an old doll's body. She used glue and paint and created a little doll with a skull head and wings on its back. It had silver paint on its fingernails because that was Marisol's favorite color. On its chest was a little red glowing heart made out of a bottle-

cap that Pichi had found the night they went outside in the garden. In his hand he held a long sword made out of a ruler with a light attached to it.

When Marisol arrived, Pichi could hardly contain her excitement. After she was wound up she told Marisol to close her eyes and hold out her hands. Then she carefully placed the doll in her palms.

When Marisol opened her eyes, her mouth sprang open and she wrinkled her nose.

"Ew, what is this trash?" she said.

"I made a doll for you," Pichi said smiling. "He has a sword. He can help us slay dragons."

"Is this Maki's fur glued to his head?"

Pichi nodded her head proudly.

"That's gross!"

Pichi frowned.

"And what is this piece of metal? Is this from my toy train? You ruined my toy train? That was one of my favorite toys. You ruined it! You ruined everything!" Marisol threw the doll on the ground and ran out of the room.

Pichi stood there, looking down at the doll. It did look like trash. She wondered how she ever thought that Marisol would like it. She was sorry that she ruined everything. She wanted to cry but no tears came.

CHAPTER TEN

Pichi was distressed because Marisol hadn't come to the toy room yet. She could feel her clockwork gears slowing down. She knew that she didn't have much longer and she started to panic. She stepped through the door of the toy room into the sunlight in the hallway.

She braced herself against the wall with one arm and slowly made her way down the hall. Maki followed her, then sprung in front of her. She was having a hard time balancing herself and was losing strength. She didn't need that springy dog under foot, so she shoved him aside with her heel and continued down the hall until she saw Marisol's brother.

"Miguel," Pichi called out, "Miguel, have you seen Marisol?"

"Nope, sure haven't," said Miguel.

"Please, you have to help me. I need winding."

"Not my problem. Find her your-self." He walked into the next room and slammed the door.

Pichi was starting to panic. She knew that if her clockwork stopped she would die. She had to find Mari-sol. She wandered frantically through the hallway. She wished that Maki was still with her so she could have his help finding Marisol. At last she reached the dining room. The table was covered in different sized platters all containing delicious meats and cheeses and piles of fresh fruit, but none of this interested Pichi, she just needed to have her key turned.

"What's this?" the mother yelled when she saw Pichi. "What are you do-ing out of the toy room? I don't need clockwork toys wandering the hall-ways while we have guests. Get back into the toy room this instant. Gregor, please, take this toy away."

"But. . ." Pichi tried to call out but she was too weak to speak and it just came out as a whisper.

Gregor picked her up by her clock-work wings, took her back down the hallway and threw her into the toy room. Pichi's gears rattled and she thought she felt something break.

An hour later, Marisol burst into the room laughing. She was arm in arm with a little blonde girl. They wore identical outfits and they were both laughing.

Marisol saw Pichi crumpled in the corner and came over to her and wound her up.

"What are you doing lying in the corner like that anyway?" she asked.

"You have a tick-tock, too?" said the blonde girl.

"Ya, isn't she pretty?" said Marisol.

"Not as pretty as any of mine," the blonde girl said, crossing her arms in front of her chest. "I have four tick-tocks and they are all prettier than this one."

The blonde girl turned away from the doll. "But I'm getting too grown up for them. I was thinking of throwing them away."

Pichi saw Marisol's face and felt embarrassed. She wished she was pret-tier so that Marisol's friend would be impressed.

"You said you'd show me your cos-tume collection," said the blonde girl.

"Oh yes, let's play dress up," said Marisol, leading the other girl away from Pichi.

Pichi followed the girls to the cos-tume room.

"Can I play too?"

"Tick-tocks don't wear clothes," Marisol said.

"This game is for real girls only," said the blonde girl.

Pichi didn't know what to say. She extended the wheels in her feet and rolled slowly backwards through the labyrinth into her little room. She sat there looking at walls that Marisol had helped her decorate. She had painted a mural on the walls with giant flowers and little fairies flying amongst them. There was a frog with three tongues and a giant eyeball creature named "Grog" that helped them on their dragon quests. Pichi pretended like she was playing dragon with Marisol. She imagined the story that she would tell the next time they were under the covers with their flashlights.

CHAPTER ELEVEN

Pichi knew just which stairs to avoid stepping on when sneaking out of the toy room at night so that she wouldn't make any noise on her way to Marisol's bedroom. They had not been playing together in the middle of the night for over a week now, and Pichi missed her company.

That night when she got to Marisol's room everything was different. All of the drawers to her bureau were open and all of their contents had been emptied out on the floor. Marisol sat in the center of the room with clothes and books piled around her. Her dark hair was wrapped up into a tall bun on top of her head and her brow was wrinkled in concentration.

Pichi wheeled over to her, carefully avoiding the messy piles. On top of the bed were four large luggage cases, lying open like empty coffins.

"I have a special adventure for us to play tonight," said Pichi.

"I can't play tonight," said Marisol.

"Why not?"

"Well, for starters, can't you see that I am busy?"

"What are you doing?"

"What does it look like I am do-

ing? I am packing for school."

"So?"

"So? I'm too old to play games with dolls and I am leaving for school tomorrow."

"You're leaving?"

"Yes."

"For how long?"

"For a long time."

Pichi felt like her clockwork gears had been ripped out of her chest. She never considered that Marisol would ever leave. What did she mean that she was too old to play games with dolls? Pichi isn't a doll, she's a real girl, Marisol said so herself.

Pichi didn't know what to say so she got on her knees and reached out to hug Marisol. When she put her arms around her, Marisol's body felt rigid, like it was made out of wood. Pichi didn't feel herself tingling like she always used to when she put her arms around her before. Marisol's hair felt itchy and her pale skin made her look like a ghost.

Pichi let go of Marisol and the girl kept sorting her piles of things.

"Just go back to the toy room, will ya?" Marisol said.

CHAPTER TWELVE

Pichi sat at the window with Maki as the car drove Marisol away in the morning. Maki made a whining noise that Pichi had never heard him make before, and she nuzzled his furry gray head under her chin. She noticed that he needed winding and she wound him up. He sprang to life and danced around her as if he'd already forgotten that Marisol had left, or he at least didn't understand that she wouldn't be back.

Then Pichi started to panic. What would happen to her now that Marisol was gone? Who would come to wind her up each morning? Was she doomed to die? No, she wouldn't have that, she needed to figure something out.

She looked at Maki. She could wind him up and keep him going but could he wind her up? She looked at his patchwork fur and springy legs. There was no way. She would have to get someone else to wind her. None of the toys in the toy room would be able to help her. She would have to go to Miguel.

CHAPTER THIRTEEN

Pichi was afraid of Miguel. Nothing inside her felt good about asking for his help but she could think of no other option. When she went to Miguel's room she was nervous, she had never been in a boy's room before. It had a funny sweet fungal smell and everything was decorated in dark colors and it looked empty. When she walked into the room her foot passed through a red beam of light a few inches from the floor and an alarm went off. A computerized voice said "Intruder Alert, Intruder Alert" and then from a secret doorway behind a bookshelf Miguel emerged.

"What do you want?" Miguel said, pulling a book from one of the shelves and pressing a button hidden inside to shut off the alarm.

"I need you to wind me up," said Pichi.

"What will you do for me?" asked Miguel.

"What do you mean?" said Pichi.

"I will wind you up if you steal me three chocolate bars from the kitchen," said Miguel.

"Um. . ." said Pichi.

"Now," he said.

Pichi made her way to the kitchen. She was careful to avoid being seen. When she approached the pantry she heard strange noises coming from inside. She bent down and looked through a crack in the door.

"Stop making so much noise you naughty boy or I'm going to have to punish you," said a woman dressed in a short black dress and lacy white apron.

"I am a naughty boy," said Marisol's father.

The father stood naked with his back against the pantry shelves. The maid stuck an onion in his mouth and wrapped cheese cloth around his head to hold it in place. Then she pulled a wooden spoon out of the pocket in her apron and smacked his bare thighs.

"Mmmmmmm," the father mumbled through the onion gag.

"I have all sorts of ways to punish you today," said the maid.

She pulled an assortment of other items out of her apron pocket and held each one up to show him before setting it on the shelf next to her: a pair of tongs, a garlic press, a lemon zester, a mushroom brush and an ice pick. Pichi noticed that next to the ice pick was a stack of chocolate bars. How was she going to get the chocolate for Miguel? Pichi knew she couldn't go into the pantry.

Pichi turned around and searched through the cupboards near the pantry. She heard footsteps coming from the hallway. So she hid inside one of the cupboards, pulling the door closed, but leaving a little crack so she could see. The cook walked into the kitchen and pulled a big canister off the counter. She carefully measured flour into a bowl. She added sugar and an egg to another bowl and turned on the electric mixer. Then Pichi saw that on the counter behind the cook were two chocolate bars. She waited until the cook walked over to the refrigerator and Pichi popped out of the cupboard and wheeled across the kitchen grabbing the two chocolate bars from the counter on her way out the door back into the hallway. She squatted down to go faster and rolled all the way back to Miguel's room.

"Where's the other one?" Miguel asked as Pichi handed him the two chocolate bars.

"I. . .um . . ." said Pichi.

"I said *three* chocolate bars," said Miguel.

Pichi wasn't sure what to say.

"I'm going to have to punish you," said Miguel.

Pichi thought about the maid. Miguel burst out laughing.

"I'm just kidding," said Miguel, "You can make it up to me tomorrow."

Miguel wound Pichi up. He put his hand on her thigh and traced the grapevine lines etched into her skin. Pichi felt the lights on her hips flicker.

CHAPTER FOURTEEN

The next day Miguel asked Pichi to steal money from the mother's purse. She always kept her purse on her vanity in her bedroom.

"Are you sure I should do that?" Pichi asked. "I don't think it's a good idea stealing money from your mother. What if I get caught?"

"You owe me from yesterday," Miguel said. "Do it or I won't wind you up."

The mother's bedroom had a canopy bed with red silk draped from floor to ceiling. A wooden fan turned lazily above the bed causing the silk to billow slightly in the breeze. Giant white calla lilies grew from black pots. A large glass door led out onto a veranda. The door was open and bougainvillea flowers crept into the room on spindling vines. Next to the bed was the vanity.

Pichi wheeled along the tile floor and she grabbed the money out of the mother's purse and stuck it inside a pocket-like compartment in her stomach that she opened by pressing her belly button. After she put the money away, she looked at herself in the tall curved mirror attached to the vanity. She wished she looked more like Marisol. She wished she had rosy cheeks instead of shiny brass ones.

Pichi looked down at the makeup on the vanity. Marisol's mother had everything laid out in an organized way on top of a silver tray. She pulled the top off a tube of lipstick and applied it to her smooth metal lips. She puckered her lips in the mirror and imagined what the lipstick would look like on Marisol. She wished that Marisol was there right now so they could put makeup on each other and play together. She had been so lonely since Marisol left.

Pichi lazily dropped the lipstick on the floor next to her and picked up the big goose feather powder puff. She dipped it into the cylindrical powder container and dabbed the puff against her face, feeling the powder sink into the grapevine creases etched into her skin, it tickled. As she removed the powder puff from her face she noticed a little circle of red on the feathers from touching her mouth.

"What are you doing you wicked doll?" the mother screamed at Pichi.

Pichi looked into the mirror and saw the mother coming up to her from behind. The mother snatched the powder puff out of Pichi's hands and accidentally stepped on the lipstick that was laying on the floor causing it to smear across the tile.

"How dare you touch my things. This is unacceptable," said the mother. She grabbed Pichi by the key in her back and dragged her out of the room. Pichi's feet scraped against the tiles, drawing a line of red lipstick from the vanity to the door. The mother tossed Pichi out the door and slammed it shut yelling, "Don't ever come in here again or I'll dismantle you."

As Pichi landed on the tile floor a piece of her knee broke off and clattered down the hallway. All the lights on her body lit up red in pain.

CHAPTER FIFTEEN

Pichi walked into Miguel's room, lipstick smeared across her lips and feet, her kneecap still missing.

"Oh Pichi, are you trying to look pretty for me?" said Miguel.

"I got your money," said Pichi in a low voice. She pressed her bellybutton to open up the compartment in her stomach. She reached in and Miguel said "Allow me," and he grabbed her wrist and pulled it away from her stomach.

Miguel stepped toward Pichi and pulled her wrist behind her body and held it against her lower back with one hand. With his other hand he reached into Pichi's stomach purse and slowly ran his fingertips along the inside lining.

"Kiss my neck," he said.

Pichi felt queasy. Miguel held her tightly and pulled the money from the purse, then he snapped it shut. Pichi kissed his neck and it left a red lipstick mark in the shape of a heart. Then he shoved her face first into his bed.

"This way my friends will think I've been with a girl," laughed Miguel as he wound her up.

CHAPTER SIXTEEN

Pichi sat in her room working on a new doll. She had taken more parts from the toy room and this time she was determined to make something worthy of Marisol. She took apart a Barbie doll and glued a picture of Marisol's face to its head. She dressed the doll in a miniature outfit she made out of Marisol's old clothes.

"Want to play dragon?" Pichi said to the doll.

"Oh yes, let's get Grog to help us," said Pichi in a higher pitched voice as she bounced the Marisol doll on her knee and looked up at the eyeball creature painted on her wall.

Pichi played dragon with her doll and looked forward to the day that she would be with the real Marisol again.

CHAPTER SEVENTEEN

Pichi came into Miguel's room. He had already turned off the alarm, because he was expecting her. He was sitting on his bed and told her to come sit beside him. He told her that she didn't have to do anything for him that day.

"Just sit still and let me look at you," Miguel said.

Pichi sat still.

Miguel wound her up very slowly. While he was winding her up, Miguel reached around and cupped her light bulb breasts. They glowed a very low light. Electric currents pulsed through Pichi's chest as Miguel gently rubbed his finger in a circle around her nipple.

Miguel reached his right hand down his pants and rubbed himself. He came around in front of Pichi, bent forward and licked her nipple. Little sparks passed between his tongue and her metal skin.

When he sat up he had his penis exposed.

"I want you to lick me now," he said.

Pichi shook her head no.

Miguel grabbed Pichi's hand and forced it onto his penis.

"Yes," said Miguel.

Pichi pulled her hand away from Miguel and ran out of the room.

"Come back here!" he yelled.

Pichi ran through the hall, knocking down a maid carrying a basket of laundry, and hid under a table in the toy room until she was absolutely sure Miguel wasn't going to come after her.

CHAPTER EIGHTEEN

Pichi played with Maki. They were playing fetch in the toy room and Pichi thought it was funny how Maki sprang all over the place, sometimes even bouncing off the glass ceiling.

"Maki, here doggie," said Pichi.

Maki bounded back through the labyrinth, carrying the Marisol doll delicately between his metal teeth.

"Good doggie," Pichi took the doll from him and replaced the face on the doll with another photo of Marisol wearing a different expression. Pichi had cut out pictures of Marisol and pasted them all over the walls to her room. She played with the doll and changed the photos in order to animate Marisol's expressions.

"Isn't it fun playing with Marisol?" Pichi asked Maki.

Pichi threw the doll and Maki ran after it. She knew she was kidding herself. The doll was no substitute for the real Marisol. Pichi looked up at the stars projected onto the ceiling. Maybe Marisol was somewhere looking at those same stars. Pichi thought those stars might bring them closer together like the night in the rain.

CHAPTER NINETEEN

The next day Pichi wasn't sure if she really wanted to go back to Miguel's room. The previous time had been really weird and she felt awkward and embarrassed. But the mother had threatened to dismantle her and the father was never around and the servant's weren't allowed to mess with the family's possessions unless ordered to. That left him as the only option.

"I've been waiting for you," Miguel said.

Pichi felt sick to her stomach. She approached the bed and Miguel already had his pants off. The skin around his scrotum was darker than anywhere else on his body and the tip of his penis was glowing bright red.

"I want you to suck it," Miguel said.

"I told you no," Pichi said.

"If you don't do it, I won't wind you up."

Pichi looked down at his penis, there was a tiny pearl of white liquid coming out of a hole in the tip. It looked like an eyeball crying a milky white tear.

Miguel said, "Come on, you can't last all day, you need me to wind you up so you're going to do it."

"No," said Pichi.

"You can't say no to me you bitch," said Miguel. He grabbed her arms and threw her down on his bed. He jumped on her back and shoved his penis against her. She struggled underneath him and he fumbled around trying to find an opening to jerk off with but Pichi's crotch was as smooth as a Barbie doll.

"What the fuck," Miguel said, bumping all around on top of her.

Pichi's lights glowed red.

"Ooo, you look sexier with those red lights," said Miguel.

Pichi sqeezed her face in pain as Miguel flipped her over onto her back, still pinning her arms down. With his tongue he pressed Pichi's bellybutton and her little belly pocket popped open.

"Oh ya," said Miguel as he slid his penis into Pichi's stomach. Miguel thrust in and out several times and then shuddered and fell on top of Pichi. She felt her stomach fill with slimy liquid and Miguel's penis went limp inside her.

Miguel rolled over and shoved Pichi off the bed. She looked up at him and said, "Aren't you going to wind me?"

Miguel ignored her.

Pichi tried to stand up but she was too weak. She crawled up to the edge of the bed and pulled on Miguel's arm.

"Miguel. . ."

"I'm not going to wind you,"

"But I'm going to die. . ."

"You didn't do what I said," Miguel pulled his arm away from Pichi, "Get out,"

"Miguel," she cried.

"Now."

Pichi crawled out of the room and back toward the toy room.

CHAPTER TWENTY

Pichi sat in the toy room barely able to move. She wanted to die, she couldn't go through this anymore, she didn't know when Marisol was going to return. Maki came springing into the room and dropped the Marisol doll in Pichi's lap. She saw Marisol's smiling face glued onto the doll and knew that she had to survive and find Marisol again.

She looked around the room and noticed a giant stuffed whale doll with a large open mouth big enough to climb inside. She crawled over to it and wiggled around until she felt the bottom of her clockwork key rest inside the whale's mouth. Then she let the weight of her body sink and she slid down to the ground until she felt the key turn slightly. She had to stand up straight again and reposition herself so that she could turn it a bit more.

It took Pichi all day and all night just to turn herself enough to give herself the strength to keep turning herself. She thought she would never be able to keep this up, but the threat of death kept her going even when she felt too exhausted to continue.

Maki sprung up from time to time when he needed winding and she took a break to help him out.

CHAPTER TWENTY-ONE

"Move those barrels right over there," came the mother's voice drifting into the toy room.

Pichi heard a loud rumbling noise and crept around the corner to see what was going on.

"I want all of this cleaned out in the next 24 hours," said the mother.

Pichi saw two men in blue jumpsuits and yellow hard hats standing at the edge of the room. One of them was wheeling a cart containing big blue barrels.

"Don't worry about sorting through any of it, I just want it all thrown away," said the mother.

Pichi popped the wheels out under her feet and rolled over to the mother.

"What's going on?" Pichi asked the mother.

The mother looked down her nose at Pichi.

"Oh, you're still around?" said the mother, "Well, Marisol is too old for toys, I am getting rid of them all."

"But what will happen to me?" asked Pichi.

"Good riddance, you were getting into too much trouble around here."

The mother hurried off and left the two construction workers there to clean things up. They worked all day, putting all of the toys into the barrels. Pichi saw the walls of her room knocked down as she was wheeled out inside one of the barrels. She saw the men chase down Maki and stuff him into a different barrel, but when they tried to put the lid on they found he was too big to fit completely inside. They cut his head off his spring neck, and tossed his head into a different barrel. Then a lid was put on top of Pichi and there was nothing more she could see.

CHAPTER TWENTY-TWO

Pichi didn't know how long she was in the barrel but it had been a bumpy ride. She knew she had to get out of there and find Marisol. After she kicked repeatedly, the barrel lid eventually popped off and she lifted herself out into the daylight only to see a vast landscape of twisted metal, tall weeds, and dirt. Corpses of rusted vintage cars formed cathedral like spires around mountains of junk.

Pichi ran over to the other blue barrels and pried them open one at a time. When she got to the last one, Maki's dismembered head was laying on top with his tongue hanging out.

"Maki!" Pichi cried out, cradling his head in her arms. She was alone. She gently put Maki's head back in the barrel and closed the lid like a tomb.

Pichi stepped carefully through the dirt trying to avoid sharp objects. She wandered down through the mountains of junk and came to a small grove of trees. Hanging from the tree branches were dozens of decapitated doll heads hung from rusted meat hooks. The heads looked like they'd been there for years, their hair matted to their heads from the rain and their cheeks caked with mud. The doll's glass eyes winked at Pichi as the heads swayed in the breeze. She started to feel afraid and lost.

Pichi climbed over piles of electronics, old TVs, and dismantled farm equipment. Her foot slipped on a cigar tube and she tumbled downhill wedging herself between a giant plastic Jesus figurine and a mountain of medicine bottles. Then she heard a noise above her.

"There's one," the voice called.

Out of nowhere, a crowd of clockwork toys came up over the mountain above Pichi and looked down at her. She scrambled to regain her footing and ran in the other direction. But she wasn't fast enough and the crowd caught up to her.

"Welcome to El Bario," said a tall skinny clockwork man.

"Please," Pichi said, adjusting her lenses to the harsh lights gleaming off their brass bodies. She stretched her arms out keeping the other toys at a safe distance. "What's going on?"

Pichi looked around at the faces. The tall skinny clockwork man had a face like a jack in the box, he wore a motley jester's hat and his torso was a giant spring. Next to him was a lithe ballerina standing permanently on one foot in a white tutu stained with rust and dirt. She looked like she had been beautiful once but the rouge had rubbed from her cheeks and her hair had been chopped off. Above her, hovering low in the air was a miniature clockwork plane and its tiny pilot wearing a leather hat and goggles called down to her in a high pitched voice, "Hello," and waved a gloved hand above his head.

"We are the Noodles, we work for Dr. Garcia," said the tall skinny man, "My name is Jack."

"Who is Dr. Garcia?" asked Pichi.

"Dr. Garcia runs El Bario, he keeps us wound up and we help him find the others," says a big furry stuffed lamb in a sing-songy voice.

Pichi wonders if maybe these people can help her find Marisol. She says, "Do you know Marisol?"

"Marisol?" said the ballerina.

Jack said, "No, but Dr. Garcia knows everyone. Come with us, we'll introduce you to him."

"Well, I have to find Marisol," said Pichi. "And, if I leave here, she won't be able to find me. All her things are here."

"Marisol was your owner?" asked Jack.

"Yes, she is the most beautiful girl in the world and . . ." Pichi stumbled, her clockwork was winding down and she couldn't stand up straight.

"Here, let us help you," Lamby sang as he leaned his thick curly fur against Pichi to prop her up.

Jack extended his spring torso and curved himself behind Pichi to wind her up. When she was all tightened, she sprang to her feet.

"Are there any more like you?" asked Jack.

"Like me?" asked Pichi.

"Tick-tocks," Jack said.

"I've never seen any others until today."

"That's what we do. We look for other tick-tocks and take them back to Dr. Garcia. Sometimes he is able to give us new bodies, synthetic bodies that don't have to be wound up."

"And you think he might know where Marisol is?" asked Pichi

"Well sure, if any of us need to know something we ask Dr. Garcia," said Jack.

Lamby nuzzled his head against her back, giving her a shove in the direction that Jack was leading. The tiny pilot buzzed around her head.

CHAPTER TWENTY-THREE

Pichi floated along the raft with the other toys down a river winding through the mountains of trash. Then they reached an archway that led to an underground city inside of the hollowed out mountains. Pichi lit up all the lights on her body to guide their way through the dark tunnels.

After a few moments, the arched ceiling started to open up and she could see buildings with lights in the windows. The buildings were constructed with adobe made from mud mixed together with bits of glass and doll limbs, car engines, sunglasses, pink flamingoes, old records and computer screens. Pichi saw other clockwork toys moving about behind the soda bottle windows of the buildings.

"Who are all these people?" asked Pichi.

Jack said, "We are all tick-tocks like you. We were all once human and were turned into toys and given as gifts to rich children. But all children grow out of their toys and this is where they are thrown. Dr. Garcia loves the toys. He helps all of us. He's a very good man and a smart scientist. He has figured out a way to transfer our brains into new bodies that don't require winding, so we can go back into the world and lead normal lives."

"Then why are you still clockwork?"

The jack in the box looks down at his hands, "It hasn't been perfected yet. It only works on one out of every three clockworks. But the rest of us have made a home here and we help Dr. Garcia rescue the other toys that have been thrown away."

"Maybe if I get a new body I can go to school with Marisol," said Pichi.

"Stop thinking about your owner," said Jack. "Don't you understand, she's gone, you've been thrown away. She might have loved you once but now you must start a new life and we're here to help you."

"You're wrong," said Pichi, feeling her gears tightening, she didn't like Jack's tone of voice, she wasn't sure if she really wanted to meet this Dr. Garcia or if these people were just getting in the way of her finding Marisol. If they weren't going to help her then she would have to find another way. But she knew that she wouldn't last long if she didn't have someone to wind her up. Her best chance was to try and get a new body. Then maybe Marisol would see her as a real girl and they could play dress up together and they would be happy together forever.

"Welcome home, Noodles," a voice said from the shadows. "What have you brought for me today?"

CHAPTER TWENTY-FOUR

Dr. Garcia wore skin-tight green spandex pants and a green sequin half-shirt. His hair was hot pink and stood straight up on his head like a feathered hat.

"Oh! What a beautiful creature you are," said Dr. Garcia as he ran his green-painted fingernails along Pichi's clockwork key.

Pichi sat in Dr. Garcia's workshop. There were gears and tools piled on long tables and a giant vat of blue bubbling liquid in the far corner.

"I hear you are looking for someone," Dr. Garcia put his hand on Pichi's shoulder and looked into her bicycle wheel eyes. Pichi saw herself reflected in his brown eyes. He looked at her tenderly, reminding her of Marisol.

"Do you know Marisol?" Pichi asked.

"Marisol. . ." Dr. Garcia rubbed his chin and wiggled his ears. "Nope. I don't think I do. Who is she?"

"She's my best friend," said Pichi, "and she left for school but I don't know where that is."

"I see," said Dr. Garcia. "I tell you what sweetie. I can't help you find your friend, but I might be able to release you from your clockwork prison. I can put you in a new body."

"Jack told me about it."

"Well, I have to warn you, it doesn't work 100% of the time. But if the procedure doesn't work, I want you to know that you will always have a home here with me."

"Okay, but I'm going to find Marisol either way." Pichi stuck out her chin and pushed out her chest pretending not to be nervous.

"We can get started right away, if you like," said the doctor.

Pichi nodded. "As soon as possible."

Dr. Garcia smiled at her. He took some measurements and had her stand on a scale. Pichi's metal parts clicked at him as he lifted her arms and examined her waistline.

"I'll need some time," he said. "But we'll begin soon enough."

Then he sent Pichi out of the workshop and told her to enjoy herself while he made the necessary preparations.

CHAPTER TWENTY-FIVE

Pichi was terrified about the surgery not working but told herself it would be worth trying because if she got a real body then Marisol would like her again and they could be together. She walked around in El Bario checking out the buildings.

She got lost among the winding streets of the underground junkyard town. Then she found an open pit filled with broken tick-tocks piled within it. It was like a toy graveyard. Dolls with no hair and crossed out eyes, lying legs akimbo criss-crossed on top of each other. There was a toy elephant that had been dissected, a mouse that was missing its arms and legs. And most disturbing of all, the remains of a clockwork girl very similar looking to Pichi with her belly pocket ripped out and clockwork gears spilling out of her eye sockets.

Pichi ran away from the pit and back through the winding streets, her gears ticking faster and faster until she came to a crowd of tick-tocks gathered together in a circle staring at something happening in the center.

Pichi approached the circle and peeked between the arms and legs of the people in front of her until she saw two clockwork men in the center wrestling each other. The men wore unitards and had bulging metal muscles. The lights on their body were lit up bright red and they circled around each other, slapping each other on the shoulder, each one trying to provoke the other.

Pichi noticed that the lights on the people crowded around the wrestlers were all blinking in unison.

"What's going on?" Pichi asked the girl standing next to her.

"A wrestling match," said the girl as if Pichi was completely clueless.

"Why are they fighting?" asked Pichi.

"For fun," said the girl.

Then Pichi noticed the smiles on the wrestlers faces.

"They're wrestling toys, it is what they were designed to do."

Pichi watched as the clockwork men tackled each other. Whenever one of them landed a blow, a metal piece on the other man's body would flip over to reveal a fake bloody wound. The girl told Pichi their skin was double-sided metal on swiveling joints. When they got hit it didn't actually hurt them, it just looked gory.

CHAPTER TWENTY-SIX

Pichi went to the doctor's workshop the next day to have her surgery.

"Just try to relax," said Dr. Garcia.

Pichi's lights were flickering all over her body. Her gears felt like she was wound too tight, the wheels on her feet were spinning even though she wasn't standing on them.

"I'm going to slowly open your chest panel," said Dr. Garcia. "This shouldn't hurt, but let me know if you feel any pain."

The doctor unscrewed her ribcage and Pichi felt his fingers caressing the gears inside her chest. It didn't hurt but it made her feel funny. Then she felt a sharp pinch and she blacked out.

CHAPTER TWENTY-SEVEN

Pichi woke up for the first time. She looked down at her arms and instead of shiny brass they were fleshy pale skin, just like Marisol's. Pichi was more excited than she had ever felt.

"Oh good, you're awake," said Dr. Garcia. He walked over to her and put his hand on her forehead. "The surgery was a complete success."

Pichi smiled and reached her hand around her back and felt where she used to have her clockwork key. It was just smooth skin. She touched her head

and felt hair, she pulled the hair in front of her eyes and saw that it was black just like Marisol's had been. She was happy.

"Would you like to see the new you?" asked Dr. Garcia.

"Yes," said Pichi.

Dr. Garcia wheeled a mirror in front of Pichi. She stood up, without thinking, her new legs working perfectly. She looked in the mirror and saw a woman, about 5'6, who looked to be about twenty years old, slender, long thick black hair, with black grapevine tattoos covering her pale skin where her etchings once appeared.

"What?" Pichi said. The woman's mouth in the mirror moving with her speech. "Wait, is that me?"

"Yes," said Dr. Garcia. "Don't you think you're beautiful?"

"What did you do to me?" cried Pichi. "This is horrible. I am not a woman, I am a little girl. Marisol will never like me now. She won't even recognize me. . ."

"Calm down," said Dr. Garcia. "You see, these bodies never age, so I could not have given you a girl's body. If I had then you would never grow up. You would be trapped as a girl forever. But this way you are already in a grown body and you will look young forever."

"But now I can never see Marisol again."

"You need to forget about her," said Dr. Garcia, "we will help set you up with a new life. You can be free to live your own life. You never have to worry about being wound up again."

"But, all I ever wanted was to be a real girl again so that Marisol and I could be together."

"You will forget about her in time,"

said Dr. Garcia.

"No, I won't forget about her. You don't know what kind of friendship we had. There will never be anyone like Marisol."

Then Pichi wiped at her face, trying to clean away the strange liquid that was leaking out of her eyes.

CHAPTER TWENTY-EIGHT

Pichi walked over to the gallery window. Painted on the window was a sign that said "Garcia's Gallery."

"Miss Garcia, could you please tell me about this piece over here," called an older woman. The woman was draped in a colorful shawl and had oversized gemstone rings on every finger. She stood next to a clockwork sculpture; it was a giant toy elephant with a tiny dismembered mouse running atop a spinning wheel inside its gutted clockwork body.

"That is one of my own creations," said Pichi walking over to the woman. "I take discarded toys and give them new life through my artwork." Pichi's tattooed skin was showing through the mesh fabric of her blouse. She wore a black pencil skirt and high-heeled shoes. Her fingernails were painted silver and her black hair was cropped in an asymmetrical bob.

"You have the most amazing things in your gallery," said the woman, "No wonder you are world famous for your clockwork shows."

A lot had happened to Pichi since she got her new body. She spent several years in El Bario helping discarded tick-tocks. But after a while she moved to the city and got her own apartment. She started showing her clockwork creations on the street, then at galleries, and eventually opened a gallery of her own. She blended in with society and even if they thought of her as an eccentric artist, most people that met her never learned of her past.

A young woman walked through the door. She had long black hair and brown eyes.

"Excuse me a moment," Pichi said to the bejeweled woman in the shawl. She walked over to the young woman, "May I help you?"

The woman stood admiring a life size clockwork doll sculpture. It was hanging from the ceiling by invisible string so it looked like it was hovering in midair by two large wings made from wire mesh with ribbons woven through them in butterfly patterns. The butterfly wings fluttered as the doll was lit up from the inside with tiny flickering colored light bulbs. There were small wheels attached to its hands and feet. It wore a crown of roses on its head.

"I really admire this work," said the young woman, "I am looking for the person who runs this gallery."

"That would be me."

The young women clasp her hands in front of her chest and said with a huge smile, "I am so happy to meet you, I am here to talk to you about the apprenticeship."

"What is your name?" asked Pichi looking at the woman; she was wearing a form fitting dress with a deep plunging neck. Her skin the color of moonlight.

"Marisol Yvonne Reyes-Jimenez."

Pichi's breath caught in her chest. It felt like she was wound too tight. She hadn't heard that name in years. She looked at the young woman more closely and thought *could this be her, could this be my Marisol?* Pichi had tried to forget about Marisol, but not a day had gone by that she didn't think about her in some way. She wasn't sure how to react. Did Marisol come here looking for her?

"Have you been looking for me?" asked Pichi.

"Oh yes, I have admired your art for years. I am in grad school studying art history and the Garcia Gallery is world renowned."

Marisol's brown eyes held their gaze. She brushed a lock of her thick black hair out of her face and twirled it around her finger. Her heart shaped lips smiled.

"Miss Garcia," said the woman in the shawl, "Do you still have that painting you showed me last week?"

"Yes, the one with the three-tongued frog?" said Pichi, "I have it in the back." She leaned in and whispered to Marisol, "Excuse me one moment."

Pichi went into the back room. Grabbed the piece of art from the shelf and then froze behind the doorway when she heard the two women talking in the gallery.

"Miss Garcia is the master of re-claimed clockwork artwork," said the woman in the shawl.

"Yes, I know. Everyone knows of her," said Marisol.

"Rumor is that she used to *be* a tick-tock herself and that's why her artwork is so intimate," the old woman said. She twisted the lollipop-sized jewel on her ringed index finger and stared at Marisol, "So, are you going to be her new toy?"

"Excuse me?" said Marisol.

The old woman laughed, false teeth slipping inside her pink-lipstick mouth, "That's what we call all of Pichi's apprentices."

"Did you say Pichi?" asked Marisol. Her eyes widening as she turned her head to look for Miss Garcia.

"Yes, that's what her friends call her."

"Pichi..." Marisol said.

As Pichi stepped out from the back, carrying a painting in her grape-vine-tattooed arms, Marisol's mouth widened. Their eyes met as she stared at the gallery owner's face, which was becoming more familiar by the second. Even though Pichi's eyes were as human as hers, she imagined that they were spinning like bicycle wheels.

DAVID AGRANOFF

LOCATION:
The vegan junk food capital of the
world – Portland, Oregon.

STYLE OF BIZARRO:
Punk Horror

BOOKS BY AGRANOFF:
Screams from a Dying World
Hunting the Moon Tribe
Vegan Revolution...with Zombies
Last Warriors of the Earth
Demons of Winter
Wizard of Shaolin
Bootboys and the Wolfreich
Goddamn Killing Machines

DESCRIPTION: David writes revolutionary dark bizarro fiction
ranging from horror, fantasy and science-fiction. Often laced with
his own radical political views, some times deadly serious and other
times with biting satire, each book is a world of its own and David
prides himself making each work a unique expeience.

INTERESTS: Straight edge, Horror fiction, Horror movies, Cyber-
punk, Science fiction, Veganism

INFLUENCES: John Shirley, Richard Matheson, Clive Barker,
Phillip K. Dick, John Carpenter, David Cronenberg, Martial arts films
of Tusi Hark, Ching Siu tung and Yuen Woo Ping. Argento, Fulci,
Norman Spinrad, John Brunner, Octavia Butler, and Daniel Quinn.

WEBSITE:
davidagranoff.blogspot.com

PUNKUPINE MOSHERS OF THE APOCALYPSE

Year 35

Dressica held her stick over the fire and watched the bottom of her marshmallow blacken slowly. The fire snapped and she felt its warmth on the clean shaven sides of her head. The old man looked across the fire and smiled at her. His features were as weathered as his leather jacket, there was no one older back in town. He was more than the wise old farmer on the hill, he was her uncle Max. The other children had fallen asleep more than an hour ago, but Dressica couldn't sleep, she wanted to talk to her uncle.

"You need to sleep."

Dressica shook her head.

"Not tired."

Most of the other children were afraid of the old man, but the school made them come out here and learn the basics of farming. Max was a mystery, he rarely came out to shows, still wore the skin of animals, didn't seem to want anything to do with life in the city. Max popped a handful of nuts in his mouth and chewed.

"Kids never admit to being tired. Why is that? You want to be a grown-up right? Grown-ups like sleeping."

Max's dreadlocked mohawk was gray at the roots. His walking stick laid at his side was almost his full six feet and wrapped in vinyl stickers. Names of bands Dressica had never heard of, Circle Jerks, Black Flag and Bad Reli-gion. She only knew they were bands that played shows before she was born. Dressica turned her eyes away from the fire.

The lights of Crassville shined across the high desert. This was the furthest she had ever been from the city in her six years. She knew there were farms and smaller villages through the land of Dischargia, but she had never seen them. Uncle Max's farm was as far as she had dared to go.

"Uncle Max, will you be honest with me?"

The wind turned the fire, and lifted her uncle's hair.

"About what love?"

"I think you adults are lousy liars."

Dressica didn't trust her mother, didn't know who her father was and the teachers seemed more interested in engineering, farms, guitars or anything but history.

Max snorted and took a drink from his canteen.

"Is that so?" Max looked up at the sky and back at her. "The Punks got old just like everyone else. Adults sometimes feel they have to lie to kids to protect them."

"I can take care of myself."

Max laughed at her and stoked the fire with a stick. Little bits of flame escaped toward the sky and when the flame lowered the old man had a sour look on his face.

"Your mother told me you have been asking about the nether lands beyond Dischargia. No such lands exist. Nothing more than myth." Dressica felt ready to explode. Max had been her only hope, he didn't give a shit what anyone thought. He was *Max-imum Damage*, punk vocalist and mosh pit gladiator of the highest ranking. She stared at the scars on his head. He survived more shows than he had any right to. Then despite the cheers of his legion of fans in Crassville he left. He walked away to grow salad greens and ginger root, only coming into the city to sell his crop at the market. She wanted the truth from him, Max sat across the fire and lied through his broken teeth. Dressica kicked the fire pit.

"Bullshit."

Max sighed and looked over her shoulder at the tents set up on the edge of his corn patch. Max patted the ground next to him. Dressica looked back at the tents, everyone else was asleep. They were alone. She walked around the fire and sat next to him.

"I didn't lie, but there are things you must understand. If I tell you, it must remain our secret." Max said just above a whisper.

"I won't tell anyone I swear."

"What year is it Dressica?"

"Thirty-five."

"Here in Dischargia, yeah, it is the year thirty-five. Beyond the red line it is the year twenty-twenty-two."

Dressica's jaw dropped just thinking about that many years. It was impossible to consider.

"In the year nineteen-eighty-seven, there were many tribes with massive cities and they waged a great war. So you see I didn't lie. The great lands of old are gone."

Dressica felt like the air had been let out of her bike tire. She had always hoped there was life beyond Dischargia.

"They can't all be gone."

"They're gone, and it's a good goddamn thing they are. The world of old was driven by greed and hatred."

Dressica used a rubber band to tie back her green hair. She shivered in the cold and moved closer to the fire. She watched the flame.

"Sounds scary?"

Max smiled at her.

"You like the music in the city?"

Dressica smiled and thought of the bands at school. Raging punk rock, the children of Dischargia got their first guitar and drum lessons at five. If they didn't show music aptitude, they were taught engineering or farming.

"You like your clothes? Your piercings?"

Dressica looked at her holey jeans and played with her nose and lip rings. She didn't understand why Max was asking her.

"If you like the way of life we have here in Dischargia, then you'll never cross those red lines on the map. Because if anyone is still alive out there..."

Dressica waited for him to finish. Max looked up at the night sky and back at Dressica.

"Go to bed."

"But Uncle Max..."

He stood up and turned his back to her. He never brought up the subject again. As far as anyone knew, Dischargia was the world.

CHAPTER ONE

Year 45

Dressica tightened her grip on the microphone and took a deep breath.

"One, two, three four!"

The band launched into a blast of high-speed punk and the circle pit swirled in front of the stage like the outer edge of a hurricane. Dressica leaned over the crowd and spit the lyrics to her favorite song. Blood splattered across her face and for a moment she dropped the mic, she wiped the blood free from her face. Bodies rammed into each other, fists were thrown, legs stomped to the beat. It was like crowded bus had broken out into a riot.

Reality Asylum was a big venue and had the meanest pits in all of Dischargia. When Combat Vehicle hit the stage the chaos was at a high. Dressica looked out into the crowd and saw a figure skanking his way across the floor. The pit cleared like the dead sea for him. A Razorback, Raz to his friends.

Three long blades grew out of his back and two smaller blades were attached to his arms. He swung his arms as the song slowed down into a beat with more groove. Dressica looked into the eyes of a drunk mosher who pumped his fist at the front of the stage. He didn't see Raz circle the pit behind him. The blades slit across his back and the man screamed like a baby, his blood drenched the stage monitors.

Raz wasn't alone, a leather jacketed man named Ike entered the pit covered in spikes just as the song ended. Dressica looked at her band mates. John, her guitar player hit a few notes and started tuning. The crowd waited impatiently, they milled around on the blood slick floor.

"How you doing tonight, we're Combat Vehicle."

"No shit! Really?" Raz called out and laughed.

Dressica moved on the stage in front of him and stared. Raz smiled, his hair was spiked in liberty spikes so tall he ducked in every door way he entered. They crowd was thick with spiked mohawks. It was the genetically engineered razors that came out of his back and arms that made Raz punk as hell.

"So Raz, why didn't the scientists give you a dick when they gave you those razors huh?"

The crowd oohed, and Raz held up two fingers. John hit a note telling the rest of the band he was ready. Raz pumped his fist.

"Stage dive!"

The band started playing their next song but Raz got the chant going.

"Stage dive! Stage dive!"

Dressica had enough. The crowd ran at each other and became a riot of bodies and the sound of bones breaking could be heard over the band. Dressica didn't start singing...

"Fuck you Raz."

This is why people came to see Combat Vehicle, uncontrolled chaos. Dressica jumped off stage and put her right thumb and pinky together. She felt a burst of energy travel up her spine. The crowd cleared as she landed in the middle of the pit. Long sharp metal quills burst through the skin on the back of her neck. She put out her arms and the quills snapped through the back of her shirt and down the length of her legs.

Dressica felt the music shake her quills, she moved through the crowd, her fists and legs pumping to the beat. She was queen of the pit. If anyone ran into her they would destroy their own bodies. Dressica spun through the crowd like a windmill. Ike the Spike laughed and ran into the circle. Raz screamed and was the next one in.

Dressica touched her thumb to her index finger and relaxed as the quills receded under her skin. She sat down on the couch set up off the stage and looked at the tattered remains of her shirt. John, her guitar player, pushed his large amp past her and winked.

"Great show Dress."

Dressica lifted up her hands. They were covered in blood and shaking, she wiped the blood on her shredded pant legs.

"You should see your face."

Dressica closed her eyes at the sound of Dez's voice. He was a great engineer, had rebuilt the city's solar panels, and in his off time he worked for her.

"It's not my blood dude, the quills worked perfect."

Dez stood over her, He shook his head. His dyed green hair and spike belts looked fresh. He had gotten dressed up for this night on the town.

"They worked great, but they could be a bit longer."

Dez pulled out an electric clipboard and used his thumb to scroll through his notes.

"If I make them longer it will cause internal scaring, or worse."

Dressica could always feel the quills under her skin, in her heart she knew they could not be longer, but she needed something to compete.

"Who is engineering for Raz?"

Dez looked up from his pad, concern was written all over his face.

"Whoever it is, they're not from Crassville, maybe from Blitz. Whoever it is they're good. You keep getting in the pit with him, you're going to die."

Dressica wiped her forehead with a towel. She shouldn't have been surprised it took this long. Dez only worked for Dressica because he had a crush on her. Every time she walked away from a show he gave her the same speech. He knew he would never talk

her out of it; she lived for the pit, spent every quiet moment thinking about the thrill, the rush she got when she danced her way through the madness.

"Come on you can walk me home while you lecture me."

They stepped out into the cool night. Two shows broke up in different venues along Rimbaud Avenue. Street vendors sold bootleg cassettes and food. Dozens of people were lined up waiting for grilled soy products at the tofu dog stands. The street barbers were dying hair and cutting fresh mohawks. So many barbers were working that they sounded like garden crews mowing lawns. They had used up their solar power and few of the barbers had assistants pedaling away to generate power.

Typical Friday night in Crassville.

Dressica led them to a food stand without a line. A woman sat behind the stand. Her dreads were tied back, her feet up on a chair, and she was reading Crassville peace punk newspaper.

"What does pit gladiator need to do to get some food around here?"

The woman looked up from her paper and looked past Dressica's eyes to the cuts on her forehead.

"I have potatoes. Home fries with a rosemary ketchup."

Dez made an approving sound.

"Dez, I'd like you meet my cousin Isa."

Dez couldn't help looking at her right arm. It was mechanical, hidden by a sleeve. He could tell a lot about its design, the engineer in him was impressed. The arm was lost in one of the most famous pit maulings in all of Dischargia. It happened during a Combat Vehicle show down in Blitz, the least politically organized and most chaotic town in the world. The legend was that, by the time the song was over, Isa was screaming on the floor and Dressica had used her cousin's severed arm to chase Raz out of the club.

Isa awkwardly worked the serving tools. She wasn't new to the disability, but new to cybernetic arm.

"I wondered why you weren't at shows…"

Dressica pointed at the peace paper sitting on her chair. Isa ignored her and scrapped the taters from the pan. The tension was so thick Dez took a step back. Dressica shook her head.

"So you're some kinda of peace punk now."

Isa's mechanical arm creaked and wheezed unnaturally as she held the paper container of potatoes out for her cousin.

"Just take them and go."

Dressica put her mutual aid credits on top of newspaper. The credits acknowledged to the council that Isa had traded community aid. Dressica turned back to Dez who walked ahead of her. When they sat at the table and opened the container Dez still had one eye on Dressica's cousin.

"Didn't Raz do that to her?"

"Eat your potatoes," Dressica said as she unfolded the fork on her multi-tool.

CHAPTER TWO

Max walked across his field, on his belt a small radio faintly played the song *Wild in the Streets* by the Circle Jerks. He just had one more thing to do before he could go back into his cabin at night. He only played music because the he didn't like the stuff the kids to-

day called punk rock. Even here in the field at night you could faintly hear the sounds of shows down in Crassville.

He had fond memories of shows before the Great War when punk was rebellion, not culture. The shows were dangerous and you were likely to break a bone or nose from time to time. They happened in rented warehouses and all kinds of funky places. Often when the owners saw what happened they shut down the shows. The cops would break them up. The cops, Max thought about them and laughed.

People didn't die in the shows in the old days; if you fell down, someone picked you up. It was an unwritten law of the slam pit. Max understood why the council made the decision to make shows so violent, but after years of pit fighting it seemed senseless to him. Punk had become safe and normal. The culture was growing too fast and had been watered down.

His soy fields blew in the wind, he knew he would have to harvest them in the next week. He would have to trade food for some workers. That meant going into the city. Max sighed in frustration as he walked up to his wooden irrigation control. He expected to be brushing away mosquitoes, but the air was clear.

Max grabbed the wooden handle and lifted the latch. He stepped back but the water didn't pour out as it always did. Only a tiny drop of water, more like a tear, rolled out and pathetically hit the ground. Max climbed up the wooden structure. There was no water coming down from the river that headed into town.

Max used his walking stick to balance himself and swung to the ground. It wasn't a huge river but it was usually the width of a two-car garage. When he stepped onto the river bank he saw the extent of the problem. Only a small trickle continued between two large rocks in the middle of the empty river bed where just earlier today he had seen the water flowing normally.

He looked up the river at the mountain to the north. It was a hundred miles or more away, beyond what the council had determined was the red line. The end of the world, at least, as far as the next generation was concerned. It had been thirty years since anyone crossed the red line.

Max squeezed his walking stick and walked toward the city. He knew what this meant. A town meeting.

CHAPTER THREE

"If you want to speak, enter an agenda item on your boards, or raise your hand and the moderator will put your name on the stack."

Dressica heard the voice call out from the speaker system in the great hall as she and Dez walked past. Dez kept walking but Dressica stopped when she saw her Uncle Max sit down in the third row of seats. The great hall was built to seat over a thousand people, and anyone could access the video feed from their TV's. She had heard the tone calling for the meeting, but like most Crassville residents she ignored the bell.

Only thirty or so citizens, mostly elders, gathered in the room. Dez stopped and squinted as Dressica stepped inside the hall.

"I thought you were tired," Dez followed her like puppy.

The council members sat down.

They all had multi-colored hair and wore spiked and studded clothing held together with safety pins. Eve-al the second longest serving member of the council was moderator. She tapped her gavel. Slowly, members of the community piled in and the red light went on the live camera.

Keith Tesco, a councilor from the north side of town, stood up.

"I donate my position on the stack to Max – former vocalist of Max-imum Damage and a farmer with excellent mutual aid standing from my district."

Dressica found a seat in the fifth row as her Uncle stood up.

"A dark time has fallen upon our land. The river no longer flows from the north."

Murmurs spread around the crowd. A young man sitting beside Dressica spoke out of turn.

"But the water is supposed to come from the edge of the world."

Uncle Max looked at the young man and pointed.

"The elders in this room must face the truth. The holes in our story will tear this community apart."

"Does the floor accept a follow-up question?" Eve-al asked.

Max nodded and she continued, "I understand your concerns, but we don't know what is taking the water."

"I contacted the farmers to the north. The flow stopped this evening; somewhere just below the red line."

Dez shook his head at Dressica, but this only confirmed what she knew all along. Something lived in the lands to the north. One of the young council members signaled a follow-up question and Max nodded for him to speak.

"The red line is the last space before the end of the world."

Max shook his head.

Dez looked at Dressica. He whispered, "I knew the world was bigger than Dischargia."

Dressica agreed but shushed him anyway. Uncle Max spoke to the camera.

"We taught you a story, you had no reason not to believe. Life comes from the river, why wouldn't its flow start beyond our world. We can't force your heads in the sand, there was a world out there!"

Shouts broke out. People stood. Fingers were pointed. Eve-al beat her spiked hammer on the table and brought the crowd to attention.

"Some of us grew up hearing tales of lands beyond the red line. I admit I never believed, but it would seem something is killing our river."

"It's a monster!" someone called out.

"Fuck you all!" someone else called out.

Eve-al rapped her hammer. The council conferred, a moment later a resolution was typed and transmitted to electric clipboards around the city. If the citizens of Crassville reached a consensus, a team would be formed to travel to the red line. Dressica picked up the pad in front of her seat and entered her mutual aid number. She stared at the pad and watched the votes. A few voted in favor of the resolution, but hundreds of citizens around the city blocked it with 'no' votes.

Dressica watched her uncle Max sit down. He dipped his head in sorrow. Dressica typed her name into the stack, no one else wanted to speak. She stood up.

"I'll go!" Everyone in the hall turned and looked at her. "That is why we have so many 'no' votes. You're afraid that you will be called to cross the red line on behalf of punk kind. I know there is more to this world and I'm not afraid."

Uncle Max looked up and smiled at his sister's young daughter. He looked at his clipboard. The votes were changing. Suddenly 200 votes became "yes."

"I'm a pit gladiator, I don't fear a line on the map."

"I'll join you." Uncle Max used his walking stick to push himself back up. More votes switched over, now only thirty lone citizens blocked. Dressica sighed. The peace punks were afraid that we would start fights beyond the red line. She knew it.

"I'll go."

Isa walked into the hall. Everyone turned to see the former pit gladiator walk in. She had a peace symbol on the butt flap hanging over her gray pants.

"Someone has to be a voice for peace."

Dressica watched her clipboard as twenty-nine votes shifted. She looked at Dez, he looked up at her. He hid his clipboard but she knew who the last vote was.

"Were gonna need an engineer," Dressica whispered.

"One warrior, a cripple, and an old man." Dez shook his head. A wave of frustration rolled around the room.

"Change your vote asshole!"

"We'll die without water!"

"Eat dog shit you fucknut!"

The shouts came from around the room. Dez stood up.

"I won't change my vote."

"I'm in!" The voice came from the back of the hall and Dressica dropped her clip board.

Raz stepped into the room and there was silence except the sound of the spurs on the back of his combat boots. Both Dressica and Isa shook their heads. Dressica was about to say *'hell no'* when she heard the signal. *Consensus reached.*

Dressica looked at Dez and could've punched him.

CHAPTER FOUR

Dressica Killmaiden slung a rifle over her shoulder and waited by the 'Welcome to Crassville' sign. She was your typical second generation woman. She thought it was patriarchal to blindly follow tradition and take the name of her father's band. She was proud of her mother, loved her, and so when she was of legal age she took her mother's band name as her own. Her mother seemed haunted by the old world, although she like many elders and first generationers never admitted to the existence of lands and lifestyles beyond the red line.

If Mama Killmaiden were here she would try to talk Dressica out of this mission, probably block the vote. But she wasn't, and Dressica was an adult capable of making this journey. She heard the spurs first, Raz led the team to the city gates. Even as the team trained, he didn't look at her, and Dressica never looked at him. Uncle Max had his hair tied back and two shotguns crossed on his back in slings. Isa had throwing knifes strapped to her legs. The same ones she had used for years in the pit.

"Where is Dez?"

Dust blew in the air as something massive came around the corner. Dressica unslung her rifle ready to fire at whatever monster was upon them.

"Back, back!"

The team pulled out their weapons, Dressica loaded a round into the rifle's chamber. She had never actually fired a gun at anything besides targets. The dust slowly cleared. It was car, a large Ford Mustang with its roof cut off. Its body was haloed by barbed wire, its wheels covered in sharp spikes. It was painted like a shark's open mouth. Dez stood up in the front seat.

"Need a ride to the red line?"

"I almost shot you."

"I smell potatoes?" Isa said sniffing the air.

Uncle Max walked the length of the car.

"How did you get one of these old things moving again?"

Dez jumped out of the car.

"Been working on it for months. I call it a hybrid, it's run partly on recycled cooking oil and a system of pedals."

Dressica leaned over the barbed wire. There was no floor in the vehicle, just six sets of bike pedals. A crowd gathered behind the car. Eve-al and Keith Tesco of the council had led a group of citizens to the city line. They only had three days for the team to train. The water only returned for two hours. It would only be a matter of days before the entire crop collapsed. There wasn't enough rain expected for months to come.

"Dressica," Eve-al stepped forward. "The hopes of our great society rest in your capable hands."

Dressica slung her rifle and jumped into the muscle car. She sat behind the driver's seat and positioned her feet on the pedals. Raz jumped in next, the car bounced with his weight. Isa and Uncle Max waited for Dez. Once they all were in the car they locked their feet into the pedals.

Dressica put the car into drive once she heard Uncle Max strap in behind her. Eve-al walked toward the car, she smiled at Dressica but went past her. She leaned safely over the barbed wire to whisper into Uncle Max's ear.

"Tell them why."

Dressica could barely hear it over the damage she had done to her ears. Eve-al stood up and walked back to stand with the crowd.

"Rock on!" The council woman yelled.

"Pedal!"

All five of them pedaled and the car revved to life. The stereo blared *Rise Above* by Black Flag. As the drum beat kicked in, Raz pumped his fist.

"Fuck yeah!"

Uncle Max nodded and smiled as they rolled away.

"Get us some fucking water!" Keith Tesco screamed and shoved his fellow councilor. Eve-al pushed him back. The crowd began to slam into each other as the car rolled away.

"Rise above! We're going to rise above!"

The crowd chanted and moshed as the mustang rolled out of Crassville on its journey with destiny.

CHAPTER FIVE

Dressica had worked up a pretty good sweat. When they got enough energy going with the pedals the engine would kick in. It would only take a few minutes before the tape deck would slow and the music would cue them that it was time to pedal. They took a road up a hill away from Crassville. They saw a few farms along the side of the road but mostly empty dessert. Isa stood up every couple miles and looked through binoculars at the river.

The flow had not increased. The mountain that had always been a snow capped dot became larger as they pedaled closer. Raz got bored easily and spent a lot of time releasing his razors and sharpening them. He didn't seem to notice that it made everyone nervous.

Dez looked over the man's shoulder at the blades. They only came out a few inches from his skin, but it had been enough to damage Isa's arm. Raz looked back at the young engineer out of the corner of his eye.

"Think you could do better?"

Dez laughed.

"I have done better. Once Dressica is in the pit you can't get close to her."

Raz retracted his blades with a snap, he flexed and you could see the steel casing under his skin. He turned and looked at Isa. He grinned.

"Sorry about the arm."

Isa started pedaling. They were coasting down the road, she didn't have to pedal but it kept her from ripping out Raz's throat. She sat there silently. Uncle Max tapped Raz on the shoulder.

"You know, when I was your age, the pit was a celebration of unity."

Isa smiled at him. The old man continued, "We danced together as outlet of aggression. When someone fell, we picked them up."

Raz turned and looked at the old man.

"Fucking hippie."

"Have you ever seen a hippie?" Dressica asked.

"No, but I read about them."

"Bullshit, hippies are a myth. They

never existed." said Dressica.

Uncle Max took his niece's mechanical hand into his own and shook his head.

"Is it really so fun?"

Dressica smiled just thinking of the excitement of the pit.

"Fuck yeah, the pit is awesome. The energy, the emotion."

Isa shook her head.

"It's all bullshit. The council uses it as population control."

Dressica saw the red line border in the distance, or she would have told Isa she was being crazy. Dressica squeezed the wheel as they sped down the road. The pavement ended and they slowed before they reached it. A single red line of paint went across the road and continued as a crude barbed wire fence. A small sign was attached to the fence.

'Do not cross the red line, this spot marks the end of Dischargia. Enter the Phantom Zone at your own risk.'

Dressica jumped out of the car and walked to the line that she was taught never to cross. Dez followed her. Just the idea of crossing this line went against everything they had been taught since they were children. Isa stood in the back seat and looked into the distance with the binoculars. She thought she could see a continuation of the road, but a fog bank hung around the base of the mountain.

Raz pounded on the dashboard.

"Lets fuckin' do it."

Dressica turned and looked at her Uncle.

"Tell us why?"

"Why what?" Uncle Max played dumb.

"The other elder, she told you to tell us why. I think she meant the red line. Or maybe something even bigger."

Uncle Max waved her back to the car.

"It is not the time."

"We're about to cross into the Phantom Zone, it's fucking time."

Raz jumped in his seat like an excited chimp.

"Those are fuckin' lyrics man," Raz started pedaling and the stereo came on. He ejected the tape in the deck and put in a mix he made. *Sick Boy* by G.B.H. blared through the speakers. "Let's go!"

Uncle Max smiled and let the classic punk song give him a reason to stay silent. Dressica jumped in the car and put the vehicle into drive. Dez still stood at the line, he shook his head.

"No, there is nothing across the red line."

"That is fucking elder talk dude, don't be a wuss." Raz screamed over the music.

"Get in or walk back, your choice." Dressica said and inched the car closer to the line. Dez jumped into the back seat and Dressica floored it. They blew past the line and Isa let out the breath she had held.

The car picked up speed as they disappeared into the fog coming off the mountain.

CHAPTER SIX

They couldn't see anything as the car cut through the fog. Raz screamed and laughed. Dressica turned the volume down as the mix tape rolled on to an Angry Samoans song. Dressica felt the power weaken as Dez took his feet off the pedal. Dez looked over the side of the car and felt his stomach drop. He shook Dressica's seat.

"Turn around! Stop! Fuck!"

Dressica leaned over the side and looked. She couldn't see the ground under them, just fog.

"It's all true, there isn't anything beyond the red line," Dez screamed like a baby.

"Keep going!" Uncle Max yelled.

Dressica stopped the car. The fog smothered them, they could barely see each other. Isa groaned as the fog surrounded them. It wasn't even night yet but they couldn't see. Dez looked nervously around. Dressica hit the steering wheel.

"Tell us the truth now!"

Dez and Isa looked afraid and desperate.

"Turn around Dressica!" Isa screamed.

Dressica turned in her seat and looked at her Uncle.

"I was never sure if you made it up or not, but when I was a kid you told me something about the world, was it true?"

Uncle Max took a deep breath. He ignored the question.

"Keep going forward, you'll find a road."

"Fucking knew it!" Raz laughed and turned up his tape. Dressica kicked the eject button with her foot. The tape spit out and silence returned except for the hum of the hybrid engine. Dressica never took her eyes off her uncle.

"I want to know what, but I also want to know why? What did Eve-al mean when she said 'tell them why?'"

"Ok," Uncle Max nodded. "It was all Reagan's fault, you see he was..."

PSSSSPAT!

An arrow landed in Max's shoulder. He screamed. Dressica turned to see a giant beast at the edge of the fog that stood on four legs taller than the car. A man sat on its back holding a bow and arrow.

"Drive!" Max screamed and he coughed up blood.

Raz stood and ejected his arm blades. He swung at the large animal, it stepped back.

"Leave the horse alone!" Uncle Max pulled one of his shotguns free and fired. The man on the beast flew off its back and his head came down in a shower of brain matter. Dressica turned to the wheel. Everyone pedaled as she hit the gas. They moved forward and felt a bump as they came up on a road. They sped smoothly through the fog until it finally started to clear a little.

More of the giant beasts galloped beside them on both sides. They heard a sound like a lawnmower as a bike with a motor pulled up on the right side. The man on the bike loaded a shotgun. Raz jumped up and swung his arm-blade at the biker's throat. Blood sprayed and the bike fell away.

"Keep pedaling!"

The car sped past the four legged beasts, it seemed the riders were holding them back. Dressica didn't care if they were allowed to go, she just wanted away from them. Isa stood and looked at the river bed through binoculars.

"I can't tell if it's flowing or not. We need to get closer."

Dressica pulled the car off the road as close as they could get to river bed without running into trees. She stopped the car and Isa jumped out. Dressica turned around, Uncle Max had pulled out the arrow and the blood poured out on to the seat. His eyes barely opened. Dez looked through his pack for the first aid kit. Dressica knew it was too late.

"I didn't lie to you." Said Uncle Max with his last breath.

Dressica closed his eyes. Dez pulled out the first aid kit.

"Put it away."

Dez pushed it back in his bag. Isa walked back to the car.

"The river flows a bit more up here, but we need to keep following it."

Dressica looked up at the sky. The sun was going down.

"We bury Uncle Max and then in the morning we find the bastards taking our water."

CHAPTER SEVEN

Dressica watched the sun rise over the mountain, it was in those first moments of light when the fog burned off. In the distance on the far side of the mountain she could see the lights of a village. It was smaller than Crassville, but well lit even at dawn. Dressica looked through the binoculars, to the east of city, large fields rolled with crops. Even at this distance she could see the irrigation system.

Raz fell asleep sitting up against a tree, Isa slept close to their fire, and Dez who never spent time outside of Crassville slept on the back seat of the Mustang.

The sun poked over the ridge and shined on Raz. He woke up almost instantly. He jumped a little and his blades came out. Dressica laughed. He looked around and when he saw no one there he retracted his blades

"See anything?" Raz sniffed.

Dressica pointed north.

"A city," Dressica broke a small branch in frustration. "They are diverting the river."

Raz kicked Isa awake. She smacked his foot with her mechanical hand.

"Fuck you."

"Wake up sleeping beauty it's time to kick some ass."

Isa sat up, Dressica pointed to the city and handed the binoculars to her.

"We have to talk to them, they probably don't realize that we need the river too."

"Are you daft?" Raz laughed. "They were riding on monsters and killed Max. You can't talk to them."

"It was misunderstanding, that's all," said Isa.

Raz laughed and jumped up. He stomped on the fire, putting out the flames under his combat boots. Raz reached down like he was going to pick Isa up. Dressica stepped in between them and released the quills in her right arm. One of the sharp quills poked Raz's neck just enough to prick a tiny hole in his skin.

"You calm down right now. Were going down there, offer them something to help, that is what we do, mutual aid."

Raz smiled, Dressica was close enough to really get a good idea what food was stuck in his teeth.

"What are we going to do if they don't want anything from us."

"Then the pit starts."

CHAPTER EIGHT

Dressica guided the car down, she squeezed the steering wheel a little tighter as they pulled up to a large sign.

WELCOME TO GOLDWATER!

In the distance they could see homes in row after row of straight lines, each one of the homes had a small patch of short green stuff that looked like prairie grass, but it was green not yellow. None of the homes had band posters on the outside, none of them had stages built out front. One of the large beasts came running toward them down the main road.

"Quick! Turn!" Dez screamed behind Dressica. She turned the car toward the first street of homes. Dressica looked at the street sign - *William F. Buckley Drive.* The car sped past home after home of well manicured lawns.

"What the fuck is this place?" Raz yelled.

Dressica had never seen buildings so plain. They didn't look lived in like any homes she had ever seen.

"Are those houses?" asked Dez.

"I don't know."

"Look! People!" Isa screamed.

The car slowed down as they came up on a man on the grass in front of his house holding a hose. He was wearing a plain white shirt with no band logo on it, he had something on his feet that didn't look like boots. His skin was pale white and didn't have a shred of tattoos. He barely had hair on his head; just a small patch hair that was the color of pubic hair. Dressica laughed, he had pubic colored hair on his head.

The car rolled up beside the man and his jaw dropped as well. He looked at them in shock, the water just fell on his lawn. Raz stood up and ejected the razors on his arm.

"That's our fucking water bro!"

The man dropped the hose and ran back toward his house. The door opened and a woman in a strange white skirt and a plain looking blue shirt stepped outside. She had a full head of un-dyed hair the color of dessert straw. When she saw Dressica and her group

she screamed.

"What the hell are they?" The woman yelled as the man pushed her into the house and slammed the door.

"What the fuck are you?" Raz yelled back as he jumped out of the car and picked up the end of the hose. "Here's our fucking water."

Raz drank from the hose. A group of men came around a corner on the back of the large beasts. Raz rubbed his hands together. Dressica jumped out of the car and Isa followed her. Dez stayed in the car too afraid to step out.

"Keep it cool Raz."

The men stopped their large animals and soon after, a huge crowd of people came out of the houses. The people looked strangely plain. None of them had mohawks, dyed hair or wore normal boots. They had plaid shorts on and plain white shirts without a single band name on any of them. The crowd surrounded them. Dressica counted at least five who were holding shotguns.

Dressica put up her hands. Isa and Dez quickly raised theirs.

"Raz, raise your hands!" Dressica said just loud enough for him.

Raz raised his hands. One man stepped forward in the crowd. He had a gold star pinned to his chest. Dressica thought that must be some symbol of authority. The man spoke.

"I'm the sheriff for these here parts. Who are you? Where did you come from?"

Dressica breathed a sigh of relief, they all seemed to speak Dischargian.

"Some kind alien weirdos!" A woman in the crowd yelled.

"Us weird? Look you fuckers." Raz pointed at her and she stepped back in the crowd.

"We came from a land beyond

the red line," Dressica said. The crowd gasped.

"There is nothing alive below the red line," the sheriff said.

"We come from a land below the line called Dischargia."

The sheriff shared a long glance with one of the men holding a shotgun.

"Lady, the red bastards dropped a few nukes on us but this still the US of A."

Dressica looked at Isa wide eyed. Raz looked back at them, both had fear in their eyes. No one their age back in Dischargia believed The United States existed for real. It was something the elder bands talked about in abstract. This awful brutal country promoting violence, war and greed. That encouraged conformity and brutal repression of self expression. It was like an ugly monster that punk parents sang about in songs to scare children into behaving like good punks. No one really believed in this story or the monsters at the center of those songs whose names stuck fear in the elders.

"We crossed into America?" Isa whispered.

"Fucking myth," said Raz.

The sheriff watched them carefully. Dressica stepped forward, guns were raised. Dressica kept her hands up.

"Look we need to talk about the river?"

The Sheriff shared a long look with the man holding the shotgun next to him.

"Lady, I think we should take to you to Chancellor Reagan."

Dressica took a step back.

"Did you say Reagan?"

Her stomach instantly twisted in knots, the ultimate boogeyman himself. The name spit in anger in more songs of the elder bands than any other. The bastard Reagan, the man whose name Max spoke with his dying breath. The man responsible for all evil in the world - Reagan.

Raz had heard all the songs, too. He reacted out of sheer panic. Raz swung his bladed arm and he spun in classic pit move. He closed his eyes, imagined his favorite TSOL song, and slammed through the crowd to the beat in his head. The whole front row of the crowd fell bleeding to their knees. One shotgun blasted, but it just sprayed busted pavement in the air.

Dressica touched her thumb to her pinky. She spun like a top and her quills came free in time for her to roll her body against the crowd. Screams sang through the town of Goldwater, the crowd didn't have it in them to riot - they ran. The sheriff pulled his pistol and fired at Dressica. She moved too quick and his aim was off. Isa threw a knife at the sheriff and it hit him in the leg.

Dez jumped into the front seat of the car but couldn't start it without lifting his head, he was too afraid to do that. The sheriff came up behind Isa and kicked the back of her knees, she fell to the ground and the sheriff put his gun to her temple.

"Stop or I'll kill her."

Dressica stopped and in a single motion her quills retracted into her body with a snap. Raz stopped in place but his blades were still out.

"Fine, take me to your leader."

CHAPTER NINE

The guard held on to Dressica by her mohawk and pushed her through the main street of Goldwater. Crowds of freakishly plain looking people stared at their team as the sheriff had them pushed through the street. Raz looked ready to explode, but the sheriff walked at the front with his gun still pressed against Isa's temple. At first, some of crowd yelled at them and many laughed, the older people just shook their heads in disbelief.

As they made their way through the main street, Dressica heard the sound she had waited days to hear. The flowing river. She looked over to the side and saw the blue water flowing through the river toward a large dam. It was a large deep river here close to the mountain. The guard pushed Dressica by twisting on her mohawk. Dressica almost released her quills out of pure anger.

"Keep moving!"

Dressica obeyed, hoped the guard would talk to her.

"Where does the river go after the dam?"

The guard kept pushing her silently.

"Does it go to your farms?"

They reached a tall building, It had at least twenty floors, the tallest Dressica had ever seen. It looked like it was built out of glass. The sheriff pushed Isa inside. The building felt like a refrigerator, once they entered, cold air blew out of slots in the walls. Even Raz got gooseflesh and shivered. They all piled into a small room with silver walls and the door shut. Suddenly they were all packed in tightly together.

The sheriff and the guards made disgusted faces. Raz laughed.

"What's wrong you have to take a dump?"

The sheriff shook his head.

"No, but it smells like you people did."

Raz looked at the sheriff and laughed.

"At least I don't look fuckin' weird like you?"

The men holding them captive laughed. Sheriff got up in Raz's face.

"Have you looked in mirror freak?"

A bell dinged, a robotic sounding voice spoke.

"Welcome to Chancellor Reagan's penthouse."

The door opened and revealed a wide open room with glass walls. It looked like the room was floating in midair. The guard let go of Dressica's mohawk but the sheriff and the four guards kept their guns pointed at them. Dressica walked as close to the glass as she could.

She could see the mighty river just below them being diverted in a water plant that serviced the houses. She could see forests being torn down by work crews. Beyond the crews taking down the trees there were fields of animals lined up. A row of animals were being led single file into a building. Dressica knew these barbarians were eating those animals. North of the city, more trees were being destroyed and homes were going up in their wake.

"Well, what do you think of my empire?"

Dressica turned around to the sound the raspy voice. There were two large desks at the end of the room. Dressica walked toward them. A man sat behind the desk on the left. He was old, shriveled, with black greasy hair.

As Dressica got closer, she couldn't see any eyes. Just open sockets. The desk on the right had a woman behind the table. Her eyes were gone too, her skin wrinkled and her graying blond hair was boofy.

The man's right arm lifted but his hand stayed frozen. Dressica heard a voice but his mouth didn't move.

"Those damn reds thought they could destroy us didn't they Maggie?"

The woman's arm shook. Dressica watched carefully, the woman's arms were attached to sticks. Someone covered by a black curtain sat behind the office chair and was directing these "people." Dressica stepped toward the desks. The guards and the sheriff all readied their guns. Dressica lifted her hands.

"Who am I speaking to really?"

The Reagan puppet moved around in exaggerated motions behind the desk.

"I am chancellor Reagan! Savior of the American dream. And you may call my partner Prime Minister Thatcher."

The Thatcher puppet clapped and spoke with a ridiculous accent Dressica had only heard between songs on Damned and Sex Pistols bootlegs.

"Oh thank you, for saving the world my sweet Chancellor."

The two puppets took a moment to blow kisses to each other. Raz squeezed his fists in frustration. The Reagan Puppet moved as if scanning the group with his empty eye sockets.

"And just who the hell are you freaks?"

"My name is Dressica Killmaiden. I come from a land down river call Dischargia," Dressica pointed out the river. "This is your empire?"

"I thought Gorby was weak," The

Reagan voice giggled and the puppet moved to the sound. "That was before he blew the piss out of our silos in Turkey. Crazy red splotch mother fucker. I'll have you know, little lady, we leveled Moscow like a truck stop pancake."

"I don't care about the old world."

"It's coming back darling." Thatcher said.

"It took a few years," The Reagan puppet pointed out the window. "But I promised the American dream would be reborn. Hamburgers, banks, no trees causing pollution and goddamn it the lowest tax rate possible."

"For the wealthy right? My mom played me songs about Reagan," said Dressica.

"Songs about me?"

"It's how my people pass down history, and those songs told of a boogeyman. An evil creature that was bent on exploitation. I thought it was an exaggeration. I think you believe all the myths, that is why you are pulling the strings that you do. I'm asking you to think for yourself. That is ultimate law in my land."

Dressica stepped toward the window and pointed out.

"Your river flows down stream and provides the water for my people. Surely we can work together and share the river."

The Reagan Puppet knocked the pictures of Nancy Reagan and their children off his desk onto the floor.

"My America! My river!"

Laughter came from the curtain behind the desks. The sound of two women laughing. A woman rolled forward on a scooter, her gray hair was pulled back in a tight pony tail.

"I warned you about these vulgar

punk rockers." The old woman's voice was shaky.

Another old woman moved forward on mechanical legs, her body robotic. Wrinkled, stretched skin hung off the old woman's only functioning biological piece - her head. Brown dyed hair, curled in a perm, shook as she moved. Blood flowed through tubes around the mechanical body back to the head. It spoke.

"Tipper's right Ronnie. They want to undermine our new America."

"What should I do Nancy?"

The robotic Nancy-bot moved forward each step set off a cascade of mechanical parts.

"Public execution."

The Reagan and Thatcher puppets clapped. The guards stepped forward, Dressica looked at Isa. Silently Isa agreed, they had tried to talk and now they had to act. Dressica jumped on to the Reagan puppet's desk and ejected her Punkupine quills.

"Hey Ronnie, Just say no!"

Dressica swung her quills at the puppet, but it dropped to the ground. Isa kicked the knee of the sheriff and he went down. Isa grabbed the pistol out of his hand. Nancy-bot jumped on to the desk and swung at Dressica with inhuman strength. The mechanical arm bashed into her quills. Dressica screamed as the quills bent under her skin.

"You fucking fucker!" Nancy-bot screamed as she hit Dressica again. Dressica hit the Thatcher desk. The puppet of the prime minister hit Dressica but she batted it away. Raz swung around with his blades and cut the belly of one of the guards. The guard's guts raced to floor as he fired off one shot. The shot went wide of Raz. The blast hit the old Tipper lady in the face, she never had time scream as her head exploded in a rain of brain chunks.

"Guards! Seal the building!" The Nancy-bot called out. Two of the guards disappeared. Dressica looked at the Nancy Reagan robot standing on the other desk. The robot waved her forward. The guards disappeared into the elevator. Raz punched the door after it closed. Dez walked over and pushed the down button.

"It won't work, you're trapped here until I kill you." The Nancy-bot said and laughed. Dressica stood up and shook out her quills.

"Sorry lady we're going down."

"In less than a minute the entire population of Goldwater will be surrounding this building ready to kill at my command."

Dressica looked at Raz.

"You're going to have to force Dez."

Raz laughed as Dressica ran the length of the table and bear hugged the Nancy-bot. Dressica pushed them both at high speed into the window. It shattered on the Nancy-bot's back. Dressica closed her eyes as they flew out the window. The last thing she heard was Raz yelling.

"Fuckin' A!"

They fell faster than Dressica thought possible She clung to the Nancy-bot and opened her eyes to see the river coming toward them. She hoped it was deep enough. She closed her eyes and held her breath just as they hit the river.

CHAPTER TEN

Dressica swung her arms and legs in the wild flow of the river. Her head popped over the surface of the water for a moment. Just long enough to hear Dez screaming bloody murder and then the plop of the rest of her team landing in the river. Dressica held her breath as she fell back under the water.

After a few seconds of struggling she got to the surface. Raz and Dez struggled to get above the water. Isa had grabbed on to the broken dead body of the headless Nancy-Bot.

"Grab on!" Dressica screamed. "We'll float down to the dam!"

Raz had to pull Dez toward the Nancy-bot. The whole team held on. Crowds had gathered on the shore line. Raz shook their flotation device.

"Where's the fucking head?"

Dressica shrugged. The water was cold, and they were moving quickly toward the dam.

"Paddle to the right!"

They started shifting their weight so they would move toward the shoreline where the main control center for the dam was. On the far bank, the sheriff ran trying to catch up, shots were fired but they were moving fast enough down the river. The sheriff was barking commands. They passed an armory and a truck depot before they rolled up on the dam.

"They are going to have someone meet us there."

Raz nodded. They rolled up on the beach. The water collected behind the dam. Traps and ducts were built to divert the water around Goldwater. Dressica was the first on the beach, she unleashed her quills seconds before Raz opened his razors. A shot blast knocked up sand at Dressica's feet but even sopping wet she moved too fast for the Goldwater cop. Dressica spun and stabbed him with her quills. She took the shotgun from him in single motion. The three other cops protecting the dams almost shit themselves. They certainly didn't fire.

Raz opened one up with his arm blades and spun to take out another cop with his razorback. He grabbed a machine gun and threw it back to Isa who caught it with her mechanical arm and fired bullets in their path scaring the cops out of the way.

Dressica was the first in the control center. The room was filled with blinking lights, and monitors. Raz tapped the screen on one monitor.

"The whole city is coming down on us Dressy, what's the plan?"

Dressica stared at all the blinking lights. She had no idea. Dez walked up to one of the computers and pushed lots of buttons.

"It's perfect really."

"What's perfect Dez?"

Dez turned and looked at Dressica.

"I closed everything off."

Raz hit his shoulder.

"You fucking wank, we need the water. Open it up."

Dressica hugged Dez. He squeezed her tighter than was appropriate but she didn't care right now. Dressica traded Isa guns and opened the firing chamber.

"The dam is brand new, and not strong enough to hold it all."

Already they could hear the dam creak, and it felt like the earth shook.

"Follow me to the truck depot!"

Dressica shook out her quills before turning to the equipment. She fired thirty rounds into the control equipment. Red sirens went off, warning signals. The dam was ready to blow.

Raz flipped off the room before following Dressica down the hall. When they stepped outside, an un-armed crowd had gathered. Dressica spun through the crowd, some of them fell away screaming, others ran. Dressica could see the frustrated cops coming across the river in boats. They were almost to shore in firing range when an explosion rocked everyone standing to the ground.

The dam had broken apart. The armed men on the boats fell over into the water as the river gave way. The speed of the water increased with each second. Dressica ignored the screams and panic on the river. She waved her team into the truck depot. Dressica looked around for a minute.

"Find the mechanics shop!"

Isa pointed to a garage, with four huge trucks opened up like they were in mid surgery. Dressica saw what she needed.

"Grab the empty tire tubes!"

The team ran into the shop and Dressica grabbed an empty tire tube.

"Hell yeah were tubin!" Raz laughed and grabbed his tube. In the background they could hear explosions and cries of panic around Goldwater. Dressica found a pump and quickly pumped air into her tube. She wasn't sure how Raz and Dez did it but their tubes were full and they were heading toward the river. Both Isa and Dressica fought to pump up their tubes.

Dressica pushed on the tube and it felt firm. She put the cap on her tube seconds before Isa. They ran to the river. In the distance before them the dam had almost completely broken apart. Lock after trap on the side of the dam snapped and broke apart like they were

made of twigs. Dressica ran to the river bed and put her tube in the water.

"Stop her!"

The Reagan puppet was set up in the back seat of a convertible that had small America flags on the hood. Dressica could see the puppeteer laying the back seat. Dressica lifted her middle finger

"Fuck you Reagan!"

Dressica was the last to sit across her tire tube and roll into the river. The power of the unleashed river picked them up and in a matter of seconds Dressica disappeared down the river.

CHAPTER ELEVEN

Sheriff Newt took a deep breath as he walked into Chancellor Reagan's penthouse. The view of the river flowing down stream still stung after a week. He walked into the office holding the Nancy-bot's head by her permed hair. It was amazing the perm held after sitting in the river stuck to a stump. But that stump kept the decapitated head from flowing down river.

"Oh thank god you found my dear Nancy," said the chancellor. The sheriff even heard sobs. Chancellor Reagan's arm went up and a headless robotic body clunked forward from behind the curtain. The Sheriff held the head up. The robot's arms reach out for the head and positioned it on top of its body. It made a few squishy noises as the head fit into place. The robot stabbed the head with two tubes. When the third tube went into the head, the eyes shot open. The robot turned around and vomited week old river water and a dead frog on to the chancellor's desk.

"Nancy?"

"Goddamn it Ronnie what happened?"

"Uh well..."

The Nancy-bot moved away from the desk and looked out the window. No one had even begun repairs on the broken damn. The river flowed naturally down toward the red line and beyond. The Nancy-bot could see the lawns dying in the suburbs of Goldwater. She saw empty fields where they had released the cows they didn't have water to support.

The Nancy-bot turned and slammed her mechanical fist on his desk.

"I swear Ronnie, one day I'm gonna destroy that Dressica Killmaiden!"

"Well Nancy, what can I say, they beat us. Those goddamn punk rockers, they beat us."

MATTHEW REVERT

LOCATION:
Melbourne, Australia

STYLE OF BIZARRO:
Pubic Absurdism

BOOKS BY REVERT:
A Million Versions of Right
The Tumours Made Me Interesting
Stealing Fred Savage

DESCRIPTION: Matthew Revert is absurdity's whore. His writing explores the lack of sense in all things and plays with the notion that nothing is ultimately wrong or right. He is most comfortable in the gutter and sees profound things in filthy places.

INTERESTS: Music, Film, Species, Banality, Musing, Procrastinating, Sitting Quietly, Cooking, Panting, Lids, Intonation, Self-deprecation, Smarm, Reading, Anxiety, Variety shows, Mood lighting, Restless Leg Syndrome, Jowls, Bee Stings, Onion Tears

INFLUENCES: Chris Morris, Nikolai Gogol, Jacques Rivette, Flann O'Brien, Věra Chytilová, Russ Meyer, Tom Waits, Bela Tarr, Armando Iannucci, Diamanda Galas, William Klein, Keith Rowe, David Cronenberg, Zbigniew Rybczyński, John Waters, Frank Henenlotter, Jay Munly, Jorge Luis Borges, Nurse With Wound, Luis Bunuel, Nick Cave, Fred Savage, The Power Glove, ↑, ↑, ↓, ↓, ←, →, ←, →, B, A, select, start

WEBSITE:
clockworkfather.wordpress.com

A MILLION VERSIONS OF RIGHT

It was certainly no surprise that what I had once referred to lovingly as 'the gentle little rub' had eventually become frenetic masturbation, resulting in my first orgasm. Under the bed that one lunch time hiding from my clockwork father. I was excited and disgusted, my pockets chock full of scabs. My hands were adorned in filthy fingernails, all chewed and torn. I laid there under the bed, cribbed among uncomfortable refuse. The sound of approaching footsteps combined with the sight of a looming shadow panged excited nerves throughout me. I jerked quickly, my breathing heavy and then there was an experience of overwhelming build. A distinct sense that this feeling couldn't elevate any higher overcame me. When that point of no return had been reached it was nothing but intense pain. My toes curled, my lips were bitten into leaking sores, sweat lathered me. That was the first time I ever ejaculated a moustachioed tiler.

The moustachioed tiler climbed down my erect shaft and immediately got to work. Retrieving all the tools he needed from a seemingly infinite back pocket, he began to lay miniscule tiles upon my stomach. It wasn't long before my entire lower torso had been well and truly tiled. The tiler extracted a thermos and a sandwich from his pocket, sat down and had a break. With his gruff exertions, sweaty brow and dirty white overalls, the tiler was a sight to behold. He chewed upon his tiny sandwich, spitting out chunks he didn't like.

When my clockwork father finally vacated the house I remember squirming my way out from beneath the bed. The tiler appeared angry at the inconvenience these movements caused.

"Sorry," I whispered, as if atonement was necessary.

He momentarily stopped eating his sandwich and stared hard, right into my eyes. A very awkward silence ensued. I had the distinct impression that I shouldn't move at all, lest I further irritate this strange little man. I watched as he retrieved a cigarette from his upper front pocket and started exhaling the filthy smoke into the room. There was little I could do.

So there I laid, pants around my knees. A good half of my body entombed in miniature tiles. If there was one thing to be said it was that this tiler had a remarkable work ethic. If only he would stop tiling for a while and get off my body. Burning with hunger, I remember desperately wanting to get up. Stomach acid was knocking against my insides like waves to a shore. Each stomach grumble forced barely spoken profanity from the tiler. I figured it best to stay where I was. My penis was pathetically exposed and flaccid, my urethra still recovering from the enormous stretch of the moustachioed ejaculation.

Hours passed and my clockwork father was due home any minute. My entire body was tiled except for my face and genitals. I assumed this was an attempt by the tiler to maximise the shame and embarrassment I would feel when my father found me in such a peculiar position.

The sound of the car rumbling up the driveway struck me with fear. The tiler cruelly laughed to himself despite the fact the situation was anything but amusing. No, it wasn't a laugh as much as a verbalised rictus.

My father's footsteps clopped up the front steps. He unlocked the door and entered the house. He gently closed the door behind and began making his way ever closer toward his son's sheer embarrassment and shame.

I lay prone, tiled to the hilt. That tiny bastard was eating a sandwich that never seemed to end. The crumbs had achieved an alarming accumulation in his moustache. I could clearly make them out despite their microscopic nature.

The words of my father upon entering my bedroom still ring in my ears to this day. In a screeching tenor he exerted the words, "Now fuck me if you ain't covered all up in tiny tiles!"

My father moved closer, eyeing the moustachioed tiler as he ate his sandwich. "One thing you should know, son, is that when faced with a situation such as yours, when you ejaculate something untoward, you should respond in a manner that is at least equally as untoward as the ejaculate."

In fascination I stared as my father. Without the slightest hesitation he picked up the tiler in a pinch of his fingers. The tiler dangled ever so awkwardly in my father's grip but remained as apathetic as ever. Once my father nabbed the little sandwich right from the tiler's tight little grasp the apathy turned into a miniaturised rage. My father just laughed in a self-assured way as he inserted the tiler into his anus.

"I'm just going to keep him there," he said to me with a pleasant wink.

He turned around and walked toward the lounge room. Moments later I heard the sound of the television coming to life.

Still laying flat, covered in tiles, I pondered what my father had said. He was undoubtedly right, as the tiler certainly wasn't a problem anymore. It was as if my father had demonstrated the positive nature of fighting fire with fire. Birthed from the cock but destroyed up the arse. It was an understandable conclusion to his little life. That it was demonstrated with such ease still dazzled me and filled me with an admiration for my father that I'd never previously experienced. My father was somehow a little less clockwork.

I remember the mild sensation of pain as I peeled the tiny tiles from my ravaged body. Each tile cluster stung my skin as if tearing off a bandaid. With the deed finally complete, I stood straight up and examined my naked body in the mirror. I was covered head to toe, excluding face and genitals, in a red, itchy rash. *Tile rash,* I thought to myself, *what a peculiar development.*

I lay in bed, covered in itch and deep contemplation. Looking back on it now, I feel as if I was robbed of my first orgasmic experience. Where I should have been reflecting on the strange physical sensations that shot through my body, all I could see was the gruff face of the apathetic tiler as he munched on his bloody sandwich. This would eventually affect my sexual life deeply. Suffice to say, during moments of sexual intimacy the tilers face continues to invade my fragile thoughts. It has ruined many a promising night. To this day I call it 'the flaccidity of the tiler's curse'.

* * *

My first ejaculatory experience may have been my first visit from the moustachioed tiler but it certainly didn't prove to be the last. As you may imagine, the outcome of my first act of self-love filled me with trepidation. The situation I found myself in was unfortunate. As a pubescent teen I was in a near constant state of intense arousal which was perpetually at odds with my fear of masturbation. I would go to bed at night and pray to a higher power I didn't quite believe in, to ward off the potentiality of a wet dream. I may have been able to reject the masturbatory temptation in the waking hours but I had little control over myself when in a state of sleep. Wags at school would boast of the sticky mess they awoke to on a constant basis. I would have loved to wake in a sticky mess; my concern however, was that I would awake covered head to toe in tiles and tiny breadcrumbs, unable to move.

The pretty young things in my class would invade my dream state regularly and it was only a matter of time before this translated into an unconscious eruption in my lower regions. This eventuality did indeed occur. It had been nearly three agitated years since my first and only orgasm.

That night, in my dreams, the girls pranced about in their short little dresses, winding me up like a toy, willing me to snap like a faulty twig.

The next morning I awoke, and like I did every morning, patted my sleepy chest, feeling for tiles. I breathed a sigh of relief as my chest was still naked as the day I was born. I threw back the blankets ready to start the day. But, the sticky, wet sensation in my pants became apparent. I couldn't quite believe it. By all accounts, it appeared I had successfully orgasmed without the appearance of a tiler. It aroused me instantly and masturbatory thoughts entered my head immediately. Wary of the time however, I had to shelve them.

The next day at school was full of braggadocio on my part. Sure, I had bragged about my wet dream prowess before but this was the first time I had actually experienced a wet dream to back it up. I boasted loudly and proudly to all and sundry. Quizzical stares assailed me from the chums and wags as my enthusiasm was in direct contrast to my previous, untrue boasts. I'm still not sure whether two and two was ever successfully put together but that is by the by.

I was determined to masturbate myself into a gooey stupor upon my arrival home. My erection had been a barely tamed beast all day. I felt it could sense the possibilities. Tentatively, yet excitedly, I threw myself on the bed and went to work. I clung to myself ever so tightly as I jerked and pulled the last three years of repression away. The moment of climax was a terrifying yet brilliant one. There was that split second where I feared the worst but the worst simply didn't come. Instead I erupted all over myself in pure ecstasy. The tiler, for whatever reason, had been vanquished from my loins.

This was my ticket to pubescent paradise. My life became a dizzy blur of climax and seminal fluid. No tiler, no problems. It wasn't until my first real sexual encounter some years later that the tiler reappeared and caused all manner of problems for me and my ill-fated sexual partner.

* * *

I met her in crying class. She was struggling with the basic methodology involved in crying ribbons. I approached her with pure intentions, failing at the time to notice her exquisite beauty. She sat pathetically with a second generation beginners ribbon hanging lifeless from her right eye. I asked her if she needed help. She accepted. Her acceptance revealed a shame in her voice. I found the display of shame endearing. I gently tugged on the ribbon, being careful not to irritate her eyeball. The ribbon slipped out, her eyes blinked frantically as if shaking out the cobwebs, 'Ribbon Jitters' they were called according to the literature. We got to talking. There was a mutual affection and it wasn't long before we were what the other wags called an 'item'.

Sexual intercourse was the inevitable conclusion of our trajectory. Our affection had grown rather deep and the 'love' word had been used on more than one occasion. As it happened, the intercourse was a result of passionate spontaneity. My clockwork father was out for the night at a 'dreary old function.' We were alone in my room discussing matters of interest. The conversation arrived at the topic of nipple wheeze. We lost ourselves in passion. I was blissfully inside her before I could fully comprehend my actions. Our awkward movements had a resonance of innocence that was purity embodied. As is common during one's first sexual encounter, it was all over relatively quickly. The moment of climax was problematic. For the first time in years I felt the familiar discomfort as my urethra stretched beyond reasonable limits. My deposit was a treacherous one. It quickly became apparent that I had just ejaculated another moustachioed tiler, only this time into my sweetheart.

* * *

I had pulled out too late. It was post-coital devastation of a most unusual kind. I could detect the look of concerned confusion in my sweetheart's eyes. I owned up almost immediately. I explained in detail about the tiler and the high probability that he was now residing somewhere in her vaginal tunnel. Her tears flowed endlessly. Between sobs I was implored get it out at any cost. My efforts to calm her down via Rastafarian impersonation were an instant failure. I asked her to wait while I sought out a torch to shine directly up her region. Although I was gone mere seconds I'm sure it felt like hours to my poor little sweetheart as she sobbed wretchedly. Coils of smoke were floating from between her legs, filling the room with the scent of tobacco. I requested my sweetheart remain deathly still as it appeared the tiler inside her was smoking a cigarette. She fanned at the smoke as it attacked her pretty face. I asked her to part her vaginal walls, which she did in a surprisingly ladylike way. I shone my torch deep within her, searching out the moist crevasses. I could just make out what appeared to be a little hand, waving about a cigarette like some form of diva. I informed my sweetheart that I could see him and she again implored me to hurry. With a long-handled spoon I scraped about inside her, trying to ensnare the tiler. He was definitely privy to my intrusion as he dodged about, attempting to find sanctuary within the limited space available. Above me, my sweetheart squealed in a discomfort that

I'm sure she viewed as pain. The real pain unfortunately was soon to come. As if the tiler was aware of the love I felt for my sweetheart he began to stab at her insides. I felt every little stab and slash. Her squeals of agony were intensified. I felt helpless as I desperately reached for the horrid little man. I did eventually manage to get his kicking body out but I tore my sweetheart up rather badly in the process.

With the bastard tiler in my tight grip I surveyed the scene. Bits of my poor little sweetheart seemed everywhere around the room. Needless to say, my carpet was sodden. My stony gaze returned to the squirming, little tiler in my hand, the source of so much misery in my life. My first sexual experience had concluded with the death of my first true love. I felt worthless. My mind began to occupy itself with thoughts of the tiler and what I should do with him. I was at quite a loss until I remembered the previous actions of my father. That day, laying on the floor, covered in tiles, my father had indeed come to the rescue. His actions were so sure. He did what he did with barely a thought and it had worked. *One thing you should know son, is that when faced with a situation such as yours, when you ejaculate something untoward, you should respond in a manner that is at least equally as untoward as the ejaculate* These were the strange words my father had said.. With conviction I slid the moustachioed tiler into my tight anus.

* * *

The tiler's presence was by no means muted. I could feel every movement as he writhed about my inner workings.

A profound sense of discomfort overwhelmed my being as I contemplated the purpose of my actions. On top of the discomfort was the feeling that my bowel tract was at that very moment being tiled. Just how long the tiler was to remain inside me I didn't know. The first few minutes had been extremely unpleasant and I shuddered at the possibility that the fate which had befallen me was a permanent one. How was I to go about my basic toiletries or even walk appropriately given the constant clench required to keep the wretched tiler inside? Clearly I needed to consult my father in the matter, which is precisely what I did.

I awkwardly walked toward my father in a style that could best be described as an elongated crab. He was in his sitting chair watching his stories. I wasn't aware of my father's televisual tastes but the show seemed especially unusual. There was a man on the screen, among the shrubbery and the hat he was wearing was clearly incorrect. In a mild panic I averted my gaze. My father looked up at me, examining my blood spangled body. Rather than a shocked or horrified reaction he simply nodded knowingly with a degree of genuine warmth that momentarily elevated me from the emotional doldrums I had been lost within. Explaining the situation in detail, with several well-timed points of the finger toward my backside the gist was understood completely. He informed me that although *he* had chosen to dispose of the tiler via his anus, it wasn't a path that I needed to take. He looked me square in the eye and repeated something that will resonate within me for the rest of my life:

"There are a million versions of right."

Those were his exact words. They circulated throughout my mind as I tried to grasp their import.

I spent a great many weeks with the tiler inside me as I couldn't find any alternative solutions to my woe. My precarious bowel movements were infused with miniature tiles and cigarette butts. I spent some time mourning for my sweetheart on the odd occasions where my mind wasn't obsessed with the beast inside me. I had completely stopped attending classes and accepting guests into my home. These were dark days as I retreated more and more within myself, almost shunning the reality of the world around me. My father's words were still but an unbreakable cipher in my mind. Any efforts made to convince my father to expand upon his statement were met with a solemn shake of the head and inexplicable gesticulation. Descending deeper into a private hell I beat upon walls with bare fists and slapped my weeping rump, trying to knock the tiler about. He remained very much alive inside me, assumedly remaining so via a back pocket full of never-ending sandwiches and God knows what other edibles.

When an unfortunate situation removes all vigour from life there comes a time when you must seek a conclusion. It appeared as though having the tiler inside me simply wasn't working out as I'd planned. My bowels were pregnant with a life that irritated me to a completely unreasonable degree. After many sleepless nights I finally arrived at the decision it was time for the tiler to go. I simply couldn't tolerate his presence anymore. He had ruined all that was worthwhile about my life and if *it* didn't end soon I feared my life would.

The bowel movement was dramatic in the worst possible way. Based on the sensation of my anal stretch and eventual tear, I was sure the tiler had grown in size. Sprays of gassy blood painted the toilet bowl murky red. Tiny tiles shattered upon impact with the porcelain. Stools of the most improbable shapes, colours and consistencies rocketed from my tiny hell hole. Then there was the smell! The fetid, miasmic stench engulfed the toilet room. I felt as if caught in a death tempest. Eventually, with much pain and applied pressure, the object of my woe slowly began to slide out of me. Bloody flatulence and splatterings of faecal inhumanities accompanied its exit from my worn and torn body. When I thought the pain could get no more severe I finally felt the tiler exit me completely and drop into the toilet stew with a mighty splash. I sat upon the toilet for upwards of an hour as I tried to assimilate the intense pain and fatigue I was feeling. When I had sufficiently recovered, it dawned on me that I could hear no sound whatsoever coming from the toilet bowl. I expected to hear the angry tiler splashing around, fighting for breath and swearing emphatically in my general direction. I tuned in closely to the minutiae of sound within the room. I concentrated so deeply that I heard the blood rushing through my veins but still, no thrashing, splashing tiler. *Could it be true? Was the tiler dead?* I was almost too scared to look. I had to psyche myself into it. I slowly stood up with my pants still around my ankles and stared hard into the revolting bowl. Nestled within the grisly muck, exactly where I would have expected to find the tiler I found something else; something that filled me with immense concern. If my eyes weren't deceiving me, instead of the tiler's body, all I could see was a rather large black stapler!

* * *

My mind was in cartwheels of wretched confusion. I immediately picked up the stapler, completely unaware I was subjecting my hand to pure filth. I held the stapler up, studying it. Toilet juice ran down my arm. I was far too preoccupied with the reality of the stapler to be overly concern. Before I knew it I had entered into tiny mental spasms. I ran from the toilet room, stapler in hand, arms flailing, pants still at my ankles. A wall, which I swear should not have been there, eventually cut short my little episode by knocking me out cold.

I awoke to my father standing over me, staring down, face full of concern. I was covered in blood, tiles, faecal matter and cigarette butts. The stapler was still firmly in my grip. Once again my father had found me in an unfortunate situation with my genitals exposed. Through a daze of concussion I relayed the events which had just occurred. He nodded, as if completely unsurprised by my experience. He helped me up into a chair, looked hard at me and simply said, "Have you tried the stapler yet?"

I watched him walk away, taking position back in front of the television. I sat for a while, once again contemplating my father's words. Everything appeared so simple to him. Perhaps the truth really was that simple. Perhaps I had let this whole situation work me up into a ball of neurosis for nothing.

I showered thoroughly, scouring every speck of my body several times over until I felt sufficiently clean. The stapler had been soaking in a cleaning solution that I'd purchased from a discount balm factory. By the time I was dried off and changed, it too was sufficiently clean. I took it with me into my bedroom and sat it on the desk. I ruminated for a while before I worked up the gumption to test its functionality. I squared a short stack of loose paper and readied the stapler for work. The result was an utter failure. There were roughly ten sheets in the paper stack and the staple barely penetrated the first couple. I kept subtracting sheets, seeking the threshold. As it turned out, the threshold was only three and even this appeared a struggle for the bowel stapler. This was the tiler all over again, I could sense it. He had seen fit to make my life unpleasant from the first moment I ejaculated him all those years ago. I didn't know whether he had turned himself into the stapler or whether it was a naturally occurring phenomena but it fit his modus operandi to a tee. I cursed his wretched name. I picked up the wretched stapler and motioned to hurl it against a wall. I stopped. I couldn't bring myself to do it. I placed it back on the desk, glared at it, cursed the tiler once more and finally sought refuge in my bed. I fell asleep almost instantly with a conviction to never have an orgasm again.

* * *

The older you get the more difficult it seems to repress your sexual urges. At least this was my experience. I had blossomed into a rather attractive young man. I was understandably attracted to women and they me. I avoided relationships and situations that would provoke unwanted urges. The unpredictability of an urge-inducing situation was a constant problem. For instance, I might glance across and see a lady tying her shoe and nearly explode in my pants there and then. Life was a frustrating struggle and of course I eventually garnered a reputation for being either stuck up or of homosexual proclivity. To tell them the truth was not an option. Shortly after my 25th year another wet dream struck.

* * *

I woke up completely draped in tiles save for my face and genitals. There was another moustachioed little monster, sitting on my chin, blowing foul smoke into my face. I passed out

* * *

When I awoke the second time there was another tiler. They were fighting each other. Throwing tiles and kicking at shins. I watched the strange spectacle for some time completely enthralled. Unusual feelings began to well within me. Staring at these little men, these little men whom I was responsible for creating, I felt somewhat like a god. Even if their purpose in life was to cause me discomfort and frustration I was still their creator. Not even *they* could deny me that. I freed my right arm from its tile encrustation and began to masturbate ferociously. The ejaculation birthed forth yet another tiler from my weary penis. This tiler instantly joined the first two in their brawl. I kept masturbating, again and again. Each new ejaculation introduced new tilers into the fight. They were all identical with their moustaches and little white overalls. Hours

passed, days passed, I lost all track of time. When my body finally gave in there must have been close to a hundred tilers. The ongoing fight was full of violence. There were bloody corpses strewn throughout my room. Those still alive wouldn't give up. They were each determined to be the only one.

* * *

Once again I awoke to the sight of my father standing over me. As my vision cleared it became apparent he was holding my testicles in his hand. They were no longer attached to my body. I slowly scanned the bedroom. There were no more tilers. What I plainly saw was a large black garbage bag. Through a small hole in one side a miniature, lifeless arm poked free. My anal stapler was still on the desk. It hadn't been disposed of. As I stared once more at my severed testicles in my father's hand I pondered. My father had stopped being clockwork long ago. This further proved it. He carefully inserted my testicles into his anus and walked away, calling back, "This is just another version of right."

CONCENTRATION
TONGUE

It started as a mere curio—writing the word 'shoes' on standard, lined paper. I was introduced to writing the word 'shoes' by my good friend, Carl. He had been doing it for a few months and in that time, had become extremely proficient at writing that particular word. I couldn't see the allure at first and was initially reluctant to engage in the activity. Carl suggested that I tag along to one of the group sessions he attended twice a week. He assured me that participation wasn't necessary and if it made me feel more comfortable, I could simply watch from the sidelines. Being a Tuesday night, I had nothing better to do. At the very least, attending Carl's 'writing the word 'shoes' group' would break up the monotony my week usually contained.

* * *

The writer's group itself had no single locus of operation. Each new class was held at the home of a member, based on a simple rotating roster. The class I attended took place at the house of a lady called Linda. Thinking back, it was really Linda who inspired me to participate in the hobby. She wasn't particularly attractive, interesting or intelligent, but there was this mosquito-like lingering quality that was strangely alluring.

I didn't just jump in and start writing the word 'shoes' though. After Carl introduced me to the enthusiastic group of 20 or so members, I was guided to a well-cushioned spectator's seat. A bowl of salt and vinegar chips sat within easy reach and I was far too weak-willed to deny its tangy charm. So I sat, stuffing my face with chips and watching. The members sat about the lounge room. Some were lucky enough to get a couch or an armchair but most had to resort to stools, fold outs or the ground. Then, in a strange unison, each pulled out a lined piece of standard paper and with tongues jutting from mouths in concentration, they began to write.

The writing continued ceaselessly for exactly 90 minutes. The vigour in which they carried out their writing was admittedly admirable. It was Linda who I watched the closest though. The concentration that played about her face summoned beads of perspiration to pop on her brow. Ropes of watery drool swung from her lower lip. Her writing hand scrawled in near-religious fervour. I could honestly say that never in my life had I exhibited such passion… for anything. It made me feel inadequate somehow.

After the writing component of the meeting concluded, a discussion was initiated. I was asked directly to share my thoughts on their hobby. I felt singled out unfairly but had a determination to speak truthfully and candidly. I admitted that although I couldn't fault their obvious commitment, I didn't understand the general thrust behind what they were doing. The choice of the word 'shoes' struck me as arbitrary and I let them know this. I queried the need to pluralise the word and wondered if perhaps 'shoe' would have the same effect. It would certainly sound less awkward in general conversation. Each and every one of them laughed at my apparent display of 'naivety'. I was told outright that the only way I could hope to understand their hobby was to partake in it myself. They urged me to try writing the word 'shoes' when I arrived home. They were adamant that the act itself would be enough to help me understand.

I had a pretty strong conviction to ignore the group's suggestion. That was until Linda approached me. I was waiting in the driveway for Carl, feeling a little annoyed by the attempted indoctrination. I was inhaling deeply on a cigarette when I felt a tug on my shirt. I jumped at the unexpected intrusion, sending Linda slinking backward like a startled animal. I apologised profusely and asked her what she wanted. I was expecting more writing the word 'shoes' related propaganda but instead, with grave tones, Linda warned me never to participate in their hobby. The way she uttered the word 'hobby' was ominous and cold. She told me that if I went down that path, it would mean the end of my life as I knew it. A few tears mapped her face and the way she shook was contagious. I wanted to know more, but she ran off, ducking behind some sparse shrubbery before I had a chance to question her. I could clearly see her behind the shrubbery. It was a poor choice of hiding spot, but if she was so intent on avoiding me, I wasn't going to push it.

* * *

I didn't talk much to Carl on the drive home and for whatever reason he didn't try talking to me. I guess he could sense the agitation his group had caused. Linda's words were percolating in my headspace like rotten coffee and scolding my brain. It was at this stage that I became certain that I would at least try to write the word 'shoes'. I'm a fairly simple guy to work out when it comes down to it. Tell me not to do something and I won't stop thinking about it until I've given it a go. It's the reason I only have two toes and the reason my last dog was called Mrs Felch.

That night, kneeling in my bedroom, stuck in a pose that approximated veneration, I placed a sheet of standard grade, lined paper on my bed. With a common, mass-produced ballpoint pen, I began to write, a little cautiously at first:

Shoes

I leant back a bit and stared hard at the word on the paper. A strange sensation coursed through me. It was the unmistakable feeling of having written a word, only with double the intensity. I wasn't sure why the word had such an effect. I tried experimenting with other words:

Lip

Tuckshops

Quarry

Mint

Bradley

There was no doubt about it. The feeling garnered from these words contained nothing beyond the typical base level sensation associated with the writing of a standard word. There was something about 'shoes' that simply hit all the right buttons. I even tried removing the pluralisation, but sure enough, the elevated feeling was nowhere to be found. My desire to keep writing the word 'shoes' began to far outweigh my desire to understand why it was important. For the rest of the night I remained on my knees, writing the word again and again. With each repetition, I felt stronger and more alive. This was coupled with an ambiguous sense of achievement.

* * *

Morning hit and I was alarmed to find I had spent the whole night writing the word 'shoes'. It was also confusing to note that despite the hours dedicated to the activity, I had only written it 12 times. There was no logical reason that such a short, simple word should take so long to write.

All I wanted to do was get better. I knew I could increase my writing speed if only I could spend a little more time. A quick glance at my clock revealed that time wasn't something I had. Work was looming and despite an urge to call in sick, I did the right thing and left the writing behind. It would still be there when I returned.

The morning commute made apparent the immediate change that had occurred within me. Rather than concentrating on the pop music coughing through my headphones, my mind was on the fellow commuters. Usually these people passed me by in a blur of early morning humanity, but today I couldn't help but wonder if any of them liked writing the word 'shoes'. I studied each face closely, trying my best to ascertain whether I was looking at that face of an enthusiast.

I cast my mind back to the writing group. I tried bringing the face of each member into mental focus. The only commonality between them all was a distinct expression of devotion—of commitment. This wasn't a trait I could readily project upon any of the faces on the train. It wasn't a complete write off though, because on a few of them, I could swear that the word 'shoes' appeared on their foreheads. I wanted to approach these people and kiss them.

Work turned out to be a waste of time. I spent the day finishing an overdue report and felt a sense of relief upon completing it. This relief was short-lived when my supervisor, with eyes aflame, threw the report down on my desk. He demanded an explanation and looking at the report, I could understand why. Rather than mapping the quarterly

growth of the glove department, I had written, very carefully, the word 'shoes' repeatedly—19 times in all. I felt my stomach twist into a knot and squeeze out its contents... right onto my supervisors loafers. I was given an official warning, a liberal spanking and sent home to think about things.

* * *

I had always been an exemplary employee and the warning should have imbued me with fear. I knew that fear was the appropriate reaction but I couldn't summon it. Instead, without a second thought, I resumed writing 'shoes'.

A few hours later, I picked up the phone and rang Carl. I was eager to attend another meeting. I was eager to see Linda again. What I wanted more than anything was to sit at Linda's side, our concentration tongues jutted, both of us writing 'shoes'.

The phone seemed to ring for years before Carl finally answered. He confirmed that a meeting was scheduled for Friday and gave me the address. I tried writing it down but all I managed was a feeble 'sho...'. I tossed the paper aside, hoping that my memory would recall the address. Staring at the crumpled paper with the half written 'shoes', a feeling of anxiety slapped my face. I immediately retrieved the paper and continued writing.

The meeting was only two days away but in my mind that was a million eternities. There was still a part of me that understood the stupidity of my impatience, but that part was quickly growing smaller. What was it about writing that word that made me want to share the experience? Why was any of this important? These questions weren't asked in hope of finding answers. They were just a way to kill time.

* * *

The feeling was unmistakable. I was now one of them. Less than a week since my initial exposure to the word 'shoes', I was already a convert. Everyone else in the group stared at me, beaming sickening smiles... all except for Linda. Despair painted her face like makeup. I felt guilty, but I was already too enslaved to my new 'hobby' to let guilt stop me.

Carl cautiously admitted that the group met nightly. He was concerned that admitting the extent of their involvement would turn me off. He may have been right, but the thought of nightly meetings was music to my ears.

As the group were taking their seats, I tried to find a spot next to Linda, but she insisted on avoiding me. Thankfully, by the time I had started writing, any feelings of rejection had dissolved into nothingness.

While writing, I could feel myself sinking deeper into strange bliss. Memories of the life I'd lived up to this point were beginning to dissipate like smoke from a quenched fire. None of this scared me. It empowered me. The only fear I now possessed was the inevitable end to the current writing session.

When the end arrived, I felt like crying. Looking around the room, it was clear I wasn't the only one. Some members from the group were openly weeping. Each clutched their paper close. I looked for Linda, eager to share the moment with her. She was gone.

* * *

I found her perched awkwardly in a tree, caressing a dishevelled robin. I traversed the tree to join her, falling several times in the process. She steadfastly avoided eye contact and although this annoyed me, I admired the stubbornness involved. We sat silently for a while, adjusting to the presence of the other. The itch to write 'shoes' kept threatening to steal my focus, but I managed to keep it at bay.

Linda eventually broke the silence by asking why I didn't listen to her. I didn't have an answer. She didn't push for one. Instead she tightened her grip on the robin and started scratching the word 'shoes' into the tree truck with its beak. I envied her makeshift writing implement and cursed myself for not having one of my own. I fumbled for a cigarette, manoeuvred it to my mouth and managed to light it without falling from the tree. I inhaled hard, watching the glowing, orange tip as I did. An idea occurred. Rather than wrestle with the appropriateness of the idea I simply acted.

I removed the cigarette from my mouth and began burning the word 'shoes' into my arm in painful, ash-ridden circles. My weak body gave birth to pathetic wails. Linda snapped her head, saw what I was doing and leapt at me. I instinctively flinched and watched as she fell from the tree. The cracking sound her body made as it hit the ground inspired a mouthful of vomit, which I swallowed uncomfortably. I flicked the cigarette away and slid down the tree. The rough, barky surface tore the skin from my palms.

I scrambled toward Linda's body, which considering the brevity of her fall, was badly broken up. She coughed up a rope of blood and stared at me. The word 'shoes' danced across her bulging eyeballs. It looked beautiful and I wanted to dive in. My reverie was cut short by Linda's hand, which clenched my collar and pulled me close. Through floating bubbles of blood she thanked me for releasing her. With the gravest tones I've ever heard, she then warned that there was no escaping for me—that I was already trapped. The gurgled words concluded with the explosion of Linda's unremarkable head. Thousands of tiny, bloody shoes rained down upon me, coating my body and blinding my sight.

I didn't notice the fire that my flicked cigarette butt had started until it was much too late. It was disposed of without thought and I wasn't to know it had flown through an open window. My eyes were still coated in Linda's mini-shoe goo, which meant that I smelt and felt the fire before I saw it. Screams from within the house upset my ears. I stumbled blindly toward the chaos, feeling the heat intensify. I didn't feel capable of helping, but felt the need to at least be nearby as a show of support.

Sirens began to fill the air, eventually drowning out the screams of the burning group members. I tried swallowing my vomit several more times before capitulating and allowing it exit. I was approached by a man with the accent of a paramedic who wrestled me to the ground. He screamed at me to remain calm, again and again, and assured me he was going to help. I felt something warm and sticky mash into my eye sockets. When enough shoe goo had been removed I learned that it was the paramedic's tongue.

With a workable level of vision back, I pushed the paramedic away and crawled toward the burning house. I pressed my skinned hands against a scorching window and peered inside. The crispy, blackened corpses of the group members sat in the living room like macabre statues. Each of them still adopted writing poses. It struck me that each of them had resumed writing the word 'shoes', even as their bodies were burning. They were all too obsessed with their hobby to save themselves. It was at this point that I decided to give up smoking. The havoc my cigarette butt had wrought was too much for my conscious to bear. I decided to focus solely on writing the word 'shoes'. At the very least, it was cheaper than smoking.

* * *

Several weeks had passed since the fire. I remained bound to the confines of my home, feverishly indulging my hobby. I sent a letter of resignation to my workplace, but I'm pretty sure it consisted of nothing other than 'shoes' written repeatedly. It didn't matter. I was free now. All of my time now belonged to writing that beautiful word. I had grown quite good at it too. I could now write 'shoes' an average of twenty times per hour. If I maintained this level of improvement, in a few years I'd crack a word a minute.

My first interruption came courtesy of a sharp knock at my door. This shook me. I had reached a point wherein the existence of others had slipped my mind. All of a sudden, this forgotten world beyond my hobby was intruding. I only answered the door with the intention of giving the intruder a vitriolic piece of my mind. The words never had a chance to leave my mouth. The man standing at the door looked familiar somehow. He held a penny whistle and embraced me in a way that definitely suggested he knew who I was. As if on autopilot, I returned the embrace and watched as he recoiled in disgust and pinched his nostrils shut. It was this nose pinch that kicked my memory into gear—I'd remember that thumb anywhere. It was my brother, Chris.

It turned out that Chris had been kicked out of Thailand for accidentally breaking it. He was now on my doorstep begging for a place to stay until he could get his affairs in order. No matter how much I craved solitude, I couldn't bring myself to turn away my own brother. I allowed him inside.

A few steps later, Chris froze in shock. He dropped his penny whistle and surveyed my lounge room. It was the first time I'd seen it from a distance. Paper, crowded with the word 'shoes', was strewn about the room like a new carpet. Where I had been sitting was smeared in excrement. This explained my brother's nose pinch and filled me with a flush of shame. No hobby was worth forgoing basic hygienic necessity and yet, this is what I'd resorted to. As this thought simmered in my brain, I spotted a scrap of paper that hadn't been written on yet. I dove for it, like I was trying to save a child from the path of a careening truck. With my jutted concentration tongue, I began to write.

My brother marched toward me and snatched the paper from my hand. I swiped at him like a cat but lost my balance and fell. I was writhing in my own waste while my brother read the paper. I convinced myself that, upon reading that intoxicating word, Chris

would suddenly understand. This flawed conviction was a great condolence. But the condolence turned to horror as I watched him scrunch the paper into a ball and swallow it. I was livid. I scrambled toward his legs and bit at his calves, but he simply kicked me away.

I was powerless to stop Chris as he forcibly bound and bathed me. It's not a nice sensation to have a family member scrub away the faecal encrustations from your arse with a toilet brush. When he deemed me sufficiently clean, I was left to soak in the tub in order to 'calm down'. It was easy for him to say. He wasn't the one tied up and needlessly kept away from his hobby. My brain screamed until little jets of blood blew from my earholes. It formed a puddle beside the bathtub and staring it, all I could think was 'inkwell'. As I looked at my fingers, all I could think was 'pen', but with my arms bound, I couldn't dip them into my makeshift inkwell. I manoeuvred myself painfully, until I was able to bob my nose in the puddle. My nose was now the perfect writing implement and the tiled bathroom wall was the perfect writing surface. I began writing 'shoes' triumphantly, only to be cut short by my brother's fist.

* * *

I was tied to my bed. Chris sat at my side with a handful of paper adorned with my handwork. He then asked a question that was impossible to adequately answer. He wanted to know why I was so obsessed with the word 'shoes'. I tried to explain the attraction using overblown, poetic language, but I couldn't convey it. Eventually I just implored him to try writing the word himself.

I shivered with envy as I watched him take up the pen and paper. My hands wanted to leap from their enslavement. Instead I bit a bulbous chunk from my bottom lip and winced as the beautiful pain engulfed me. My brother's hand was moving easily across the paper. Too easily. There was no way on earth he was writing the word 'shoes' that fast. He was cheating and what's more, he looked completely unimpressed. I begged him to show me the paper. I refused to believe he could be so mindlessly efficient on his first attempt. He looked disgusted as he waved the paper about my face. I cried without restraint. Sure enough, Chris had written 'shoes' about 50 times, quite legibly too. I accused him of being a closet hobbyist. He must have learned some superior method from a yogi in Thailand. I called him a hypocrite and spat bloody spit in his face. He stormed out of my house, leaving me tied to the bed.

The hours my brother was gone were the worst of my life. My whole body was screaming and there was nothing I could do to loosen my restraints. The pen he had been using sat so close, yet painfully out of reach. I spat blood down my front, hoping to miraculously form my beloved word, but it was no use. The blood itself became hundreds of small, red shoes. They marched off my body, leaving me more alone than ever. I started trying to hold my breath in the hope I'd suffocate to death. It just wouldn't work.

* * *

Chris eventually returned with a package under his arm. He didn't say a word to me, just sat with his back turned and played with whatever the package held. I wanted to know what he was doing. I pleaded with him to tell me. I was completely ignored. I tried to close my eyes. Tried to sleep. It was no use. He stood up quickly and jammed a needle into my neck. I screamed in pain.

He sat five more syringes filled with murky liquid by my bedside. He told me they were for later. He told me the needles were full of heroin. I deduced that this meant my neck had most likely been injected with heroin. I could feel myself getting drowsy, which wasn't exactly unpleasant. The pain I was feeling began to fade into warm shapes. Before my eyelids fell shut, Chris explained that if he was going to have an addict for a brother, he wanted me addicted to something sensible.

In my mind, I saw myself sitting at an antiquated bureau. I was dressed so well and I looked so happy. I was writing the word 'shoes' in a mesmerising cursive that filled me with satisfaction. My lips sandwiched the most glorious concentration tongue. I felt so alive. My brother had given me a gift, an addiction that allowed me to further explore my hobby. I'd never have to stop writing that beautiful word again.

THE GREAT HEADPHONE WANK

She tells me to shut the fuck up and that little nightly zone I so carefully create for myself vanishes; like it never existed. I muster up a huff and flick off the stereo. The sound cuts out immediately and I'm left in an uncomfortable silence. My ears begin to adjust and pick out night-time noises, usually ignored by those blessed with the ability to sleep. She has already drifted off. I stare into the back of her head through the darkness, resenting her completely.

I admit I'm prone to melodrama but music is important to me and without it I just can't sleep. Or, if I do manage to shut down, my sleep is infiltrated by damaging thoughts. There's something magical about the sonorous ebbs and flows of a trusted CD. It lulls me into comfort; it massages my brain. I'm lost without it.

Fucking Nadia! She's snoring already. I have no doubt that she could sleep through my most ferocious death metal album at full blast. She could find warm slumber during the chilliest black metal. I try not to think the worst of people but she's doing this solely to punish me; I'm sure of it. I clutch my music to me like a security blanket and it clutches me right back. Tonight my blanket has been shredded.

I lie awake in bed with my wide eyes staring at the ceiling. Fearing the dancing shadows, I masturbate while thinking of limes.

* * *

Nadia counteracts my miserable, insomnia-ridden mood with sickening cheerfulness. She's eating toast and passing comment about something on the television. I have no time for it.

"You really pissed me off last night!" My words drip with involuntary venom. She stares at me with surprised eyes.

"What are you on about?" she finally says.

I enter damage control. "Shit, sorry babe. I didn't mean to sound like such a fucking prick. I just had trouble sleeping 'cause you made me turn off my music." Fuck I sound pathetic! A smile crosses Nadia's face as she comes to grips with the petty childishness I'm displaying.

"You're kidding me right? You haven't been brooding all night have you?" Her lack of respect sends a spike of anger to my brain. I repress it admirably.

"I'm having a shower," I respond as a means of escape, knowing full well she will have left for work by the time I get out.

I hear music in the stabbing shower water. It cleanses me metaphorically and physically.

* * *

I hate my job thoroughly. It's so redundant that my not doing it would affect the world in no perceivable way. I work for a company called Astenburger Ltd. My job is to yell at walls in order to test their emotional fortitude. The company founder, Leonard Astenburger, claims that walls absorb the emotional state of anyone who comes into contact with them via a process similar to osmosis. Over time, the weight of a wall's emotional burden can lead to degradation and instability. Unsubstantiated documentation presented by Astenburger himself claims that many lives have been lost due to the collapse of emotion charged walls. This claim has been scientifically refuted ad nauseum but due to a core group of supporters and stakeholders the shady operation continues. This rakes in considerable money for the company and Astenburger personally. Of course this doesn't translate into much money in my pocket.

"You shit! You smell like old tits! Why don't you give a fuck to your father?"

The wall gives no indication that it has absorbed what I'm yelling. Company policy dictates that no less than 90% of what I yell must consist of inexplicable insults. I yell more in one week than most people probably yell in their whole lives. My throat is covered in a leathery callous. I have developed formidable vocal stamina.

The various instruments used to measure the emotional fortitude of a wall before and after yelling spit out esoteric data. I send this data to a department which specialises in the analysis. The results of the analysis are little known among those outside a key circle of managerial types. Annual reports are circulated under the guise of transparency but these reports are virtually impenetrable and go largely unread.

I shout myself hoarse for 8 hours. The day ambles along at a painfully slow pace. The thought of arriving home and soothing myself with music normally calms me enough to deal with my miserable days but Nadia fucked that up the arse with a knife.

I'm tired and angry.

* * *

People have a way of surprising you and sometimes this surprise is even a good thing. I arrive home in woeful spirits having spent my nightly train ride rehearsing polite yet hateful things to say to Nadia. Before I have a chance to unburden myself I am confronted with a parcel placed atop the doormat. It's lovingly gift wrapped and addressed to me. My inner child is excitingly clicking his heels. There's a card attached that says:

Dear Michael,

Get a good night's sleep, okay!
You can be such a baby sometimes.
Don't worry numb nuts, I still love you.
(a picture of a smiley face)

This way we both win!

Lots of love,
Nadia

I tear into the delicate package, unsympathetic to the time and care taken to wrap it. I'm dumbstruck. Entombed within is a simple set of headphones.

"You like?"

I look up. Nadia is leaning against the doorframe wearing nothing but one of my old, large t-shirts. A large smile beams from her face. She looks fucking good.

"Now I can sleep in silence and *you* can sleep to your music."

The solution is so simple that I make a mental note to kick myself later for not having thought of it.

"This is great! Thanks!" I can't think of anything more appropriate to say. I feel light, as if a chronic constipation has been lifted. Nadia strides over with her arms spread wide, wordlessly imploring me for a hug. I fall into her arms and loose myself in her idiosyncratic odours, the odours that you only recognise and appreciate with time—individual like a fingerprint. We retreat to the bedroom and fuck painfully. Desperately.

* * *

After dinner we're both relaxing on the couch, Nadia with her head on my shoulder watching television, me staring at the headphones which I have now removed from the packaging. I try them on, prompting Nadia to reposition her head. Unconsciously, she doesn't want to get in the way. The headphones feel incredibly comfortable. After a few seconds I barely know I'm wearing them. I can't wait to lie back in bed and drift off, beautiful sounds feeding my starving ears.

The late night news possesses a hypnotic monotony that has lulled Nadia to sleep. I roll with it by gently nudging her awake and suggesting that bed may be in order. I wave my new headphones at her in anticipation. Barely awake, she smiles at me with genuine warmth and love. The opposite of this smile would kill you dead.

The bed sheets feel cold and smooth against my naked legs and the pre-sleep lamplight fills the room with warm ambience. Nadia and I engage in a mandatory hug, which ends the pre-sleep ritual. Unbeknownst to her, I silently fart several times. This is common.

This is love.

Nadia has rolled over onto her side as I plug the headphone jack into the stereo. I carefully place the headphones on my head. I visualise a king being crowned and immediately curse my delusions of grandeur. I turn the stereo on and the mechanical sound of a preloaded CD whirs into life. As I lay back I flick the lamp off, the room is minutely illuminated by the stereo's blue display. My finger easily finds the play button on the remote despite the lack of light. I could perform every function on my stereo remote in the blackest void. My tactile memory is strong.

My anticipation drags the split seconds out as I wait for the first track to start. My eyes are closed, every atom in my body prepared for sustenance. Through the left headphone speaker a slapping noise fades to life. It's not until the meaty groaning begins in the right channel that I become completely confused. I flick the lamp back on and stare at the stereo. The display indicates that the CD is playing. I skip forward a couple of tracks only to be confronted with more slapping sounds, more groaning. I remove the headphones in a mild panic. I strain my ears, hoping that somehow the sounds I'm hearing aren't originating from the headphones. There's nothing to hear except the heavy breathing of Nadia beside me. I hold the headphones to my ear once more and there it is, clear as day. The same masturbatory sounds. I throw the headphones down on the bed beside me, while attempting to massage the stress from my brow. My eyes shift back and forward between the stereo and the headphones. I snap myself out of whatever reverie I'm in, intent on justifying the entirely odd phenomena. Without much thought, I pluck the headphone cable out of the stereo. Intensely loud, blastbeat ridden death metal pours into the room. Nadia wakes with a start, unusual for her as she will sleep through almost anything.

"Fuck, Michael! Use the head-phones!!!"

I dive toward the stereo's power button, cutting the sound off abruptly.

"Sorry babe, you don't under-stand…"

"Just let me sleep."

She rolls over, ignoring me, leaving me to deal with the situation alone. I don't dare make a sound.

* * *

I try numerous CDs and every stereo in the house. The sounds differ from track to track, album to album but essentially it's all wanking; a vast cornucopia of wanking. Some of the wanking carries a strange, dignified air that fills me with immediate envy.

I cower pathetically in the corner of the lounge room, which suddenly seems so foreign and foreboding. The occult headphones are plastered to my ears, vexation drowning my brain. The ceaseless masturbation crawls into my ears, pulling me in, ensuring I am part of each and every groan, pant and slap. The physical and mental exhaustion merci-fully knocks me out at about 4 am.

* * *

Nadia finds me the next morning splayed out in the lounge room, fast asleep. The headphones are still stead-fastly attached to my ears. When I don't respond to her concerned voice she begins to kick me until finally I stir.

My body is caked in dry, sticky sweat and my face is stained with tears. In a daze I remove the headphones and stare blankly, right into her eyes.

"What the fuck, Michael?"

Dull shards of understanding and perception emerge as my body tries to reboot. My brain attempts to scan for the appropriate wording to explain myself but I feel as if the wanking has erased everything.

"Have you been here all night? What was wrong with the bed?"

My only response is to feebly hold up the headphones, offering them to Na-dia. "Listen," is all I can say.

Tentatively she takes possession of the headphones while staring at me as if I were a stranger. Her body language places a psychological distance between us and it terrifies me. I watch closely as she listens and starts to hear what I've been hearing.

"What the hell are you listening to, Michael? What is this shit?"

She throws the headphones down and gives me an accusatory stare. I prop myself up against the wall, engaging in the conversation against my better judgement.

"It's wanking, Nadia."

"Yes! I can hear that it's *wanking*! Why the fuck are you listening to it?"

"It won't stop—it's ceaseless and I don't know where it's coming from."

"What do you mean 'you don't know where it's coming from'?"

"It's the new headphones you got for me. Wanking is all they will play. No matter what CD I put into the stereo, it comes out as wanking."

"What shit are you on right now, Mike? You're scaring the hell out of me."

"I fucking *wish* I was on something.

At least then there would be a fucking explanation."

Nadia continues to stare, clearly unable to process what I'm saying. Painfully I stand up, using the wall behind me for support.

"Look, I know alright! It's crazy, I'm going mad! I am completely willing to accept the fact that I've snapped and this is all some fucked up hallucination."

Nadia slowly shakes her head involuntarily. Tears slowly creep from her eyes.

"Nadia please—prove to me that this is a hallucination. Take the headphones, get them to play music. *Please*, prove that I'm going mad. I need a shower; I'm going to be late."

I limp away, leaving Nadia behind to wrestle with the situation. I need to wash away the stink of my undoing.

* * *

I'm working up the strength to start pouring abuse at the blank wall in front of me when I receive a phone call from my supervisor. I hold the phone to my ear half expecting to hear masturbation. Instead I'm subjected to Dean's intolerable smarm.

"Hi, Michael. Dean here."

"Hi, Mr Hayes." A familiar sense of dread always accompanies these chats.

"How you travelling, Michael?"

"Fantastic, never better."

"Good to hear. We need to have a chat, Michael."

"About what, sir?"

"Best not to discuss it over the phone. Come to my office this afternoon. Does two sound good?"

Silence at my end.

"You still there, Michael?"

"Umm… yes sir."

"Two pm this afternoon. Does that suit you?"

Mr. Hayes hangs up before I have a chance to yay or nay the proposition. I'm hardly in a position to bargain but even farcical democracy is better than nothing.

Whenever someone asks me for a chat my defences tweak automatically. It feels like my internal organs are coming loose and rattling around my torso. The simpler they ask, the more devastating the result. At least that's been my experience. I envisage absurdly melodramatic scenarios in my head, one of the worst being Mr Hayes questioning me about '*all this masturbation you've been listening to*' and then whipping my bare arse with rhubarb. Most of the scenarios usually follow a typical, '*you're fired*' type trajectory and result in me walking home forlorn. There's usually an equally forlorn looking puppy following me. We don't befriend each other, I think he's just attracted to the scent of my misery. I picture myself explaining the job loss to Nadia and watch as the guts of her financial security are violently ripped away. I watch her walk out the door, in too much of a hurry to put pants on. She'd rather expose her shame to the world than spend a second longer with me. She walks along the side of the road, thumb jutted out, imploring the perverts of the world to give her a ride—to take her away from me. A car load of horny men pull up beside her, Nadia enters the car without as much as a glance back in my direction. I never see her again and my life enters a period of total ruin.

I have this nasty habit of letting

my imagination sprint away from anything resembling logic. By the time I'm even partially aware it's usually too late. The damage has been done. Two pm will arrive with funereal dread. I spend the remaining hours before the 'meeting' staring blankly at the wall I'm supposed to be abusing. I cast my mind back to the headphones and have an unusual urge to use them. There's something about their masturbatory consistency which appeals to me. It seems ordered somehow. Despite the confusion and discomfort, when I put on those headphones I know exactly what I'm going to get.

* * *

"It's your readings, Michael. You don't appear to be eliciting any response whatsoever from the walls you're testing."

My teeth grit as I suppress boiling rage. Mr. Hayes sits calmly across from me, a passive perversion accentuating every hate-filled chunk of his being.

"Can you explain these results, Michael?"

His smile momentarily disappears and I become aware of the unnatural fluorescent light bathing his office.

"I follow every procedure to the letter including the abuse to non-abuse ratio. Perhaps there's no response to get."

His smile returns, brighter and more sickening than the office lights.

"Michael, Michael, Michael… I'm disappointed in you. Are you to tell me that you have no belief in Astenburger's theories?"

Of course I have no fucking belief, I think. My answer is only slightly more tactful.

"Look Mr. Hayes, I'm just doing my job. Mine is not to question why."

I notice his eyes bulge. In a flash he gathers his composure and attacks with more rehearsed bullshit.

"Any man worth his salt should question *why* on a minute by minute basis." He places his hands in his pockets and begins a slow walk around the office. "Did you know that in your department you remain the only employee to have sustained a zero result?"

"No sir, I did not know that," I say feebly, without any thought of defending myself.

"How does it make you feel?"

"Fairly ambivalent either way, sir," I say coldly, devoid of emotion.

"You really need to shape up, Michael. I'm officially putting you on notice. You have two weeks to get your act together. Am I understood?"

I nod gravely.

"Excellent! You may leave now. I sincerely look forward to seeing you here again under more positive circumstances. Please believe me when I tell you that I don't *like* doing this sort of thing. I guess in reality I'm a bit naïve, Michael. I have this unquenchable ideal that we can all work together harmoniously."

A revolting smile crosses his smarmy face as he extends his hand out toward me. Against my better judgement I shake it. I coat his palm in my nerve-induced sweat.

* * *

"YOU FUCKING CUNT! YOU FUCKING CUNT!! YOU MOTHERFUCKING CUNT!!!'

I'm screaming at the top of my lungs to a wall that really doesn't give a shit. "What the fuck do I have to do to you? What do I have to say? PIECE OF ELDERLY SHIT, WHY DON'T YOU GO AND BLINK PISS!!!"

My efforts strike me as particularly fruitless. I punch the wall, skinning my knuckles and leaving a streak of blood behind. To my addled mind the blood appears to spell the word *pathetic* and I really have to agree.

The urge to resign from this sham of a job multiplies within me. In the end its pure fear that stops me. The status quo may fill me with hate but there's something to be said for comfort. I stare hard at the instrumentation, willing it to fudge a reading. I'm sure dodgy instrumentation accounts for every reading registered by every other employee to date. I seem to have been cursed with instrumentation that refutes Astenberger's theories even more vehemently than I do. In a way we're allies in a house of fools. I can't deny that a large part of me would feel incredibly disappointed if a reading were to occur. I still have some semblance of pride.

I cast my mind back to my psychopathic night spent with the headphones. My mind is far too sleep-deprived and hazy to formulate any meaningful theories. I know what I heard but I won't discount auditory hallucination, except that Nadia heard it too! She clearly said that she heard it. Unless I was hallucinating Nadia's reaction too. She may have been saying the exact opposite and I was contorting her words into what I needed to hear, in which case I am the very definition of crazy. She's probably packed up her bags and left. I'll arrive home to find that bitch gone with a hurriedly scrawled note in her wake:

Michael
You make life hell. I'm outta here.
Fuck off and die!

Die! Die! Die! Die!

Sincerely,
Nads

It's just like that bitch to fuck off when I need her more than ever. She could make it so much better. All she has to say is, "Michael! You're right. I hear it too, let's fuck." Instead she pisses off with a carload of dirty perverts. She's telling them the most vulgar lies and the lousy cunts all snigger and fidget while they feel her up en masse.

Breathe Michael, breath.... I feel as if every screw has come loose. I've worked myself up into an unbelievably stupid, inane panic. I'm too scared to go home... *but I need her. I need her more than ever. She's my anchor—she's an unmoveable calm, devouring my pathetic tumults.* I think my thoughts are trying to kill me.

The walls refuse to respond. Nothing I say is good enough.

* * *

The train ride home was wretched. I had to fight the urge to ask strangers what I should be yelling at my walls. There's a perpetual feeling that everyone knows exactly what to say except me. My decisions are wrong, my choices are wrong—everything I have a hand in is wrong. I anticipated Nadia with equal parts intense need and dread. She wields the power to proclaim me sane or other.

Approaching my front door I slow down exaggeratedly, like a mime walking against invisible wind. I fumble with the house keys, dropping them on the doorstep. I can only assume this is a deliberate ploy to buy more time. The time I try to buy seems to correlate directly to the creeping dread expanding within me. *I just have to open the fucking door!* The door is a clotted bandaid, which I'll tear off as fast as possible, I don't care how much skin it takes.

I step cautiously over the threshold and enter my dimly lit house. The curtains are drawn, only slits of dying sunlight are granted entry. The vibe in this room stings my brain. The walls and furniture seem to cut at Dr. Caligari angles. I pick up on a bread trail of empty, contorted CD cases. I follow the trail through the house, arriving in the bedroom. I'm confronted with the hunched, shivering shadow of Nadia cowering in the corner with strips of daylight cutting searing lines through her body. The image chills me to the bone. I flick the light on, trying to douse myself in the safety of its basking glow. I wish I hadn't. Under the stark illumination lie hundreds of horribly shining CDs. The viscera from the empty cases which have led me to this point. I notice ten or so headphones like my own strewn about the refuse. Nadia stares directly into my eyes. She seems lost. Her eyes are choked with thick, jelly-like tears. She's wearing the headphones. Unseen pressure building within her forces her upright like a tortured jack-in-the-box. She rips the headphones off, throwing them against the wall.

"Babe, what's wrong?"

"They never cum, Michael! They just keep wanking and wanking but they *never* cum!"

She keeps repeating they never cum, over and over, lost in delirium. I take quick, nervous strides toward her and shake her hard by the shoulders.

"Come back to me Nadia. What the fuck is this?" Something registers in her eyes, the light of reason shines.

"I've tried every CD in the house. They all do it! I thought perhaps the sounds were coming from the headphones themselves but....."

"...but what, Nadia?"

"They all respond to volume control, track skipping and random play. The wanking stops when the CD stops. It doesn't make any sense."

Nadia gestures toward the other headphones with a shaking arm. "I went to the store, the store where I purchased your first set. I got every one they had in stock. None of them do it. It's just the set I bought for you!"

I stand a while, pondering Nadia's maniacal words, an uncontrollable smile dances across my face. "You know what this means don't you, Nadia?"

She stares blankly, I answer for her, "This means that I'm *not* fucking crazy! *You* hear it plain as day. So the only question is, where the hell is this shit coming from?"

"You tell me, Michael! I've been asking myself that question all day. I can't stop listening to it. They NEVER cum!"

I hadn't thought about it before but Nadia was right. The masturbation was ceaseless without any hint of climax. There was just perpetual momentum, a clockwork toy, winding up without release, without breaking. It was a disturbing thought. Who did these disembodied auditory signals of self-gratification belong to? Why were they being channelled through those headphones? These questions simply led to new questions like rancid bog bubbles rising to the surface.

Looking at Nadia, wrapped in a blanket and warming her hands with herbal tea, I feel uncontrollably choked with tears. I resent her for breaking down. She's my rock, Nadia's not allowed to crumble. Whatever we've been subjecting ourselves to has been affecting us in a deeply psychological way.

"Nadia?"

She slowly turns her head to face me, waiting for me to continue.

"Let's fuck."

After gently placing her herbal tea on the coffee table she crawls on top of me, cocooning us both within her blanket. We claw at each other ferociously, trying to dig deeper into the other's body. I bury my nose into her raw armpit, allowing the miasma to thrive within me. As we fuck, we cry. Our unstoppable tears intermingling. We thrust in agony, achieving a mutual orgasm, unlike the poor souls in the headphones. Afterward we remain entangled, sobbing and quivering. This is how we remain until morning.

* * *

I choose not to shower after I wake up. I'm seeped in Nadia's scent and I feel safe that way. Nadia calls in sick and returns to sleep on the couch. I'd follow her lead if my position at work wasn't so volatile. I move in for a goodbye kiss, inhaling her morning breath deeply. She smiles warmly at me before drifting back off. I stop to stare at her one last time before leaving for another day of demeaning, disempowering labour.

I arrive at work dishevelled but on time. It appears my next assignment is a residential wall. We don't usually get residential assignments and the fact I've been handed it has me thinking that I'm getting wound down, faded out. Give Michael the ephemeral shit while the *real* employees focus on the commercial walls. I fill out the necessary paperwork and head back to the train station.

My mobile rings half way through the trip. It's Mr. Hayes.

"Michael! How are you today?"

"On my way to the job I was assigned, sir. I'll be there in about half an hour."

"No rush, no rush. Treat yourself to a nice cup of coffee on the way."

The smarmy bastard!

"I personally requested you for this job, Michael."

"You did, sir?" I feel like saying, 'no shit!'

"Yes I did, Michael. I like you and I would like nothing more than for you to succeed. This residential address is a shoe in!"

"Why's that, sir?"

"The house I'm sending you to is nearly 90 years old! Those walls have had plenty of time to suck up some emotional waste. You can't fail. I doubt whether you'll even have to insult them, just tip your hat. The meter readings will be off the chart!"

"I'm not wearing a hat sir."

"Michael, you really crack me up! I'll talk to you soon sport. Don't disappoint me!"

"I'll endeavour to do my best . . ." He hangs up before I finish the sentence. What a cunt!

I turn into a small residential street lined with large oak trees that form a canopy of sorts. The whole damn place is doused in shade and sickening happiness. The street itself is quite short and

I reach my destination in a matter of minutes despite my amble. On the way I step on a dead bird. I consider this an omen, although I can't decipher it. The house in question certainly looks as old as Mr. Hayes said it was. I half expect him to be waiting inside with a stopwatch saying, *this was a test and you're late!* I wouldn't put it past the prick. I pass through a decrepit wooden gate that still holds endless charm despite its decay. The front garden is noticeably overgrown, yet it feels deliberate.

The elderly lady who answers the door smiles warmly before proclaiming, "Astenburger is a wonderful man. Thank you ever so much for coming."

Great, who else but an Astenburger nut would pay for this sham service? I keep these thoughts to myself and slide past her fat thighs. The house smells like a holding cell for those about to die. I attempt to enter my 'professional' mode, which to my critical ears sounds painfully forced.

"Pleased to meet you, Mrs. Webber, I'm Michael. It's always a delight to meet Astenburger admirers among the general public."

In my head I envision my clone performing a sloppy operation on me. Afterward my family gather to celebrate my transformation into the world's most pathetic eunuch.

"My husband and I have been avid followers of Mr. Astenburger for many years now."

I nod politely. What else can I do?

"Which wall will I be working on today, Mrs. Webber?"

She claps her wrinkled hands together joyously. "Follow me, this way, this way!"

Mrs. Webber has more life and energy at 80 than I've ever had. If she dropped into the splits I wouldn't be surprised. A childish desire to push her over rapes my mind. I slap the thought hard, putting it to rest.

I follow Mrs Webber through a long hallway into a well lit, sparsely furnished room. She gestures to a large wall and begins to reel off her story while I set up the instrumentation. I pay little attention. It takes on the ambience of muzak.

"That wall you're looking at has quite an incredible history. I've lived in this very house since the day I was born. My father built this house with his bare hands. Do you have any idea what dedication such an act entails? Of course you don't! The younger generations are all impatient and lazy—no offence intended. It's just that you all want things right away—now! You're all more willing to pay someone else to do the job for you than to do it yourself. That's all by the by I suppose.

"My father, god bless him, lost something in that wall. My father was obsessed with limes, had been ever since he was a nipper, or so I'm told. He had a tree out back in his childhood home. He loved that dear tree. He was never happier than when he was harvesting limes. He was involved in a never-ending search for the perfect lime. At least he thought his search would be never-ending. Shortly before the construction of this house began he ventured to the very same lime tree from childhood for one last harvest. Like a gift from god he saw it—the perfect lime! Did he snatch it up? Yes, indeed he did! In the weeks leading up to the construction of this house he wouldn't be seen without that lime in his proud, working man's hands.

"That's not even the best part. When I was a little girl he'd tell me that he discovered the perfect way to preserve the lime. He claimed that it would NEVER rot! Can you believe it? Apparently the perfection inherent in that lime imbued him with a complex theoretical capacity. He was able to adapt and execute this preservation method in a matter of days. Something must have happened along the way though—I never did see the lime. My father told me he lost it. Simple as that! I've spent my entire life contemplating that lime. You want to hear my theory? Of course you do! I believe that somehow during the construction of that wall, the wall you're here to test, the lime became trapped. I'd bet my bottom dollar that waiting inside that wall is a pristine lime, preserved to perfection! I never did have the heart to tear it down though. If it's in there, it'll communicate with us! I'm counting on Astenburger's methods to make contact with my father's crowning achievement."

I stare up at Mrs. Webber who is still lost inside her vacuous fantasies. I want to be anywhere but here. The instrumentation has been set up and I appear to be sipping from a cup of tea I don't remember being given. Mrs. Webber's ponderous story largely washed over me but I heard the word limes mentioned on numerous occasions. She seems nice enough, a bit starved for attention perhaps. Sexually speaking I wouldn't want anything to do with her—I don't even know why I'm thinking about it. She's still standing politely just outside of my field of vision. I have to get her out.

"Sorry Mrs. Webber, it's not permitted for clients to witness the process. I hope you understand."

She looks disappointed but she nods warmly and leaves me alone.

I feel self-conscious about screaming profanity with elderly ears in the adjacent room. My insults come across more as whispered suggestions.

"Hey flatty. Would you mind giving me a response? I'm about to be fired don't you know? I'll rub my cock on you. That'll get you going, you garden hat."

I take a step back. I'm clearly just embarrassing myself. As the day bleeds on I spend more time contemplating the wall than actually insulting it. I visualise it as a manifestation of my employment. It sprouts great wings and flies away like a toaster on a screensaver. My waning motivation concocts images of me attempting to capture the wall with a butterfly net. I get within striking distance, swing the net with all my strength and watch as it shatters upon impact. Shards of twisted metal skewer my body. I retrieve a white, blood stained flag from my pocket and wave it about. I surrender! The wall comes crashing down, the growing shadow darkening my world. Pitch black.

* * *

I arrive home after another shitful day and find Nadia once more in darkness, the headphones secured to her ears with masking tape. She claims that the headphone masturbation is evolving into an obsession. I ask politely if I can spend some time with the headphones to which she begrudgingly agrees. For the next hour I absorb the masturbation cathartically as Nadia watches impatiently. Rather than reclaim the headphones afterward, she throws me against the wall and violently pulls down my jeans. For the first time in months she gives me a blowjob— probably the best blowjob I've had in years. It's as if her life depends on it, as if she's trying to swallow me whole. For inexplicable reasons, Mrs Webber enters my headspace several times throughout. I shake her visage away as best I can. Nadia's mouth is firmly clamped around me when I ejaculate. After she swallows, she slowly stands up, looking confused. To my bewilderment, Nadia claims that my semen tastes exactly like limejuice. I shrug it off as a psychological distortion on Nadia's part until she exhumes a lime pip that has mysteriously wedged itself toward the back of her mouth. The rest of the night is spent taking turns with the headphones while the other watches. I leave Nadia with the headphones while I make my way wearily to work.

* * *

"Do we have anything yet?"

Mrs Webber looks hopeful. She reminds me of a child, a child I was about to disappoint.

"Sorry Mrs. Webber, it will take a couple of days for the preliminary data to be analysed. You'll receive a full report bearing Astenburger's insignia."

Although it clearly isn't the answer she's looking for, the mention of Astenburger's insignia sets her eyes alight. Mrs. Webber ponders the thought for a while and suddenly starts sniffing the air like a cat.

"You know something, Michael? You smell more strongly of sex than anyone I've ever met. I can almost see the sex wafting from you." How do I respond to a comment like that? I stand dumbfounded for some time.

"I haven't showered in a couple of days"

"It doesn't offend me any but I'd recommend a basic hygiene regimen. Especially when you consider that you're representing Astenburger."

"I'll certainly keep that in mind, Mrs. Webber." I make my way hurriedly over to the wall and arrange the instrumentation haphazardly. Mrs. Webber voluntarily leaves the room. Once more I have a cup of tea in my hand I don't remember being given. I stare the wall down confrontationally.

"I will break you, you fucking son of a bitch! I'll poke your tits out with a dirty spoon and feed them to your mother. I WILL BREAK YOU!!!"

This continues for some time before my hoarse voice gives up. I seek Mrs. Webber out. I have an uncontrollable urge to ask her a few questions. She's on the toilet, door wide open. She looks terrified.

"What are you doing? Get out of here!"

"I just have a few fucking questions, Mrs. Webber."

"Are you going to rape me?"

"NO! I am not going to rape you. I just have some simple questions I need you to answer."

"At least allow me my decency."

"You get your fucking decency AFTER I've asked you the questions."

She begins to sob in that inimitable way elderly ladies do.

"Look, stop crying. I'm not going to hurt you."

"Just ask your questions and leave me be."

I get right to the point. "Why do you believe Astenburger's bullshit theories? What evidence out there suggests that any of this is even remotely true?"

"More to the point, what are you doing working for Astenburger when you clearly don't believe in his theories?"

"It's a job—people need money—I'M PEOPLE, MRS. WEBBER!!!"

"Are you going to rape me?"

"NO!!! I'M NOT GOING TO FUCKING RAPE YOU!!!"

"Why not?"

"Why not? I'll tell you why the fuck not: because I DON'T rape people. Get that out of your fried mind."

"Is it because you find me unattractive?"

"No, it's because I don't believe rape will get me anywhere. I have no desire for power over anyone. Plus, let's be honest, Mrs Webber, you're 80 years old. I don't make a habit of fucking people more than twice my age."

"If I asked you politely, would you rape me?"

"If you asked me politely it wouldn't be rape would it!"

"Would you consider making love to me? I'm a virgin, Michael. I need love, even if it's only physical and fleeting."

"I'm sorry, Mrs. Webber, there's no way on earth I could do that."

I watch closely as the mood in her cataract-stricken eyes turns cold. I can feel the environmental mood change.

"How do you think your employer would react when I tell them you harassed me like this? How do you think the Police would react, Michael?"

I wince as reality sucker punches me in the gut. The weight of my folly crushes me to dust.

"How can you be a virgin, Mrs. Webber? How does anyone in this day and age stay a virgin? I thought you said you were married?"

"I'm not of this day and age, Michael. For me, the topic of sex never came up until it was too late. Now, are you going to love me Michael?"

"There's a problem that I don't think you're considering."

"What's that?"

"In order for me to 'make love' to you, certain physical reactions need to occur, certain physical reactions that given the circumstances, aren't probable."

"You're talking about erections aren't you, Michael?"

I nod emphatically.

"Don't be foolish, you're more erect than you've ever been."

I look down at my trouser fronts and sure enough, my penis is painfully erect. I'm in danger of bursting through my jeans. There isn't a hint of arousal anywhere in my body, yet physically I'm all ready to go. Perhaps my body is simply trying to save me from myself. Keep me out of harm's way. I capitulate.

"Where do you want to do this?"

"Follow me to the boudoir, Michael."

She rises from the toilet, trousers still at her ankles and waddles toward the bedroom. I follow.

* * *

"I need to know that you love me, Nadia. I feel lost and I'm relying on you."

"Where's this coming from?"

"I had a horrible day at work. The sort of day I can't even begin to describe."

"I love you more than you'll ever admit to yourself. I love you so much it causes pain."

"Life is horrible pain."

"The pain of my love is wonderful."

"I need to take the headphones with

me to work tomorrow, Nadia." The look of fear on her eyes drowns my heart.

"You'll get them straight back. Please, Nadia, I need them."

She paces the room, rubbing her chin with dirty hands. I can already sense that the solution she's looking for doesn't exist.

"You can take them, Michael, I won't stop you. Please don't keep them from me. When you're not here they're all I have."

I comfort Nadia with everything I have, which, admittedly, isn't much. I stroke her knotted hair and kiss her unwashed neck. She cries into my chest and I feel the warm damp of her tears as they seep into me. I find musical qualities within the crying. As it continues, it strikes me: I haven't listened to music in days. This is the first time I've even thought of it. I spend significant time with the melancholy symphony, willing Nadia's demons away while ignoring my own. That night we perform acts of unspeakable passion. We can't stop.

* * *

I make my way back to Mrs. Webber's. She still appears entranced in post coital bliss. I arrange the usual instrumentation along with the headphones. I ask if she has a portable stereo. She fetches me one immediately.

"What on earth are you doing, Michael?"

I ignore the question. I hate her questions. "Can you get me a CD, Mrs. Webber?"

"What CD do you want?"

"It doesn't matter. Anything."

She spends some time foraging around for a CD that won't embarrass her. She returns with a pile of five or

so. I grab the first one my hand touches, dropping the rest. The plastic clatter elevates Mrs. Webber's anxiety and she takes a cautious step backward. I load the CD roughly, intent on getting the job done. Sleep deprivation retards my coordination and every basic movement becomes a matter of second and third takes. The CD is loaded. I fumble with the headphone jack. On the fifth or sixth attempt I get it plugged in.

"Michael! What is this? Tell me what you're doing. I could call your supervisor at the drop of a hat."

"Shut up or fuck off, Mrs. Webber."

She takes several more protective steps backward, finding solace against the adjacent wall. The icons on each stereo button, which indicate the function, have faded with use. I cycle through them all, searching for 'play'. When I hear that magical sound of the CD whirring into life I pump a fist of internal victory. Holding up the enigmatic headphones against my ears I listen for the masturbation, making sure it isn't an isolated phenomenon. It isn't. Wanking fills my headspace instantly. I turn the volume up as far as it will go and press the headphones firmly against the wall.

"What are you doing now, Michael?"

"I'm waiting."

"Waiting for what?"

"When it happens, we'll both know."

An air of excitement buzzes within me as I wait. I have no idea what it is I'm waiting for but I'll wait as long as it takes. The instrumentation refuses to register anything out of the ordinary. I cast my mind to Nadia. She must be pacing the house in a powerful state of insecurity—fuck I love that crazy bitch! She needs the headphones more than me. I feel horrible for depriving her. It's like scooping a fish from a pond and throwing it on the bank to flop around in agony. It isn't hard for me to envision Nadia as a helpless fish, drying under the blazing sun. Flopping and flailing in concentric circles as her life ebbs away. I shed a tear which feels like a nail forcing its way through my duct. The instrumentation refuses to register anything out of the ordinary. I think about my job—I think about all jobs. The lack of purpose chokes me. My bank account remains at a constant level of stifling oppression, willing me to keep going, filling me with fear. How many jobs could be removed from the world without consequence? I've never met a single person who does anything worth a damn. The instrumentation refuses to register anything out of the ordinary. Sex! This absurd drive, which satisfies for mere moments before we're compelled to need it again. On more than one occasion I've dreamed about tearing my cock off and firing it into hell's cunt, where it is swallowed and forgotten. My testicles manufacture generations of potential people, all of which die a quick death in a condom or the shower drain. I perform millions of abortions daily and nobody cares. The day my seed grows is the day I owe my sincere apologies to the world…

The instrumentation is going fucking nuts!

A rumbling sound, like a localised earthquake, shakes the room. Mrs. Webber lets out a deathly scream. An enormous crack traces its way from ground to ceiling. Steadfastly I keep the headphones pressed against the wall. More cracks form and dance randomly over the surface. Mrs. Webber is cowering in the corner, entranced yet terrified. A small portion of the wall crumbles away, giving birth to a plume of plaster dust. More sections crumble and fall, covering me with dust and debris. Before long I'm holding the headphones against nothing. The wall has turned to rubble. Both Mrs. Webber and I are powder white and blinking through the dissipating plume. My instrumentation has thrown up vast quantities of data and the blinking light indicates that automatic shut off is imminent to avoid overload. I stare at where the wall used to be, taking in the mound of rubble. Mrs. Webber dives with surprising agility toward the debris and frantically starts to sift through it.

"The Lime! The Lime!" she yells.

I get down beside her, compelled to aid in her search. It doesn't take long for a green, circular shape to emerge. I pluck it up and hold it above my head. Mrs. Webber falls back sobbing. I can't believe the condition the lime is in.

"The lime! You found the lime! I knew it would be there. I found my father's beloved lime!"

Slowly I hand the lime to Mrs. Webber's shaking, hungry hands. She carefully takes the lime from me and holds it before her eyes. With tears flowing, cutting trails through her powder white face she looks warmly toward me and says, "Mr. Astenburger is a FABULOUS man."

I let the events and Mrs. Webber's words sink in before saying, "You know something Mrs. Webber, you may actually be right."

Ever so gently she wipes the dust from the lime with her shirt, cleaning it with love. She studies the lime ever closer, eventually her expression changes. The awe has vanished.

"You know Michael, this lime really isn't *that* perfect at all. I've seen hundreds of limes more pristine than this at the supermarket. This is actually a little disappointing."

* * *

I exit Mrs. Webber's home. Nadia is waiting for me. She must have followed me. Sweat is pouring from her body and she is visibly shaking.

"Michael! The headphones, Michael, give me the fucking headphones. I need them, Michael, please let me have them."

I completely die inside as I hand the headphones over. Everything Nadia was has been distorted beyond recognition. She snatches them from me and begins to run.

"I'll see you tonight, Michael. I'm sorry."

Her voice trails away and she's gone. Instinct tells me that she's gone for good. Right there, on the footpath, I break down and cry. A few passers-by give me a wide birth and utter things amongst themselves. *Goodbye Nadia.*

My mobile phone shears through my pain and despair. The display indicates that it's Mr. Hayes. I hold the phone against my ear half expecting to hear Nadia crying.

"Michael!"

"Hi sir."

"What the hell happened?"

"I got a response, sir."

"You're fucking telling me you got a response! The remote data feed is off the charts! How?"

"Persistence."

"Can you meet me in two hours at the office? I have someone here who wants to talk to you."

"I'll be there."

"See you then, Michael, see you then."

* * *

Until this day I had only seen Astenburger in photos. Now, there he was, sitting in front of me, eyes gleaming. He was a man in his late 60s with snow white hair and black rim glasses. He reminds me somewhat of Colonel Sanders.

"I'm sure I don't have to tell you who this is," says Mr. Hayes, full of pride.

"Of course not. It's a pleasure to meet you, Mr. Astenburger."

Astenburger leans across the table to shake my hand. He has the smooth hands I'd imagine aristocracy to have. "The pleasure is all mine Michael. You look terrible. Are you alright?"

"To be honest sir, it's been a fairly taxing day."

Astenburger's shrill laughter fills the room, followed closely by the laughter of Mr. Hayes. I've never seen the office and I don't even know who it belongs to. It has a blurry, maniacal edge to it, which disorients me.

"I'm sure you have, I'm sure you have. Now, Michael, I came here today to thank you personally. The readings we received from you have been triple-checked and there is no doubt regarding the certainty of the results. I believe that what you did today single-handedly validates my assertions more than any theory I can wretch forth. How on earth did you do it?"

"It was all just a big wank, sir."

A stunned silence replaces the joviality. Mr. Hayes stares at Astenburger, searching for the correct response. Laughter fills the room once more.

"You are a scream, Michael! Seriously though, I'll have you fill out a report detailing the events. I can essentially guarantee a hefty raise coming your way."

* * *

The scene I walk away from resembles a cardboard cut-out of reality, faces frozen in rehearsed emotion. Everywhere around me there is overwhelming heat and suffocation. I make my way to the bathroom. The mirror reveals several coagulated wounds mapped across my face. Beyond these I search for that spark which makes me who I am. There is no spark to be found. I am officially empty. I hear Nadia's voice tripping down stairs in my head, fading away into nothing. I dive after her but she's already gone—broken and gone. I leave work, resolving to never return again.

Approaching my house I can't quite shake the feeling a mausoleum might elicit. The sky around me is sympathetically overcast and grey. I vomit down the face of my front door where I find a note that reads:

Michael,

Every part of me loves you. You subvert my hell and I give you nothing in return. You deserve so much more than me and I'll never be more than I am. Please find it in your heart to hate me with everything you have. Anything less would crush me.

I've taken the headphones, Michael, I need them. I won't be coming back. I can't come back. There's something I haven't told you. Remember how the masturbation in the headphones never resulted in orgasm? I was

proven wrong, Michael. Eventually it did. The disembodied voices came in me en masse, drowning me in their seed. I think I'm pregnant, Michael. My skull is engorged with life. I don't know where this process will lead me but I do know that I need to be alone with the father. The father in the headphones. I can't say what I'm about to give birth to, but I will love it with everything I can muster.

You still mean more to me than anything. Other than my child, I can't imagine anything coming close. I'm in pain, Michael. I am in such neverending pain and I don't know how to cope. When you picture me, picture me leaving. You have to kill your love for me.

Love eternally,
Nadia

I skulk through the house, kicking CDs out of my path. Every room is infused with our combined BO, which reminds me instantly how far we both slipped. I have an urge to open every curtain and window to flush the place out but I can't be bothered. Instead I begin sifting through the CDs littering the carpet, trying to find something to suit the mood. I settle on a mid 90s Funeral Doom album that I didn't even know I still had. I contemplate emptying my bladder and maybe inducing some more vomit but I do neither. I pop open the tray in my stereo and place the CD inside. With the sticky remote gripped tightly in my hand I fall back on the couch. I hit play, close my eyes and resent her completely.

ANDREW GOLDFARB

LOCATION:
San Francisco

STYLE OF BIZARRO:
Illustrated Weird Humor

BOOKS BY GOLDFARB:
The Ballad of a Slow Poisoner
 Slub Glub in the Weird World of
    the Weeping Willows
A Hundred Horrible Sorrows of
    Ogner Stump

"Genuinely creepy. Like early David Lynch." - Shannon
Wheeler, creator of *Too Much Coffee Man*

DESCRIPTION: An unholy marriage of Walt Disney and H. P.
Lovecraft, Goldfarb draws strange creatures doing strange things in
a strangely endearing fashion. He employs old-fashioned comic art
techniques and a warped sense of humor to express an absurd world
view that sees the universe as a seeping hotbed of innumerable
terrors.

INTERESTS: One man band, comix artist, black velvet painter,
patent medicine salesman

INFLUENCES: Evocative of offbeat comix masters like Basil
Wolverton (Mad Magazine) and Jack Cole (Plastic Man), the exis-
tential horror of Lovecraft and Poe, Dada, Surrealism, Voodoo and
the warm winds that whisper through the willow trees at midnight,
calling your name.

WEBSITE:
www.ognerstump.com

REM AND MOREL SMITHE WERE TWINS JOINED AT THE HIP. THEY DIDN'T GET ON TOO WELL ⁓ TRUTH BE TOLD, WHATEVER BLOOD FLOWED BETWEEN THEM WAS BAD.

SEEING AS HOW THEY NEVER SAW EYE TO EYE ON ANYTHING, THEY DECIDED TO DUEL TO THE DEATH, WAY OUT IN CONGAREE SWAMP

THE BROTHERS SMITHE WERE STANDING KNEE DEEP IN THE BOG, KNIFE AND AXE AT EACH OTHER'S THROATS, WHEN THEY BEHELD A STARTLING SIGHT.

RISING OUT OF THE WATER WAS A WELL-DRESSED TORSO OF A MAN, BUT WHERE THERE OUGHT TO HAVE BEEN A HEAD, THERE WAS INSTEAD A GIANT HAND, WITH AN AWESOME UNBLINKING EYE IN ITS MIGHTY PALM.

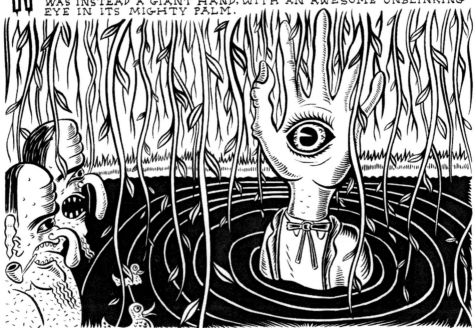

THE THING STARED AT THE BROTHERS SMITHE~ ITS PENETRATING GAZE SEEMED TO BORE DEEP INTO THEIR SOULS.

AND THEN IT SANK BACK INTO THE SWAMP, AND THE BROTHERS KNEW THEY HAD TO TELL THE WORLD WHAT THEY HAD SEEN~

ROM THAT DAY FORWARD, ALL HOSTILITIES WERE FORGOTTEN BETWEEN OREM AND MOREL, FOR EACH NEEDED THE OTHER'S TESTIMONY TO BACK UP THE FANTASTICAL STORY OF WHAT HAD RISEN FROM CONGAREE SWAMP.

ND SO IN THE END THE EYE HAND OF THE CAROLINAS WAS A BRINGER OF HARMONY AND GOODWILL THAT HELPED THE BROTHERS SMITHE TO FOREVER BURY THEIR HATCHET.

the Tea Party

WORDS — RACHEL BELLINSKY
PICTURES — ANDREW GOLDFARB

TEA TIME WITH FRIENDS IS A PLEASURE
BUT ALWAYS BEFORE IT'S DONE
SUDDENLY I SNAP AND JUST LIKE THAT
I OFF THEM ONE BY ONE

YES, I REMEMBER THE VERY FIRST TIME
MY COURTESY TURNED TO MURDER
MISS MARGARET INSULTED MY BISCUITS—
BUT I NEVER MEANT TO HURT HER

I WAS REACHING FOR THE BUTTER KNIFE
POLITELY AND SUBLIME
WHEN IT ACCIDENTALLY SLIPPED
AND LANDED ON HER 15 TIMES!

THERE WERE BLOOD STAINS ON MY WHITE GLOVES
THE GUESTS, THEY WERE APPALLED!
AND THEN I HAD NO OTHER CHOICE
BUT TO GIVE IT TO THEM ALL

A LOVELY SUNDAY PARTY
WHAT IS MORE DELIGHTFUL THAN THAT?
EXCEPT MAYBE THE HORROR ON THEIR FACES
FRAMED BY THEIR DAINTY PARTY HATS

MY PARTIES START WITH GOOD INTENTIONS
BUT THEN I MUST CONFESS
I RUN OUT OF SOCIAL GRACES
AND THEN START RUNNING OUT OF GUESTS

IT'S NOT THAT I DON'T TREASURE THEM
~DON'T MISCONSTRUE MY MEANING~
MY VISITORS ARE ALL QUITE CHARMING
BUT MOST ESPECIALLY WHEN THEY'RE SCREAMING

NOW FINGER SANDWICHES ARE MADE FROM REAL FINGERS
AND MY TARTS ARE TO DIE FOR
THE PASTRIES ARE FILLED WITH THE PIECES
OF MY GUESTS FROM THE DAY BEFORE

I HOPE I HAVE NOT DISSUADED YOU
FROM SHOWING UP FOR TEA
I EXPECT TO SEE YOU THERE AT NOON
AND FINISHED UP BY 3 ～

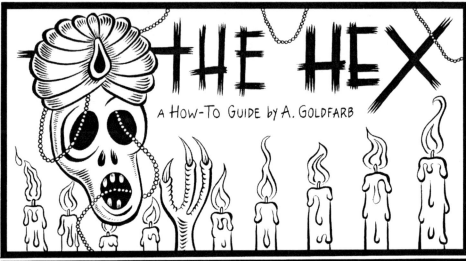

pardon us, o astral fanatics. we were hoping to take a peek at your star-scope, to ascertain whether those lights in the sky are luminous rocks or holes in the cosmic fabric.

VERILY, THEY ARE NEITHER. OUR WORLD IS A HOLLOW GLOBE, OF WHICH WE ARE ON THE INSIDE...

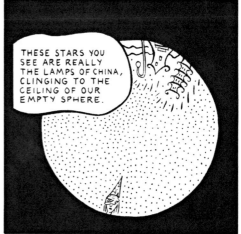

THESE STARS YOU SEE ARE REALLY THE LAMPS OF CHINA, CLINGING TO THE CEILING OF OUR EMPTY SPHERE.

BUT DON'T TAKE MY WORD FOR IT ~ COME OUT BACK.

SWEET BETHUSELUH!!

3

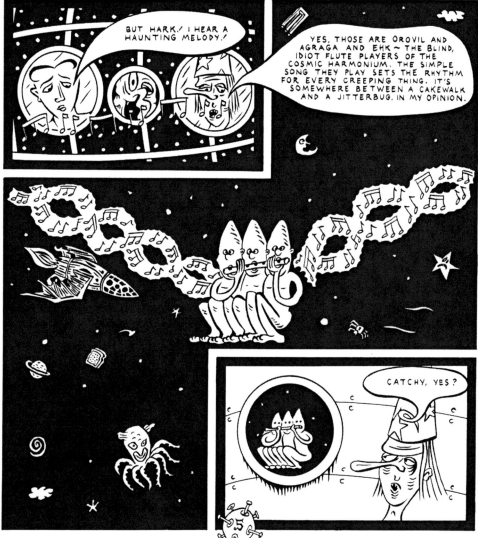

THE SOMNAMBULIST'S LAMENT

featuring three of
OGNER STUMP's
one thousand sorrows

by Andrew Goldfarb

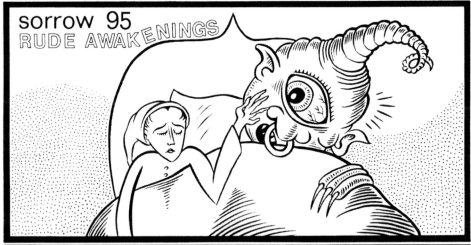

sorrow 95
RUDE AWAKENINGS

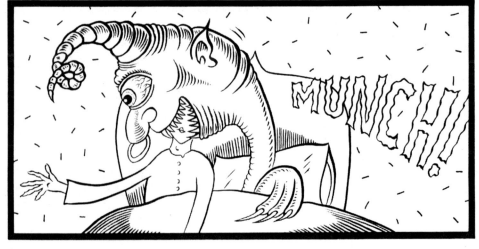

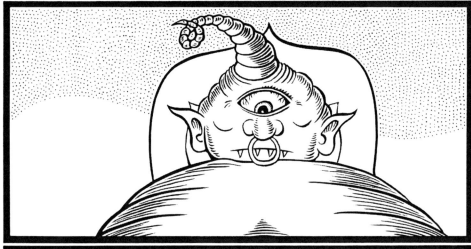

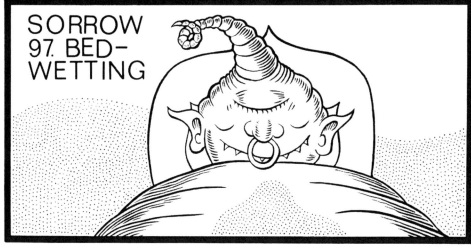

JEFF BURK

LOCATION:
Portland, OR

STYLE OF BIZARRO:
Punk Pulp

BOOKS BY BURK:
Shatnerquake
Super Giant Monster Time!
HomoBomb
Pothead
Sex and Death Camp
Dinosaurs Attack!
The Slaughterhouse Thrills
Shatnerquest

"Like Lloyd Kaufman and Sam Raimi's mutant offspring . . ." - Wil Wheaton

DESCRIPTION: Like the literary equivalent to a cult B-Horror movie, Jeff Burk writes violent, absurd, and funny stories about punks, monsters, gore, and trash culture. Everyone normally dies at the end.

INTERESTS: Giant Monsters, Comic Books, Tarot, Propaganda, Chaos Magick, Bacon, Beer.

INFLUENCES: Futurama, Troma, William Shatner, Pinky and the Brain, The Clash, Grant Morrison, Godzilla, Crass, David Cronenberg, Star Trek, Warren Ellis, Carlton Mellick III, The Grand Guignol, Edward Lee, Aleister Crowley, Batman, H. G. Wells, Leftover Crack, Alan Moore, Andy Warhol, Eli Roth, Stan Lee, Chumbawamba, Tales from the Crypt, The Dead Kennedys, Wonder Showzen, PFFR, Drugs, and Sleep Deprivation

WEBSITE:
jeffburk.wordpress.com

CRIPPLE WOLF

1

Nightmare at 40,000 Feet

He didn't really want to kill the baby but he did it anyway.

He snatched the infant out of its mother's arms and sunk his teeth into the baby's soft chest. It squealed like a stuck piglet.

The mother's screams pierced his ears. He bitch-slapped her with his hairy paw but she kept screaming, staring at her mutilated baby dangling from his other claw. He swiped at her again and, at that exact same moment, the plane hit a rough patch of turbulence. His claw sliced cleanly through her neck and the rocking of the cabin sent the head bounding into the overhead storage compartment and straight off into the middle of a row of passengers.

Panic exploded in the crowd.

He snorted, his senses aroused by the blood, sweat, and fear in the recycled air. The infant convulsed in his claws. He lapped its blood with his wide flat tongue and then tossed the little pork chop aside.

He spun and wheeled toward his next victim.

***

"Now boarding Fetish Flights #33 to Portland, Oregon, United States."

The nurse pushed Benjamin Kurtz in his wheelchair to the end of the line. Well, she wasn't really a nurse. Her plastic form-fitting uniform and thigh high boots gave that away. But Benjamin had paid her good money to take care of his *every* need during his stay in Tokyo, and getting to the airport was one of his needs. He shifted in his chair, wishing he had to take a shit so she could clean him off one more time before he left.

Benjamin served four tours of duty in Vietnam. On the first, a stray piece of shrapnel ricocheted off his helmet. Nothing but a miracle could explain how he had sustained no physical damage. But after that, his memory was never the same.

On his fourth tour, while on patrol, he was attacked by a wolf. The attack put him in the chair and there was something else important but he didn't remember. He spent a while in the infirmary, dead from the waist down, and that's where he developed his diaper fetish. Having those young nurses, still fresh from medical school, wipe the shit from his ass excited him in ways he never before dreamed.

When he was returned to the States, Uncle Sam no longer having use for a crippled soldier, he found out he had a wife. He had just plain forgotten. She had moved on with her life and remarried and, after a few months, he had completely forgotten about her again.

The diaper fetish stayed.

Disability took good care of him and he saved up so, once a year, he could take a vacation to Japan. In the States he occasionally got lucky with a cute premed, but most of his nurses were old, fat, hags. In Tokyo, there were establishments that catered to his specific needs.

That's where he met . . . well, he didn't remember her name anymore. Her name didn't matter, what mattered was how she filled out that uniform.

Benjamin eyed the other passengers waiting in line. Near the front was a guy with a bright blond bihawk chatting up a young girl with purple hair. Behind them were two more punks talking amongst themselves. There was a guy who looked like a body-builder, a Japanese Elvis, hippies, and even two fools dressed like clowns.

The normal clientele for Fetish Flights.

The line moved forward and Benjamin took notice of the man directly in front of him. He was wearing a long brown trench coat that was at least two-sizes too large and an oversized brown fedora pulled down to hide his head. In the crack between his coat and hat, it looked like his neck was covered in purple spandex. When he stepped forward, in-between his jacket and boots, Benjamin could see the man was wearing purple tights.*He looks like a real pervert.*

Soon, Benjamin was at the front of the line. The ticket taker was a knock-out blonde wearing a fetish outfit made of strips of black leather connected by metal rings.

"Welcome to Fetish Flights," she said, taking his ticket, "enjoy your flight."

"I'm sure I will," he said, staring at her nipples poking through the leather. "But I do need some . . . special assistance."

That's what made Fetish Flights, Fetish Flights. Their staff catered to anyone's desire; the men were Adonises, the women Aphrodites. All were dressed in the finest, and most revealing, fashion of the discerning fetishist.

She glanced down at his ticket. "Of course. We'll have a stewardess attend to you momentarily."

She pushed a button at her station and an even bustier brunette wearing even less came up to Benjamin. His nurse left and the brunette pushed him down the ramp onto the plane. She wheeled him to his handicap seat, which was right next to the boarding door. Next to him was a young, wholesome-looking, woman holding a very small baby. He grimaced at her, sometimes people accidentally ended up on Fetish Flights due to their extremely discounted fares.

"Don't worry, he's a heavy sleeper," she said when she noticed Benjamin looking at the child. "He won't be one of those screamers on the plane."

She rocked the baby and said, "It's a full moon tonight. I hope we can see it from the air, it should be beautiful."

Benjamin nodded. A full moon. That seemed important. But he couldn't remember why.

***

Abdul Omar, otherwise known as Lawrence Talbot on his passport, stared at himself in the mirror of the tiny airplane bathroom. Some days he found it hard to believe it was himself staring back. His hair was two inches long and rather stylishly spiked. He rubbed his smooth chin and remembered a time when there was a bushy beard there. He smirked at himself. With his The Clash t-shirt and blue jeans, he looked just like one of them.

All a part of deep cover.

He pushed a button on his shoulder, so subtle and hidden that only he knew its location, and his forearms popped open revealing two hollowed out compartments perfect for smuggling.

From his left arm he removed

a switchblade. He snapped open the weapon, admiring its six inch blade. He snapped it shut and slid it into his font pocket.

Abdul took a taser out of his right arm and stuck it into his other pocket.

He snapped shut the compartments and pushed another hidden button on his hip. He lifted his shirt and opened the chamber in his chest. Inside was twelve pounds of C-4 hooked up to a small control panel. He reached in and activated the panel. He knew that when the time came, the explosives would add destructive potential. At the very least, if anyone tried to stop them, he and Mohammad (who was in the next bathroom going through the same preparation) could just take down the whole plane.

Abdul shut his chest and pulled his shirt back down. He smoothed out the picture of Paul Simonon smashing a bass guitar on his shirt and took one last look in the mirror. The clothing, even the bands and logos on them, had been a part of his cover story. To make his story viable he had to immerse himself in this hedonistic culture. He had to watch the TV shows, read the books, and listen to the music. Surprisingly, he found himself enjoying The Clash. The punk group was just randomly selected for him, but the heretic white men actually had some lyrics to which he could relate.

He left the bathroom and walked down the plane's narrow aisles. He stole a quick glance at Mohammad, who was already seated and flipping through an issue of *Wizard Magazine*. As he sat down, he picked back up the cheap paperback he had been reading, *The Conqueror Worms* by Brian Keene. Just some piece of horror dreck

and another part of his assigned cover. He read while softly singing under his breath.

"Death or glory. It's just another story."

Abdul awakened to the roar of over three hundred passengers.

Great Allah, how long was I asleep? People were standing and screaming and crying. Abdul thought they must already be at the assigned point and Mohammad was making his move.

He sprung to his feet and flipped out his switchblade.

"Everyone! Stay calm and no one will be hurt!"

His voice was not even audible over the chaos in the cabin. He realized that no one was even looking at him. They were all looking at something behind him. Abdul turned around and stared.

A hairy beast was in front of him. Its large paws and arms were wrapped around a man wearing a black latex catsuit while its snout was buried deep in the man's neck. The animal and man were soaked in blood.

The animal's eyes shot up and locked with Abdul's. The thing tossed aside the latex clad corpse and howled like a wolf, its snout dipping down and then straight up in the air. Its thick brown fur was shaggy and matted with gore.

Abdul was frozen. Apart from the fact that he was looking at a monster, there was something else terribly wrong with it. The beast, who was obviously male, was sitting down in the aisle like a human in a chair. Then what he was seeing clicked.

It's in a wheelchair . . .

The creature rolled forward, using

its hirsute paws to gain speed. Abdul leapt to the side, throwing himself over vacated seats. He wasn't quick enough. As he jumped, a large paw swiped at him in midair and dug a hole in his stomach just below his hidden chamber. The claw caught hold of his intestines and the creature continued to wheel down the aisle.

Abdul convulsed in shock and couldn't move. He watched his insides unravel and get pulled across the plane. He could just barely turn his head to see the monster run down an old woman in a ball gag and corset. Then his vision went black and white and he could smell roses. Then nothing.

***

Kiichi was nodding his head to the fast beat of the Stance Punks songs playing on his headphones when Kana started to shake him. Kiichi tore off the ear pieces.

"Hey—" he stopped when he heard the screams. Kana stared at him with wide-eyed fear through her hot-pink bangs. Kiichi turned to Yousei, who was already on his feet scanning the cabin.

Kiichi, Kana and Yousei all played in the same punk band, Mouthful of Ants. After three years of playing together, their career took off with their fourth album, *Land of the Rising Scum*. At the record release show they revealed their new live gimmick. Before they went on stage, they all drank a homemade cocktail of fake blood and syrup of ipecac. For the first five songs of their set, all the members of Mouthful of Ants projectile vomited fake blood across the stage, crowd, and each other. That caught the attention of Epitaph Records and then the

world. Which placed them onboard the double-deck, wide-body Airbus A380 flying from Tokyo, Japan to Portland, Oregon, U-S-A!

They had dreamed of this moment for years, their first world tour. All that stood between them and their first show on American soil was a thirteen hour and forty-seven minute flight. Well, that and whatever was scaring everyone so much. Kiichi didn't want to die in a plane crash—not before they played New York City.

He stood up to try and see what was happening. It seemed everyone in the passenger area was standing and yelling. The plane held three hundred twenty-five people in this cabin alone. Kiichi strained his neck but couldn't see what was causing the panic. The three punks were seated in the back of the plane, on the left, next to the windows. Whatever was causing the commotion was happening in the front, to the right.

The girl with the purple hair's body flipped into the air, bounced off the ceiling, and crashed into the middle section of the passengers. People fled toward the back of the plane, climbing over seats and each other to get away from whatever was coming.

"Mega uncool," said Yousei.

***

The beast tore through the people, it did not pick any specific targets, its claws slashing and slicing through flesh and plush seats alike. The fear-stench of its prey electrified the air. Sometimes it brought some juicy morsels to its mouth, but it wasn't killing for food. It was killing for fun.

***

People tried to get away but there was just no place to go. A Japanese man dressed as Elvis tried climbing over one of the seats but the creature grabbed his feet and pulled him in close. With a single motion, the beast slashed into the man's gut, sending blood and viscera spraying into the air.

A crusty old man had ignored the fleeing crowd and remained in his seat. His pants were down around his ankles and he was furiously whacking off. A spray of blood from the slaughtered Elvis hit his exposed penis and delivered just the lubricant he was hoping for.

The beast turned to the man and roared in his face, covering him with blood-speckled saliva. The man jerked faster.

The monster grabbed the man's gore-coated cock with one paw and his balding head with the other and tore both off his body in one easy motion. The beast bit into the man's severed face, cracking the skull, and pulled out a snoutful of brains. It threw the penis at a screaming woman and it bounced off her forehead.

"Filthy beast, pick on someone your own size," came a voice from behind the creature.

The cripple wolf turned its hairy maw flinging mucus, slobber, and gore.

Standing in the aisle, between the monster and the rest of its intended victims, a man wearing a purple facemask and a purple spandex bodysuit struck a defiant pose, hands on his hips. On his chest was a shiny yellow "S."

The people behind him cheered. Their savior was here. The one and only, Star Spangler!

The monster spun its wheelchair to face the purple challenger. It howled and pushed forward, hard. The Star Spangler ran toward it, drew back his fist, and punched the creature with the force of a Panzer III right on its snout. The last person The Star Spangler hit this hard was the self-proclaimed "indestructible" Destroyo. That blow had knocked the villian's head off his body and through three-blocks-worth of walls before finally coming to a stop in a second grade classroom. The Star Spangler spent time in therapy after that, but he got better.

The hairy thing shook its head, quickly recovering from the resounding blow. Then reached out and sunk its claws deep into the The Star Spangler's forearms. It held the hero firmly in place with his arms outstretched. Blood ran freely from the wounds and began to pool on the floor. The Star Spangler grimaced, trying not to show the pain. The crowd fell quiet.

The beast pulled The Star Spangler's arms further and the cabin filled with the sharp sound of splintering wood. The hero let out a high pitched scream. Then the passengers closest to him began screaming as well. They fell to their knees as blood poured from their ears. His super vocal chords had shattered their ear drums.

With a quick tug, the thing pulled both of The Star Spangler's arms from their sockets. He shrieked as blood from his stumps sprayed across the cabin.

The monster swung the right arm like a club, smacking The Star Spangler across the head. He dropped to his knees and his left arm came slamming down. The Star Spangler crumpled as the beast brought both his shiny purple arms down on top of him again and again.

It roared and tossed the arms aside. Then grabbed its wheels and rolled over the fallen superhero.

***

Dax Thompson flopped back in his chair.

"Ahhhhh . . ."

The coke surged through his brain and everything went sharp.

"Whew! Damn Chavez, this is some fine shit."

Chavez took a drag on his joint and adjusted his headpiece, "Told you."

Dax flipped up the tray table and it slid down next to his seat. He leaned forward and looked out over the Pacific Ocean. Chavez and he had been piloting transpacific flights for going on five years. The two got along great, their hedonism providing a quick bond. While their behaviors unnerved some of the flight staff, and would surely terrify the passengers, they had an impeccable record. If anything, all the drugs helped them to focus. Especially when it came to these nearly fourteen hour marathon runs.

Black lights gave the cockpit an eerie glow. In the center of the console, an undulating lava lamp bubbled martian-green in the stoner-light. Bob Marley played over the cockpit's private speaker system.

Dax loved these night runs over open water. On the darkest nights, it felt like he was flying through an abyss. And then the lights of land would begin to twinkle in, like he had just traveled through dimensions.

Or there were nights like tonight. A bright full moon filled the sky, not a cloud obscured the water beneath. The light danced off the black water that seemed to stretch out forever in every direction.

"It's a beautiful night. Times like this, with nothing below and nothing above. Really makes you think," Dax said.

Chavez smirked, "Shit, are you getting into one of your Thoreau mood again?"

"*Chavez! Dax! Are you there?*" Shelly's voice cut in through their head pieces interrupting the reggae. She was one of the stewardesses and she sounded frantic.

Chavez pushed a button on the center console, "Chavez here, what's up?"

It was hard to understand what she was saying. It seemed like there were people screaming in the background. "*. . .back cabin . . . it's killing everyone!*" And then she cut out.

Chavez and Dax exchanged a look.

"I'll call Daryl," said Dax.

The Airbus was a modern marvel of engineering. It was one of the largest commercial airplanes ever built. The plane had three main passenger compartments—two on the lower deck and one on the upper. The two lower ones were the business class accommodations. The back cabin, where Shelly called from, was the larger of the two and capable of holding three hundred twenty-five passengers. The front cabin was smaller and held one hundred fifty. The upper deck held two hundred fifty seats for first class. At full capacity, the plane was capable of transporting seven hundred twenty-five people, and this night's flight was nearly full.

With such a large number of passengers, the airline staffed the plane with fifteen flight attendants to care for their needs. Five were assigned to the upper deck and the other ten were split into two teams for the business class. Shelly led the back cabin with a staff of seven. Daryl was in charge of the three for the front.

Dax pushed the button for the front cabin, "Daryl, you there?"

"This is Raymond."

"Yo Raymond, what's going on down there? We just got a strange call from Shelly."

"Don't know yet. There's a lot of screaming from the back cabin. Daryl went to check it out."

"Copy, keep us up to date."

"Will do."

Dax flipped off the intercom and the music returned.

He turned to Chavez, "What the fuck you think that's all about?"

***

The screaming started in the back cabin and did not stop. After two minutes, Daryl decided he should go check it out. He left Raymond in charge. He jogged to the curtains that divided the two compartments, his uniform's chains and metal rings softly clanging. Worried passengers eyed his chiseled frame as he went past. He stopped and listened to the screams and the sounds of fighting. He was pretty sure he could smell blood.

As he grabbed a hold of the curtain, images of terrorists and slit throats filled his head. He was totally unprepared for what he saw when he pulled it aside.

The cabin looked like a slaughterhouse. Corpses and body parts littered the floors and seats. Blood was splattered everywhere, even on the ceiling.

Most of the surviving passengers cowered at the back of the cabin, hud-

dling together. Others climbed over the seats like they were trying to get away from something.

Daryl scanned the room and saw what was causing the carnage. A large hairy animal of some sort was tearing its way through the people. Limbs, bodies, and gore, flying in its wake.

He grabbed the intercom handset on the wall next to him and pushed the button for the cockpit.

"This is Daryl. Get the marshals. We have an animal loose in the back cabin."

***

Agent Willis came back to his seat and sat down next to his partner. He had just been called to the cockpit over an emergency that was apparently happening in the lower cabins.

"What's going on?" asked Smith. A red foam ball bounced on the end of his nose.

Willis snickered.

"Shut up, man. You don't look any better."

Both agents wore red foam noses, rainbow colored polka-dot jumpsuits, blue over-sized shoes, and white gloves. Their wigs, however, were different. Willis had a neon green mad-scientist hairdo and Smith had a skull-cap with a bright blue frohawk.

Their cover was always assigned before flights. But the agency really fucked it up this time. They were told there was an international clown convention happening in Portland and the Japanese branch of the International Federation of Clown Sciences and Enthusiasts would also be on their flight. But Willis and Smith were the only two clowns on board.

"I'm sorry, I can't help it," answered Willis as he controlled himself. "Seems there's some kind of animal loose in the back cabin."

"An animal? What kind?"

"Don't know. Someone probably just snuck their dog aboard."

"Alright," Smith stood up, "let's take care of this."

Willis followed him and they descended the narrow stairwell to the lower level. Their shoes squeaked with each step.

As soon as they were down, a strong copper smell attacked their nostrils and screams assaulted their ears. They drew their SIG P226s and went to the dividing curtain where a visibly terrified steward was standing and passengers, some with terrible injuries and covered in blood, were running through.

Next to them were two heavily pierced, scantily-clad, punk girls with huge tits. They saw the guns and gasped. One threw herself at the other, "Hold me, I'm scared."

"What's the situation?" asked Smith.

The steward pulled back the curtain and the agents saw the massacre that was the back of the cabin. Both agents held their guns out and went in.

They rushed down the aisle toward the beast mauling a young woman in a metal brassiere. They stopped about ten feet away and each fired a shot into the back of the thing's head. It dropped the woman's body and pivoted to face them.

"Head into the next cabin," Smith yelled and motioned with his head backwards. Some passengers understood and ran down the opposite aisle.

"Are you seeing what I'm seeing?" asked Smith.

Willis turned his attention to the animal; a shaggy, gore-soaked combination of wolf and man, sitting in a wheelchair.

"I think it's crippled," commented Smith.

The beast began wheeling toward them at a speed that would win a gold medal at the Special Olympics.

Both agents opened fire.

In order to be an armed Air Marshall, one must be an expert marksman. Just one stray shot could depressurize an entire airplane. Agents Smith and Willis were the best deadeyes in the business. Every shot they landed should have been a fatal blow but the thing did not even slow down.

It slammed into them, wheeled past slashing its claws, and spun around to face them. Both agents now lay on the floor with their polka-dotted legs cut off at the knees. The men helplessly thrashed about while they bled out.

The beast, satisfied at the disposal of this nuisance, spun to see the people running down the opposite aisle towards the next compartment.

It howled and wheeled toward the escape route.

***

"Oh shit," Daryl said to Raymond as they watched the monster wheel straight at them.

Daryl glanced at the people still trying to get out, there were still a large number coming down the aisles and they were only slowing each other down. He looked back at the monster and knew that it would be upon them soon.

"We have to shut the emergency doors," he said to Raymond.

"But there are still people in there."

"That thing will be here in moments."

Raymond hesitated and then nodded. Both of them went to the sides of the entryways and hit the emergency buttons. As a security measure, the plane had automated steel doors, eight inches thick, which could be activated at a moment's notice. In the event of a hijacking, the doors could isolate the affected area from the rest of the plane.

Passengers continued to rush past and when the doors started to slowly slide over, the crowd surged forward. Daryl and Raymond stood back as people continued to squeeze through. Then the doors shut, cutting off the back cabin.

People begged in both English and Japanese for the door to be opened and then a loud crash resounded and the creature hit the doors. The screaming rose in volume and then fell as the few survivors in the back cabin were scattered away from the steel doors.

Daryl looked over at Raymond who was visibly shaking. The front cabin was now filled with lucky passengers who had escaped the massacre. People were crying and covered in gore. It was hard to tell who was actually hurt and who was just splattered.

"Gather up the other attendants and help anyone who's hurt," he said to Raymond.

He then went over to the intercom and rang up the cockpit.

"Daryl here, I think we got it contained."

***

Kiichi, Kana, and Yousei reached the doors just as they snapped shut. They were immediately pushed forward by the other passengers attempting to escape. The force of all the bodies pressed them flat against the doors. Hands reached around and banged on the steel and voices pleaded for them to open.

"Scene's turning Dennis Hopper," Yousei strained to be heard over the crowd.

Kana nodded and pointed to their left, the direction they just came from. The three wormed their way through the mass of bodies.

Then the beast attacked from the opposite aisle in a fugue of sharp teeth and claws. People flew into the air as its wheelchair plowed forward. The thing slashed blindly and tore through soft flesh and bone.

The three punks broke into a full run toward the back of the plane.

The rear back cabin had a small hallway that led to four bathrooms and a service/cooking station for the flight attendants.

Kana ran into the cooking station. There was a steel counter with cups built into it containing all the silverware. She grabbed from on the cups and spun around with the weapon held out.

It was a plastic spork.

"Spastic," she shouted and threw the utensil to the floor.

Other passengers had seen the punks flee to the back and they were now seeking shelter in the same area.

Kiichi and Yousei were still at the end of the hallway, right by the seating area, frantically searching the doorframe. Kiichi glanced up and saw the monster was still tearing into people at the opposite end of the back cabin.

"Spicy," Yousei exclaimed as he found the button that activated the panic doors. The steel barrier started to slide across. Right before it closed completely, the beast turned and met Kiichi's eyes from across the cabin. It growled and the door shut tight.

***

"People, please try to stay calm."

Raymond's voice boomed over the front cabin's public intercom. In the crowd, the flight attendants, along with a few passengers with basic first aid knowledge, worked to provide medical help for those that needed it. The injuries were many and severe. Some needed tourniquets for lost limbs, others were just being made comfortable until they bled to death. People were understandably panicked and control needed to be regained.

"I've been talking to the cockpit."

That got the passengers' attention. The front cabin quieted and, oddly, the smell of blood seemed to grow stronger.

"The animal is contained—"

As if on cue, the monster howled from the other side of the steel doors.

"—and we are closer to Portland than we are to Tokyo, so our only option is to continue on to our destination. The pilots have been in communication with PDX and medical and security help will be waiting for us. We just need to wait this out until we land."

"And how long will that be?" someone in the cabin yelled out.

Raymond paused and composed himself, "Six hours."

2
The Curse of the Cripple Wolf

Sister Mishka Holloway picked up the baby while everyone else ran past it. It would have been easy to mistake the child as dead; its chest was split open and on the floor was a small tendril of intestine.

But when she almost stepped down on the body, Sister noticed that its tiny chest was moving ever so slightly. The poor thing wasn't dead yet. Instinctually, she scooped up the bloody infant and, holding it close to her habit, she ran.

The rest was a blur, but suddenly she found herself locked in the small hallway that led to the bathrooms and kitchen. She sat down and leaned against the wall.

There were six other passengers—the three Japanese punks, a shirtless

American man with the physique of Stallone (steroid-infused *RAMBO III* years) flexing at no one in particular to console himself, and a young American hippy couple. It looked like the man's lower ribs had been ripped away. His dreadlocked partner tried to console him through a stream of tears as she held in his guts through blood-stained tie-dye.

Sister looked down at the child and gagged. Its torso was torn so wide she could see the tiny heart beat and small lungs expand and contract like spongy bellows.

She rocked the baby against her breast and softly hummed "Hey Diddle Diddle" while she waited for it to die.

***

The Star Spangler opened his eyes and tried to prop himself up. For some reason he couldn't get his arms to work. Then he remembered—they were gone. Fortunately, his healing powers had immediately sealed the wounds and he didn't bleed to death.

With some struggle, he sat up and then got to his feet. He looked around the cabin. Apart from the numerous bodies, it appeared he was alone. Then he heard growling and scratching. He turned and saw the monster attacking a metal door at the back of the cabin.

As if alerted by some sixth sense, the beast immediately turned its head and locked hungry eyes on him.

"Fuck." The Star Spangler turned and ran the other way. He heard the squeak of the monster's wheels as it raced after him.

The front exit was blocked off by another steel door. The Star Spangler kicked it and yelled for someone to open.

He turned his head and saw the beast was right behind him.

"Fuck," he screamed and round-house kicked the creature. The thing immediately grabbed his leg and, effortlessly, wrenched it back. The limb tore away at his waist and The Star Spangler was left balanced on one leg.

"Fuck," he screamed once more and the monster began to beat him with his severed leg.

***

Raymond heard the struggle on the other side of the door as the monster claimed another victim. He wanted to help the person out, but opening the door could mean death for everyone else in the front cabin.

The cabin was too noisy for anyone else to have heard the attack. Daryl was organizing a retreat to the upper cabin. The monster was in a wheelchair, so if it got free, he figured it would probably have a problem with the stairs.

Most of the passengers were already on the upper level but some of the extremely injured were too hard to move. Raymond walked across the cabin passing at least two dozen people missing limbs or trying to hold in their guts. Attendants and some passengers assisted the wounded as best they could, but the plane just wasn't prepared for this kind of emergency.

Daryl handed juice boxes to some of the passengers. He saw Raymond coming and waved him over. The two stewards went to a corner of the cabin free from any passengers.

"I was thinking," said Daryl, "I think I know what that thing is."

"Yeah?"

"A werewolf."

"Come on," said Raymond.

"No, think about it. It's a full moon tonight and that thing was in a wheelchair. What kind of animal needs a wheelchair?"

Raymond didn't have an answer for that.

"And, I'm pretty sure I saw an older guy in a wheelchair get on during boarding."

"I wasn't paying attention to the back cabin."

"A werewolf," Daryl leaned in closer, "we got a fucking werewolf on the plane. You've seen the movies, right? You know what that means?"

"We need some silver bullets?"

"No . . . well, that too, but think about it. What happens when a werewolf bites someone?"

Raymond felt the blood rush out of his face. He turned and looked around a cabin full of people nursing bite wounds.

***

Mohammad sat in an overstuffed chair in the upper cabin. There was no enjoying the niceties of first class, not with Satan having sent a minor to thwart his mission. For what other reason could that beast be here? He saw it kill Abdul, but it would not kill him. No beast would stop him.

He stood up and walked toward the front of the cabin. The stewards had set up a service station and were offering people food, drinks, and alcohol—all free of charge. Several weak willed passengers were already passed out drunk.

He asked for an orange juice and the stewardess gave him an apologetic smile. She shook her head "no" with over-enthusiasm that made the various metal chains and rings of her uniform jingle.

"Sorry, we're all out. We do have plenty of Cucumber Pepsi and lemon vinegar Kit-Kats."

Mohammad raised an incredulous eyebrow. "No, thanks."

He turned around and headed back to his seat.

The cabin the monster had attacked was the most populated of them all and, while the upper cabin was packed tight, it seemed like there should have been more people. He walked past two young women, their skin covered in tattoos and piercings. What little clothing they were wearing clung skin-tight to their bodies, soaked with blood.

They held each other, softly crying, and then one gently kissed the other. The kiss deepened and they began groping each other, blood soaked breasts sticking together, lip piercings tangling in their passionate embrace.

Mohammad scoffed and hurried past.

The devil really was going to great lengths to stop him but he was ordained by Allah. Nothing could get in his way.

He took his seat and leaned his head against cushioned neck rest. He closed his eyes and concentrated on the weight in his chest. Not only would he be striking a blow against a symbolic Satan, he would even be taking out one of his personal servants.

Mohammad closed his eyes and imagined the rewards awaiting him in heaven. There was no way he was letting the plane land in Portland.

***

"This is Fetish Flights number thirty-three we have an extreme emergency, repeat we have an extreme emergency."

The only response over the radio was static.

"Fucking nothing," said Dax.

"That's impossible," said Chavez.

As soon as the animal had started attacking, Dax and Chavez radioed a distress call to inform Portland of their situation, but they got no response. The equipment all seemed to be working fine but even when they tried radioing other planes they got only dead air. Normally, even out in the middle of the ocean, they should be able to pick up both Tokyo and Portland and at least a dozen other flights.

They both sat silent for a moment. They couldn't even count the number of flights they'd piloted together but there had never been any problems. Now that they had one, they were all alone.

"You've got to be kidding me," said Chavez.

"What?"

Chavez pointed at the instrument panel and Dax saw the problem immediately. The compass was spinning around wildly. Its needle pitched back and forth rapidly. The LCD readout with their speed suddenly dropped to zero and then changed to 999 and back to zero. The altitude indicator jumped up and down widely. The GPS just turned off.

The plane, however, stayed steady and gave no sign of a problem.

"We've got a real problem here," said Chavez.

Dax nodded and did the only sensible thing he could think of, he snorted another line.

"Alight," he said, "there's a monster on our plane, we lost contact with everyone, all the instruments are malfunctioning, and we still have four hours until Portland." He lit another joint, hit it, and passed it to Chavez.

He grabbed the throttle and pushed it forward. The plane picked up speed and the speakers started blaring Slayer's "Angel of Death."

"Fifty dollars says I can get us there in three and a half."

***

Sister Mishka Holloway realized that the infant was no longer moving. She held it out in front of her, its swathing bathed crimson. She slowly unwrapped the child and was stunned when she saw, instead of having died, the baby was completely healed. Where, just an hour before, there was a large gash, now was completely smooth pink skin.

The child's chest slowly rose up and down.

Sister began to cry. Finally after everything that had happened, God gave them a miracle.

The baby opened its eyes and looked right at her. It cooed and smiled, opening its mouth wide. That's when Sister saw its gums were bleeding. Small pointed teeth burst through the tender flesh and the child suddenly had a mouthful of needles. Its tiny body began to thrash and it sprouted a thick coat of brown fur.

She cried harder as the child transformed into something closer to an animal than human.

It leapt out of her hands and dug its tiny claws and teeth into her neck. The claws pierced her throat, grasped her windpipe and with a quick pull, wrenched it out of Sister's neck. She gurgled and fell limp. The baby werewolf giggled.

***

"Allah, protect me . . ." Mohammad whispered as the cabin erupted.

The low drone of people crying and talking was suddenly replaced with screams of panic and people frantically scattered in all directions. Mohammad stood up and saw fur covered monsters attacking people everywhere. It looked like anyone bitten by the beast had been similarly transformed at the exact same moment.

A very pregnant woman staggered by, her jaw missing and tongue flapping about at an odd angle. Her stomach was slashed open and the head of her unborn fetus dangled out of the wound. A werewolf pounced onto her back knocking her straight to the floor and sunk its hungry teeth into her swollen belly.

The two pierced lesbians were still making out despite the slaughter surrounding them. A monster towered over them and grabbed each one by the back of her head. It pulled them apart and then slammed them together. Their heads smashed in a soupy mixture of blood and brains.

Mohammad reached into his pockets and took out his knife and taser. He climbed over the seat in front of him while the beast gorged on the woman's corpse. A monster rushed him from his side and he shot the taser. The creature thrashed and crumbled to the floor. Another came at him from the front, climbing over a row of seats. Mohammad slashed with the knife cutting through both of its eyes.

He scanned the cabin for an escape. Everywhere, people were fighting and dying, overwhelmed by the beasts. Right next to him was the staircase leading to the lower cabins. He didn't see much of a choice, so he ran down the stairs.

***

Daryl was attending to an elderly woman with blue hair, two broken legs, and half her face missing from a bite when she transformed. It happened quickly and Daryl was taken off guard and didn't react. The bitch slashed forward and ripped into his pants, tearing his testicles completely off. She swung her other paw and scooped out his face as if it were nothing more than silly putty.

Raymond was across the cabin watching as, in the exact same moment, every injured person changed into a beast and assaulted their caregivers. A few tried fighting back but immediately fell to the inhuman strength of their attackers.

Above him, he heard screams and the sound of struggle from the upper cabin.

He ran to the intercom and was about to call the cockpit when he saw a passenger run to the metal door between the cabins. The man was obviously panicked and just looking for a way out when he hit the door open button. Raymond spun to stop him but he was too late.

The door slid open and the wheelchair bound werewolf burst through and ran right over the man who opened the door.

***

Kiichi, Kana, and Yousei were huddled by the steel door, trying to formulate a plan, when the man started screaming. They all turned to see the baby werewolf gnawing at the dead woman's neck and the injured boyfriend, now werewolf, disembowel his former love.

The body builder was just standing still, staring, and screaming like a little girl.

Both creatures immediately leapt at him and he went silent as they took him down.

"Speed Racer time," Yousei yelled as he hit the door open button.

All three punks spilled out into the back cabin. They took a quick look around but the original monster was not to be seen and the other steel door had been opened.

The boyfriend-wolf dropped the corpse and charged them. It sprung at Kana knocking her down. Kiichi immediately delivered a steel toe to the thing's temple. Yousei grabbed a suitcase from the overhead compartment and used it as a battering ram to knock the monster off Kana.

Yousei pulled her up when Kiichi noticed the The Star Spangler on the floor. He was missing both arms and a leg but he was still alive.

"A little help?" he said.

"Come on man, pogo," Kiichi said as he lifted The Star Spangler up.

"Very funny."

The Star Spangler precariously balanced himself and hopped forward on one leg. "Oh this is gonna suck."

There was a howl and they all looked back. The wheelchair-wolf was zooming straight at them. The punks climbed over the center seats leaving The Star Spangler alone in the aisle. He hopped forward as the beast gained on him. Then the footrest of the wheelchair hit him in the ankle and The Star Spangler fell on top of the monster. The two rolled forward, the beast blinded by the superhero.

The punks watched as the tangle of man and beast wheeled down the aisle and plowed straight into wall at the end.

Kana clapped.

The werewolf pawed at The Star Spangler and grabbed a hold of his remaining leg.

"No. No. No."

The beast tore off the last purple limb and tossed it aside. It held up the torso in front of itself. The Star Spangler could see bloodlust in the monster's eyes and drool dripped down its chin. The Star Spangler had no way to defend himself, unless you counted biting and it was doubtful that would accomplish anything, but he refused to beg or cry. If this was it, he was going out with dignity.

The werewolf cocked its head and then tossed the torso aside, having lost interest in its victim.

While the monster was toying with The Star Spangler, Yousei spied Abdul's body, the taser and switchblade lying next to it. He didn't question why that man had weapons, he just grabbed them.

"Power time."

He tossed the taser to Kana and all three punks took off through the doorway into the front cabin.

They were met with a feeding frenzy. The transformed injured passengers had slaughtered their caregivers and were feasting on the corpses. Mouthful of Ants froze in the doorway. The creatures were too consumed with the carcasses to notice them.

Kiichi saw one of the flight attendants hiding behind the back rows of seats. He crouched down on the floor and was almost completely hidden from sight. Their eyes locked and the attendant held up a finger to his pursed lips. Be quiet.

Kana pushed Kiichi forward as Yousei took the lead. The three crept down the aisle. They slow stepped, careful not to draw any attention from the dozen creatures in the cabin.

They passed a werewolf that was missing the lower half of its body and lapping blood off the floor. It saw them and hunched over the puddle, growling, protecting its treat.

They got to the stairs that lead to the upper cabin and crept up them. Yousei took point so when they reached the top he signaled with his hand for them to stop. He slowly peaked his head out. To his right was the upper cabin, where apparently most of the passengers had congregated.

The room was an even bigger bloodbath than anything on the lower levels. At least two dozen werewolves were feeding, fighting, and two were even fucking amongst the seats and corpses.

As the plane pitched ever so slightly, a thick river of blood ran running down the aisle and flowed down the stairs. Kana clapped her hands over her mouth so as not to vomit, worried that the sounds of her retching would attracted the beasts.

Yousei looked to the left. There were the large metal doors that led to the cockpit. Since the plane was still in the air, the pilots must still be OK. He looked back at his friends and motioned with his head in the direction of the cockpit. They nodded.

"Stay silent hill," he whispered.

He took Kana's hand and she took Kiichi's. The three slowly moved out of the stairwell into the upper cabin. Just like below, all the beasts were engaged in their own activities and took no notice of them.

They were inching toward the cockpit door when the intercom blared to life.

"This is the cockpit, can someone please respond? Is there anyone out there?"

At once all the monsters perked up and turned in the direction of the cockpit and saw the three punks.

"Fucking Jar-Jar," grumbled Kana.

***

"I don't get it," said Dax, "what happened to everyone?"

To punctuate his statement there was suddenly banging and muffled cries coming from their cockpit door. Dax and Chavez both looked back.

"Well let them in," said Dax.

Chavez got up and unlocked the door. He opened it and three young people decked out in black leather, multicolored hair, and covered in piercings and tattoos spilled in. Behind them, from floor to ceiling was a wall of brown fur, claws, and gnashing teeth.

He slammed the door shut and the monsters slammed into it. The door shook but the strong steel did not budge.

Dax turned and looked at the punks getting to their feet and saw that Chavez's face had gone white.

"Dude . . . what's up?"

Chavez sat back down at the controls and took the joint from Dax. He hit it long and hard.

"Will one of you tell me what the fuck is happening?"

"Mega mecha werewolf horde," gasped the female punk.

Chavez stared at the punk and passed her the joint.

"Rasta," she said grinning.

Chavez turned to Dax, "I'm way too high for this shit."

3
Werewolves on a Plane

Mohammad climbed over the bodies in the back cabin. He found it surprisingly easy to get back there. Most of the monsters were too concerned with their kills and those punks distracted the others leaving him free to move about the lower section of the plane.

He searched through the bodies and found Abdul. His friend was mangled with most of his insides now outside. The upper part of his chest was untouched. Mohammad found the hidden button and Abdul's chest flipped open. Inside were the explosives, still armed and operational.

Mohammad was relieved. Allah was still watching over him.

He removed the bomb as he heard howls from the upper deck and the sound of heavy creatures moving about. The punks must have gotten the monsters excited and they were searching for more prey they may have overlooked.

He pulled out the bomb and looked around. He headed to the bathrooms and service station at the back of the cabin. The area was empty, with the exception of two mutilated corpses.

He pushed the button shutting the emergency doors and slumped to the ground. His body was sore and tired but he was still alive.

On the floor next to him was a small one-foot-wide hole that had been torn into the aircraft's floor. He paid no mind.

***

Raymond was still hiding in the seats when he heard the horde moving down the stairs. The werewolves were on the move. Those damn punks must have gotten them excited.

The beasts began to flow down the stairs into the cabin, sniffing the air and growling.

Raymond knew he had to get out of there.

He crawled beneath the seat in front of him. He didn't know where he was going. The cockpit crossed his mind but all the monsters were blocking the stairwells. Then his back bumped into a seat and the fetish wear on his uniform rattled.

A growl sounded next to his ear. He turned, and there, still sitting in the wheelchair, was the damn beast that started this all.

Raymond got to his feet and backed away from the snarling creature. His back hit the wall and he found himself next to the emergency exit.

Then a crazy idea crossed his mind.

He looked around the cabin and there looked to be fifty werewolves staring back at him. Each one drooling and eyeing him with desire.

He reached his hands back and found the emergency lock. He clicked it off.

His movements were slow and calm, he didn't want to excite them just yet. The pack crept forward. The wheelchair wolf held its position in front of him and continued to growl.

Raymond paused for a moment and tried to think of something positive, some good last note to go out on. But he had nothing. He had no family. No love in his life. His career and constant travel had made keeping even basic friendships impossible. Hell, his cat died last year.

He looked around the cabin as the monsters bore down on him.

"Fuck ya'll," he whispered and opened the door.

***

"Mother-cunt-fucker. What now?" Dax yelled as alarms went off all over the cockpit. The punks were sitting on the floor and the five had been passing joints around constantly. The punks were kind of weird, especially how they talked, but he and Chavez did manage find out from them that the plane was filled with werewolves and, most likely, they were the only five people left alive.

But there was a bigger problem. He knew Chavez noticed it as well but hadn't said anything. One of the few instruments that will still working was their odometer. According to it, they should be over the west coast of the United States right now with Portland just a scant half an hour away. Instead, open ocean and black skies stretched out for forever in front of them. Even if the odometer was malfunctioning and even if they weren't going as fast as they thought, land should be in sight.

Dawn was also due forty minutes ago.

"We got decompression in the front cabin," responded Chavez

"What's our altitude?"

"You know damn well the altimeter is not working."

"Shit, OK let's hope we can do this." Dax snorted another line. "Hold on," he directed as he began to take the plane down.

If they didn't get the plane below 20,000 feet in a matter of minutes the entire plane would depressurize, exposing them all to extreme cold and a dangerous lack of oxygen. They would be knocked unconscious.

***

When Raymond opened the door, it flipped outward with such force that it surprised him. He suddenly found himself outside the plane hanging onto the door handle. His body pressed flat against the plane.

Monsters, corpses, and luggage flew out from the doorway in a constant stream. Raymond screamed, not in terror but primal rage at the beasts. Now they were the ones dying.

He saw the monster in the wheelchair come flying out with the other debris.

Got you, you bastard.

He pulled with all his strength toward the doorway. He had resigned himself to dying when he opened the door but now he was willing to fight for survival again.

He felt the plane pitch down and the pull became less strong. Dax and Chavez must still be alive and they were trying to pressurize the plane. There was still a chance of making it out of this.

Through the grace of God he managed to pull himself into the doorway. He held onto the doorframe tight and the plane kept going lower. He looked into the cabin and it seemed to be empty of almost everything. The oxygen masks had lowered and were whipping about from overhead compartment.

There was something bouncing around in the cabin. Raymond struggled to make out the shiny purple blur. It suddenly was headed straight at him and then he heard the blur screaming.

It shot straight at him and Raymond was able to register the blur as a torso with a screaming head right before it hit him square in the chest. The force sent him and what was left of The Star Spangler out into open air.

***

Dax leveled the plane when he reached what he thought was a low enough altitude, there was no real way to be sure. But they were not knocked out, so he must have been successful.

"I think we're OK," said Dax.

One of the punks shushed him.

The cockpit got quiet and they all listened. Beneath the floor came a strange scratching sound.

"What the hell is that?" asked Chavez.

Suddenly, all the instruments in the cockpit began sounding alarms or just shutting off.

"We've got massive failure across the board. We're losing control of all vital systems," Dax informed.

A hole burst open in the floor and a small furry blur burst out. The baby werewolf began bouncing around the cockpit like a basketball slashing and biting. All five started screaming and blindly striking at the creature.

Kana took out the taser and struck forward. The beast squealed and hopped on top of the instrument panel. It giggled and its claws dug into the controls, damaging them even more. Chavez smacked it with the back of his hand and the little monster grabbed their bag of coke and dove back into the hole it emerged from.

"What the fuck just happened?"

"I think a baby werewolf just stole our coke."

"This is getting stupid!"

Kana grabbed Dax and started shaking his shoulder to get his attention. She was pointing frantically out the window toward the left wing of the plane.

Dax squinted, trying to see what was going on. "There's . . . something . . . on the wing of the plane."

He could see a large blob on the wing of the plane but he couldn't make sense of what he was looking at. The lights on the wing blinked on and off, briefly illuminating it. He saw what it was but it took his brain a moment to make sense of it.

The werewolf in the wheelchair was on the wing, somehow staying in place. The wind whipped the thing's fur against its body. The beast howled at the moon and Dax swore he heard it above the noise of the plane.

The beast began to tear into the wing, prying back paneling, and attacking wires.

"Oh . . . oh, this is so bad," said Chavez right before the plane started violently rocking side to side.

"OK," said Dax. He took his hands off the steering joystick and sat back examining his ruined instrument panel. He pushed a button and the speakers blasted, "Ziggy Stardust" by David Bowie.

He felt surprisingly calm as he lit up what he knew was his last joint, "Try to hold onto something. We're going down."

"Let's rock and roll," Yousei nervously said.

***

Mohammad woke up in the hallway. He must have passed out from exhaustion. He could feel the plane going down.

He assumed that he had slept through the rest of the trip and that they were landing in Portland. This was what he was waiting for. He pulled up his shirt and opened the hidden compartment in his chest. He armed the bomb and closed his eyes, saying a silent prayer.

There was a screeching sound and he opened his eyes to see a miniature werewolf coming out of the hole in the floor. Some kind of white powered was covering its snout.

"Praise be to Allah," he said and the bomb went off.

***

In the cockpit they heard and felt the explosion. The plane was only a few yards above the water when the bomb blew. The cabin split open and the cockpit was sent rocketing forward, flipping over.

Kiichi saw Chavez's chest cave-in as he was thrown into the steering joystick.

The punks went bouncing around the cockpit and Kiichi tried to reach out to one of his friends but his head hit the ceiling and the world went black.

***

Kiichi was aware of the wet and the cold but nothing else. Then he felt open air and his lungs gasped for oxygen.

He opened his eyes to see Kana and Yousei leaning down over him, grinning.

"Nine lives," said Kana.

"Like a mongoose," said Yousei laughing.

Kiichi shook his head and regained his senses. He sat up and looked around. The three punks floated atop an inflatable emergency raft. About a hundred yards away, the burning wreckage of the plane was slowly sinking below the waves.

"Flyboys?" he asked.

Kana shook her head, "no."

He grimly nodded. At least the three of them had made it.

High above them, the full moon illuminated the open ocean and the last bit of wreckage sunk beneath the water.

Yousei started shouting and pointing. Kana and Kiichi turned and looked in the direction of his finger. Through the darkness they saw another raft drifting in their direction and there appeared to be someone on it.

All three began yelling and waving, they were so happy they weren't the only survivors.

The other raft drifted closer and all three punks fell silent when they got a good look at it. In the center of the raft, still sitting in the wheelchair, was the cripple wolf. It howled at the moon and waved its paws eagerly in their direction, like it was trying to will them closer—and it was working.

The two rafts were approaching each other at a quicker speed. The punks dropped to their knees and tried in vain to paddle with their hands in the opposite direction but the cruel ocean currents were too strong.

In moments the two rafts were touching and the werewolf lunged forward, falling off its wheelchair but directly on top of Yousei. He screamed as the werewolf tore into his stomach. Kana jumped on the beast and pulled out the taser. She tried to shock it but weapon was soaked with salt water and rendered useless.

The wolf reached back and grabbed the top of her head with its powerful paw.

Kiichi rushed the creature and it lazily backhanded him, sending him flying through the air right onto the other raft. He sat up and Kana's shrieks reached an unnatural pitch. He managed to get to his feet just in time to see the beast pop Kana's head from her body.

He froze in shock and the beast tossed her corpse overboard. He noticed that Yousei was still alive and moving but for some reason he was smiling. Yousei's hand made a quick motion and something metal flew through the air toward Kiichi. He caught the object and looked down to see he was holding the switchblade they found onboard the plane.

The sudden movement attracted the werewolf's attention and it turned to face Kiichi. The punk flicked the blade open and moonlight glimmered off the weapon.

Yousei flashed him devil horns, "Rock and roll forever."

Kiichi returned the sign, "Party every night."

The werewolf howled and slashed Yousei's neck, finishing the kill.

Kiichi flipped the weapon in the air, caught it by the blade, and whipped the knife straight at the center of the raft. There was a loud *Pop* and the raft quickly began to deflate. The beast saw what was happening and frantically began to try and crawl back to the other raft where its chair was. Its movements only pushed the air out faster.

Yousei's corpse went beneath the water and the monster thrashed about with its arms. Its legs hung useless and the beast slipped beneath the waves.

Kiichi looked over the side of the raft and watched the monster desperately try to doggie paddle, its muscular arms and wet fur slapping against the water. Bubbles erupted to the surface as it lost its struggle and sunk below the waves. Then the ocean was quiet and Kiichi was alone.

He collapsed. His body weak and soaked to the bone. He rolled over and threw up, his nerves beyond shot. With great effort, he managed to sit up. The monster's wheelchair still sat on the raft. He snorted in disgust at it and pushed the contraption over the side into the water.

Far off in the horizon, the first rays of the long-delayed dawn finally broke, the sky just beginning to turn the deepest shade of purple. When the first stabs of yellow pierced the sky, Kiichi began to laugh and cry.

HHHHHOOOOONNNNNNKK-KKK!

Kiichi turned around. Not more than a few hundred meters away was a small fishing ship. He waved at the vessel and lay back down in the raft.

Now he was just laughing. He survived. He would live to see another day.

He felt so good that he didn't even notice the bite wound on his ankle.

GARRETT COOK

LOCATION:
Illinois

STYLE OF BIZARRO:
Chainsaw Noir/Neopulp Expressionsism

BOOKS BY COOK:
Murderland 1:h8
Archelon Ranch
Murderland 2:Life During Wartime
Jimmy Plush, Teddybear Detective
Cart Fop, Fart Cop
Wrongside
The Wake at the House of Dead Cats
The Bacongirl Diaries
Requiem for a Hockeymask
Murderland 3: Godless

"Garrett Cook's work has an edge…
and it's at your throat." - Robert Dunbar

DESCRIPTION: Garrett Cook is a purveyor of dark moral fiction, pulp that blurs the boundaries between high and low culture, twisted nightmares of a Jungian bent and grindhouse Punch and Judy shows. His work presents us with heroes of questionable character but an unquestionable capacity to take on adversity. He also wants you to laugh at the worst things you can imagine.

INTERESTS: Japanese science fiction, Unpleasant Things

INFLUENCES: Dante, Franz Kafka, Lewis Carroll, James Joyce, William Burroughs, Harlan Ellison, Kurt Vonnegut, H.P Lovecraft, Robert E. Howard, Stan Lee, Jack Kirby, Alan Moore, Frank Miller, Bob Dylan, The Ramones, Nick Cave and the Bad Seeds, Todd Browning, F.W Murnau, Edgar Ulmer, Val Lewton, Lon Chaney Senior, David Lynch, Satoshi Kon, Dario Argento, David Cronenberg, Tobe Hooper, Tom Savini, Roger Corman.

WEBSITE:

thegarrettcook.blogspot.com

RE-MANCIPATOR

CHAPTER ONE

He pulled out of her and saw a smile that had seldom been real. It had been a smile for the milk fund and for movie magazines, a smile seldom shared in earnest and seldom a genuine postcoital gift.

"It should always be like this, Johnny Booth," Norma Jean, whispering into his ear, combining these words and a few small, affectionate bites at the same time, "it should be like this, forever."

John Booth's face, which was seconds ago the very picture of joy and serenity, turned into hard plastic.

"We can stay here," Norma Jean explained desperately, "we can stay here and we can survive and build a life."

Booth hated when he had to look away from her. He looked away, but he wasn't going to be silent or to pretend nothing was happening as men often did with women. He knew her history and all of the chances at happiness she had lost and the ones that weren't about happiness at all. Which is why it pained him to say what he was about to.

"Norma Jean, I could be happy with you anywhere. There isn't a world so awful that it wouldn't be brightened by wakin' up next you for the rest of my life. But, baby, I fucked up the world and I've gotta go out there and unfuck it. There's no way around it."

A lot of things could be said about the girl and her acting skills—stiff, naïve, inhuman, awkward, incapable of speaking like an adult—but there was something she could do that few actresses could do like she could, and that was cry. Besides pills and disappointments, she had tears to spare and when he said that he was goin' out to unfuck the world, she proved it.

"You can't go out there, Johnny, you can't. You gave me another chance, you made me happy for the first time. There's never been a man who made me happy, Johnny Booth, and you know it. What about me?"

He answered the question by grabbing her face and kissing her. It was rough, it was aesthetic, it was a celluloid kiss from a real man's lips, it insisted on being filmed, but still it was just for them. She dried her tears. She understood.

"So it's like that, Johnny?"

"It's like that, Norma Jean."

She smiled and crawled under the bed, giving him a view of one of the finest asses to grace the silver screen as she did. If things weren't so emotional and he didn't have to go, he'd have wanted another go at her. When she emerged, she had the flamberge. She knelt before him and presented it. He could feel his legend crackle, he could feel the story the image could build, the power and the beauty of being handed a magic sword by Marilyn Monroe.

"May you kill many Lincolns," said Norma Jean, solemnly.

"You know I will, Norma Jean," John Booth replied and they left the bedroom together.

Musashi was in the hallway. It was not surprising. He never slept.

"You're going now," he said. Many of Musashi's statements sounded like questions and many of Musashi's questions sounded like statements.

"Yes, I'm going."

"Good?" It sounded like a statement but Booth could tell he was asking him.

"It will have to be."

"Good."

"Yeah."

"Remember what I taught you."

Booth laughed.

"How could I forget? You're Musashi Miyamoto."

In the kitchen, Homer was blowing smoke from his hookah at Herodotus. Although blind, he could tell about where the historian was. Herodotus wished he could use the hookah himself but couldn't, being a cat and all. The smoke blowing ceased when Homer heard footsteps.

"That you, Booth?" he asked as Booth and Norma Jean entered the kitchen.

"No, it's seven Lincolns," said Herodotus, holding back a snicker.

Homer jumped to his feet.

"Shit! This is what I've been practicing for. Get my sniper rifle, cat, it ends tonight!"

The cat rolled his eyes. Homer, being blind, of course did not see this.

"Of course it's Booth, you crazy blind bastard. And that's not a sniper rifle. It's a saxophone. I've been fuckin' with you because you ate my good cheese."

Homer blew smoke in the cat's face again, but this time it was not out of generosity but malice.

"Asshole."

Booth hugged the blind bard.

"Thanks for everything."

"It was nothing, if anything I ought to thank you for the story you've given me. They're a hell of a commodity for bards."

Booth rubbed Herodotus behind the ears.

"And thanks for what you've done. You've been a hell of a sport, too."

Herodotus purred.

"It wasn't all that bad, Booth. I'm honored to know a man who's as willing to right a mistake as you are. Good luck and give 'em hell."

Booth nodded.

"I will kill many Lincolns."

And at that, John Booth stepped outside, flamberge in hand into a hell of his own making, a nightmare world built on a foundation of lies to do what any good man with access to a big sharp blade ought to do—make history.

CHAPTER TWO

Noctys Blakblud, Gothrocker General of Washington, DC, tossed a sack of Marilyn Monroe parts at John Hbooth's door instead of knocking. He figured it would be louder and a more rockin' kind of thing to do. Hbooth did not respond on the first toss, so he tossed it again. The noise was squishier this time. Hbooth had heard the first toss but since it was 4 am and he'd worked until 2:47 creating Marilyn Monroe from soulstuff and Historion particles, Hbooth was slow to rise. Hearing the second toss and having a vague idea why it had sounded squishier, had to be a sack of body parts. Hbooth ran for the door like a bat out of hell before a third one occurred. Sure enough, an angry Noctys was holding a bloody sack.

"My liege, it's four a.m...."

Noctys took a swig from a bottle of rubbing alcohol.

"Yeah, but I've done a shitload of coke, Hbooth!"

"I take it Marilyn is in that bag."

"Yes," snarled Noctys, "your shitty-ass Marilyn Monroe is in this sack."

This instantly made Hbooth defensive. He took pride in the fruits of his candy man talents.

"You realize that wasn't a clone or anything, that was Marilyn Monroe. So, my Marilyn Monroe was not shitty, but perfect...and it seems you have killed her."

Noctys flipped Hbooth the bird.

"Perfect, my ass! This Marilyn couldn't swordfight worth shit!"

Hbooth rubbed his temples with two fingers. His brain was starting to ache.

"I brought Marilyn Monroe back to life, constructed this flawless copy of her body and you got in a swordfight with her?"

"A flamberge fight to be precise. What did you think I was going to do with her?"

Put his dirty, rockstar hands all over her large, round wonderful breasts, breathe all over her shining alabaster skin, stick his syphilitic prick into her... Hbooth was almost kind of relieved that it had come down to a flamberge fight. Feeling her soul as he reconstructed her with candy man's gift and Historions, he felt her poetry, her despair and he longed for her, wished he didn't have to do what Noctys told him, wished he could have run away with her and not left her in the care of this addlebrained rockstar creep.

"Did somebody tell you Marilyn Monroe would be good at swordfighting?"

"It was a fantasy of mine. And you work for me and you make these fantasies happen with your dead people powers. The candy man can!"

Hbooth was a candy man and that was what he could do, so Noctys was right. He just wished he didn't have to.

"You didn't need to bring me the corpse. I don't reanimate corpses. I use my talents and gather Historions and soulstuff to..."

Noctys tossed the sack at Hbooth. It hit him in the chest and knocked him to the ground.

"Boring! Make her again! Make two so I can race 'em!"

Hbooth sighed. Rockstars would never understand the concept of candy men. The candy man could, but there was only one thing any candy man could do.

"You'll have to talk to Juanita. She's the one who can duplicate things."

"You're stupid and boring, Hbooth. You're totally like that ancestor of yours that killed Lincoln and ruined society. Thanks to your piece of shit ancestor, rockstars will always rule!"

Noctys got on his dragon-shaped motorcycle and sped off, laughing and chugging rubbing alcohol. Hbooth wished he had some to chug. Noctys was right. When his ancestor (who shamed the family so much that they put a silent "h" in the front of their names) killed Lincoln, he had doomed America to centuries of rule by idiots and eventually rockstars. The new president Amber Honeylove could use a bullet in her head, if she didn't have a candy man that could make people bulletproof on her staff. If only there were still men like Lincoln, men who could stand up to the rockstars and lead America to freedom. If only...who can take the sunshine, sprinkle it with dew, cover it in chocolate and a miracle or two...the candy man can.

CHAPTER THREE

"History," said Herodotus the cat, "is bullshit. The sooner people realize this, the easier the world will be to fix. It is mutable, easily manipulated, and vulnerable to the machinations of evil men. You'll get more truth out of those yarns that Blind Fuckin' Willie McTell spun for wine money."

"But history's the only true thing. By its definition, it has to be the only true thing."

"He's right," the bard chimed in, "it's bullshit. Anybody can make it, anybody can break it."

CHAPTER FOUR

The words were not "Sic Semper Tyrannis." "He's sick, he's mental, it's rabies!" said John Wilkes Booth as he pulled the trigger, knowing what the lizard worshippers at Bohemian Grove had put into the negro-loving Yankee president. He had used his skills as an actor to infiltrate the grove and find out why nobody had stopped him from trying to free the slaves and what he had seen, the orgies, the giant owl, the talking reptile statues...too much for most men's sanity to bear. But he was stronger than most men, strong enough to pull the trigger on a sick and deadly president, no matter what it would take.

CHAPTER FIVE

"Our boy's gonna kick her ass," said Noctys, beaming with pride.

"Yup, this debate's a lock."

Amber Honeylove had taken off her clothes and was now violently humping the microphone. This was how her debates usually ran—lewd, naked and showered with candy, dollar bills and applause. Hbooth was worried about Abe. He looked green and sickly, like he might not make it. Was his patch-job flawed? Couldn't be. He recited the mantra to himself.

"Who can take the sunrise, sprinkle it with dew..."

"...cover it in chocolate and a miracle or two," replied the Voice of Wisdom, "the candy man can."

Hbooth inhaled and exhaled repeatedly to calm himself.

"I didn't fail, I didn't fail, I didn't fail....the candy man can."

And indeed he could. But he did not know about his ancestor or the fatcat plot or what was called Abies by the fatcats as they sipped pandasperm at Bohemian grove. He did not know that bringing back Lincoln intact, brought back one scary motherfucker. He also did not know that Lincoln's first impulse when losing a debate was to bite his opponent on the arm. Which he did. Hard. Blood gushed from Amber's butterfly-tattooed arm as he took a good chunk out of it.

"Give 'em Hell, Abe!" shouted Noctys from the third row as he carved an inverted crucifix on his bare chest.

Hbooth shook his head.

"Noctys, I think something's wrong."

Noctys slapped Hbooth in the face.

"I don't fucking pay you to think!"

Amber should have called in her secret service goons to put an end to the feral president but biting was one of Amber's hundreds of fetishes. She pounced on Lincoln, ready to return the favor. Lincoln did not particularly know what to make of this, but knew that he wanted to eat her, so kept biting. And as he tore off bits of excessively tanned smooth teenage girlflesh, she began to change. Her head was expanding, becoming longer, more angular, more like his. Tufts of hair were appearing on her face and her bones were cracking and reknitting themselves. Her thick teen popstar legs were becoming long, spindly and stiltlike. In short, she was turning into a tanned, large-breasted Abraham Lincoln, complete with a fleshy pink stovepipe hat growing out of the top of her head like a tumor. Lincoln's eyes widened. He cackled maniacally. He embraced his pornographic teenie-boppelganger.

"Lincoln loves only Lincoln!" he screamed before shoving his tongue down her throat.

For the first time in several years, Noctys was legitimately concerned.

"Hbooth, I shouldn't have ordered you to bring Lincoln back to life."

Hbooth slapped himself in the forehead.

"And I shouldn't have brought Baudelaire back to life so you could get tertiary syphilis from him. I also shouldn't have told you what Baudelaire and syphilis were."

"I quite agree. You should be punished. I could fuck you and give you syphilis."

"Uh...that would be REWARDING me." It was a lie but Noctys would certainly believe it.

The tall spindly Lincoln monster that had once been Amber Honeylove disengaged from Lincoln, feeling a greater urge for carnage than carnality. Surprisingly fast for such a gangly, addled creature, she lunged at one of the secret service agents, dragged him to her with her Lincolnlong arms and began chewing on his face. As she chewed, his bones broke and knitted as they had in her, and the big pink stovepipe of flesh grew out of his skull. She and Lincoln laughed together.

"Lincoln loves only Lincoln!"

The secret service man bit another secret service man who bit a cameraman who bit another cameraman, who bit another cameraman who bit a girl in the first row who bit the girl next to her who bit another that bit another in an orgy of biting and Lincolning. The audience was applauding.

"Lincoln! Lincoln! Lincoln!"

"Bite 'em all, Abes!"

"I want a beard like that!"

"I want to be tall!"

"I want to be a hero!"

"Anyone can be president! Even a woman!"

This would have been an excellent time for everyone to flee in terror and evacuate the auditorium but this was America and in America, you can't be afraid of Abraham Lincoln and the approval of their peers, rabid Lincoln monsters, or not told the audience that everything was cool and there was nothing better to be than Abraham Lincoln.

Noctys joined the crowd rushing the crowd of Lincolns that was rushing the crowd.

"Make me president! Make me president!"

"Noctys, he's a monster!" Hbooth protested.

Noctys flipped Hbooth two birds.

"So am I! So are all of us!"

Hbooth decided to rush the exit instead of arguing with Noctys, who, sadly enough would probably be better off as a Lincoln monster. As the only person fleeing, it was not very difficult to reach the exit. What would be difficult was to figure out where the hell to go next. He hopped on Noctys' dragon-shaped motorcycle and got to thinking. He only got to think for about a block before his thoughts were interrupted. Horribly interrupted.

Turned out en route to the debate, Lincoln had already bitten several people and those several people had been ravaging through town claiming other victims for an hour. For rabid undead Lincolns, a one hour head start was plenty.

CHAPTER SIX

Hbooth took off the blindfold. Five. Wasn't bad. Wasn't good either. Five hatless mannequins did not mean hope for the future by any stretch of the imagination. Musashi grunted. Hbooth was taken aback to discover that it was Musashi's approval grunt.

"Doing better."

"Thank you, Musashi."

Musashi punched Hbooth in the gut. His fist was like a meat tenderizer.

"Only the weak man accepts compliments!"

"I am sorry…"

Musashi punched him again.

"Only the weak man apologizes!"

"O-okay…"

Another punch.

"Only the weak man stutters!"

Hbooth put the blindfold back on and readied the katana. Musashi started the stopwatch. Slice, slice, slice, slice, slice, slice, slice, slice, slice, beep. Hbooth removed the blindfold. Seven sliced hats, one mannequin nicked on the shoulder. Musashi grunted a slightly nicer grunt.

"Better."

"No, still bad."

"Good! You start to get it!" Musashi smiled and killed the bottle of rice wine he'd been chugging.

"Thanks, I thought I was doing…"

Musashi smashed the bottle over Hbooth's head. It didn't hurt much. Noctys had broken a lot of bottles over his head in his day.

"Everything okay?" asked Homer, having heard the sound of the broken bottle and rushing to find out if all was well. Herodotus was on his shoulder.

"Hrmmm," Musashi grunted.

"Oh, good. How many dead mannequins?"

"Seven," said Hbooth, "but it's not good enough."

"I agree," said Herodotus, jumping down from Homer's shoulder and lying on the floor to clean his genitals, "especially for a man descended from someone who was famous only for killing Lincoln. You should be a genius at killing Lincoln."

Homer raised an eyebrow.

"In Ancient Greek, there is no H. It's just a rough breathing."

CHAPTER SEVEN

Stovepipe heads as far as the eye could see, skinnytall wobbly unmen biting, clawing, homogenizing, making everybody the man that history had loved so dear, the rabid lunatic slain by the hanged patriot, secret weapon of the fatcats of Bohemian Grove who passed the Holy Grail around and drank to the end of mankind, to a world where everyone was one rabid monster president that could be easily controlled with reptile mind control techniques. They kissed a photo of John Hbooth, praising his mistake and themselves for their centuries of fake history. They knew if they made a hero out of Lincoln and a monster out of Hbooth somebody would bring back Lincoln and the Historions would duplicate the disease exactly.

A Lincoln walked onto a city bus, sat down beside an Asian male to female transsexual. Took a bite out of her arm. Took a bite out of her neck and her bared thigh. Made her greenish, made her lanky, made her head extend. The Lincoln crossed the aisle, moving onto the next seat, as the greenish, bearded miniskirted Asian tranny Lincoln stood up to take the bus by surprise. One-armed Vietnam vet en route to the welfare office got bitten. The Abies gave him back his arm, to choke, grab and scrape, to drag the fleeing screaming Elvis impersonators en route to the Council of Elvises meeting by their throat, bring them to his sharp-toothed mouth, rend their throats and make them like him. The courageous driver tried to crash the bus, martyr himself before the illness could spread, but trannies, grannies, Elvises and Vietnam vets with Lincolnized faces wouldn't let it happen. Instead, the bus careened into a group of nuns on a walk with some children in wheelchairs, kept going and then crashed.

Fire and impact were not enough, burned though they were, scarred though they were, the Abies reknit their bones and rekindled their thirst for flesh and their desire to homogenize the world and make it Lincoln. Nun corpses, crippled children corpses, granted the breath of life by disease, malice, egocentricity. Child Lincolns on stunted long Lincoln legs and Lincolns in torn nuns' habits joined the band of burned monstrosities to find more to rend and rip and reconstruct.

CHAPTER EIGHT

Ragtag street people with makeshift spears and flaming Old Granddad molotovs tried to fight back to little avail. The Lincolns were hungry for their selfhood, hungry for the taste of Lincolnfree flesh in their mouths and the thrill of knowing that there would be one more of them. Lincoln loved only Lincoln and that was that. They weren't doing so hot until Charlie Battleaxe showed up.

Before the Lincolns came, Charlie Battleaxe was an urban legend, something homeless parents used to remind their kids not to talk to heavy metal has-beens. Before Noctys Blakblud took over, Gothrocker General wasn't a job. The furthest a Gothrocker could progress in the government was District Gothrock supervisor and DC was a town run on Metal. But, Noctys was louder, dumber and more willing to cut himself to entertain voters and Charlie was reduced to living alone in his trillion-dollar fortress of a mansion without any butlers, maids, prostitutes or candy men. So, in his loneliness, he roamed the streets killing homeless people with a battleaxe. It wasn't out of malice or contempt—he just couldn't come up with a better way of reaching people.

Charlie Battleaxe didn't want anybody honing in on his murder and the Lincolns seemed like they would do just that. So, the fat, red, bearded, tattooed, metal has-been and Viking manqué took up his axe for the people. He rushed into the fray, eyes afire, heart full of anger and sorrow, and started taking heads. Smiling, awash in arterial spray, he screamed out.

"Thank you, Minot!" was all he could think to scream. The feeling of pride left him momentarily, thinking he was back at the Minot, North Dakota Civic Auditorium opening for Quiet Riot again. The delusion vanished when he realized that the Minot, North Dakota Civic Auditorium six and a half foot tall Japanese tourists with stovepipey flesh growths didn't try to throw the snapping severed heads of bearded housewives at him. He decapitated the bearded Lincolnized Japanese tourist only to find that its head was rolling around on the ground trying to bite his foot. Since he was wearing sandals, he didn't dare kick it, but since he had a battleaxe, he buried it in its stovepipey growth.

"Lincoln loves only Lincoln!" it screamed, unable to articulate its pain in any other way. He brought down the axe again, splitting open the growth.

"Thank you, Minot!" Charlie Battleaxe was hoping more blood would spray out. It did not. What did crawl out were a bunch of tiny lizards with Abraham Lincoln faces who were foaming green stuff at the mouth.

"Lincoln loves only Lincoln!" they squeaked before melting into a puddle of green, foamy lizard goo.

"Thank you, Minot!" he screamed in reply, slicing another Lincoln's stovepipey growth in half. Lincoln lizards, green stuff and goo yet again. The homeless survivors took shelter behind trash cans, rooting for Charlie Battleaxe but still too frightened to help him out. The Lincolns grew more zealous, gathering around him in a bigger, tighter knit group, ten at a time. But Charlie Battleaxe wasn't standing for it, Charlie Battleaxe was a creature of heavy metal psychosis, wanton violence, deep-seated, misplaced half-retarded wet brain rage, something a man from the 1860's couldn't understand, even as a rabies-inducing zombie juggernaut.

CHAPTER NINE

"Be careful," warned the statue of Herpetarch Slyxx'ks'h, "she is a phenomenal swordsman and very familiar with the works of Musashi."

"Panic not," said Kennedy's fatcat clone assassin, "I've made several phone calls as the president. She is demoralized; been doing too many pills. Jackie and I can easily defeat her."

Jackie Kennedy nodded as she sipped her strength-enhancing pandasperm reptile cocktail.

"That little blonde bitch is good as dead."

The fatcats laughed as they invented crack to spread through the ghettoes and injected monkeys with Anthropoid Infecting Dark Sorcery, an acronym which they would later claim meant something else.

"Your confidence pleases me. Let us only hope that her skills never fall into the hands of the Booth family."

The fatcats laughed again.

"Forgive me, Herpetarch," said Frank Sinatra, "but there's no way. Marilyn dies tonight and we'll make it look like an accident. I've already gotten her addicted to sleeping pills through the mob psychiatrist I had taking care of her."

The fatcats laughed again.

As night fell, Kennedy's fatcat

clone came to the door.

"Johnny? Is that you?"

"It is in fact me."

Through her sleeping pill haze she could have sworn he didn't have his Boston accent. He hadn't been using his Boston accent much. Probably because that cunt Jackie made fun of him for it so much. She had always thought something was up with Jackie, but Frank had said it was just jealousy and Frank was a smart guy. Frank knew people. Frank could be trusted.

"Johnny, I'm sad. I'm lonely, Johnny."

"It is beautiful and ironic that in your loneliness, you are not alone."

"Oh, Johnny, you always know what to say."

The Kennedy clone from Bohemian Grove was in, Marilyn's nightgown hit the floor and a champagne bottle was uncorked. All was going according to plan for the reptiles.

CHAPTER TEN

"We need a war council," Marilyn suggested as she swung the sword at a Lincolncougar.

"A war council? How are we going to get a war council?"

"You could make one."

Hbooth wasn't too sure about the idea.

"What if all the people on the war council have egocentric zombie rabies?"

Marilyn took a moment to respond, since she was just narrowly avoiding the Lincolncougar's teeth.

"I don't think that's going to happen, Johnny."

CHAPTER ELEVEN

Hbooth hit the gas hard on the dragon-shaped motorcycle, wondering what the hell there was to do beyond dodging Lincolns and getting someplace safe so he could maybe think of a way to undo the mess he'd caused out of hatred for rockstars and love for Marilyn. Sweet little Marilyn would certainly not approve, sweet little Marilyn would say… she'd say…shit. Shit! Shit! Shit! This was no good. No fucking good. Marilyn was at Noctys' mansion, a mansion whose door Noctys had just driven through on his motorcycle. A mansion with a mural of Jefferson Davis painted on its side, which would surely irritate the Lincolns. Hbooth found himself wishing he was one of those candy men who could go from one place to another just by thinking of it. Instead of one of those candy men whose ability to resurrect the dead doomed civilization. At least there was only one of those. Too bad that one was him.

A group of Deadheads had just been bitten by some hip-hop loving Tommy Hilfiger'd suburban poseurs whose stovepipes had torn apart the black winter hats they had previously used to show how cool they were. Now they were much cooler and had much bigger hats. Now they were like most of the people they admired, now they were like almost everybody. Hopefully not almost everybody. How fast could this have spread? Hbooth discarded his thoughts of epidemiology and resumed motorcycle survival thoughts. Unlikely motorcycle survival thoughts.

"Lincoln loves only Lincoln!" he screamed.

"Lincoln loves only Lincoln!" one of the Deadheads shouted as the Lincolnizing process finished up.

"Lincoln loves only Lincoln!"

"Lincoln loves only Lincoln!"

The hip-hop and Deadhead Lincolns were fooled by this simple gesture. If he could try it on every other Lincoln between there and Noctys' mansion, it would be fine. If it worked. These Lincolns caught on a few seconds too late, started their stilty shambling toward him when he was already out of sight and all he needed do was take a shortcut down an alleyway to make them forget he had existed. He hoped it would continue to be this easy. He zoomed down another busy street, trying the mantra on a Lincolnized prostitute and a recently Lincolnized cop who must have been stupid enough to try to arrest her for Lincolnizing a gawky, Lincolnheaded French poodle that barked hungrily for flesh.

"Lincoln loves only Lincoln!" the prostitute shouted.

"Lincoln loves only Lincoln!" the cop shouted back.

The French poodle was not convinced. With his beast-sharp nose he knew what Lincoln smelled like and what Lincoln did not and what Lincoln didn't smell like smelled like food zooming by on a motorcycle. Luckily for Hbooth a six foot high French poodle on Lincoln legs was not much of a runner; unluckily for Hbooth, the French poodle had already bitten an Irish wolfhound and a Chihuahua that were sniffing around for survivors not far from him. On its long new legs, the Irish wolfhound was almost as fast a motorcycle, and the Chihuahua, its skinny, tiny body skittering like a spider on bony Lincoln limbs, actually was.

Though the jump was awkward, the Chihuahua made it, clinging to the back of the motorcycle to get at Hbooth, who had to drive with one hand as he punched it in the face. Hbooth was distracted, driving slower, potential prey not just for the wolfhound and the Chihuahua, but for a mass of Lincolns down the street that heard the motorcycle and knew that it meant people. By the time he managed to gouge out the Lincoln Chihuahua's eyes and toss it off the motorcycle, it was the least of his problems.

If Hbooth had been listening for it, he could have heard Charlie Battleaxe calling out "Come back!" Charlie had been dispatching Lincolns for several minutes (a pretty long time considering the Lincoln attacks had only been going on for about an hour and a half) and he showed no signs of tiring and stopping. Lizards and goo everywhere. Homeless people applauding him, though still wanting nothing to do with the fight. Life was good and now the bastards were running. After he heard the sound of a motorcycle he took off. He ran after them, axe held aloft to see what it was they were chasing after and chased them in turn.

This is how Hbooth and Charlie Battleaxe met up. Hbooth was trapped between the hungry Lincolns Charlie had been fighting off and the Lincoln dogs that had been chasing him. He figured he was good as dead or good as Abe. But, Charlie Battleaxe had no problem with splitting a couple stovepipes from behind so he could see what they were after. And when he did, he was happier to split a lot more.

"Blakblud! Blakblud!" he growled as he split two stovepipes in one wide battleaxe arc.

Noctys' dragon-shaped motorcycle

had at one point been Charlie Battle-axe's most prized possession, a badge of authority and metal supremacy. But, during the election Charlie had been so sure of his rock supremacy over Noctys that he bet his motorcycle. He lost that bet and lost the cycle, and it was many of the factors leading to his downward spiral into homeless axe murder.

"Blakblud, you bastard, you're mine!" Lincoln after Lincoln fell at Charlie's axe, so many that the Irish wolfhound ignored the motorcycle to pounce on Charlie. It made a more valiant attempt than any human Lincoln as of yet, actually using its mass and bestial fury to bring him to the ground and prep him for a bite. Still, even a monster dog couldn't get between the crazed metalhead and his custom motorcycle. Charlie found the strength to split the dog's stovepipe head, roll the corpse off, and jump at the motorcycle.

Hbooth rolled out of the way just in time, leaving Charlie flat on the pavement, prey for more advancing Lincolns, who'd been converting homeless people as Charlie dismembered their brethren. As he gunned it toward the mansion, Hbooth hoped the metalhead would stay down, though he was frightened at the thought of such a fierce man being converted into a Lincoln. He didn't know what to feel when the fierce metalhead stood up again; pursuing the motorcycle, forgetting how much faster it could go than he could.

Hbooth idled the bike and got off. It occurred to him who this was and why he was chasing him.

"I'm not Noctys, Charlie. I'm his candy man. And I need to get back to his house safely. When you get there,

you can break anything you want, you can piss all over his collection of original Goya paintings, you can make sexually explicit phone calls to his mother. Whatever. I hate the bastard and he's probably a Lincoln by now anyway. I'll even give you the bike if you let a friend and I hide out at your place."

Though street-crazy and in a slaughter-fog Charlie saw reality once more, his head jerking into alertness with a gesture that would have been suitable for a stalking Michael Myers. He remembered that Noctys usually did not wear a shirt, was usually covered in cuts and meaningless tattoos and was usually very quick to proclaim that he was Noctys, while this guy was quick to deny it. Noctys also wasn't afraid of most sharp things, so wouldn't have tried to flee. Wasn't Noctys. It was Noctys' poor, long-suffering candy man. Damn good candy man. He'd always wanted this guy instead of his candy man, who had the power to turn diamonds into cheese and vice versa.

"Damn, I know you. You ain't Noctys at all. Good for you. Goth rocker general or not, I still got a feelin' like it would suck being that guy."

"I think so too. But not to worry, he's a Lincoln now."

"Good. It ain't like I ever needed an excuse for killin' but damned if it ain't nice to have one every once in a while, besides, you know, that I'm out of my fucking mind."

"You might be out of your fuckin' mind, Charlie, but you figured out how to kill Lincolns."

Charlie shrugged.

"I just didn't like those damn arrogant foofy skinhats. They make me real mad."

Hbooth surveyed the devastation

Charlie had wrought. There were more corpses than he could count. Not that he tried very hard, having stopped at about 27, but he could see there were a lot.

"Shit, Charlie, I can see that."

"I wouldn't have voted for that cocksucker that's for sure. You and me got a lot in common, John Wilkes Booth, you come from a family of Lincoln killers and I'm a damn good Lincoln killer."

The hairs on the back of Hbooth's neck stood up on end. He still didn't want to be thought of as a descendant of John Wilkes Booth.

"Different Booth. I'm Hbooth with an H."

"Suit yourself," said Charlie, "then you drive and I kill."

CHAPTER TWELVE

"That sounds awfully simplistic."

"Not to me," Homer chimed in, "it makes a lot of sense."

Musashi grunted. Possibly in agreement.

Marilyn poured another glass of champagne with vodka.

"He's not just any cat, Johnny. He's Herodotus."

"But…"

"Just go to the theater," the cat said slowly in a tone that a five year old would have found patronizing, "and do what you do, but backwards."

"I don't see how I could travel in time."

"Just revise history," said Homer, "it's easy. I did it all the time."

"That doesn't make any sense."

"That's because it's bullshit, time travel, raising the dead, history, it's bullshit. It's bullshit, Booth."

CHAPTER THIRTEEN

"Who can take the sunshine, sprinkle it with dew…"

"Cover it in chocolate and a miracle or two," replied the Voice of Wisdom as Hbooth carefully wove together the Historions that made up Marilyn. It felt nice feeling her soul and the contents of her life coming together. He felt a creepy urge to lick it since he thought it would taste good, in spite of the sourness and the bittersweet quality of it all. It certainly smelled nice enough. She certainly smelled nice enough. He picked up some things he had missed as he examined and joined with her soul the night before. Such as her passion for samurai culture and swordsmanship. Noctys had been right. Must have been a coincidence, one of his many misfiring neurons misfiring correctly. Well done, Hamlet-monkey, well done. Too bad it had ended so badly. She didn't like the cuts at all, didn't like…when Noctys snuck up, tasered her, impaled her on his sword and then put a sword in her hand when she was down to make it look like he won. Durable soul in spite out of all the times it had succumbed to despair, wasn't feeling "oh, the misery of being impaled!" but rather "I could've beaten that bastard, I'm sure his technique was inferior."

She stepped out of history, shimmering in one of her gowns from *Some Like it Hot*, and kissed Hbooth on the cheek.

"Oh, it's you, you wonderful boy!"

He blushed.

"Hi, Marilyn."

"That wasn't as long as the last time."

Hbooth tried not to laugh. It would've been at the ingenuousness of the statement not at the stupidity if he had, though.

"No, it certainly wasn't. He wanted you back."

She smiled. Her eyebrows fluttered.

"Really? He wanted me back?"

"Well, you know…"

She hung her head. Her smile disappeared and she commenced searching Hbooth's nightstand for champagne. Hbooth had anticipated this and had purchased some.

Marilyn slapped him. She placed a hand on her chest.

"My goodness! What kind of a man keeps champagne in his nightstand all the time."

Hbooth was shocked. He couldn't find a reply. She shocked him again, when she started to giggle.

"I'm just pulling your leg, Johnny. Why don't you get some ice?"

He smiled and nodded, still tongue-tied by love. He went to the kitchen and got a bucket of ice. Hbooth kept lots of buckets in his house for when Noctys would drop in. Seemed like that man couldn't go five minutes without excreting SOMETHING, blood, urine, vomit…had to be some way he could get away from working for the kind of man who required his employees to keep dozens of buckets in their house for his bodily fluids and the bodily fluids of others he spilled. He was relieved that he could find one that hadn't been used yet.

Marilyn applauded his return.

"My goodness, champagne in your dresser, ice buckets in your kitchen. You're like the Ritz, Johnny."

He poured her half a glass with some ice. He anticipated her next question.

"Vodka?"

"Next drawer down."

"Incredible."

When she poured the vodka, it was oddly dainty, hitting the rim exactly.

"I'm such a hypocrite, sometimes, Johnny," she said, with a tinge of melancholia, "I study Bushido and I can't stop drinking. Then again, how do you stop drinking when you spend your time with Sinatra and the Kennedys? Hmm? It's difficult, Johnny, it really is. Actress, woman, lush, samurai. What's a gal to do?"

Again, Hbooth could not find an answer. Marilyn giggled.

"You're quiet, Johnny, I like that. Not often that a man will just sit and let a girl talk like that. Except for when he doesn't care what she's saying. But you care, don't you?"

"Yes."

"Well, there's one word. You drinking?"

"I…"

She poured him a glass of champagne. He took it. He could use one.

"Thank you."

She touched his face.

"No, thank you. Not every day a guy brings you back to life, even if it's his job."

He leaned in closer.

"I'd do it even if it wasn't my job."

"I know you would."

A big fat, awkward silence sat down between them with crossed arms, shaking its head disapprovingly. It couldn't be seen but they knew it was there. Hbooth backed up.

"Noctys should be here in a couple of hours to pick you up."

Marilyn poured and downed a drink in one move.

"Well, somebody thinks highly of his prowess in bed."

"Marilyn, I…"

She silenced him with a kiss. He felt like his heart was going to implode. He leaned back in and put his hand on her thigh. Then she shocked him again by breaking the kiss and standing up.

"John Hbooth, you are a coward. You're a chicken-shit slave to a rock and roll idiot and I will have nothing to do with you. You have a fantastic gift and you don't use it for anything but serving that sword-swinging psychopath in a leatherjacket."

She locked herself in the bathroom and cried. He pounded on the door, trying to reason with her as a courtesy, not because he thought it would work.

"Marilyn, I'm sorry. I can't do anything with you. I've brought you back for Noctys and while he's still in charge of me, I can't be with you."

"Well, why's he in charge? Can he bring back the dead? Is he smart? Is he useful? Is he amazing? Why's he in charge?" she shouted through the door.

"Because he's a rockstar and rockstars are in charge."

She opened the door.

"I bet his music's terrible," she said, pouring herself another glass of champagne.

Hbooth laughed as he poured himself one.

"He has a song called Niggersperm Magic Machine."

"Jesus. Why couldn't jazzmen run the country?"

"Not popular enough."

"I know, but most of them don't do anything worse than reefer."

"I suppose they don't."

They lay together, thinking about how Noctys was coming and when he came they were going to be separated, until he broke her yet again. He didn't want to see her brought to him in parts. There had to be something else that could be done. But what? He was bound to serve his rockstar master and while his rockstar master still lived, he couldn't violate the candy man's oath and use his power for himself. Not while Noctys lived…or not while Noctys was his rockstar liege. He'd been thinking before about how he was a candy man, how he could make the dead come back to life and how the world would be better if rockstars no longer ruled. As the plan materialized completely, a smile devoured half of Hbooth's face, just as his next decision would devour the world.

When Noctys arrived, Hbooth didn't hesitate to present the idea.

"My liege, before you go, I've got a candidate who can beat that bitch Amber good."

Noctys did something he seldom did in his loud, stupid rockstar life: he listened to the proposition.

CHAPTER FOURTEEN

"He's sick, he's mental, it's…"

The scream did not occur. The shooting did not occur. The death and historical canonization of Abraham Lincoln and the demonization of John Wilkes Booth did not occur. Before Booth the much elder's pistol fired, Booth the much younger got the drop on him with his Historion gun. Firing rapidly accelerated Historions with the consent of existence, Booth repented for something that was one hundred fifty years from being his fault in order to make sure his own sins would not be committed at all. He turned a villain who should have been a folk hero into fading particles of myth, a story nobody would ever think to tell or to retell, a name that would show up instinctively on tips of tongues when people would talk of history's villains and disappear because it wasn't the right one. Hero or villain, there was nothing left of him.

Booth the younger shuddered as the Historions undid his ancestor, knowing that only moments later, he would start to come apart in incomprehensible ways. There couldn't have been a John Booth, could there? There wasn't a man descended from another man who should have been but wasn't, there wasn't a man that destroyed that man since there was no man to destroy. Claws and rending hooks of bullshit history, bullshit physics, bullshit myth, bullshit fictions were yanking on him hard. Eating every scrap like dogs by the dinner table, they left only a sense of profound emptiness that filled the theater, an emptiness that nobody could explain but everybody felt.

"Don't mourn me," Lincoln said to the theater, "don't mourn me, because I think I have rabies of some kind and I feel violent and stupid and empty, the world feels emptier somehow. Lincoln loves you, America, so forget Lincoln, forget him!"

Lincoln jumped off the balcony onto the stage, hoping to finish himself off in a dignified but flamboyant manner. He did not. As John Wilkes Booth had after jumping down from the balcony, Lincoln only broke his leg. But, he had publicly proclaimed he was rabid and looking to die a hero's death to a crowded theater. The consequences of yelling fire would have been mild in comparison. Cast and theatergoers descended upon the president, beating, kicking, biting and rending him. Knowing somehow that it was for the better, Lincoln died with a beatific smile on his face, even as the patrons of Ford's Theater beat, molested and mangled him, pounding his head against the stage until it burst open and hundreds of little lizards crawled out.

CHAPTER FIFTEEN

"I'm starting to get exhausted," Charlie complained as he punched a Lincolnized pony in the face, "Most days I only kill five or six things with an axe. Today, I've killed like ten!"

"I think it's more like a few hundred, Charlie. You're very good at killing things with an axe."

"Yeah, it's just that and Metal. When we get to Noctys' house can I do some Metal?"

Hbooth hoped he wouldn't.

"Sure, Charlie, you can do all the Metal you want."

"Good, because I fuckin' love Metal! Even more than I love killin' things with an axe!"

The pony's stovepipe was thick. It didn't snap so quickly as a human's, which didn't look good for Charlie. To make matters worse, a twelve-year-old anorexic Lincoln in a pink party dress sat down on the pony's back and began grabbing at and trying to bite Charlie. With one hand, he punched the pony in the face, with the other he hacked at the stovepipe.

"Can't you drive this any faster?" Charlie shouted at Hbooth.

"Not faster than a Lincolnpony."

"I hate when these things are animals!" As a chop from Charlie left the pony's stovepipe hanging by a thread, the pink party dress girl caught hold of the metalhead's face-punching arm and prepared to take a bite. Time slowed down to a crawl as she prepared to clamp down her jaws on him and the axe prepared to disconnect the pony from its pipe. A fang grazing skin, a flap of stovepipe flying, screams of tiny lizards, a startled twelve year old letting go as the pony beneath her crumpled and died. A Metalhead's eyes widening in terror as he realized how close he'd come to becoming one of them. The motorcycle finally creating some distance from the wandering Lincolns. It was a tense few seconds.

A tense few seconds that got tenser when they reached Noctys' ill-protected mansion. Tenser because Marilyn was inside and the place didn't even have a door, tenser because while Lincolns tended to go after other food when prey was out of sight for more than a few seconds, and they weren't too far away to be found, and tenser because Charlie was growing tired. His muscles were tense, he'd nearly been Lincolnized and the deep reservoir of violence in his heart was starting to dry up. As soon as Hbooth idled the motorcycle Charlie held out the battleaxe.

"Hbooth, I can't fight anymore. You're going to have to be the one who kills Lincolns."

"I don't know if I can do that."

"You want to save your girl?"

"Yeah."

"Do you feel bad about making all those damn Lincolns?"

"I only made one."

Charlie glared at him. Hbooth did not object to the glaring since he knew it was quite justified.

"Fine, I'll take it," said Hbooth.

Hbooth took the battleaxe, not too sure if he could even swing it but pretty sure he might have to. Surer when he noticed Noctys' pet polar bear, now several inches taller, teetering on undersized skinny legs and sporting a goatee, a Lincoln face and a stovepipe hat. Hbooth wet himself. Most people would have. Polar bears are gigantic. Lincolnized polar bears were colossal abominations against nature. The battleaxe felt woefully insufficient. Hbooth himself felt woefully insufficient. His whole life he had been mocked for being descended from the man who killed Lincoln and now, he was in a position where he was responsible for returning Lincoln to the world and would have to kill him several times. Hbooth briefly contemplated suicide. The contemplation was very brief as the only thing he could commit suicide with would be the battleaxe, which was not very good for suicide at all.

He held the battleaxe over his head, telling his body to go in there and charge, to prevent Charlie from being eaten or Lincolnized by the furry, white death god. Hbooth had known that sooner or later working for the kind of asshole that thinks he needs a pet polar bear would cause problems and he was proven right. All that could be done was to charge the bear...the beloved sixteenth president bear. To charge the bear like an assassin, an endangered-species-killing presidential assassin. Hbooth's body did not charge. It quivered, then it froze. Then its eyes widened as it watched Charlie Battleaxe's head bitten off by the Lincoln bear. Then it fainted dead away when Charlie Hatbox's head grew back, albeit elongated, stovepiped and equipped with a very familiar goatee.

In what might have been a faint-based hallucination, Hbooth met the Greek poet Homer on the steps of the Lincoln Memorial. He fainted again at the sight of a gigantic bronze Lincoln. He awakened once more at the Lincoln Memorial and fainted once more. The process repeated itself six times before Hbooth gained his bearings and realized that he was probably in a faint-based hallucination and even if he wasn't, Lincolns couldn't Lincolnize statues.

"Hi," said Homer, "are you John Hbooth? I'm blind, so you could be anybody."

"Yes," said Hbooth.

"You've fainted eight times in the past five minutes."

Hbooth was grateful Homer couldn't see his face turning scarlet. He was already embarrassed enough that he'd fainted eight times in front of the author of the Odyssey.

"Sorry."

"You should be."

"I am."

"Good."

"Good."

Homer produced a joint out of thin air and lit it.

"I've been sent here by the Voice of Wisdom. You fucked up. But, there is hope, yet. There's always hope, although the Voice of Wisdom likes to hide it in the damnedest places. Like zombie-ridden wastelands."

"So what should I do?"

Homer offered Hbooth a toke. Hbooth declined. Homer shrugged.

"Well, you need to assemble a war cabinet using your Historion powers. The cabinet must include me, Miyamoto

Musashi and Herodotus. But, the Voice of Wisdom will only give you enough soulstuff to make Herodotus into a cat. Probably because it's funny."

"And this will resolve the Lincoln problem?"

Homer shrugged.

"Hell if I know. But you've got a lot to learn about history and heroism and they're the people to teach you."

Hbooth's eyes opened and he found himself on the back of the dragon-shaped motorcycle. Marilyn was driving.

"Marilyn?"

Marilyn did not confirm it was her; she was busy cutting the stovepipe off a Lincolnized panther with her flamberge.

"How the hell did you survive?"

Marilyn did not answer again because two Lincolnized gorillas were meeting their doom at the edge of Marilyn's keen blade.

"Oh."

Marilyn giggled.

"What, you didn't know I'm one of the greatest swordsmen in history? I'm no Musashi, but I've read the Book of Five Rings so many times…"

"If we survive, you might get to meet him."

Marilyn made the face Marilyn Monroe made when she got surprised.

"Really, Johnny?"

"Sure thing. We've got to get somewhere safe."

"Well, I stole some house keys off a dead Viking. Will those help?"

A tiny snowflake of hope dropped on Hbooth's tongue. It tasted of pollution, ash, and carcass but it was a start.

"Yes, turn right here."

Marilyn turned right, slicing through a Girl Scout troop and a freakishly tall Abe-headed pangolin and as they rounded the corner, they both caught sight of Charlie's veritable bunker of a mansion, built from thousands of electric guitars magnetized to steel walls. Swinging pendulum blades hung from the trees and half-buried landmines promised death to all intruders. It might not have been possible to be completely safe from Lincolns, but at Charlie's house, they'd be pretty close. Here, they'd be able to relax, build the war council Homer had told them to, and, hopefully, find some way to clean up this mess.

CHAPTER SIXTEEN

The Bohemian Grove fatcats almost choked on their pandasperm when they saw what the spy satellite orbiting Charlie Battleaxe's house was recording. They embraced each other, crying and screaming and begging the Herpetarch for answers and salvation.

"You have failed me," said the Herpetarch, "you have failed yourselves and reptilekind alike. You sicken me, you sniveling bastards."

"Please, oh Godking of lizards," said Frank Sinatra, who was of course not dead at all, "you must help us! He's going to ruin everything."

"No," the Herpetarch replied, his tone quite firm, "you've failed and you can fuck up society for yourselves. If there's anything you can do it's that."

Sinatra shook his fists and began to cry.

"We're fucked! We're fucked! It's the end."

"Relax," said Mykle Hansen, placing a hand on his old friend's shoulder, "it's not over yet. All we have to worry about is John Booth. The guy's got nothing going for him but a magic sword and some kind of hoodoo pistol."

Madonna wagged a bony finger at the world famous author. The two had never gotten along. Yes, Hansen had invented Twitter, allowing the fatcats to spread cancer faster than ever, but he often overlooked the bigger picture and seemed to be in it more for the pandasperm and slaves than for the reptiles. Madonna was always in it for the reptiles.

"Again, you miss the point, Hansen! John Booth is a candy man capable of manipulating Historions to bring back the dead. If he reverses the process using a Historion pistol, the history we've created is going to be fucked up for good!"

Hansen waved Madonna's wild theory away, although he secretly knew that her knowledge of Arcanoscience was far greater than his and she was probably right.

"Ha! That's a good one. There's no way he could come up with that. It's too crazy by half!"

Hansen and Madonna were both right. While it was certainly true that nobody was nearly as crazy as Madonna, Hansen was wrong in that Booth had discovered that by reversing his Historion reconstruction process, he could destroy the history the lizards had fucked up...for good. Hansen was right to point out that Booth had nothing but a magic sword and some kind of hoodoo pistol to take on every Lincoln between Noctys' house and Ford's Theater. Watching Booth step out of the mansion into a city overrun by hungry Lincolns, Mykle Hansen looked pretty damn smart for being so cynical.

Booth was at once terrified and

dead calm, his faith in himself unwavering, though perhaps devoid of context. *I am invincible for some reason. I am a hero for some reason. I am a hero because I have decided to be one and heroism is bullshit. I will make history because I can and history is bullshit. Herodotus the cat told me so.*

He breathed deep, readied the sword and tried not to count, tried not to think that it was his fault. Tried to be nothing but a man swinging a sword above his head to open up several disgusting growths and let loose the hideous lizards inside of them. The seven-year-old girls who had become Lincolns were not in his mind innocent children he had fucked up by reviving a rabid president, they were pink tubes full of lizards, the grandmothers were bearded old ladies with lizards in their heads, the wheelchair-bound veterans were monster presidents on wheels that could not be suffered to live.

Hansen and Madonna looked on in shock, through the cameras to see the bringer of Armageddon transformed into a knight of redemption as had been written in books of The Lizard Scriptures that the Herpetarch had insisted were Apocrypha and therefore none of anybody's concern. The Herpetarch lacked the perspective of a Greek historian in a cat's body, a historian that would have reminded him that Apocrypha means bullshit and history is bullshit, so…

"Dino, Sammy, I'm comin', I'm comin'!" screamed a desperate Sinatra as he shot himself in the face. As a woman with no loyalties who could not resist fresh blood, a hungry Madonna stopped panicking about Booth while she slurped up the mess that used to be the chairman. His face bits tasted

like victory, for she had been cochairman for all this time. Hansen shrugged, taking Madonna's seat and summoning more slaves to top off his pandasperm and add a few shots of Secret Reptile Spacevodka. Maybe the Lincoln plan had fallen apart, but at least he'd earned a promotion.

Ironically, as Madonna was ingesting the vital fluids of her former boss, Booth had come face to face with a familiar figure. This Lincoln had wandered a fair distance from the Civic Debatodome and had, as Booth had figured before, been better off as a Lincoln. As a rockstar and a politician, Noctys Blakbludd had not been especially efficient, but his biting and Lincolnlove had led to over a thousand converts including a Galapagos tortoise that had escaped the zoo. Booth really enjoyed killing this particular Lincoln. He wished he could kill him twice. But a hundred Lincolns into the Lincoln phalanx was an opportunity just as good.

A hat! An actual hat. And a real stovepipe hat meant he had found the cause of many of his sorrows…at least the cause of his sorrows that was not himself. As he brought down the magical flamberge to do what Booths did best, he thought of the film The Lost Boys and how killing the head vampire turned everybody back into people. That would have been really great. It's a shame Lincoln had become a rabid zombie thing instead of a vampire.

Lincoln crumpled and died and the world was still mostly Lincolnized. People were still empty, rabid abominations gnawing on everything that wasn't like them. There was a long, cylindrical tube on everybody's head still and inside it there were still lizards.

If Ford's Theater weren't in sight, Booth would have been pretty depressed.

CHAPTER SEVENTEEN

Marilyn parted grave dirt and history as she angrily dug her way to the surface. She was going to make the fake JFK pay for leaving her for dead and replacing her lover. She'd make Jackie pay too. The Voice of Wisdom speaking in falling leaves and tiny fluctuations in temperature told her to get a rifle and go to Dallas. The Voice of Wisdom often told people to get a rifle and kill the president, yet most of them and most of their doctors and family members always said it was a bad idea. Lucky for the Voice of Wisdom and history at large that Marilyn was pissed off that she'd been left for dead by a fake president and his fatcat bride.

Even having just crawled from the grave, it was not difficult to find somebody who would pick up a hitchhiking Marilyn Monroe. If it weren't for the grave dirt, she'd have been able to leave the trucker star-struck and unable to make her pay for the ride with a blowjob. It wasn't too bad. She didn't swallow and a presidential assassination was more than worth the taste of sperm on her breath. The trucker's name was Oswald and he was very happy to save Marilyn some trouble and let her borrow his rifle. He was going to the book depository to find a book on how to best adjust the scope on his other identical rifle.

She lay down on a nice grassy knoll where she could get a good view of the fake president's car, took aim and made history. History omitted the greenish lizard goo that came out of the head wound and that the president was actually an impostor, but other than this, Marilyn's lucky shot made a pretty big splash. She rose to her feet, ready to flee the scene only to find the president standing behind her. She didn't mind that this was probably the end. At least she'd killed one impostor. It was disconcerting that there were so many of them, but she didn't have a hell of a lot to live for anyway and if this one was going to finish her, then there wasn't a lot that she could do.

"Norma Jean," said Jack Kennedy, "I don't know if I can explain it, but somewhere else I was somebody else who loved you and suddenly I wasn't this person. But I can feel the love and I can feel that we've got great things ahead of us."

They joined hands and began a grueling odyssey to find someplace safe. History said neither of the two dead American heroes was ever seen again, but history, as Herodotus the cat said, is bullshit. Love isn't.

KRIS SAKNUSSEMM

LOCATION:
Melbourne and New York

STYLE OF BIZARRO:
Hexotic Fetish / Totemic Dream

BOOKS BY SAKNUSSEMM:
Zanesville
Private Midnight
Enigmatic Pilot
Sinister Miniatures
Eat Jellied Eels and Think Distant
    Thoughts

"Saknussemm spins imagery like a freak Lewis Carroll."
- East Bay Express.

DESCRIPTION: A psychotropic puzzle box adventure.

INFLUENCES: Swift, Sterne, Kafka, Burroughs, Cortazar, Philip K. Dick, the Marquis de Sade, Jung, Cantonese opera, Indonesian shadow puppet theater, Japanese monster movies, David Lynch, Captain Beefheart, Outsider Art, 1950s-60s psychological experiments, the histories of deviant sex.

WEBSITE:
www.saknussemm.com

SPARKLEWHEEL

Night time. Warm. Humid. A vast, mostly uninhabited fairground with weird giant clown heads leering out of the darkness of closed attractions…statues of goofy characters off in the distance of dead rides looking sinister now…abandoned booths…broken lights sparking…silhouettes of people, not clear enough to be certain of their intent.

We arrive at a ride that is still running. It's like a huge roulette wheel, which can ratchet itself up the central axis as it whirls. The man running it has a white redneck face but the body of a black bodybuilder. No one is in any of the car-containers near us—the few people there are all on the other side of the circle and we can't see them.

The ride begins and the spinning starts to get really intense, the feeling heightened as we lift higher off the ground, seeing both more of the fair and less, with the shadows and the shutdown sections. You take notice of the rhythm of the rising and revolving and say, "It's like a sex machine." I say, "Yes, and like a time machine."

Then we start to get really hot… touching each other…kissing…and then we think what it would be like to fuck while on the wheel, flying around this haunted fairground. You've got this flimsy mint julep dress on with no panties and I'm wearing microfiber cargo pants. You're wet and ready. It's easy for me to pull it out and slide into you. You can ride me while we speed

higher and harder around and around.

No one can see because we're up too far from the ground and moving too fast. You rise and squat—and pump, feeling my whole cock inside you, thickening even more with the texture and the pressure. At first you ride me, just like a merry-go-round, me playing with your tits. The texture is perfect. Squishy, but not soaking. Tight like a mare's grasp…so that I can feel the walls of you suck in around the head and shaft like a deep muscular mouth. I start bucking up inside you to meet your grind, pulling your skimpy cotton dress up so your ass is fully exposed to the warm wind blowing past, and I can peel the cheeks back, getting the whole meat of you in my hands…from your moist puckered asshole to your quivering flanks that I slap with my hands as the pressure starts to rise and you shove in against my chest to rub the shaft against your clit.

I ease a finger into your ass, which is dripping and loose now…your breasts free of the dress and my mouth moving between the nipples, which look bigger to you than you've ever seen them, hard and wet and pointing out…almost wanting to be bitten off.

The ride seems to accelerate in time with our hunger…like a mania we've infected the machine with…and just as we're both about to come…there's a massive wrenching sound and a blast of what looks like neon starlight…then steel and live wires go whipping past our heads and the limbs of someone on the other side of the wheel fly by and we feel this rush of dizziness as the whole ride snaps from the axis and tilts madly, hurling us into the air, still fucking.

We only become disentangled when we land...in this lagoon-like marsh on the other side of the fairground. We can see the faint glow of the few ride lights reflected off the underbelly of low clouds, but it seems like a million years ago. There are shouts and sirens, but they get muffled and more distant very quickly. We've fallen into a kind of swamp. Half-submerged holiday cabins and mired bulldozers covered in lichen and moss lurk all around us. There are gas flares and burbling pockets of bubbles rising. Inner tubes float...and a big fiberglass ice cream cone that looks like it was shot at by a rifle. Then you feel something brush against your leg and you let out one of your squeaks. Maybe it was a mud turtle. Maybe it was something else. There are clearly other things in the water than just algae-coated shopping carts and stolen road signs. We both start to panic a little, wondering what we've fallen into.

Then we see it misting into view—like a mirage—until the iron and timber emerge. It's like a houseboat...or rather...it's like a farmhouse built on top of a rusted barge or channel dredge. We swim for it...the flaking ladder on the near side. You climb up first, your dress ripped down the back, and when you reach the top, your butt is right in my face. For a moment, I forget everything else that's going on. I want only to fuck you in the ass, right there on the deck of the barge. Then an owl swoops down with a plump, sopping water rat in its talons, and I remember what's just happened. We don't know where we are. We might've fallen into

toxic sludge. And who in the hell lives in this floating house? Are we really alive still?

There are a couple of foggy lights on and some music playing. Something sappy and lost in time, like a Jackie Gleason record. Music to pour a martini and get the girl into bed by back in the 1950s. We're freaked. We're wet, we appear to be unhurt...but we need help. So we go inside. No knock. The screen door is open.

There are more mosquitoes inside than out, but at first it's kind of a strangely cheerful scene—reassuring compared to what we were expecting. My dick is still hard from the image of your ass arched up before me when we climbed onboard, but we can't be fooling around right at the moment.

The room we've entered is a homey old farmhouse kitchen with awful green and yellow painted cupboards and cheesy knickknacks everywhere—a refrigerator armored in souvenir magnets...what looks like a frozen dinner now steaming on the table, as if whoever lives there was just about to sit down and eat. We call out but no one answers. We wait but no one comes. So we peek into the next room.

There's a candle in a screened lantern barely burning, but it's enough to light up the walls and we see them all staring down at us. Animal heads. Hundreds of them. From deer and wildcats to pigs, donkeys, even mice. They've all been expertly mounted, but crammed together. The candle casts a glow down the hall to the rest of the house, and we see there are more animal heads—fish, snakes and birds.

Cats. Dogs. Horses. We shit ourselves. The whole place is a grisly taxidermy museum, but oddly innocent and farm-like. The contrast really gives us the shudders. And still no one answers. No sound in the place. Just the swamp noises outside...the burbling of the water, the hiss of escaping gas...and the jut and bump of the barge rubbing against sunken or drifting bits of debris.

After a moment of fussing and arguing about what to do, we decide to check the whole place out. I take the candle and we do a room-to-room. Every chamber is exactly what you'd expect a quaint old farmhouse to look like—except for the stuffed animals. Frogs, rabbits, even a couple of eerie clown heads from the fairground. Plastic thankfully.

But in what is sort of like the parlor where a television sits, there's a table laid out with a miniature trailer park on it. The detail is remarkable. Perfect little Winnebago's and older enclosures. Tents. Toy cars and itsy bitsy people, like expensive mold-cast figurines...willow trees made of strips of cardboard and torn flannel. Everything is exactly proportioned... and there's a curious sense of order to the layout...all the people and vehicles positioned around this gleaming silver miniature Airstream trailer. And then, at the same time, we realize...

The miniature trailer park is laid out like a kind of board game.

Just then, we hear a sound outside that brings us to full alert.

The sound...is actually two sounds. One is disturbingly near at hand—but impossible to place. It seems to be an extension of our inner turmoil, as if the hypersensitive channels of intimacy and anxiety between us have escaped and are now animating the bizarre houseboat. The other sound is clearer and more immediately compelling. A rush of water...as if the barge has cut loose from the sludge and gurglings of the swamp...the reed tussocks and the carcasses of metal...and is now in some swifter flow...heading toward we know not what. We bolt outside to the deck, bumping into each other, dropping the candle in the caged lantern in our hurry.

The sight outside is mind stopping. The barge has indeed wandered out of the lagoon and is quickly slipping into a genuine bay.

Before us are two things. Closer at hand is a ferryboat, like the Staten Island ferry, only the size of a very large cruise ship. Every single window is lit and blinking fiber optic cords festoon the sides so it almost looks alive. The odd thing is that people keep leaping off the top deck, which is a long way down to the water on a boat that size. They fling themselves off like they're drunk or stupefied, splashing and whinnying. Fragments of clothing follow them down...old-fashioned hat racks...newspapers and magazines... and money. It's as if whole cotton bales of currency have been torn apart and flung over the side. The bills waft down in the lights like leaves on fire...all over the harbor...some blowing past us as the barge lurches, gushing into the stream of the bay.

The second and even more imposing thing we see is a city with spot-

lights slitting back and forth—and skyrockets that may either be fireworks or bombs spurting overhead.

Part of it is like Laughlin, Nevada, crowded up against a palisade of cliffs...but with colossal faces carved in the rocks...billboards collapsing down the embankment...the signs of campfires and shelters in the clefts. The part overlooking the water looks more like Louisville or Memphis, an American river city, but with hallucinatory Asian and Middle Eastern influences. Like Damascus on the Mekong. It's hard to be certain of anything because the city is literally falling down as we look at it. Enormous demolition equipment is attacking it, like dinosaurs smashing a model village. We can see looming cranes and wrecking balls swinging, lit by anti-aircraft lights. There are men with luminous green hard hats all over the wharf area...with gauze facemasks...and people with lunch boxes for heads or parking meters. It's like a City of Idiots...completely demented. Except for one huge pillar of scaffolding. Within this framework, thousands upon thousands of people hang, scurry or climb like spider monkeys...all wearing signal orange jumpsuits and headlamps. There are so many they give shape to the structure, making it a skyscraper—but writhing with instability and change. Every so often one of the scalers plummets—but their place is instantly taken. More and more swarm from below, driving the others higher, until the building has a true and sustaining shape even when some of the individuals fall.

Only when we have gawked at this scene for a few moments...trying to take it all in...make sense of it somehow...do we realize that the lantern we'd left behind in the farmhouse has set the place ablaze. The windows and doorframes crackle with the heat, shattered glass from the panes raining down over the deck, flames whooshing out. We're heading into a collision course with the giant ferry of lights and jumpers and snowing money...on a barge with a burning farmhouse roaring...approaching a city gone insane.

Somehow, the whole frightening pandemonium of the situation charges us. We wanted trouble and bright lights—and we've got it. In spades. Our best option looks like jumping ship before we smash into the ferry—the barge might well survive in sections—but we recognize that we might get eaten up by the screw propeller or flounder to drowning in the wake. Plus, we're feeling a little flush in the luck department remembering the roulette wheel ride. Then two things happen.

Out of the wildfire farmhouse charge these people with animal heads—they must've been behind the walls—imprisoned or secretly watching us—we'll never know, because they rampage off the barge into the bay, the flames flaring out when they hit the water. The whole structure explodes as they do, and almost sends us into the drink with the repercussion. Then we hear a voice from down on the water. We think it's one of the animal head people who's okay and now calling for help. But it's not. They're gone—too badly burned.

It's a big fat guy in a life raft. Only

he doesn't have hands. Arms, but no hands, and so he can't row very well. He's in even greater danger than we are of being crushed by the ferry because he's just in a little inflatable. But if we were in it and were rowing, we could get to land. So we jump. No words between us…nothing. Except…

At the last second, you turn around and run back into the farmhouse, with timbers crumbling down and flames pouring out. I think, this is it. She's cracked. She's dead. Charred. Gone.

And then you reappear. You're clutching the Airstream from the trailer park board game. Your dress is on fire. And you run right past me, grabbing my hand as you go…and we leap into the bay as the farmhouse really blows…lumber, melting fridge magnets and scorched animal heads hailing down behind us.

We hit the water about 15 feet from the life raft and swim toward the fat man, who's waving his stumps at us. You're closer. You make the raft. Then you do something I'm secretly really grateful for, but shocked to see. The moment you're settled in the spongy little yellow boat—that looks so very small up against the nearing ferry, you let go of the Airstream, pick up one of the oars and smack the fat man in the side of the head, knocking him over the edge. I scramble in and pick up the other oar, with him nearby in the water, still conscious and beginning to flail. When he gets close enough, I nail him over the head as hard as I can. You started it and I have to finish it—and I instinctively understand your point. We don't know him. We don't owe

him. There's ash and destruction all around, we may already be dead and in some Inferno. We have only ourselves.

Then I start to row like holy hell. But I'm a very good rower. Have been since I was a kid. We slip out of the ferry path just as it hits the barge, the iron and steel of it doing more damage to the ferry hull than vice versa. But the incinerated farmhouse slides off the back into the harbor taking all the animal heads and miniature people secrets with it…extinguished in a last fire swirl of disintegrating studs and a monstrous belch of steam. The ferry plows on, passengers still chucking themselves off, the lights still twinkling, a wicked gash to fore from the barge impact spraying water and ruptured wood over our heads. But we're too busy tumbling in the waves and trying to stay in the raft.

We row toward the city. There are fires up and down the shore. Some seem to be consciously lit bonfires of furniture and driftwood—or smaller cooking fires. Others are the smoldering bodies of cars and machines. We don't have much choice but to try to land. The raft is too small to risk crossing the harbor, and we have no idea where we're going. There are people outside the rings of fire along the quay and the spit of rocks and sand—all of this below a wall of broken cement and razor wire beneath the city. Some people are surf fishing, oblivious to the chaos around them. Others seem to be engaged in what looks like a paintball game. Farther down, in the shadows from the spot fires and the lights of the self-destructing city, it looks like uglier

things are happening. Rapes, dismemberments, unknown rituals.

Back behind us, people begin shoving cars off the ferry as water surges into the damaged hull. We can't tell if they're desperately lightening the load to keep from going down—or enjoying the vandalism—because they cheer whenever a car goes over and splashes into the black bay, the ferry still churning forward even as it takes on water.

We have to turn our attention back to bringing the raft in while avoiding the rocks and stuff along the shore. There are oilcans and plastic bottles everywhere in the dirty foam. Other things look sharper and more dangerous. But we come in on the waves from the ferry and drag the inflatable up toward these granite seawall reinforcements. I carry the miniature Airstream under my arm like a breadbox.

Once we're up below the glare of the city on the other side of the wall, we see that we've pulled in right in front of two Slavic-looking men. One is sitting by a stick fire with a sheep on a leash, as someone might with a dog. The other has a row of great clamshells laid out on the sand, which seems to percolate with a squishy kind of residue as we step across it. If the shells were smaller, he'd look like a street vendor of knock-off jewelry. As it is, they look more like shelters. They're big enough for people to sleep in.

"Good thing you made it," the Clam Man says and blows a huge jet of snot.

We're not at all sure about that. There's something distinctly creepy about both of them, and as we look around, it's clear they live here. They've got a larger raft with an outboard motor on the back, cooking utensils and a whole lot of what looks like recently stolen electrical goods, all hooked up to a diesel generator covered in grime. But at least they're not cutting people's limbs off. Yet.

I start to ask a question, but then I realize I don't know which one to ask first. The Clam Man cuts in before I can speak.

"There's a rain comin'...better take cover in a shell. First night's free."

The idea of climbing into one of the giant clamshells doesn't do much for either of us. Rain seems to be the least of our problems.

Then a series of fireworks explode overhead and we feel the first drops of the storm. Heavy, burning drops. It's like the magnesium of the rocket flares have mingled with the moisture from the sky. Down the beach and over the rocks we see the silhouettes of people scrambling for cover. It's not ordinary rain. It's an acid rain. Two big drops smoke on your arms and I can smell the flesh sizzle.

The man with the sheep leads the animal into a shelter that looks like a huge mailbox, and then he and the Clam Man start pulling on these Haz-Mat suits. Our skin is starting to burn. You leap into one of the shells and the lid comes down behind you suddenly and clicks like a lock. I get a bad feeling—worse than the rain—which very suspiciously seems to stop.

"What happened to the rain?" I ask.

"Oh, it comes and goes," the Clam

Man says…with a rather nasty smile.

"Then let her out," I say.

"Sure," he says. "Just give me what you've got in your hand there, and I'll open it up. Otherwise, you'll need more than a jackhammer to get that thing open."

There's a smashing sound out on the water—wood and metal giving way—the ferry is really starting to submerge.

"You'll have time to think about it," the Clam Man says, and pulls out a shining little harpoon gun about the size of a sawed-off shotgun. He points it at me while the Sheep Man drags their boat down to the water, then he backs toward it and they shove off, heading out toward the ferry, where people are still throwing things off and jumping—some of the bodies occasionally landing on the cars that haven't sunk with a sickening sound of broken bones and choking.

I figure giving up the miniature trailer is no big deal…but something makes me resist. The metal has stayed cool in my grasp and feels strangely satisfying, reassuring. Valuable. But if I give him the trailer when they get back, how do I know he'll open the shell? The Clam Man doesn't look like the kind to honor his end of any bargain. I don't know what to do—but after kicking the shell a few times and bashing it with a rock, I'm pretty sure he was right about how hard it would be to open by force. I don't even know if you can breathe inside. I start to freak out, pacing the gooey tar sand. Then I hear a voice. A woman's voice. But not yours.

It's coming from under a pile of kelp by the Sheep Man's dwindling fire. A woman crawls out, seaweed still clinging to her skin. She's naked other than the damp strands and is very beautiful, but I can see she has some open sores over her body, as if she's buried herself in the seaweed for skin relief. She tells me the men have gone out to salvage from the ferry. They're sort of pirate-scavengers. I have a little time to open the shell. But there's only one way to do it.

I have to piss all over it—and then ejaculate on it. At first I don't believe her, but what choice do I have? So I urinate all over the clamshell—and to my surprise and relief it starts to hiss and corrode, softening. "Quick!" she says. "You have to come on it too."

Great, I think. I had to have a piss—I was actually dying for one. But I'm not sure I can just get it up right there…not with people getting hacked up and a whole city falling down in flames on the other side of the wall. Then she removes some of the seaweed to show me her breasts. They're large and full, gorgeously shaped. Even with a couple of patches of sores, they're something to see. I start to think that maybe she means for me to fuck her and then shoot over the shell. But when she pulls back the seaweed from around her waist and thighs, I see her vagina is a mass of festering sores and chancres…a bacteria stain surrounding a gaping wound that she's attached leeches to in order to eat at some of the blight. Beneath the leeches, tiny white worms wriggle out of the necrotic flesh. I want to vomit—she covers herself again.

Then she approaches, kneels down on the springy sand and takes my cock out of my pants, still wet from the bay. Her mouth is exquisitely formed, with thick, sensual lips…and soon I feel them sucking me, licking and breathing on me. She runs her tongue over the head, following the contour of the glans…defining its helmet shape. Then she sucks the whole head in, taking two…and three inches of the cock into her warm wet mouth without moving her neck. More of it goes down her throat. She seems to be slowly inhaling it. I harden with the suction and the sight of her taking me. Deeper. Seen now from this angle, her sores aren't visible. She's beautiful, early 30s maybe, with scarlet hair, and big firm tits she brushes against my balls, as she lifts her head, taking my cock higher as the erection strengthens.

Meanwhile the clamshell is fuming and loosening. Dissolving. I'm wondering if you're still alive. If you can see or hear—or know what's happening. What you're thinking? What you would think?

The Seaweed Woman increases the speed of her sucking, working her soft full lips back and forth over the head, then licking the tip of the shaft. Faster. Her head is bobbing hard now, her breast jiggling rhythmically. I start to wonder what the men will do to her when they get back and find out she's helped us. Me. I feel a tenderness toward her…mixed with raw lust. Suddenly even her festering sores seem erotic. I can feel I'm going to shoot. I get ready to pull back—to pull out of her mouth and jerk over the shell.

But as my cock slips out of her mouth, which I'm reluctant to leave, I have to admit—a part of me wants to come down her throat, or to spurt over her breasts—she gasps and says, "No, I must have it! I need it for my sores. It will heal me."

I'm just about to blow. I have to make a decision. She's thrown me off completely.

"I can't!" I tell her. "I have to get the shell open."

"She's already dead," the woman says.

Something in her eyes tells me she's lying. I push her away and rush to the shell and give myself a final vigorous stroking, slurping out a gush of hot semen that shines silver in the light. The gobs hit the slowly decomposing shell and a chemical reaction starts, spreading over the surface like a phosphorescent shadow. Soon the whole clamshell is pulsing and then liquefying. I turn back to the woman who's fallen on the sand, breathless. I squeeze my cock and drip a last little pearl of cum down on her spread legs. The pus-filled infection seems to spasm and the blind white worms waver and retract. The droplet has eased some of the putrefaction. I drape some of the seaweed up over her like a blanket and her breathing quiets as she seems to black out. Just then an explosion rocks the ferry and it slips deeper into the water. It can't stay afloat much longer.

Turning back to the shell, I see you alive—squirming in a mess of what looks like tapioca afterbirth. It's wet and sticky and you're hysterical with it clinging to you—but it doesn't seem to be hurting your skin. A minute later I have you out and am leading you down to the water to wash you off.

The water isn't all that pleasant but it's better than the muck of the shell, and you're so relieved to be out of there you don't care. But now you're naked and we have to get away before the scavengers come back. I'm not sure what to do.

Then I walk you back to the remains of the shell where I've left the Airstream. The woman in the seaweed stirs as we pass. "The Sheep will give her some clothes," she mumbles.

"Who's that?" you ask.

"A friend," I say.

It doesn't even occur to me to question how or why the sheep will give us some clothes for you. I go to the big mailbox enclosure and find that inside it's actually as large as a hangar at a country airfield. There are hundreds of Vietnamese people working old sewing machines and looms in narrow rows. One of them, a youngish man who looks like he's the foreman, gets up from a bowl of clear soup and pulls some clothes out of a big pile of what I imagine are discards or defective goods. The outfit has a sweet smell of lanolin, the smell of babies and farm fields in springtime. He gives me a lamb's wool vest with a leather exterior…and these chaps things…pants cut out at the ass…with a pair of lamb's wool-lined moccasins.

I hand them to you and you grumble about running around showing your ass, but I point out that we don't have much time…and you start to think that they're sort of cool. So you suit up and

I grab the Airstream and we book out of there, leaving the Seaweed Woman either hiding more completely in the kelp, or having fled—I can't say which, and the raft with the men is coming back overloaded with things we can't see clearly.

It takes us a while to negotiate the rocks and find a crack in the seawall big enough to scrape through. There are constant fireworks or incendiaries…the clang of torn metal…the jar and quake of buildings being torn down…sirens… and mob sounds…but we keep moving…the borderland between the city and the waterline ends up being quite a bit more complicated than it appeared from below…with all sorts of hideous injured people hunkered down between the pylons and the boulders—and the sewage conduits. Catatonics. Corpses. I'm amazed how the sight of your bare ass cheers me as we flee. Everything else has been stripped away inside. Only primal thoughts remain. A good thing, as it keeps me on edge.

When we finally reach the city proper, we find ourselves on an old cobblestone street like in Lower Manhattan. An enormous flag billows up on a pole. It has the design of a $100 bill. There's a stretch of park filled with statues covered in white tarpaulins and canvas sheets…and a group of people who appear to be worshipping a fallen electrical tower they've propped up against an old brick building with marble pillars out the front. Bulldozers with halogen lights power through a wall down the street…manholes steam and water mains erupt…people in wheelchairs either stranded in the shower or

there to bathe, we can't say.

A man rushes by in a trench coat carrying a fishbowl. He yells, "The Run is on, look out! Look out!"

He trips on a cobblestone and drops the bowl, which shatters, releasing some brightly colored tropical fish. But there's no time to save the fish because mechanical thunder reverberates off the remaining buildings. A herd of MX riders sweeps out of an alley, helmeted and shining in plastic and steel. They're revving their bikes, chasing down a pack of middle-aged men in their underwear…with javelins raised…or the ceremonial swords the picadors use at bullfights. It's like the running of the bulls in Pamplona. They chase and hound—and then hurl their barbs—either nailing or running over the older men as they charge in panic, trying to get away. Some do and are greeted with bouquets of roses or lopped-off hog's heads. Others are skewered, crushed, or run down til their hearts burst. We slip into a side alley, away from the turmoil.

A carriage appears…like the kind that should be drawn by horses. Instead it's pulled by people, men and women, naked and with heavy leather blinders on.

After the motorcycle insanity, we think we can handle this slower moving group and yell, "Halt!" They do.

Perched on top of the carriage, in the driving, whip position is a decomposing cadaver in a tuxedo.

"Where are you going?" we ask.

The blindered man in the lead says, "Wherever Mr. Hugo wants."

We look at each other. Somehow they haven't cottoned on to the fact that Mr. Hugo est mort. He gone. Wid de flies. Surely they can smell him. But apparently they don't. They're just wandering around in circles.

"Mr. Hugo isn't feeling well," I say. "He wants you to take us some place. He wants you to take us to…"

And then I'm stumped. I have no idea where we should go—or where might be safe.

"The Zoo!" you yell suddenly—having looked up at the cliff and seen a rotting billboard showing a woman in a mix of park ranger / white lab coat gear holding a bunch of parrots in her oversized hand. The fading caption says… "THE ZOO IS FOR YOO…All the questions of a lifetime…all the fun of a blind cherry pull."

I go along with this notion. The zoo might at least provide some shelter. Maybe. They're usually open, park-like places with more vegetation. So we hop up next to Mr. Hugo, where the odor of decay is so much more unmistakable… but our blinkered, harnessed friends don't take any notice. They seem happy to have a destination to reach.

Except for another gang of motorcycle riders who have lassoed some young girls in bikinis and are applying white-hot branding irons to their stripped asses, we don't see anyone else along the way—other than shadows of people running and the lights of tractors down distant streets. To our surprise, one of the motorcycle wranglers whips off a metal flake blue helmet and shakes out a big mane of auburn hair. It's a hot Goth Asian woman who gives us a haughty smile that has a hint of fangs.

The Zoo turns out to be a ghastly derelict place filled with barred pits and enclosures with fake animals made of Styrofoam and peeling plaster. The only illumination comes from grim orange security lights scattered about on caged poles. The only true building is a dark glass pavilion in the shape of a hexagon. Facing it, across a lawn of garbage, is a yard filled with shacks and burrows—surrounded by a very tall steel fence with brutal spikes on top and covered over by a mesh of netting that looks like it's made of heavy gauge fishing line, the sort they sometimes use on high speed rotaries to decapitate animals in abattoirs instead of blades. Behind the bars are hundreds of dirty children…dump kids, ferals, kids dressed up like dolls—looking woeful and vicious in the sodium orange. They chant when they see us and the Airstream… "Knick-knack Paddywhack… Knickknack Paddywhack…"

We don't know whether to feel sorry for these filthy orphans or afraid. Are they rounded-up here by their own strategy—for protection—or are they the prisoners we suspect them to be? And of whom?

The answer isn't long in coming because some of them start to have seizures. Others start chanting, "Zookeeper…Zookeeper…Zookeeper!"

They point and gesture frantically…and over a rise we see approaching headlights.

The Zookeeper, who is obviously a source of profound fear for the children appears on a John Deere ride-on lawn mower, out of the dark of the supposed Savannah, which is really a wasteland of fiberglass lions, chicken wire antelope and mangled giraffes made of retaining rods for concrete walls. The figure wears a white jumpsuit with black-green mirrored headgear, like night vision goggles—and we aren't sure what this means for us—until the mower gets nearer.

To our amazement we see that not only is the Zookeeper female, she looks exactly like Yoko Ono when she gets up close. And she has a tranquilizer dart rifle slung over her shoulder. "ZOOKEEPER! ZOOKEEPER!" the kids grunt, twirling around and having these mini epileptic fits. Others moan out some other word, which sounds like *Gooper*.

"Good, I see you've brought me a present," the Zookeeper says, ignoring the wild kids and pointing with the rifle to the Airstream. "Give it to me now, and you can stay in the hippo pond. It's got the freshest water."

"We're not staying with any fucking hippos," you say.

"Perhaps you'd like to feed the children then," the Zookeeper says with an ugly crease in her lips.

"Why don't you feed them—if you're the zookeeper?" you ask.

"That's just what I mean," the Zookeeper laughs…and we realize that she intends to feed us to the children, who look hungry and savage and deranged enough to rip us apart.

"We're not going to give you anything," I say. There are, after all, two of us, and the kids appear to be secured within the pen.

"Maybe you'll feel different when

you see the Gooper," she answers and blows on this silver whistle.

The mention of that name and the high-pitched tweet of the whistle drive the feral children berserk. They're like birds in a net.

And then we see why. Out from the other side of the zoo, up closer to the cliffs, comes this towering, lumbering form. He's about 20 feet high, a kind of ogre, but oozy and dripping... leaving pieces of himself as he moves. His body is like some kind of resinous glob made up of bandages and honeycomb—chambers of bee pollen that split open and spill behind when he walks—or mud daubers' funnels that crack and powderize. His head is like a huge paper wasp's nest—yellowjackets and white-faced hornets flitting in and out. He can't in fact keep a single expression in place for more than a few seconds, because his face is whatever the insects make it out to be at any given moment. The children chant, "Gooper! Gooper!" as he nears, crying and shitting in their pants. Wherever he steps he leaves a squash of something like maple syrup or honey...American mustard...and treacle. Objects he's absorbed into his mass squish out, followed by a cloud of bees and flies.

Up close there's a disgusting odor to him of molasses and the disinfectants used in public toilets. He's dripping and weeping himself all over, his face forming and reforming with the wasps' excitement.

"Now," says the Zookeeper. "If you won't give me my present, then you'll give it to the Gooper."

I slip you the Airstream in prepara-

tion for telling you to run while I distract the monster. We know the thing can't move very fast.

A blob of yeasty-stinking brown sugar-gunk plops off at my feet...and I feel your hands take the Airstream... sliding over the smooth metal coating. As you do, there's a click in the top and the roof opens like a box. This surprises us both enough for us to look away from the Gooper and the pen of drooling children.

From out of the Airstream you extract a remarkable implement. It's like a crystalline tuning fork...but more organically shaped...like a large wishbone made of some super-fine blown glass. It's hypnotic to behold...and has the same effect on the Zookeeper, the Gooper and the children. Suddenly, the protective feelings we've had about the Airstream, which seemed sort of irrational and silly before, are now all vividly justified. The slightest glint of the object, the feel of it to the hand—it's unquestionably precious. And it seems to have an inner life to it, changing weight and reflectivity with our touch.

The Gooper eyes the wishbone, the wasps swarming to maintain his face. He makes a sound like a clogged garbage disposal and stretches out a thick resinous hand as the beeswax and dishtowels flowing inside his mass flop and slurp out in a mess of golden gelatin. He wants it—whether to eat or play with, who knows? The awfulness of it makes you drop the bone. I pick it up. It has a luminous sheen to it now—like something almost radioactive. And then when I hold it up—and I can't think of anything else to do—partly to taunt the giant—partly to try to ward it off—the wishbone catches the reflection of one of the sodium lights beside the children's pen.

A kind of prismatic effect erupts all around us—like a kaleidoscopic grenade going off. And then the shards of light stream together like iron filings to a magnet...focusing down into a beam like a laser, shooting out from the bone. When I raise the bone a little higher the ray strikes the Gooper's head and sets it on fire—the nest exploding in a ball of red flame. A sticky slab of body drops off and sends the creature toppling into the steel spikes of the children's yard, impaling the thing...so that it smushes down and begins to melt. Furious hornets fill the air like shrapnel or flecks of hot ash. The children start smearing their hands and faces into the transparent yellow-brown bulk of burning, softening jelly...and within seconds the Gooper is a puddle of caramelized honey and kitchen utensils—like some school cafeteria flooded with diabetic urine and Jell-o.

The Zookeeper is beside herself, and levels her rifle at us, sputtering and seething with rage. The light beam from the bone has disappeared and I can't seem to catch the reflection of the yard light again. I can almost hear the thud of the dart that will strike me. Or you. We're both done for...unless...

You reach out for the bone... whether you think I've suddenly frozen or not, I don't know...but in reaching for it, one of the stems seems to ting. It's a clear, bell-like, bird-like sound— just like the tines of the tuning fork it partially resembles. Hearing the sound, you strike it more forcefully with a finger and the resulting sound is now like a crystal chandelier vaporizing.

The Zookeeper drops the gun and clutches her ears. The children begin to wail like ambulances. The air reverberates in all directions. And we hear and feel it bouncing back off the darkened glass walls of the hexagram pavilion. Then...ka-smash!

All the windows of the building blast out or in...we can't tell...because fragments fly everywhere like knives... and from inside the pavilion swoop hundreds and hundreds of shrieking bats. They storm outward in a black smoke of flapping wings. Some hit us in the head—some claw or bite as they whisk past—but while we duck and swing at them, waving the wishbone between us...they cover the Zookeeper completely—like sheets of black newspaper glued to her goggled head. The white suit quickly disappears beneath them. The claws clasp on. She is simply a clump of leathery wings and feasting teeth, rolling and thrashing helplessly beneath them.

Some stray fliers the children snatch out of the air, gnawing into their wings while they're still alive. Others catch them by wing or claw and beat them on the ground before biting off their heads. Other children aren't so adept and are hit in the face, blood from the cuts leaking down their faces as they charge in panic around the pen.

Without a word we hop on the ride-on mower and I gun it over the rise. As we pass the sad, trash-strewn enclosures, lights come on and some taped message about the animals that are supposed to be on display comes on…a generic cheerful female voice talking about habitats and places of origin. Some bats and hornets trail after us, but we leave them behind when we pass through a stand of artificial trees made out of some stiff synthetic fiber like Welcome mats. The landscape opens up again into some kind of war memorial with a bronze Sherman tank the size of a chapel.

We finally reach a wide boulevard of fluted iron streetlamps and burned-out cars. Park benches have been dragged into the middle like barricades. Down the way we see the spit and glitter of welder's sparks and some kids doing tricks on skateboards. We abandon the mower. Then we hear someone shout… "Rags! Rags!"

It's an old-time rag merchant's street wagon, but not pulled by a horse. The beast of burden is a huge and deeply wrinkled gray Neapolitan mastiff, at least 10 and maybe 12 hands high, the biggest dog we've ever seen by a long shot. It looks half asleep in its heavy harness—or maybe deaf from the shouting.

Seated on the wagon is a bearded, red-faced man with a silk hat that rises and then slants crookedly and then back again, like an improvised stovepipe. He looks wasted and worn—and beside him sits a sleek black monkey that looks as well-groomed as the man looks disheveled and sick, wearing a little white robe, like a kind of priest. The man sees us, and sees how close we are and still he belts out loudly, "Rags! Rags!"

"Why would we want rags?" you

ask. "Especially now."

"You can't go from rags to riches without rags, can you?" the man answers.

We don't know what to say to that… and then the man seems to slump… not like someone who's passed out or had a stroke—like a machine that's stopped working. I look at you and see that you've held up the wishbone, and I wonder if that's what's caused the effect. Then it dawns on us both…the man *is* some kind of machine. A toy… or a tool. The owner of the wagon, or the master, is really the monkey—who seems to grasp our recognition.

"You're quicker than most, yet dumber than some," the monkey says, with sort of a wheezy little laugh. "What'll it be, rags or remnants? Shreds or patches?"

"We want to know where this place is and what we should do," you say.

"This place is here," the monkey says with another wheezy laugh, as if he's made a good joke.

"But what should we do?" you ask again…this time with some real frustration and despair in your voice. "We want to get out of here. Now!"

Maybe something of the desperation in your tone gets through to the monkey—or maybe it's because you've waved the wishbone at him—but he changes his expression quite dramatically, becoming more doglike and more human at the same time. Then he reaches over to the man, who now seems propped like a piece of furniture next to him. The monkey snatches off the man's eccentric hat and puts it on his own head. "Some questions require a hat," he says.

He sits there with the tall zigzag hat on for what seems to us like a very long time—so that we begin to wonder if he might not be some kind of machine too. But at last he comes out of his trance and makes an announcement.

"You two ask what you should do...as if I knew. So, here is what I have to say. To get away...maybe... you should try to stay."

The idea of a talking monkey wearing a big silk hat we just let go by. We've seen so many extraordinary and distressing things, we're not easily flummoxed anymore. But the actual advice, which we weren't really expecting to get, takes us both aback.

The monkey seems very pleased with his recommendation and restores the hat to the man-machine's head. When he does, the man instantly snaps into animation again and bellows, "Rags! Rags!" at full volume.

The enormous gray mastiff comes alert again too and the cart pulls off, with no more comment or any kind of goodbye from the monkey. After a while, the echo of the man's voice and the clatter of the wheels fade away down the avenue—and we're left wondering what the hell the monkey meant...and what this whole nightmare world means. Why, how—and when can we leave?

Which eventually gets us back to mulling over what the monkey advised us to do: *To get away, try to stay.*

Beyond the rhyme there does seem to be at least some element of reason to this remark. Try to find something you've lost, stop looking for it. Try to

remember something you've forgotten, think of something else. The contra nature of the counsel strikes us both as maybe somehow being on the right track.

But if we were to try to stay, where would we take shelter?

"We have to get out of this shithole war zone," you say. "It's an insane asylum let loose in a bombing range."

"We need a vantage point," I say.

So we start scanning the palisades...the crackpot sheds clutching onto the cliff face...what look like old mining tunnels with sulfur yellow lights glimmering out. Then... way above the billboards and the little encampments...we spot a plateau and some kind of kiosk. We have to wait until the spotlights that criss-cross the sky slice past and reveal more detail... but when they do...we see cables running over the void between the cliff... and another canyon wall we can't make out. There's some kind of cable car that runs over the city. And the car, which is stranded out about a quarter of the way on the wire from the plateau looks just like an Airstream trailer.

There's no escaping the similarity. It has to mean something, and so, not knowing what else to do, we set out with the wishbone, heading toward and up the cliffs to try to reach the cable car.

We walk for about two miles without seeing anyone directly, except for an old phone booth crammed full of yelping people, some of whom have clearly disjointed limbs or injured themselves in trying to fit. We sprint past not wanting to get involved—and not knowing if they're there by choice, seeking refuge—or if it's some kind of contest. Or if they've been stuffed in there against their wills. A couple of the inside faces pressed up against the spider webbed glass are unmistakably the faces of dead people.

Once we reach the base of the palisades, the prospect of actually reaching the plateau safely seems daunting. The cliffs are folded in and steep, with countless crevices and hiding places… and who knows how many hostile, paranoid, or just plain evil people—or creatures—waiting to ambush us. I'm worried about you trying to climb in moccasins. I'm feeling exhausted. The whole project seems fruitless—especially starting in the dark. And the luminous quality of the wishbone appears to register this discouragement because it sputters and pulses. Dimming.

And then, just as we're beginning to really pant and puff, slipping and starting rockfalls—and wondering when we're going to get picked off by some sniper shot, or one of us will tumble off into nowhere screaming— you start laughing hysterically. I think, shit, she's lost it. Now what are we going to do? You're laughing so hard now you let out a little teapot fart—like a note on a kid's toy horn—and that gets me laughing. We've been through so much. We may well be dead. It's all so hopeless. Your little toot acts as a pressure release and all the emotion just empties out. It's like another kind of sex. Complete, unrestrained breakdown. But together.

Only when we've laughed ourselves sick, am I able to understand that you've been pointing at something off in the dark for a couple of minutes. When this finally sinks in, I look— and look again. And I'll be damned if I don't at last see what got you snorting and breaking wind. It's an escalator system built right into the cliff. Neat and flowing like a waterfall of gridded metal. All our exertions were unnecessary. The whole system is sheltered by a tall shaft of cage…and while that means an ominous ride up…with no way out if we're waylaid…it's nonetheless a way up. And a fast one as it turns out—although our hearts pound the whole way…wondering if someone or something is waiting for us—hoping for just something like our arrival.

"If the thing suddenly stops," I say. "We try to smash through the barrier and go over the side. We don't want to be cornered and taken alive."

As terrible as that sounds, it gives us both a jolt of energy to be in such a situation. We feel more alive because of it. The dread, the anticipation—it's like an amphetamine and an aphrodisiac. I want to go first, in case there's trouble up ahead of us. But you insist on riding on the higher step. "I want you to see my ass the whole way," you say. "It's a primal thing. I need your animal. And I promise not to let another one go."

That gets us both giggling again. Our morale has lifted…and as we ascend we start to feel stronger. More together. More decisive. We're taking some active step now, not just wandering. The fear is still strong. Rich like the smell of sweat or meat. But it's sharpened us not cowed us now. If this is all a drug we're on, the bewildered lunatic phase is behind us. This is clear—bright and etched with our concentration.

The vigilant, combat-ready but optimistic mood seems to carry us upward at least as much as the moving stairs… and gives us the illusion of a shield around us. The wishbone tuning fork starts to shine more intently again.

Switchback level by chainlink landing we climb and reach the plateau without incident or sight of anyone else. Once at the top, you slip off and squat for an enormous pee, while below the fireworks thud, the juggernaut of demolition equipment rolls and crowds of masked and maimed people pound and flee like fools for slaughter.

The plateau is a lonely, barren place. The kiosk is boarded-up and riddled with bullet holes. No sign of any equipment or controls inside—no way to call the cable car back. The trash and bones of old fires lie scattered everywhere. Bras, condoms, shell casings, syringes and pieces of busted Japanese toys. But the cable to the Airstream looking car looks strong and hangs with a reassuring level of tension. In the occasional flash of the spotlights from below we see a line of seagulls perched along it. They look spectral in the gloom, but maybe benign. Spirits of opportunity.

Counting the gulls, it looks like about 200 yards out into the abyss… about the same distance you might feel you could safely swim drunk on a hot summer night to some little island in a river, perfect for a bug-embattled fuck as the fireflies blink in the saw grass. For the first time since we fell out of the roulette coaster in that other lifetime, I feel strangely confident and relaxed. And then you peer out over the edge and say, "I can't do it. I can't do heights. Not like this. We'll have to stay here."

I immediately feel my own fear rise. It's a thousand feet down at least. What was I thinking? There's no way. It's suicide. Just as insane as those wounded shadows stampeding in the ruins. Better to hold up in the bird-infested kiosk and wait for the people with the guns and the needles to show up. Maybe they won't know we're here. Maybe we can even join their tribe— whatever it is they are. The wishbone light stutters.

But then one of the arc lamps below sweeps over the car suspended out on the cable. It really does look exactly like the miniature Airstream, only full sized. We were dead right about that from down below. We can't have come this far…through so much…for this not to mean something. What other hope do we have? What other clue? Somehow, we've been drawn to the cable car. We were meant to find it—to reach it.

"We have to get out there," I say. "And I'm not strong enough to carry you. How can we do it? We have to try."

You've never looked so pale…so white you seem like a stray piece of spotlight that's come to life. As white as one of the gulls. But you answer very clearly. "I want you inside me as we go. If I have something else to think about, I can do it. And if we're going to fall, then I want us to fall that way."

You turn and give your butt a

wiggle, and then peel back the chaps in front to show me your pussy. Frankly. So innocent, and yet so lewd.

It's like the first time I ever had a chance to stare openly and unashamedly at a real naked girl. Someone whose skin I could taste. Not a centerfold on some tree fort wall or some "playmate" in a magazine dragged out from beneath a bed to jack-off to…but a real flesh female, close enough to catch her scent…to know that there is a scent to women, and that no one is exactly like the other. The terror and the wonder of it…understanding that this is where we all come from…and yet seeing past the mother-phobia and lost womb security—always switchbacking like the escalator—to some crude but pure desire…a thinking past the thinking… an acceptance of the base wants as the basis of all.

And soon, we are entwined. Converged. Slow and meditative. Slipping and sliding forward in the dark like caterpillars. We go fist-hold by pump along the thick braid of the cable, the lubricated metal smell getting us hotter, as you wrap your long legs around my waist, feeling me, barely moving inside you, but pushing, squirming forward… not just fucking you…but fucking myself into you…fucking us both along this slender strand of twined steel, as the seagulls squawk and take flight.

The windswept ashes of the plateau seem miles and years behind us… we don't remember the moment of giving way and letting go of the rock wall, kicking out into the dark air. All we are is a creature wrinkling itself along in a line…the squish and plunge of it lever-aging us closer. Closer. Closer.

It's funny, because there are so many times, as a male, when you long to fuck. To enter. To thrust. It's been a wonderful blowjob, thanks very much—the 69 has gotten me wired and wet and hard…the gentleness, the delicacy and time-taking, the snuggling and nuzzling—all these pleasures have their engorging moment, their special, needful appeal. But then suddenly all you want to do is to plunge and stab. To butt and ram. To own and occupy. You've moved past wanting pussy. You now crave cunt. You want to shove past the consensual…to the elemental. To feel cunt walls pushed apart by the strength of your hard-on. To command and control the rhythm of the drive. To spray…like a fire hose on fire…your male milk. Like starlight in a small, overheated room. To yell and pound— and pulverize. Smash out the windows and let the rain in. Fuck *everything*. You want only to groan and bellow like the animal you have to hide from being so much of the time. So many hours of every day. So many minutes of such a short life. You want for just one blood-warm second, the freedom of all evolutionary time—the right to violate. And then, for that violence, for that base-of-the-spine predatory hunting party impulse to somehow be assimilated back into normality. For your revelation of the Creature within you to have been embraced by the other's Monster…for the cunt's Hydra-Gorgon-Venus Fly-trap greedy sucking fertile vacancy to understand. Oh, to let the Creatures really loose in the company of another demon. How they throb and glisten when they have a chance. How their craving, once sated, gives back light and heat—and will. More hunger for life.

But there are other times, when one longs to be mouth-centric. To suck and pluck at slickening pussy lips. To tease the meaty little bud of clit, the female penis. And nipples…the ultimate psychosexual crisis point, firing the brain across the lobes, across the years. To not only tongue a tender, succulent female asshole—but to devour it. To feast on where your woman shits…to submit…to serve—and to consume. To give way absolutely to the oral child within. To taste. To desecrate oneself with the smear of enjoyment. To give and bite. To be humiliated and to reign supreme, literally eating your lover like a conquering cannibal. To go down and not worry about what comes up or where it leads.

And this was where I found myself now.

The inability to realize my oral fixation…the slow screw-piston enjambment of cock into vagina as a means of transport…the only means of sexual contact…this heightened my connection. And yours. Your nipples burned with want for my mouth. My fattened rod stuck up to the cervix inside you—you felt your clit tingle with the imaginary urgings of my tongue—your ass exposed to the wind and the darkness, you felt what it would be like to have my lips covering it in a rude, cheek-parted kiss. But there was nothing we could do, except wiggle and gyrate together. And not look down.

We reach the car and the simultaneous climax is like nothing we've ever felt before. Like we've burst open and spurted out all our organs. The second we grab onto the roof of the car, the shockwaves hit us…the vibration of longing and fulfillment radiating through us…turning into an almost electric current. We've done what we set out to do.

But almost immediately, the mood turns sour and anxious. We climb in and collapse onto the floor of the car, which is empty but for a silver railing around the side and an operator's console. Our muscles ache beyond description. We're suddenly famished and thinking we may well just pass out from hunger and fade to black in our sleep. We don't have any supplies. We don't have any water even! What did we expect to find up here? Just because it looked like the Airstream? How did we think we could live on nothing but wind and sex?

The gulls return, curious or antagonized. They flock and peck at the windows. You nestle into me, the wishbone between us…as we await the end… both of us believing it will be like some doomed polar explorers' mission we've read about…tragically but peacefully slipping off into a terminal daze while the wind howls outside the nylon tent—the pelting snowflakes turning into pestering, screeching gulls.

One of the ghostly white birds strikes the window with a crack of broken neck and falls out of sight. Maybe, once the pangs and cramps of hunger have passed—the delirium that will come with thirst—we'll be free. Forever free and dead.

Things go silent immediately outside as we dangle in the enlarged Airstream over the phantom city. Only distant sounds of detonation and dismay…a flicker every once in a while of harsh quartz light from below. Our thoughts give way to fatigue and surrender.

However, just as this resignation fantasy is beginning to really take hold, we hear the cry of the gulls again. They're flying about once more, but not attacking the windows of the car this time. No!

Just as the ravens nourished Elijah in the wilderness, the gulls have returned to us with food—perhaps from some looted supermarket. Torn strips of wilted lettuce and not quite molding fruit. Cans of beans and steak and onions. Bags of peas and lentils. Jerky. Chocolate! Muesli bars and breakfast cereal. Smoked ham, tinned tuna… protein…survival fat and vitamins. Everything they bring and deposit on the roof I retrieve…and we feast…not even tasting the flavors, just accepting the nutrition, the chance to keep going. Every single morsel is a banquet. Every mouthful a miracle.

We savor and gorge on the food as we wanted to orally indulge in each other's bodies before. We realize that we may have a means of staying alive for a while longer.

"This could be the solution," we say aloud—at precisely the same time.

And the moment we say this—an old man appears in the car.

"Where did you come from?" we cry again in unison.

"Whenever you pick up two words and rub them together like sticks," he shrugs. "I'm the Old Man. I won't stay long. I'm always here."

He really is old. And dirty. Like a scarecrow left out in a field of cow corn too long. But he smells good. Like lanolin…and an oven warm Cornish pasty in a paper bag.

"What should we do?" I ask.

"You keep asking that," he says, raising a hand that seems too big for his thin body. "Why don't you try driving the cable car? You've got the handle."

"Is that what this is?" you ask, holding up the wishbone.

It seems to have changed shape again, and now appears to be more of a human designed device. Industrial, although beautifully crafted.

"Why don't you try it?" he says— and points to a slot in the car's console that now, when we think of it, does indeed look like it was meant to accommodate such a shape.

"How do we know we can believe you?" I ask.

He smiles. "You mean, how do you know you can trust me? Tell me, who gave you the handle?"

"Was it your house with the animal heads?" you squeak.

"What are you talking about?" he replies. "I don't need a house. I'm the Old Man. I meant that however you came by the handle is how you can trust me."

"But where does the cable car go?" we wail at the same time.

"How would I know that?" he shakes his head. "*You've* got the handle."

"We're safe up here," I say.

"We don't know where the car goes," you add.

A skyrocket booms nearby and the aftershock sets the car rocking.

"Safe," the Old Man repeats.

We see people tightrope walking on the wires. They have headlamps on. At first there is only a couple. Then more appear. Some are wiggling along precariously or going hand over hand. Others move nimbly like rodents, closing in on the car.

"Suit yourselves," the Old Man nods. "I'm off now."

"Wait!" we cry. "You're not just going to jump!"

"No...I'm not," he answers, as if we're stupid. And that's certainly the way we feel.

"But what will happen...where are we and how do we get out?" I want to know.

"The question you should ask yourselves is how you came by the handle."

"The wires just go off into the dark," you say.

"Darkness is all there ever is until you attend to the right questions," he answers—and then disappears right in front of us.

Shit, we think.

Some of the headlamp people shimmying along the cable are nearing the car. Gulls circle around them. Balloons float up from the city below. Silver foil, bubblegum pink and satiny red Valentine hearts. One of the climbers is about to leap for the roof of the car. We don't know what they want—or what to do. It doesn't seem like a good idea to just wait there like sitting ducks. Besides, how many people can the cable support? It seems like now or never.

Once again.

So, together we slot the wishbone into the metal sleeve the Old Man indicated—and like a lever we pull it. We expect the car to lurch forward—but instead, there's a rush of wind and gulls and paper. The bottom of the car has dropped open! The floor is gone and we're left clinging on to the sides...all of the remains of the groceries blowing down over the water and the city. "Fuckersnattle!" you scream. "Fuckersnattle!"

The Old Man appears again in mid air.

"You tricked us!" you shout.

"I did not," he says, looking calm despite the draft blowing up under his dirty old coat. "I didn't say how the car runs."

"What do we do now?" we yell together. "Fall to our death?"

He frowns at us, like we're upstart kids. "I don't think you're much good at falling. Why don't you try finding. You seem to have some knack for that. Just take the handle."

He vanishes again, and we can no longer hang on...we can't...there's no choice...so we tug at the wishbone, just as a couple of people land on the roof of the car. We wrench it free and let go of the sides of the car, holding the wishbone between us...hollering at first in horror...but also high on the finality of our decision. The release.

And it doesn't feel like falling.

After a second...or another million years...the nausea of letting go is gone and we feel this pitch of pleasure and power. Just like we did back on the ride at the fairground. It doesn't make any sense—it makes less sense than anything else that's happened to us since the fairground—since as long as we can remember. And yet, it feels totally natural. Like something we were made to do and have done before. We'd just forgotten.

If we're falling, why doesn't the ground start rushing up beneath us? Why doesn't the collapsing city of tractors and spotlights and psychotic crowds get closer? If anything, the lights and the noise seem to recede. We feel this fantastic buoyancy, as if our bodies were opening up to engulf the night. It makes us laugh, like the coming-on buzz of some intense drug. Tears stream out of our eyes with the thrill of it.

People start leaping off the wires and clasping on to us like skydivers in a routine. We aren't afraid. More appear—pouring out of the cliff face and down the cable from both sides. They fling themselves off and into formation—joined by gulls and bats and balloons—and still more people who slide down the wire on chains and then let go.

Together we form this undulating circle. The people's lights flash. The ever-widening wheel we make turns, spinning around us and the wishbone that glows at the center. I look out at the spokes of the sparklewheel—the limbs and the wings and the fabric all meshed together. All the lives rippling their lights, with more people leaping, building and growing the spinning machine. Crystal. Feather. Blood and bone.

And still it doesn't feel like falling.

It feels like a new kind of travel. A new kind of home.

CODY GOODFELLOW

LOCATION:
Los Angeles, deep in the heart of
Porno country

STYLE OF BIZARRO:
Hypernaturalist Weird Fiction

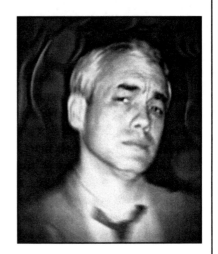

BOOKS BY GOODFELLOW:
Radiant Dawn
Ravenous Dusk
In The Shadow Of Swords
San Francisco Guidebook
Jake's Wake*
Silent Weapons For Quiet Wars
The Day Before*
Perfect Union
Black Wind
Spore*
All Cities Attack!

* Co-written with John Skipp

DESCRIPTION: Deeply transgressive metamorphosis fantasies
of a doomed collective unconscious repackaged as id-addled post-
postmodern pulp trash.

INTERESTS: Getting hit by cars, rhubarb pie

INFLUENCES: Dashiell Hammett, Philip K. Dick, HP Lovecraft,
George Orwell, David Cronenberg, Robert Williams, Salvador Dali,
Secret Chiefs 3, Swamp Thing and every genre movie from the
summer of 1982 except E.T..

WEBSITE:
www.perilouspress.com

THE HOMEWRECKERS

1. THE STORK BROUGHT ...MURDER!

I was just minding my own business in Baptismal Park at sunset, watching the storks take flight from the Southern Rookery with their cargo of newborn boys bound for the orphanage, when I got pinched by the Nuns.

One of the storks stalled overhead, a little drama as it almost plummeted out of the sky with a fresh-hatched bundle of joy in its clutches. I didn't see it hit the ground, but I didn't see it rise up into the pink clouds, either.

I don't usually get a penguin to shuttle me to a job, let alone one I hadn't cracked yet. But getting collared by Sister Mildred Crawghast was like a familiar, comfortable pair of shoes, spanking you.

Like usual, she led by snatching my neck from behind with those damned steel pincers, and tuned me up with her ruler. I went limp as a street-eel while she dragged me into her swooping cruiser.

I like girls. I know, boys hate girls and vice versa. But there's something wrong with me. I really like them. And they really hate me. I got a history. But I would be a liar, if I said I didn't get into this job for the chance to ride in cars with girls.

When I know to expect her, I carry smelling salts to come around faster. I know she has to keep up appearances. It wouldn't do for her to look soft on the competition, so she never spares the ruler.

Something had her chastity belt in a twist, tonight. Her bat-winged wimple was a squirming crinoline grab-bag stuffed with bad things that wanted out.

"Your place or mine, sister?"

Sister Mildred's jet-black eyebrows cocked at a sardonic angle that made her violet eyes the dots on twin question marks. She never dropped her chainmail veil, but I had seen behind it plenty of times, in dreams. "A client of yours... on our side of the Wall."

"Pity I haven't kept my shots up to date. How about you?"

Limbering up her ruler, Sister Mildred nodded to the milky novitiate beside her, who took my gun in her white-gloved hands. It looked cute, and might've been provocative, if she could fire it. Somebody smarter than all of us set it up so only a man, with a man's sweat and stink, could switch the safety off a gun.

Like they needed guns... I was still goofing on her when she impaled me on a needle big enough to joust with. As the suppressor 'mones started to kick in, the evil thoughts in my reptilian backbrain slunk off to their swamp, and I loosened up enough to let them take my gun. Pity... if she wanted answers, I probably would've been more cooperative while horny and homicidal.

Rubbing the hole in my neck, I tried to make nice. "You girls don't have anything to worry about, with me. I'm a professional."

"It's not you, we're worried about. Not everyone is as immune to your animal charms, as I. Now, tell me about your new clients."

I volunteered nothing, naturally. It's almost sad enough to make me rich, how many idiots think a private investigator is honor-bound to help you thwart the nuns.

I didn't know much, but I made Sister Mildred beat it out of me. She had picked me up before I even had a chance to find out how many lies they told me, never mind cashing their check.

As I knew she would, Sister Mildred filled in the blanks. A young newlywed lesbo couple, crazy in love and just setting up housekeeping in a secured fifth-floor walkup. Marian and Wildy Centinela. The sister pumped me for my angle on them, and I didn't try to lie. Dollars to dogtails, it was the hope that I might have a line on other, less reputable tradesmen than myself to get them over the Wall, or even Out. Fucked if I know where they get ideas like that. "I never even met 'em, and as for what they wanted…"

As I talked, my gesturing hand came within an inch of her knee.

At such awkward intervals, Sister Mildred's face usually folded into a scowl to cure long-pig leather, and the ruler took my full measure. But now, she launched a smile big enough to chew through her veil and bite my nose off, and her black kidskin glove trapped my right thigh. "You can't meet them or cash their checks, but you'd better figure out what they wanted, if you like being a boy."

We blitzed the Portal Veneris without stopping for the matrons and ramrodded into Sisterville with blue lights and sirens wailing. We flew up Tubman Avenue, swung right on Medea and followed the monorail down into Gertrude Gulch.

It never ceased to amaze me, how much cleaner, quieter and safer even the seediest slums on the women's side

of the city were, than any precinct in Boystown. Three generations with no men around was supposed to set them free and make them pure, but they'd just perfected their makeup. To hear them tell it, the Valkyries had next to no trouble, outside of man-trouble. And to hear them tell it, they had plenty of it, tonight.

Two cruisers and a paddy wagon were parked in front of the Anais Arms, an instant carnival of valkyries, nuns and eunuchs setting up shop in the lobby and getting barked at by the matrons.

I wolf-whistled. "One hell of a crack flying squad you girls got. You already thought to send out for a scapegoat."

The novice opened the door and herded me out onto the curb with pincer mittens. Sister Mildred stepped out after me. "Mundy," she said, like addressing a social disease, "I doubt there's a powerful enough drug to make you behave like your more civilized ancestors, but I'm not trying to pin anything on you. I was rather naively convinced that you might even be willing to help our investigation. No woman could have done this. We don't want another war. We want justice."

The Nuns and Valkyries kept order on their side of the wall. If they pinched me for more than just a free femdom session, they had to want something a lot more desperately than they wanted peace and quiet. Unless they really did like me for the murder, and were dangling the noose. Playing the angles with women is a lot harder than men. With a dick, all you have to do is draw a straight line to the nearest hole.

Lots of guys think the Sisters run a big petting zoo and rug-munching party, but they seemed all frosty business. Nuns and Valkyries held up every opposing wall in the building like caryatids. Everyone wore a mask or a veil, and the air was rife with suppressor 'mones, rosewater and fingerprint powder. And the stink of spilled blood.

When I saw the crime scene, I did not know that those images would stay burned in my brain forever, and they didn't. The horror of it still haunts me with the reminder always to carry a camera and hand lotion.

The apartment was a wreck, furniture smashed and scattered like two tornadoes had a jitterbug contest in the bedroom, the entertainment hutch, the living room and ending, as all good parties must, in the kitchen.

Two young women in matching gossamer lingerie lay entangled on the checkerboard tile floor with their hands around each other's necks. French manicured nails were still hilt-deep in one girl's face and throat, and a bread knife and a knitting needle fouled the battleship contours of her more zaftig adversary's brassiere.

They were both a bit huskier than your average Mother's Day effigy, and the one with the knives in her was a regular war-grade butterball, but if they'd brought me here to plant my filthy male evidence at the scene, I would happily have obliged, had duty not interceded with her ruler.

"Who called in this mess?" I shouted. None of the nuns deigned to answer.

A eunuch coroner told me the score. "The building matron came up, when she saw the stork circling over the building, last night. Said it was the second time this week. Brought up that—" pointing at a gift basket with oranges, carob chocolate and a big pink teddy bear.

The eunuchs were snipped from birth and halfway to sisterhood from hormones, but the nuns let them prance around, because it gives downtrodden women everywhere an effigy to stoke their hate, in case the blame for every war, pogrom, jihad, inquisition and genocide ever waged in human history ever slips their minds. And because there are still some jobs no liberated woman wants to do.

"Tasty one, Floyd," he was saying. He smiled like it was costing him money. "These were good girls. Both nurses fresh out of school, triple A-rated, neighbors say they were happy. If we can't keep them safe, then people start to talk. They're saying a man had to do this, and I can't buck it."

I knew how it looked; I remembered the Pink Bug scares, the purges, the nancy camps. The gender war had gone cold, but assholes on both sides of the wall wanted it hot again. "Cry some for me," I said back. "With no men around, some human always steps up and starts playing the heavy."

"You're still packing pipe," the eunuch sneered, sniffing the air with his grotesquely oversized, inside-out nose. "What brings you this side of the wall?"

"Blind date," I replied, as his name came to me: Doc Livermint. The eunuch chuckled and went off to sniff their sheets.

I knelt over the rigid, ripped-to-shit forms, lost in bad thoughts. I'm no perv, but something like this shook you twice as hard, when live women never let you get this close.

I asked Sister Mildred what was so special about the Centinelas. "And where's the baby?"

A valkyrie with a face like the back of a shovel snapped, "This isn't your case, dick. You're not a cop here, you're a suspect. If you don't know why they called you, then we need you like fish need shoes."

"Well, I don't want to toot my own horn, but my keen masculine detective instincts say they killed each other."

Sister Mildred went to a window and showed me the tiny crescent of glass missing from the pane beside the latch. "Someone cut their way in."

My bunions and bum ear reminded me we were five stories up. There was no fire escape. "You give this guy too much credit. He may have been bright, but I doubt he had wings."

I didn't want to knock the girls' detecting skills, but without male criminals to knock against, they just didn't have to work all that hard. Women can be fine policemen, but they don't seem to make enough good crooks. When a real piece of police work fell into their laps, they still jumped on a chair and screamed for a man to take out the nasty man who must've done it.

I poked around, tossed the trash bin, found a wadded-up raw silk handkerchief. No monogram, but it dripped perfume. Vanilla.

I went to the window and opened it. "Anyone talk to the housekeeper?" I asked Livermint.

"It's buggy as all heck, but swing away."

I went over to the little speaker grille by the kitchenette. "Hey House, what'd you see?"

"Voice not recognized." Sultry, like dry ice on glass.

"You get anything out of it?"

"No, and the floor matron's already rebooted it twice." The eunuch flashed a selection of soiled panties stuffed up his sleeve. "Hey, you want a souvenir?" All these fuckers think they have my number.

I went back to the dead girls and studied their bodies some more. Sister Mildred had to draw her ruler to separate us.

Sizzling sweat popped out of my overheated pores. The Nuns hissed and pumped their atomizers. The valkyries fingered their scissors. I was starting to turn them on.

Sister Mildred moved to lead me out. I shook her off and mopped my sweaty face with the hanky from the trash bin.

"Well, ladies," I dreamily observed, "seems to me you've got a missing third victim. And the motive, and the means, are right here."

I showed them the little white feather I found on the ledge, but none of them looked at it. They stared at my face and hissed, building to a hysterical maenad whine. In that roiling soup of hostile pheromones, I took refuge in the only source of comfort at hand, and sniffed the handkerchief some more.

I looked into the chrome mirror of the radar range. My face was caked with a mustard yellow paste that smelled a lot less sweet than the hankie it came in.

I looked down at the handkerchief I'd been dabbing my face with. It was loaded with the stuff.

"Mystery solved!" I shouted, holding up the dirty diaper.

Two valkyries puked. "Amen, sisters," I said.

Sister Mildred yoked my neck in the pincers and puppeteered me down the stairs to her cruiser. "Wipe your face," she growled.

"You have to look at it, you do it." I thought I was being pretty debonair, so I didn't notice right away that she wasn't steamed at me, so much as terrified.

"You idiot! You dirty, stupid, lecherous, rotten man!" None of it reached her eyes, but I was pretty sure she was crying. "I risked so much to bring you over here, because I hoped you'd see something my sisters wouldn't, and could give some insight they wouldn't be able to ignore. You'd better hope a man is behind this crime, because it's not the first, and if you look around, I'll bet you'll find similar murders on your side of town, too. Something big is coming, Floyd. Everyone on your side is too blood-simple to see it, but I thought you'd at least understand, what with your... brain damage."

Some speech. I tried to follow it, but the shot was already wearing off, and by the time she was done, I was picturing ripping her face off and running around Sisterville wearing it for a loincloth. Sadly, my brain was not nearly damaged enough, for her to get through to me.

It's a point of pride that my clients almost never get killed until after my per diem gets maxed out. When it happens, I need closure.

Or at least comfort.

Soon as she'd picked me clean, Sister Mildred dropped me off at the Mott Terminus gate for Boystown. I had a headache from all the estrogen, so I popped a little pink pill from the case I'd found at the bottom of the Centinelas' kitchen trash, hoping it was a painkiller, or at least a pep pill, but no dice.

I slipped out a washroom window and prowled the oppressively clean tower blocks, where everything smelled like fresh-baked cookies.

My voucher was running out. I slipped on a new street face and went out the back and down the alley, turned down Lucretia Boulevard, stopping in the Automat for a bottle of Ovaltine that I emptied into the gutter. I circled the block and went through a couple dormitories, then to a park. I lurked in the bushes until I found a woman alone on a bench with a stroller at her knee, in the shadow of the Suffragette's Memorial.

Rolling a balaclava down over my face, I stepped out of the shrubbery and pointed at her from my coat pocket. She gasped, but didn't scream. Her baby gurgled in her lap, pink paws laying bare the engorged, cyclopean eye of her left breast.

I held out the bottle. "I'll have what she's having," I said.

"You have a disgusting sense of humor."

"Actually," I said, pulling out the gun, "I have no sense of humor whatsoever."

2. DIAL Z FOR ZZZZZZZZ

You look confused.

Not that I can literally see you, of course, but I've been known to do some detective work, in between getting clobbered by nuns and sticking up wet-nurses. You also, I'll wager, look like the kind of phony highbrow idiot man-child who gets his history from funny books.

We're not big on history, around here. History is a nag. But if it'll help you soldier on through my earnest confession without skipping to the centerfold and gumming up the pages of whatever sordid rag we're meeting in, I'll spell it out.

Right after the Great War, America had all kinds of bright-eyed reformers, prohibitionists, crusaders and muckrakers clamoring to do away with everything that made life worth living. Some did it with sneaky legislation, some with axes and batshit crazy eugenicist Bible nonsense and some with test tubes and new Bibles of the germ warfare variety. It was these latter assholes, who got their fondest wishes granted.

Some righteous fundamentalist gene-splicer who probably never got laid, but a posthumous medal in the Pink Wars, came up with the final solution for fucking with other people's successful sex lives, and the answer to every unfuckable fundie's secret prayers.

They weren't aiming to start a war between men and women; they just wanted a bug that would nullify the animal attraction that made premarital sex possible. They always planned an antidote that would be administered whenever a clear-eyed couple unclouded by lust applied for and received a license to be married. But once out of the lab, the bug had other plans.

The first outbreak was in San Francisco. Men and women came down with a kitten-kiss of a flu bug and then went berserk, killing each other in the streets. It only took some eggheads a few weeks to discover what was happening, if not what caused it or how to stop it, but by then, the fever had spread around the world and commenced to chewing its own ass off. Cities burned, and every house was a battlefield. In some places, men and women drew up into factions and withdrew while society collapsed. With soldiers, sailors and so many other refuges for he-men, the men had a head start, but without women around, they turned on each other more often than not, and so it fell to women to try to make peace. Ten years of germ and chemical warfare had rendered most on both sides sterile or prone to ghastly mutations, so the truce divided up the responsibilities of every household on the back of the new, bifurcated state.

The men would build the works, grow the food and protect the divided state against all enemies foreign and domestic—from sewer crabs to ghouls and Mexicans—and the women would do all the other stuff—like making babies.

The old-fashioned way was obviously out of the question, but all men free of defects donated sperm to the hatchery and got a receipt, and their seed was sown in a handpicked egg in a little rubber oven. When the bundle of second-hand joy hatched, the product was inspected, tagged and delivered by stork to its happy, loving parent—if they wanted it. Most women raised babies, but only if they were girls. A few weirdo males tried to raise their own sons, but it seldom worked out. The rest of the girls and nearly all of the boys grew up in orphanages.

It was a tough life for a boy, but they made us strong. Anything broken, burned or cut off you grows back faster than hair, until puberty. That's why kids make the best soldiers.

Girls aren't made so tough, naturally, but they got other advantages. Smarts. Girls learn how to read and write before boys know how to talk, but boys can kill each other before they can walk.

For almost fifty years, this was how we had lived, and it worked pretty good, compared to what came before. We were polite to each other when we spoke on the phone and aside from men killing each other for any reason that came into their pointy heads, there was little reason to want it to change. We were civilized, even though not a day went by but that every one of us dreamed of killing the nearest member of the opposite sex with our bare, bloody hands.

I know what you're thinking. Again... don't know you, wouldn't want to, and I'm not psychic, but you're saying to yourself, none of that shit ever happened. This geezer is peddling hophead horseshit.

And I would've agreed with you, once. I didn't know half of that stuff myself, before I drank that bottle of mother's milk.

It felt good to get back to Boystown. The burning trash and tires, the illiterate graffiti, the laughter, screams and gunshots, felt like home. Even if every face that passed on the street was a grimace of terror, a drunken flush or a wrinkled mask of rage, at least you could see the faces and know what lay behind them.

Except for the wall that separates them, Boystown and Sisterville belonged on different planets. The red brick and brownstone buildings of Boystown sagged under a harsher gravity. The trolley lines and bootleg telephone wires twanged like the strings of a busted guitar. A hot, ionized wind off the desert scoured the streets and left a thin coat of gray dust on everything.

Dust that used to be cities and people.

Not that the streets were without novelty or color, tonight. Big posters were splashed all over every storefront and fence. REFORMER EUGENE ORKNEY FOR MAYOR! The Screws' candidate was a tall glass of curdled milk with a smile prim enough to stop a gang rape. DON'T CHANGE IN MID-CHARGE, went the incumbent rebuttal: RE-ELECT HORTON WELCH! Welch's lenticular posters knowingly waggled their eyebrows and mutton chops at me as I passed. Some inventive artist had drawn huge uncircumcised sausages that seemed to leap into Welch's grinning mouth with every step.

The Central Terminal was eighteen blocks from my office, but I knew if I hopped the trolley, I'd just be wasting a nickel. I held up a lamppost at the corner of Patton and Custer and tested out the second hand on my watch. Before it had even rounded the 6, I got picked up by a chopped Dusenberg filled with Roosters. Four pimply gunsels with Thompsons rode the running boards. The Negro chauffeur wore a freshly slaughtered chicken on his head.

"Take a load off, Floyd," Nimrod Cox braced me from the backseat and threw open the batwing door. His partner, Lummox Lardstone, climbed over into the front and beat the seat to death with his ass.

I expected one of the official police forces would snap me up, but I saw no law anywhere. Tipping my hat to whoever tipped them off, I graciously accepted their invitation.

"Quiet night," I said. "Not a Bull or a Screw in sight."

"Both Coppers' Balls are swinging tonight," Cox snarled, "uptown and down. I hear you got a better invitation, though." Three coats of pancake powder wasn't thick enough to hide the ringworm scars on his pasty face.

"I've danced plenty with cops. How'd you boys get out of serving drinks and parking cars?"

"You smell sweet, Floyd," Cox sneered. "Like that stuff, that... whatta they call it?"

"Perfume," Lummox grunted, like he hoped no one noticed he could talk. "Like dames wear." It must suck to have to be the brawns and the brains of an outfit.

I watched us turn off Custer down a nameless alley lined with speakeasies and casinos. "Hey, mighty thoughtful of you yeggs. How'd you know I wasn't headed home?"

Cox giggled at Lummox, whose upper lip stretched longer than his tie. "Must be a big case, if it's got you hopping the Wall. We wanna help. Where should we drop you off?"

"How about the Bulls?"

The giggling turned into a choked cough. Cox huffed an ether-soaked handkerchief. "Watch your mouth, dick. You're already riding in a police car."

None of his friends were laughing. Outside, the property values continued to tumble... tattoo parlors, chicken hawk cribs and gladiator pits crowded the narrow gulch that felt like it was paved with human skulls. A runaway giant pinhead dragged its trainers by its leashes out the loading door of Murillo's Roman Arena. The Roosters pinged gunfire off its armor as we passed.

"No offense, Nimrod, but I read today's paper, and you guys still run the bootlegging rackets. Two armies of cops in this town is plenty. Who're

they gonna chase, if you guys all find badges in your Malt-O-Meal?"

"Things change, Mundy. You didn't hear it from me, but Prohibition's getting repealed."

I was a little while taking that in. If I could hear it from a ham-and-egger foot soldier like Cox, I should've heard it first from the paperboy, but this was out of the blue. If there was anything to it, the gutters would soon be running with something, and it wouldn't be rotgut.

Two more drags on his rag, and he huffed, "You didn't hear it from me."

"Congratulations on your newfound respect for law and order, Nimrod, and thanks for the tip. I might just look up your old job."

He looked just like a little wasted angel, falling off his cloud. "How'd you figure, smart guy?"

"Alcohol's been illegal for over forty years, and it hasn't stopped anyone from wetting their beaks. Cops rolled over on just enough hoods to stay in the law business, and booze cost more, but the price hasn't moved half as much as bacon or milk, not since before we were born. If Boss Cloaca thinks he's gonna move uptown and start shopping for mayoral robes, he's drinking something stronger than the bathtub piss you yeggs peddle."

Someone in the car started snoring. Some feral kids chased a flaming giant rat through our headlights. But Cox was still all ears.

"You go legit, everyone can make and sell their own sauce. You either open up a war on the whole city, or you try to muscle in on the law and order rackets, which are a mug's game with way too many mugs in it. Trust me, bo: the last thing you clowns want to try to be, is respectable."

I'd gone and given Nimrod a migraine. "There's all kinds of ways to make a living, dick. All kinds of vices. We just ain't gonna run from the bulls and screws, no more. This town's gonna stop trying to be something it ain't."

We squealed round a corner and the roosters jumped off the running board to let me out. No lights out here, but the moon glittered on the black ribbon of cough-syrup river in the concrete spillway. Lummox patted me down and took my gun. I don't know why I ever took to carrying one.

"You're not cut out for honest work," Officer Cox told me, "but you ought to start looking at another trade, if you like your face how it is."

"I like it about as much as I like getting threatened by punks with someone else's big ideas stuffed in their nuts. You think you can fix it, you're welcome to try."

The goons didn't look excited about painting me with lead, but they all had bills to pay.

The searchlight on a Bull prowler interrupted our little rendezvous. "Top o' the evenin', you cock-gobblin' twists! Put your hands up and your wallets out!"

Took him long enough to do the math, but Cox figured there was no percentage in drilling me, just yet. The Dusenberg roared back the way it came with the bulls on their tail, but before it faded away, I heard the river rats stirring out of their boltholes to see what tasty morsel got left on their doorstep.

I started walking casually, like a man with a gun and a good reason to be on the wrong side of town in the dead of night. Puzzling things out kept me from running and pissing my pants.

The roosters beat the bulls and screws to brace me soon as I came out of Sisterville. Did their threat have something to do with the dead nurses, and the possibly missing baby?

This was too much to figure out, sober.

I didn't have too much trouble getting home. Something from the canal that claimed to be a woman offered me a helmet wash for a fin, and a clamdigger's special for a sawbuck. I was game until I saw the clam. The sea hag didn't even have a knife, and must've got rats to chew his dork off. Even the sea hag would've been raped to remnants if he was even a fraction of a real dame, but you want to believe, because it's as close as you'll ever get, to the real thing.

I bade him goodnight and set his wig on fire to show whoever was lurking nearby I meant business.

My stomach was bubbling over. The milk wasn't sitting still. It wanted to be cheese. I chewed over the disparate contents of my two serialized abductions, and came up with nothing staggering. Sister Mildred seemed to think somebody—with a dingus, natch—was stealing babies and killing their mothers. She also seemed to think I knew something about it. Boys got snatched about as often as wild dogs got adopted, and domestic violence in Boystown was a spectator sport. But something Nimrod Cox said about this town got my antennae in a knot.

As for his pipe dreams about the Roosters turning legit and Prohibition getting rolled back—bullshit. More likely, somebody was stirring up a war.

I should've gone to a speakeasy or a blind pig to lubricate these lines of reasoning more methodically, but my head wasn't in it. Following my troubled gut to the nearest A&P, I bought eggs, flour, sugar and baking soda, and went back to the office to bake a cake.

What the fuck are you looking at me like that, for?

3. I GET BLOWN… IN HALF

Not that I got right to making my cake, of course. It's never that easy.

Punks and newsies hollered my name as I came down my street. I'm well known, almost famous, in my neighborhood, for a number of things I'd rather forget.

Most guys who wind up in the papers don't seek to get famous. When it comes along, it crushes them, because it's the last thing they need, fame. They just want to rest when they're tired, eat when they're hungry and get showered with unconditional adoration for everything they do or say or leave in a toilet. They don't want to be celebrities. They want to go back to the hatchery.

I just wanted to do my job, and I wound up famous. That I hadn't been aced already only showed I wasn't worth killing.

I hadn't seen any Screws, but I smelled their trail like burned blood, leading back to their uptown fortress. The Screws started out as the reform party, the killjoys who dried up the booze, shut down the sporting houses and, some said, hatched the bug that made men and women hate each other. Merging with the priesthood and the trade unions—especially the prison guards—the Screws were the crusading morality police. But after Doc Mandrake's barnacle goose scheme blew up

in their faces, the Screws ended up in the doghouse, and the Bulls have taken over the city's political machine.

They're so tough, they can proudly claim to have killed more of their own by mistake, than the entire criminal element of the city. Screws and Bulls both carry badges and make arrests, but mostly, they pound on each other. Men have to create two of everything, so every creation will have someone or something to fight with.

Owing to ongoing disputes of a personal nature with my landlord, I had to sneak into my building via the neighbor's rooftop. The bullying instructor whose dojo was above my office was working late, teaching his charges to kick the crap out of a whole marching band. The bleating of nerds being bludgeoned by brass instruments covered my entrance and the claxon my housekeeper sounded. The wires to the landlord's office were cut, but the sound carried through the dumbwaiters and crawlspaces of the Arbuckle Arms.

At home, I found all my food tins gnawed open and emptied out. I haven't had rats in years. I miss rats, but they don't come around, anymore, since Iggy ate them all.

I didn't really think of him as a son. More of a pet, really.

The Screws had a pretty good plan a while back to do away with the women, and they had a brilliant backup plan to propagate the species, that they heroically sprang without telling anybody.

Doc Mandrake invented a bug that made men pregnant.

For a while, they called it Mandrake Simplex B, baby-cancer, barnacle geese and Clooney's Complaint, before they blacked it out of the news and rounded up the unhappy johns and their offspring for the glue factory.

According to public restroom lore, the initial outbreak was deadlier than the plague, as hysterical victims self-aborted and bled out. Besides the cramps and drastic anatomical redecoration such a new arrival means for a man, the whole ordeal is surprisingly bearable, once you've weathered the shocky uncertainty of the first trimester. Pregnancy runs its course quicker than most flus, and the fanged, taloned wethead baby pops out of an ectopic womb on the surface of the prostate, ready to defend itself and already knowing as much as it ever really will.

The Screws lost the last election because some crusading idiot blew the whistle on them. He lost his badge and went to jail, and wound up pregnant with an infantoma on his prostate.

Beyond keeping down other household pests, they're not good for much. It's slightly illegal to kill them, but it's illegal for them to exist in the first place. I let it have the run of the pantry and the TV, and brainwashed Ethel, my housekeeper, to conceal them from the cops.

My keen deductive instincts told me something was wrong when I found Iggy stapled to the wall. The two-pronged fork had gone through his face and into the crumbling plaster of the office's sorry kitchenette. Wherever his brains were, they weren't in his head, and he hopped to his feet when I pried it out. He didn't do chores or speak or wear pants, but a face on the small of his back looked more than a little like me and he smoked my cigarettes, and he grew out of an ectopic malignancy in my starboard scrotum, so I felt kind of warmly towards him, even then.

Like a dog.

Whoever stapled Iggy had ransacked my files and left an empty envelope that smelled like gardenias on the floor. The envelope had my address on it. They also dropped a big yellow steamer on my desk.

Ethel only added to the confusion. "You've got a lot of nerve just breezing back in, after you left like you did."

"I'm real sorry if I hurt your feelings, baby," I murmured into the intercom. "But I got all kinds of new business… maybe could afford some upgrades…"

"I wish I could believe that," she said tartly. "But you left such a mess, and you come right back in with your promises…"

"Wait! When did I leave?"

"Don't expect me to play your memory, too, Floyd Mundy. You know good and well you left not five minutes ago."

I stormed the corridor, skidding to a stop by the stairs. The elevators hadn't worked in months, but one was going down. I jumped from one landing to the next, then dropped down the shaft, catching passing railings to slow my fall. I landed on some geezer who stuck his head into the stairwell and demanded an explanation. I surfed his body to the ground floor and stumbled out into the lobby just in time to see my landlord shoot me in the back as I ran out the revolving door.

The shotgun blast cut me in half. Both halves hit the ground running and caught the Redeye Express trolley.

I turned to my landlord and raised my hands. "You sure know how to make a guy feel welcome, Bossy."

He didn't lower the shotgun. Bossy McGee was beautiful when he was angry. His creamy pale skin flushed with rage until it clashed with his tousled nest of scarlet hair, and his round hips shivered with enough rhythm to start a conga line. And his heaving double-F bosom, straining against the crushed velvet folds of a triple-whalebone corset, was a lot easier on the eyes than his eyes, which had poison shooting out of them.

"And you sure know how to hurt a girl, Floyd Mundy." Bossy lowered the shotgun to light a pink cigarette. His bouncing bosoms were both clamped to rubber suction cups that fed steady spurts of fresh milk into the wheezing pump on the desk.

"Bossy, let me explain. I just landed a case that'll catch me up on the rent, and—"

"You missed my set at the Dorado Room. And you charged in here without so much as a word…"

Bossy was all mixed up from his hormone treatments, but he qualifies enough as a she, that he has to stay in the cage in the office, and shoots a couple suitors every weekend. He took the hormones just to make the black market milk, but he's still a he-man woman-hater, so we get to keep the cow.

I've never been Biblically acquainted with Bossy, but I hated having to avoid him, because I'm addicted to his milk. That's why we called him Bossy… he pumped night and day and delivered it still warm via dumbwaiter. But nobody got the milk for free.

I pointed to the still-spinning revolving door. "That, uh… wasn't me, baby. But you thought it was, and you shot it…"

"Oh, I was just having a hot flash, and you wandered into my sights. It's only rock salt, crybaby. See?" And he

shot me in the face. I guess I had it coming.

The geek(s) who tossed my office dropped an alligator bag and a pretty credible rubber Mundy street-face in the doorway. I picked up the bag and fed it some toothpaste until it relaxed its toothy jaws and let me dig out the loot from my office. My keys, a bottle of talcum powder, and three bottles of milk, all broken. But they hadn't just raided my stash. Adding gardenias to the heady aroma of spilled milk, was the letter from the Centinelas. I pocketed it and waved to a squad of scowling Screws who rolled by in their spotless white uniforms.

My face stung so bad I cried more than bled, but I had to make nice with Bossy.

Nature hates a vacuum, but it hates sitting around alone on Saturday night even more than you probably do. (What night is it, out there, anyway? What're you doing tonight, going out to spend time with girls? There's girls there, right? You can touch one, and not draw back a bloody stump? And you're staying home with this rag? Wow, it must be the bee's knees to be you, Casanova.)

I gave him a cigarette and scratched behind his horns. Thanks to the 'mones, they came in faster every time he sawed them off, so he'd just given up. "So how about floating me a couple ounces until payday, baby? It's not just for me… I need to bake a cake."

Bossy recoiled from me like I was made out of pus and old rubbers. "You maybe ought to step up the steroids, Floyd. You smell like a girl."

One of my eyes was closed over from the rock salt, but I could read the letter well enough. Which was weird, because I couldn't read it before.

I could read money, street signs and addresses and such just fine, college queer. I could've asked Ethel to read it if she wasn't such an idiot and a stoolpigeon, that I had to poke out all her spying eyes. So I'd just puzzled out the time and place for the meet, and left the couriered letter on my desk. And got collared by the nuns, which is where you came in.

In elegant handwritten purple script, the letter read:

Dear Detective Mundy,

Please excuse this unorthodox entreaty, but obviously, I could not call upon you in person, and we have little faith in the discretion of telephone switchboard matrons. But the urgency of our predicament demands forthright assistance that we are quite unable to procure, on our side of the Wall.

My wife and I recently had a baby. No need for congratulations, and please allow us to rely upon your utmost confidence. For the circumstances surrounding our joyous arrival are such that we must needs leave the City at once. A mutual acquaintance of ours recommended you as someone who could be trusted around women, and a steady hand in a crisis. We have saved a small fortune in ration coupons and even some cash, which we are willing to trade for conduct out of the city limits. It is direly urgent that we be out of Sisterville before the next Election Day. Please forgive me for not elaborating further, but I will explain everything if you will only meet me tomorrow at the southern rookery in Baptismal Park today at 3PM. I assure you that, given the changes approaching, you will not regret our rendezvous, or taking up our cause.

Mrs. C

The big words and fruity grammar made my head hurt, but I still knew what they meant. That made my head hurt even worse.

But I worked on cases, not causes.

And right now, I had other work to do.

As I greased a rusty tin pan with some edible Astro-Glide I found under my desk, my phone rang. My housekeeper told me the phone was ringing.

"So answer it," I said.

"It's not for me."

"What the hell's eating you, anyway?"

"If you don't know, then I guess it's nothing. The stove is on fire. Do you want me to put it out, or would you rather I answer the phone?"

"Mundy," I snapped at the phone.

"What did you find out about the Centinela case?" The husky voice was all business, but a perverse part of me wanted to let the place burn down and go live in that throat.

"I found out I should've been asking you about it, since you sent them to me."

"I did no such thing! If the Centinelas used my name in recruiting you, though, why didn't you say so, when I picked you up?"

"I wasn't sure if I could trust you," I snapped, "and I'm twice as not sure, now!"

"You idiot! If nothing else about what you saw got through that cracked semen-jug you use for a head, it's that you can't trust anyone but me!"

"Isn't that just like a dame! Why can't you just tell me the score?"

"I would if I could… if I knew, but I can't see your side of the Wall."

"Nobody's selling black market she-babies, if that's your angle. Everybody's abuzz over Election Day."

"Another power-struggle in the monkey-house. Nothing ever changes over there, no matter who's in charge."

"Not this time. The Bulls are fixing to overturn prohibition."

"Dear Lord. It's happening, then."

"What's happening? Sister, nobody's thirsty over here, as it is. Like you said, nothing ever changes…"

She sighed so deeply I could hear her habit strain against her bosom.

"You don't have any proof a man was involved in those murders. You just want to believe you're better than us."

"Oh, we've got man troubles, alright. A woman was robbed near the terminal, last night. By a man."

"Oh, that's terrible. What did he get from her?"

"That's the sickening part. He milked her."

"Do tell. Sounds like some kind of pervert. I hope you catch him…"

"Oh, we will. The mother—"

"Yeah? What abut her?"

"She works the central bakery."

Ding! went the bell.

"Your cake is done." She hung up.

Sister Mildred was trying to tell me something, but in her inimitable feminine fashion, she either gave me too much credit for sense, or none at all.

I was sitting on a stockpile of bombshells: Boystown was going to be wet for the first time since the Pink Wars; someone was killing women or making them kill each other, and abducting their babies; and she knew

about the milk. Sister Mildred knew damned well that I'd get into trouble left to my own devices in Sisterville, so she had to have wanted me to steal the milk.

The only thing that didn't add up was that, if any of it were true, there weren't nearly enough dead bodies.

I had to get over the Wall to Sisterville. I shaved and showered, busted out my spare revolver, a blackjack and an extra pack of smokes, frosted my angel food cake and hit the streets.

I've found that if you have a good feeling like somebody's looking over your shoulder, it's best to run before it, and not look too deeply, if at all. If you do, you start running into troubles. Looking for answers, you just end up with more questions.

I had this friend, who used to think he saw God. Not one of those cheap new Boystown gods, but The God. It usually came to him when drunk, but sometimes, when he needed answers or someone to confess to, the face would simply be there, looking down from over the horizon, and it made him feel better.

Until one day, when, for totally unrelated, totally normal reasons, he talked to a shrink about some things, and the triviality of regularly seeing God came up.

The shrink was very understanding. He knew all about this phenomenon, he said. He took out a selection of wallpaper samples from the orphanages and martial Kriegergartens, and flipped through them until he came to a cheerful yellow depiction of the sun as a wise man with a beard of wavy rays that were also particles.

This should have given my friend

some closure, but instead, it made a mockery of everything he thought was real. He snapped and threw the shrink out the window, then torched the office.

He had perfect certainty, until he tried to find out the truth. It's all true, too, except for the first part. I don't have any friends.

I pegged two tails getting onto the red-eye trolley in front of the Arbuckle Arms. A plainclothes Screw hopped on and clung to the outside rail, even though there were plenty of seats. A Stutz Bearcat with twin-barrel Gatling turret cruised half a block back, like a picky john shopping for a twist. I looked out the window, reading the signs, and wondered who put all those fucking words on them. Maybe two or three people in my whole building could read anything longer than a ration coupon, but nobody needed to. Colors and noises and smells told you everything you needed to know, and if you couldn't smell trouble, the world was better off without you.

A milk truck had crashed into a cement mixer at the Octopus, the eight-way intersection at the center of Boystown. The cement mixer's driver was on a stretcher, but two ambulance companies were fighting over his body with crowbars and straight razors, and a big crowd had gathered to watch and gamble on the outcome.

The trolley ground to a stop in a puddle of milk. I jumped off and the Screw followed with his face hidden behind a newspaper. He stepped on an alley cat and slid face-first into the frothy white milk, and was fighting off cats as I jumped back on.

The Bearcat skidded through the intersection and mowed down two stretcher jockeys, but gamely came after us, all pretense of secrecy ditched.

I jumped off at the Crematorium Park terminal and ran up the steps to brace the nearest harness bull like a long-lost Dutch uncle.

A cagey geezer with salt and pepper muttonchops, the bull saw the Bearcat snarling in the trolley turnaround and swung his club at my head. "Don't wipe your troubles off on me, bo. I got enough of my own."

"Arrest me," I begged, "you fucking faggot."

"Get away from me, damn you! I'm an old man—"

The Bearcat pulled up to the curb with four roosters in it. I didn't recognize any of them. They were kids fresh out of the Army, who'd have to go piggyback to piss over a curb. The one who cranked the Gatling down on me stood on a pile of phone books. A stretcher jockey splayed broken and bleeding across the Bearcat's fanged front fender, wailing like a siren.

"Call a cop." I kicked the bull an uppercut that detached his kneecap and sent him spilling into my arms.

"Get in the sled, bright boy. Boss wants to see you." The driver's voice cracked. He smoked two cigars at once.

"Take the dicks out of your mouth when you're addressing your betters, freckles."

I can see why the gangs use any prepubescent kids they can get. They're utterly fearless, because short of cutting their heads off, you just can't kill the little fuckers. But they couldn't follow water out of a faucet without getting crossed up and shooting somebody.

Freckles was on the cusp of puberty. He had a lot to learn, but he was smarter than the others, who opened up on me and my arresting officer.

Two of them pulled out .38s and hit the bull in the back. I almost dropped my dancing partner when the Gatling opened up, but it immediately kicked free of the kid's little hands and slashed the revolving doors of the terminal and chewed up the crematorium's sooty tile façade.

I dropped under my cop and lay prone as the bulls and a gang of concerned citizens came out of the terminal shooting. The Bearcat fishtailed out of the turnaround with all guns blazing.

The bulls chased them down the street, then barked and fired their tommy guns into the sky. Drunk as poets, and none too concerned about Election Day. By the time they noticed their fallen comrade, I'd gotten out from under him and into the terminal washroom.

Not a lot of people know about the restrooms in the terminal, but there's a good reason stewbums camp out in the stalls and go berserk punching the walls. On the other side of the wall is a ladies' restroom. From the duct above the last stall, an agile, athletic fellow could easily climb the vertical shaft, negotiate the huge fan, and drop down the twin shaft into the adjoining ladies' room.

I could've kicked myself for not hiring an agile, athletic fellow to do it for me. I tore the seat out of my pants and broke the heel off a shoe climbing the duct, and the fan sucked off my hat. I got a good whiff of that maddening lady-piss perfume and lost my footing coming down and fell through the heavy steel grate into the first stall in the ladies' restroom.

Luckily, the stall was not occu-

pied. I landed elbow first on the seat and shattered the heavy porcelain bowl with my head.

Someone was knocking on the stall when I woke up. I lay in a puddle of piss and stinky cotton lobsters.

I quickly changed into my disguise, turned my creeper coat inside out, jabbed some plugs in my nose, glued on my street face and gave myself a shot of estrogen.

I said it before, and I'll say it again. I like dames. Lots of guys do. But no matter how I feel about them in general, when I get around one, I feel the bug in my blood. I want to crack their heads open on the curb and fingerpaint swastikas with their brains. I want to chicken-fry their tits in a skillet and fuck their smelly fish-holes with fireworks. And it feels like the only honest, natural feeling I've ever had in my whole rotten life.

The smell of them makes me want to do it, the sound of their voices and the thought of touching their soft, silky skin. And because I like them, I hate them even more for being what they are and knowing I'll never, ever get to have them.

If I take a shot and work very hard to control my feelings, I can go among them for a while, but I can't stick around. If enough of them got wind of me, they'd kill me in the street.

4. BOYS GO TO JUPITER...

I hopped the turnstile (no mean feat in a nun's habit) and made the Spinsterville purple trolley. The ogress matron at the checkpoint showed me her fangs, but stamped my voucher. My fake ID rooked me as Sister Ursula Leberkaessig, a nurse who worked with the invalids at Our Lady of Euthanasia. Nobody looked twice at my disguise, unless they were looking for ideas for a Halloween costume. My nose had warts with wiry white hairs with more warts on the ends.

I had to remind myself to walk like a woman, but booby-traps lay on all sides, though less obvious than in Boystown. The little differences could catch you up. All the lights had dimmer dials instead of knife switches, the doors had latches instead of knobs. And everywhere, there were plots and hanging pots of daffodils and zinnias and brushed-steel colored roses that everyone stopped to smell, as if to get directions or the latest news from their perfume.

I moved quick and kept it simple, and I was better at it than some of my fellow pedestrians. A skinny number in a long skirt with a full veil curtain hanging down from her hat brim was having trouble with her shoes. They seemed to be full of broken glass. As I passed, I caught a whiff of her perfume: ether and flop sweat.

"Jism and snails, and puppy-dog tails," I hissed as I passed.

The stumblebum tripped on his trailing hem and barked, "Blow it out your axe-wound, sister-licker!" in a voice higher than a piccolo, but hardly feminine. His falsetto went up three more octaves when he spun around and drew back his fist to punch a nun in front of witnesses. I gave him the Evil Eye sign and toddled off on my errands.

First, I went to the hospital. The morgue was downstairs, and I lucked into Doc Livermint holding down the front desk.

I slipped him a sheaf of ration cou-pons and peeled back to corner of my mask. "I need to see those girls again, Doc."

"Holy crow, dick, you're bucking for the joy buzzer. If you wanted sou-venirs, you should'a just called…"

I had to pass him a flask of apple-jack and my favorite Tijuana Bible (Popeye and Amos & Andy in "A Pulled-Pork Sammich (w/ Extra Olive Oyl)") before he ushered me into the refrigerated room. "They'd cut off my stub, if they knew—"

"They'd cut off your head, if they knew half of what was plugging it. Did the Centinelas get cut open, yet?"

Livermint led me into a dim room with a bunch of drawers, and locked the door behind us. He hauled open a drawer and then another. The sheets were tacky with seepage. "Nobody's supposed to touch 'em… orders from the top. Thought you was here about the others…"

"What others?" I asked, but I had a good idea.

I stroked their cold faces with a dab of hormone corrective cream from the coroner's shelf.

Wildy, the one with the knife and needles in her bounteous bosom, sprouted thin little black whiskers on her chin. I risked a peek downstairs and clucked my tongue. What a world. The lengths some people will go, to live in sin.

"Change the name on this one from Ms. Centinela to John Doe Tucker."

Livermint almost swallowed his dentures. "I don't know how that got by the nuns."

"They didn't want anybody to know." I looked at the other drawer. Even worse was her partner, the fat one. She wasn't so fat, anymore, but her belly slumped like a deflated medicine ball. I put two and two together, and almost lost my lunch. "Breeders. No autopsy, but they wasted no time vacuuming out her gonch." I pinched her buttocks a few times and found no blood in the corpse. I pinched a few more times, to be sure.

I checked the other drawers. Over a dozen of them had fresh nametags. "I bet you another Bible, about half these broads are smuggling plums."

However they got together, the Centinelas were freaks—a heterosexual couple who hadn't killed each other right away. I'd seen enough antique stag films to piece together what must've happened next. They got by undercover long enough to conceive a brat, but then they either succumbed to the curse of the birds and the bees, or somebody fixed it up so it'd look like they did.

That somebody had clipped them and snatched the kid before the nuns could do it must've really chafed their chastity belts.

Livermint wistfully cupped his truncated junk. "If men and women can live together, then we've all been sold a bill of goods…"

"Yeah, it's a shame they got bumped off before somebody could bottle it and sell it." A wild hair up my ass made me give Livermint the Centinelas' pillcase. "See if you can find out what these are without eating all of 'em, will you, Doc?"

Livermint wouldn't let me use his phone, so I found a booth in the hospital lobby. Sister Mildred was out, but her novice offered to take a message. "Tell her to meet her sister at the Anais Arms."

Getting into the Anais Arms a second time was tough. I picked the lock on the service entrance, shucked my dirty habit and peeled off my street face. The nuns had all gone, and a matron was back on her post in the lobby, so I had to scale the courtyard wall to the fifth floor window that I'd opened on my first visit. But the shutters were down.

I pressed my face to the steel and shouted, "Special Delivery for Apartment 813!"

"Go away!" The housekeeper sobbed. Deep shock, in my opinion, only renders robot dames hotter. "My residents are gone! I'm… a crime scene!"

"Maybe that's why somebody ordered all these flowers…"

"Flowers, you say? But surely you must have the wrong apartment—"

The shutters clanged open. I heaved myself into the darkened living room and took in the air for a few minutes before I realized I wasn't alone.

"You're no florist! Help! A man! A may-an! Intru—"

I pulled her intercom plug before she could sound the alarm.

She'd tried to clean up the mess the nuns left, but the red snow angels smeared into the dining room rug still looked like big black butterflies in the dim light from the open window.

I pulled out my noseplugs and sampled the dank, close air. Under the biting reek of ammonia and cleanser, I could still smell a faint trace of male musk, mingled with cheap gardenia perfume. The erstwhile Wildy Centinela wasn't a eunuch, so he'd have to have kept a stash of premium hormone suppressors, unless he was some kind of mutant. And if there was a fifth column of breeders hiding in Sisterville, they'd have some means of communicating, sharing resources… but they couldn't have been that organized, if they came to me for help.

The kitchen was a bust. The food had all spoiled and the housekeeper dumped it down the trash chute. I tried to remember if I'd seen the blender on the counter before. Somebody had tried to grind up a chicken and banana malted, but had burned out the motor, liquefying all those tiny little bones.

I went for the bathroom. I pushed the door open and stepped in a puddle. The toilet was backed up. The medicine cabinet was open and empty. The room glowed orange from the coils of the space heater perched on the sink. The open door tugged the heater's cord taut and jerked it off, into the puddle I was standing in.

I watched it all happen. I didn't know all that much about how electricity works, but something told me it wasn't going to end well.

The heater shorted out. Lightning shot through me, and never found the way out. My brain popped off the top of my skull like a lobster trying to escape a boiling pot.

I came to clinging to the hallway rug. My hands twisted into smoking claws. My shoes were on fire. Angels floated overhead, little chubby cherubs pissing in my face. I slapped myself until they disappeared. All but one adorable little angel, who was going through my coat pockets.

"Buzz off!" I tossed the cherubic pickpocket down the hall and tried to put my shoes out.

A shadowy figure about the size of a puppy watched me from the narrow hallway leading back to the bedroom. It might have been shadowing me all along. It was doing something to the wall, crouched into a little ball I would never have noticed, but for the tiny green glint of light off its goggles.

Slowly, I reached my hand down the far side of me, to my gun. The shadow pried the grate off the central heating duct and climbed into it.

Still woozy from the electrocution, I crawled over to the duct and jammed my hand into it. "Gotcha, ya little bastard…"

A mousetrap snapped shut on each finger.

Over my screams, I heard the duct grate in the kitchen pop off and the pitter-patter of little feet circling around behind me.

I'd have to put my gun down to get the mousetraps off. The dark figure sprang into the room and came at me. As it tottered into the plane of daylight from the window, I brought my gun up, but my finger never found the trigger.

It was a baby. Maybe two-foot-three in knitted booties, and wearing a badly recycled diaper.

I held out a bottle of Bossy's best. "Baby want a bottle?"

"Nuts to you, fuckface," she gurgled, then flung something in my face. I closed my eyes and felt tiny things bounce off me—candy, peanuts, pills—

French ticklers.

When they struck my sweat-dampened face, they erupted. They exploded all around me, a few grams of hydrophilic foam rubber under incredible pressure in tiny capsules, but instantly they became life-size synthetic harlots whose grabby claws were hardly factory spec. They could gut a man, and he wouldn't know it until he tried to eat lunch.

The pint-sized intruder skirted around my one-man orgy and dove out the open window. I struggled and kicked, but it was like wrestling Jell-O. They wriggled and flowed over me like eels. With all my might, I got my head turned to look out the window as my assailant slipped away into the sunrise on the wings of a stork.

I was still fit to be tied when I heard a sharp tongue clucking disapprovingly from the open front door. Sister Mildred drew her razor-sharp ruler and chopped the French ticklers off me. "I have to hand it to you, Ursula. You always know how to make it worse."

5. DIAL M FOR MILCHBIER

Sister Mildred helped me out with the ticklers and mousetraps, but she wasn't nice about it. "You could've told me the Centinelas were breeders."

Her sharp sigh almost blew up her veil. "I wasn't sure I could trust you," she said. "And I'm twice as not sure, now." She sat down and pulled off a glove, and added, "You see now, how complicated this is."

"You don't know the half of it. The Centinelas didn't kill each other, and they weren't offed by their own natural baby."

"The Centinelas did kill each other. But somebody poisoned them. They were both dosed with a common testosterone booster called Bulldog Elixir."

"I've heard of it. Pit fighters use it. A snort of that would put hair on a jellyfish's chest. The killer was crafty: setting booby traps, poisoning. You know what that means."

She turned away, but every shroud-ed inch of her said she knew what I was going to say. She just waited for me to say it.

"The baby that tried to clip me was a girl."

"You don't say."

"It gets worse. That diaper I found in the trash last night was a boy's diaper. That's why I thought it smelled good. And if you sift out the contents of that blender, I think you'll find the missing baby boy. The little minx was a cannibal, Millie."

Sister Mildred regarded me with new eyes. "Like you men don't eat each other... I thought you'd figured out that part, at least."

"You know, maybe I did. The milk you're giving your girl babies... it's not just milk, is it?"

"It's just mother's milk, Floyd. Our babies still come out of the vats, but we bond them with mothers who breastfeed them through their first year. They get everything they need to survive... antibodies, proteins..."

"And everything their mothers know. That's why you dames are always so far ahead. You could do the same with the boys, but you don't... or do you? What're you feeding them?"

"I don't know, Floyd, but things are about to change on both sides of the Wall."

"And you dragged me into it why?"

"I thought you'd know something... I kind of hoped the Screws were behind it."

"I wouldn't know if they were. No, somebody with brains is making these plays."

"The Spinsters—you don't even know about them, do you? They've stopped every serious attempt to find a cure for the Curse, and now... but

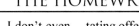

this is way over my head. I don't even know how far up it goes. Someone in the hatchery—"

"It must go to the top, at least. My little angel got away on a stork." I started to light a cig but caught a warning roll of her eyes and instead reached out to take her naked hand. "I need your help, Millie."

She didn't slap me or snatch it away. She let me touch her. I felt the heat of her skin, the breakable strength of a bird's wing. She looked at me. "No man gets into the hatchery."

"But you will," said a steely voice from behind us. I felt a jolt of shock shoot through Sister Mildred before she took her hand away and stood up.

A pair of valkyries stood in the doorway with swords drawn. The older, uglier one held a joy buzzer in her mailed fist. "You're coming with us."

"No need to use force, ladies," I said, but they pressed the stud anyway.

Sister Mildred leapt to my defense, shouting, "No!" Joy buzzers only work on male brains, so they clubbed her down with the butts of their swords.

I tried to stop them, but I was having twenty orgasms per second, and couldn't be bothered.

It was a lot more pleasant than getting electrocuted in the bathroom, but it took me a lot longer to wake up. Sometime during transit, I bit the tip of my tongue off, and my shorts were like flypaper. It honestly wasn't as much fun as it sounds. After the fiftieth jolt, it starts to hurt, and you forget to breathe. Those of you who've experienced seizures from huffing industrial solvents will know what I'm talking about. I'm sure the Sisters would have come up with a less enjoyable way of incapaci-

tating offensive menfolk, but the sexual response variation makes it possible to zap all the men in a room and leave the ladies standing.

I woke up in a wheelchair in a big glass solarium. I was parked facing a window. The sunset turned the sister city's garden rooftops to purple flames. I was no civic planner, but it seemed like the women's city was not just cleaner and safer, but much more densely inhabited. Men took pride in dodging or lying to the census, but there couldn't be more than fifty thousand of us. How many women were there?

The Wall did not quite hide Boystown, but a pall of smoke did: foundries and factories and refineries and crematoriums, and the gray fingers of arson and trash fires.

A horse-faced nurse in a white wimple kicked my brakes and tried to help me remove my "boxing glove," until she realized I wasn't wearing one. My left hand was a swollen purple sack of fractures from the mousetraps. As cold as she was, she wasn't much of a nurse. Her eyes wandered somewhere over my shoulder as she absently pricked the arm of my wheelchair with a syringe and pumped something into it.

She wheeled me through a series of frosted glass doors that opened by themselves. "Mother Superior will see you now."

The last door opened, and I screamed and tried to leap backwards out of my chair.

The big office had a big impressive desk and big oil paintings on the green-veined marble walls and a stunning stained glass ceiling. But it had no floor.

I looked down through empty

space at a gigantic ant farm. Little white worker ants shuttled tiny eggs around in an endless nest. It was the factory floor of the central hatchery, twenty stories below. I couldn't move, or I would've fallen out of my chair onto the flawless glass floor. The nurse pushed me into the center of the room.

"I love to spy on guests, the first time they see my office," said a reedy, echoing voice. "Forgive an old woman's foolishness, but it is rather impressive, isn't it?"

I looked around for the speaker. I saw a flash of carrot-hued hair bobbing behind the enormous desk and heard a chair squeal on the tempered glass floor. I looked around again, and yet again, but saw no Valkyries or nuns, no cameras or microphones. We were alone. That scared me almost as much as the hundreds of feet of hungry empty space between my ruined shoes.

"I am the Mother Superior of the Central Hatchery, but to be quite frank, I've never been too comfortable with the religious trappings of my office. Dr. Regina Barkdoll, at your service."

She wasn't wearing a veil. I wondered if it'd be bad manners to ask her to put one on. She was as tall as me, if I didn't get up (which I still couldn't). Her bright orange hair was pulled back in a severe bun that maybe added to the quizzical arch of her eyebrows. Her eyes were bright, bobbing green tropical fish swimming up against the convex walls of her goo-goo goggles. Thin lips parted in an animated, avid smile that should've got my blood flooding south. I hadn't seen a live dame's naked face in a month of Sundays, but I'd entertained dirtier thoughts while looking at Bossy McGee.

She wore a white dress that clung to her boyish figure and let me know exactly how little I was missing. If sexual attraction was the Curse, then this homely broad was the cure.

"Please forgive my lax manners, Mr. Mundy, but we so rarely get male guests… I'm quite at sea as to how to be a proper host. Would you care for some refreshment?"

I would rather have had some unguent and splints for my mangled hand, but I nodded dreamily. I'd expected a lot worse treatment, and was quite content to let the Mother Superior drop the other shoe on her own time.

Dr. Barkdoll tweaked a brooch at her throat. "Sister Hortense, bring Mr. Mundy a frosty mug of our Milchbier, please." She hopped from one foot to the other on the glass like a fidgety kid, making me nervous. "So, I must say, this is rather exciting."

"What is?"

"Why, meeting you, Mr. Mundy! It's not every day I get to meet a hardened alpha male, a cold-blooded killer. You survived prison."

I wondered if she laid out the same line of bull for Nimrod today, but all I could smell in the office was myself, and her. "I took the easy way out. I was sentenced to eighteen months, but I opted to get raped eighteen times, instead."

Her laugh was like a hen strapped into a vibrating belt machine. She thought I was joking. "Yes, you are quite a celebrity in Boystown, I understand. You were the one who uncovered the Reform Party's culpability in the Mandrake plague, weren't you?"

"Yes, I'm afraid so, ma'am. That's why I went to jail."

"Were you a private detective at the time?"

"No, ma'am. I was a Screw."

"I beg your pardon?"

"The uh, Reform Party Police. I was a sergeant, and uh, I didn't have a whole lot of choice in the matter… I was, uh… one of the infected."

She clapped her hands. "You carried an infantoma to term? That's simply marvelous. I hope we have your seed on file, Mr. Mundy."

"I'm uh, a regular donor…"

"Excellent."

Sister Hortense trotted in and bowed before me with a silver tray balanced on her hand. I'd expected some sort of piss-bitter tea or at most a syrupy fruit cordial in a wee glass, but instead, I got a frosty mug of what looked like a malted milkshake. Foamy froth sloshed over the rim and scooted down the icy glass to pool on the tray. I took it and sucked the head off the mug as Sister Horseface clopped out and shut the door.

Holy fucking shit! Alcohol! I felt the same instant glow of a good stout beer, but with the creamy undercurrent of mother's milk. "I never thought…"

"Oh, Mr. Mundy, we're not so prudish as you might imagine, over here. We enjoy a judicious tipple now and again, but this is a special brew, commissioned exclusively for our brothers and cousins in Boystown. We've always dedicated our best efforts to being good neighbors and helpmeets to our fraternal counterparts. We thought that our relations had grown to such a point that we could offer some small token of our esteem, and faith in their maturity. As it's likely that Prohibition will be repealed, we thought we'd help you all to celebrate."

This case was getting more wrinkles than my granddad's nut-sack.

"Sure, you just don't approve of them trying to live together."

"Ha! Quite impossible, as bloody history and recent events have proven. But just as the Dark Ages cleared the slate for a new vision of society, so did the gender plagues force humanity to take charge of its own reproductive future, indeed its evolutionary future! Nothing a man can break, that a woman can't fix, and look at us now! True equality, with each sex liberated to pursue its own fulfillment…"

"I meant, uh… I didn't think you could make beer with milk…"

"Oh, there were some obstacles, but we discovered a yeast that can ferment lactose… Kluyveromyces fragilis yields a less sweet, but robust, flavorful beer similar to koumiss, the drink of the Turkish Steppe peoples, though that was made from mare's milk."

"And what sort of, uh, milk is this stuff made out of?"

"Do you like it?"

It tasted kind of funny, but I'd already finished it. I stifled a belch, almost dropped the mug trying to set it on the floor. "It's swell, but…"

Skipping around my chair, Barkdoll clapped her hands and said, "Well, I suppose you know I have a number of questions for you, as I imagine you likewise have for us. There's no reason why we can't all cooperate." She steepled her fingers and pointed her long nose at me.

"I'll bite… where's Millie Crawghast?"

Disappointment clouded her features. She wore a lot of pale foundation makeup that hid her age, but some of it cracked and crumbled from the corners of her mouth. I didn't know how to play her game as well as she'd hoped. "Sister Mildred's decision to bring you into this affair was rather unfortunate, as it was an internal sorority matter. Tragically, even the fairer sex is not immune to occasional outbursts of violence."

"I'm a big boy, Mother. I don't like being spoon fed crap. Somebody's offing natural breeding couples in Sisterville. Killing men, which makes it our business. Sister Mildred—"

"—Is a devoted protector of our city, but she has rather a blinkered perception of the larger issues in play." She leaned in close. Something stronger than beer seeped out of the cracks in her makeup. "Now, these 'natural' couples of yours... how are they natural? Nature endowed humanity with the ability to perfect its own reproduction, so why would regressing to bestial rutting to roll the dice on every attribute of one's offspring be any kind of desirable development? "

"So everybody's better off with them dead. I figured you'd feel that way, since your storks delivered the assassins."

Her head whipped around so fast, a tuft of her orange hair sprang out of captivity. "What kind of nonsense is this?"

"Baby girls make great killers, if you give them the muscle and nerve tonics boy-soldiers get. I almost caught a pair of them looting my office. With unseen muscle like that, a girl could pick the next Mayor of Boystown, and rule both sides of the city."

She wrung her little white hands like she was snapping rabbits' necks. "Only a man could ascribe such base motives to a woman, but you never understood us, did you? No, you've tried to dominate, exterminate and replace us, but we've forgiven all that. No, to try to rule or wipe out mankind would be just what a man would do. We're offering you forgiveness, and a chance to know real peace, and rid the world of all its evils in one fell swoop." She pointed at my empty mug. "Would you care for another?"

I tried to shake my head, but nodded instead. I don't remember Sister Hortense coming in, but my mug was full when I picked it up. I asked her if I could smoke.

"I don't mind, if I could steal one from you." She winked conspiratorially. "They don't want us to smoke in here, but if you never get to go outside..."

I offered her one and lit it, then my own. It tasted funny, but maybe it was the beer milkshake curdling on my palate. It tasted like period-blood.

"I can't take credit for everything we've done... It falls to the Mother Superior to oversee the next generation of leaders and scientists who will usher our sorority into the future. If my eggs and milk transmitted my distilled ambitions, my frustrations, and yes, my fears, to some of our infant sisters, than I suppose I am ultimately to blame."

"They do have your lousy eyesight. Maybe you could let the next generation figure things out for themselves..."

She took a huge hit off the cigarette, hacked and coughed and threw up, choked it back and swallowed it. "God, I miss these. What brand is it?"

I looked at the handful of blurry packs in my handful of hands. I didn't recognize any of them. That fucking little she-devil who stole my French ticklers, must've also replaced my cigarettes.

I put out the cigarette in my beer

and gently set the glass down. If I looked right at my feet, I could make them move. Louder than I meant to, I said, "You've been talking in circles, lady, an' I'm sick of it—" My speech slurred.

Barkdoll leaned on me and took out another cigarette. She didn't light it. She just sniffed it once and bit into it. "You don't even know how little time you have left, Mr. Floyd Mundy. You may as well show it to me."

Tobacco shreds stuck to her cold, dry white tongue as she licked my face.

"I don't suppose you want to see my license—"

"I like the way you fill out your clothes, Mr. Mundy." She plopped down on my lap. "I want to soak my head under your hose!"

Her bony hips dug into me like a rack of antlers. Those magnified eyes chomped at the glass like green piranha. Without blinking or taking a breath, she grabbed my manhood in a strangling grip, like the stick shift of a car with a broken clutch. "What's wrong with it? Make it erect!"

"I'm sorry, Doctor, really, I, uh... joy buzzer, you know, it, uh, it gets, you know, awfully sore—"

I wondered what the hell had come over me. I'd never touched a live woman until Mildred, except in self-defense, and here one was coming on to me, and I felt nothing. No urge to fuck or fight, and no chance to flee. But I didn't want to rip her open and stick my gizmo in her aorta, either. Was I cured?

"No, I see, I see how it is... Male arousal is threatened by powerlessness. You need to have some measure of control and freedom, to respond as a natural male. I understand that."

Stretching out one coltish leg in baggy white nylons, she kicked over my wheelchair. My hands flung up too late to shield my head. I skidded backwards under the chair on the crown of my skull.

Regina Barkdoll ripped her dress open and flung it over her desk. Underneath, a crenellated white bustier with control–top girdle and a merry widow made her look more dressed up than ever.

I popped up fit as a fiddle and ready for love. "You frigid little bitch, I'll give it to you—"

Wicked hope swam up in those eyes like someone threw fish food in her glasses. "Give me what, Mr. Mundy?"

"I'm going to..." The red wave crashed inside me and rolled back. I wiped a tear out of my eye. What the hell was wrong with me? "I can't go through with whatever you've got in mind, Mother Superior. It's just not professional, and anyway... I'm involved with someone..."

She kicked off one of her stiletto heels. It clocked me in the mouth, splitting my lip. "You're not in control of your emotions right now, Mr. Mundy. But you're a fool if you think you ever were. Tell me, Floyd. How much do you remember about your mother?"

"Wow, now you're talking my kind of pillow-talk. I didn't have a mother."

"All babies have a mother, even males. Of course it's not safe for living matrons to handle them, so we have mechanical wet nurses to monitor and feed and change them. Ugly cold machines, covered in wire mesh, that conducts mild electrical shocks when the babies misbehave."

All this talk of torturing babies

was getting her hot. She squatted on the glass and dragged her bony haunches across the glass like a dog with piles.

"But not all our boys were reared so harshly. No, we're making progress, finding new ways to grant a measure of mercy, more than we'd ever expect to get back from your kind.

"Yes, some of the milkmaids are covered in soft velvet upholstery and pleasantly scented to convey a loving, nurturing environment as a bedrock for a healthy, well-balanced, confident adult personality.

"We got bored with that rather quickly, so the next experiments—the first ones I supervised, right out of the nunnery—caused the warm fuzzy mother to deliver short sharp electrical shocks seemingly at random. The feeding child never knew why he was punished by his loving mother. But it created a strain of male personality that was almost immune to the hostility response from the Chastity Curse."

"Sounds like you came close to a cure."

"Yes, the virus had wormed its way into our genes, but the answer appeared to be in simply retooling somatic brain chemistry. It was all we could do to bury our results and move on. You see, we're not about to sacrifice the gains the Curse won for us. But even that failed experiment yielded some interesting side effects."

"Such as?"

"Why, you, Mr. Mundy! Your antisocial cynicism and obsessive capacity for wrecking social norms was inculcated into your personal gestalt from the day you were hatched, and it's paid great dividends. You turned on your own fellow reformers, and you've served us well, when you thought you served only yourself. Whatever did you think your life was for?"

She was closing in. My hands came up to protect me, but I didn't have it in me to hit her. Why was she doing this to me?

"Listen, Mother, I don't know what your game is, or what was in that beer—"

"My dear stupid boy, it's the cure we've been searching for, all these years."

"A cure? Hot damn, why didn't you say so?"

"It's not a cure for the Curse. It's a cure for masculinity."

She hit me. It felt good. Biting my tongue felt great. Punching my own face felt amazing. Even the heart attack I was having felt fucking great.

"Isn't that just like a man! Only good for one thing, and no good for it when you need it!" She reached out and grabbed my tie and yanked me off-balance so I fell into her fist. I crumbled to the floor. She pounced on me, her knees like spurs, her mouth spewing jungle hate when it was not nibbling my neck. "You make everything in the world so ugly that we have to reject it, and deny ourselves the pleasures of our birthright, and when you're finally forced onto an equal playing field, you curl up and play dead—"

Her padded, conical breasts shredded my shirt and crushed my windpipe. Cackling and gasping, hyperventilating, she whipped my belt off and lowered her pelvis onto me. Wiry pubic steel wool scoured my tender flesh, and something dripped on me.

This was my birthright, the thing for which I'd been made, but never dared dream of ever doing. I'm no virgin. I've banged plenty of things, and almost as many people. But if this was sex, I could see why some geek in a lab cooked up the Curse.

It was as if a single lock snapped, and all the animals in the zoo behind my tear-filled eyes escaped all at once.

"I said NO!" I slammed an elbow into her forehead and rolled away, trying to cover my nakedness before she came hobbling lopsidedly back on her lone stiletto heel.

I reached for my gun, but of course, it was gone. I tried to catch my breath, but my lungs were a soggy pair of used teabags. My head was swimming, the room was spinning, and when Dr. Barkdoll leapt on me again, shrieking like a boiled cat, I grabbed the only thing I could reach and hit her with it.

The white patent leather pump had no heft to it, but the six-inch heel broke off in her left eye. She tumbled onto me like a bag of knitting needles.

"Oh dear, what's come over me..." she moaned in my ear, lost. "What did you do to me, you disgusting man?"

"What'd I do to you? Now, hold on a minute—"

She rolled off me and turned away in a sad play at modesty. The heel's silver tip winked at me. "I don't even know myself, anymore... I, we, we only wanted to save the human race from mankind, and it seemed like such a splendid plan, but with so little time left, I guess I thought I'd earned one last fling..."

She cried. Every broken note from that heaving steel bosom circled over us like red vultures that ate each other rather than touch our spoiled meat. So lost and desolate, and the worst part was that she wasn't alone. She'd done great evil and planted the seed for even worse, but whose fault was it that she

was an ugly little weirdo, in the first place? If someone had been trying to perfect the sexless female, then they were to blame for everything that went wrong. She'd chucked a lifetime of virtue to plunge down the rabbit hole chasing a fatal folly she'd kept contained in vats and syringes all her life. And in the end, she'd thrown herself out there with a smile and plummeted down into that bottomless chasm of love, only to end up with me.

I put my unmangled hand on her trembling, stooped shoulder. "It's okay, lady... there's a lot of bad going around... but you already got my specimens and all, what would you need, you know, the rest of me for, anyway?"

"Oh, you still don't understand, do you, you poor, big idiot? Your children aren't men, not in the traditional sense. We've got gallons of spermatozoa to work with. You're all obsolete, don't you see? We could've just done the world a favor and wiped you out, but we wanted you to understand, we wanted to share with you all that you'd missed out on..."

She looked past me, at the empty beer mug. Sniffling, she asked, "You don't have another cigarette, do you?"

I'm kind of slow on the uptake, but I went from clueless to crazy as soon as I put it together. "What'd you feed me? Talk, you harpy!"

Mother Superior crawled to the foot of her enormous desk and tried in vain to reach her high chair. "If there's a man or a woman you do care about, I'd hope they're very understanding, because you're not going to be a man for very much longer. In fact, before Election Day is over, there won't be a man left in Boystown."

She handed me something she'd kept tucked in her girdle. My revolver. "At least you can do this part." She sagged like a tired windup toy.

But she was wrong. I wasn't good for anything, anymore. My gun wouldn't shoot. I checked the drum and found four bullets. But when I pulled the trigger, nothing happened. Safety was off, nothing obstructed the hammer or the barrel. The only thing it could be was simply ridiculous.

My children, she'd said something about my children. I ran for the nearest door and kicked it open. "I WANT TO SEE MY KIDS!"

And for my sins, I saw them.

They came out of the corners of the room, moving obscenely fast on all fours, some wearing saddles or pulling little wagons. All of them were boys.

They battled and frolicked and licked my hands in frantic love and pressed me with their paws and bade me scratch their notched and branded ears. All the animals that went extinct during the bad red-letter days of the Curse were back, and they all had plug-ugly Floyd Mundy mugs.

Some with tusks and horns trampled the unruly baby animals and herded them a respectful distance away from their test-tube pater familias. I tried to gather them to my weeping breasts and suckle them so they'd grow thumbs and forebrains and turn out better than they were wired to, or at least just like me.

No, maybe this was better. At least they'd have jobs.

It took me a long time to snap out of it. I sat at the bottom of a deep hole, feeling the gentle rain of people walking on my face.

Then again, they weren't so gentle.

They jumped up and down on my head and dumped the contents of their diapers on me. Really, a second later and I would've drowned.

I lay on the glass floor surrounded by redheaded baby girls and glowering, towering storks.

A baby girl climbed up into Mother Superior's lap. Humming a tuneless lullaby, the poor spinster cooed and cuddled the rosy-cheeked imp right up until it pushed the broken heel to the hilt in her mother's head.

Storks nipped me with their brass-shod beaks and raked me with taloned feet. Tiny pink hands with nails like carpet tacks raked my ankles. A baby girl with a hand-shaped bruise across her face scampered up to me and head-butted me in the crotch. "She was old and in the way. Thanks for acing her."

She held up a joy buzzer, big as a pie plate in her tiny pink titty-clutchers. She hit the button.

Nothing happened.

"Don't thank me..." I jumped, but not for the she-devil. I grabbed the legs of her stork. My gun was useless, but I could hit the floor with it.

It took three blows to crack the glass. A rippling fault like petrified lightning split the room in half. The babies leapt back into their slings around the storks' necks and I grabbed another one by its wattled throat just before the floor gave way.

My trusty stork pals flapped for all they were worth, but we were still falling. A few babies, dead Dr. Barkdoll and her very impressive desk plunged to the distant hatchery floor amid a hailstorm of shattered glass and fluttering white feathers.

Storks clawed and bit my hands and face, but I was too busy falling to do more than rip out some pinfeathers. Maybe ten feet above the copper cooling towers of an industrial baby-maker, they changed tactics, took hold of me and yanked me upward.

It took six of them to hoist me up and out a skylight over the rooftops of Sisterville. I heard sirens and saw Valkyries racing across the rooftops and shaking their mailed fists, but nothing could catch us.

6. ...TO GET MORE STUPIDER

The storks dumped me on the roof of a warehouse just over the wall in Boystown. They splattered me with shit as they flapped away. I hopped off the roof onto a delivery van, rolled off and stumbled down the street. I almost had enough birdshit on me to pass for a uniformed Screw from a distance.

I got as far as the next corner, when they started chasing me. The street did a rhumba under my feet. Windows cracked and shattered and signs swung on their chains.

How big was the guy they sent after me? He had two little guys steering him, in a hollow convertible skull where most guys hang a hat. It was a stooge, and the biggest I'd ever seen. The Bulls breed them by putting mercury and Bulldog Elixir in their milk, which does wonders for gigantism, but leaves them with chewing gum for brains. So they make midgets a foot tall to drive them around.

The stooge threw cars aside and palmed pedestrians by their heads and threw them to try to knock me down. I darted into traffic, sliding across the hood of a Packard stuffed with reporters in porkpies and pig-masks. Their flashbulbs blinded me, but their hoots and jeers gave me something to punch.

"Private peeper perv Mundy a spy for the skirts!"

"What a scoop! Smile for the cameras, Judy Iscariot!"

"Hey Floyd, who do you hope they'll get to rape you in prison, this time?"

I gouged the driver's eyes and booted him out into the street. The rest of the pigs jumped out as I floored it. The car shot forwards about ten feet and hit something solid. I reversed and hit something that grabbed my bumper and lifted the car right off its wheels.

The midgets squeaked at me to pull over. The wounded stooge screamed like an air raid siren and swung the Packard around over its head. The midgets pulled levers and threw switches and twiddled dials, but the stooge was out of control.

I thanked God we lived in a city that banned seatbelts. I kissed windshield and went through it and sailed into the air. I could see again... fat lot of good it did me.

I hit the side of a trolley and stuck to it. I drew my heater and told the conductor to step on it. He didn't have to be told twice. "You smell funny, mister," he said. "like tunafish."

The trolley slowed as it began to climb Dictionary Hill, but the conductor yanked on the lever until the trolley lurched along almost as fast as I could've walked. The stooge didn't come chasing after us. Instead, he got the bright idea to grab the trolley's power lines, and yanked on them like a leash. The electrical shock made lightning shoot out the top of his head and fried the two midgets. It tugged and kept tugging. The trolley squealed as its wheels spun useless in their tracks. Something snapped, and the trolley turned into a big dumb sled. At the bottom of the hill, the stooge waited for it with open arms and a boner like a barber pole.

Riders jumped out into traffic like ants out of a cake. I leapt out onto the roof of a hearse that charged up the hill so fast the coffins flopped out behind it in the street.

I jumped off at the next corner and tried to blend in, but the foot traffic was running to and from the accident with equal eagerness.

It was a cinch they'd be waiting for me at home, but I had nowhere else to go, and something was wrong with me. The joy buzzers and my gun could've been mechanical failures, but when that baby bopped me in the junk, it hadn't hurt nearly as much as it should've. I had a sinking suspicion about what was wrong. Call it intuition—

I stopped and leaned against a fence to catch my breath, when something grabbed my coat and tried to pull me through the chainlink mesh.

"Well, if it ain't the ol' yeller slit-lickin' dick!" Little fingers like ten-penny nails dug into my arm and ripped my creeper coat to shreds when I tore free of their grip.

I whirled around, but I knew who it was. The Rooster punks who tried to grab me and ended up pinched by the bulls. They climbed up the fence of the juvenile hall exercise yard, heedless of the voltage and the razorwire in their crazed hatred.

I backed up and gave them the finger. Freckles saluted me in kind, the way these kids always salute their elders, to flaunt their youthful invincibility. He bit into his extended middle finger at the second knuckle, chewed it off and spat it at me.

I picked the severed finger up and put it into the trigger guard of my revolver. It lit up and popped off a shot over the kids' heads.

The stooge came around the corner. None the worse for wear for dancing with the falling trolley, he shook his head until the charred midget skeletons tumbled out, and came shambling towards me, smashing one fist into an open palm.

Shooting the stooge in the face only made him uglier. He threw out his arms like a zombie, bawling like a big, lost baby, and kept coming.

I aimed lower and shot out his knees. He finally went down with a thud that upended trashcans, but kept crawling up to me on his big elbows and threw out a hand to crush me. I jumped aside. Something tumbled out of his huge paw and I picked it up.

It was a badge. A gold detective's shield, with my name on it.

The stooge wasn't answering any questions. Three different kinds of sirens carved up the night. I pocketed the badge and ran to catch up with a panel truck. The driver was a skinny gimp I knew I could yank out of the seat, but somehow, I didn't have it in me. I just ran alongside the truck with tears in my eyes until the gimp pulled over and let me jump on.

Through blubbering fits, I told him where I lived.

"Heard on the radio some peckerwood spy assassinated the Mother Superior. The slits're on red alert..."

Sure they were! I'd been set up to take the fall in a palace coup. "Did they get the guy?"

"Sure, they killed him all kinds of dead. They got a dragnet out for the nun who helped him pull it off, though. But they're saying it's war—"

I almost vomited with relief. Sister Mildred was still a step ahead of them. "So, what're the bulls gonna do about it? With Election Day only two days off—"

"That's what stinks! The Main Man decided to move the election up! The Bulls are rounding up the voters right now! Promising free beer and war with the slits, if they win. Boy, I hope they do..." The gimp took a whiff of me and a weird red glaze filled his eyes. "Say, you been rolling around in flowers, or something? You smell kind of... pretty."

I jumped off the truck at my corner and ran into the lobby.

Bossy McGee blinked me a warning as I ran by the desk, but I didn't savvy Morse code. "Couple fellows looking to rent your office, Floyd. Heard you was dead."

"Shut up, baby, I know it," I shouted back.

No wonder everyone was acting like I was dead. They were all reading tomorrow's paper.

"Did you tell them I was here?"

My housekeeper lied like anything. "I was overridden by the civic authorities. They installed a virus. I was raped, Floyd! They made me..."

The door flew open and hands dragged me over the threshold.

"Well," I said, trying to sound casual, "what's the rumpus, boys?"

Two mobs sat in my office, with my desk staked out as no man's land. I felt a momentary twinge of guilt that my office was a dump, but the bathroom was almost clean enough to piss in.

Three screws in their white uniforms held up the far wall—Inspector Onionson and two punchdrunk punks named Fufkin and Stencilton. Vince Cloaca, Nimrod and Lummox slouched in my chairs and spat tobacco on my floor. Cloaca was the Roosters' head enforcer. Just under two feet tall in lifts, he made up for it by riding a black Great Dane named Aloysius that came up to my shoulder holster. The dog had already pissed in every corner of the room, and now ambled over to lift his leg on my ruined shoes.

Cloaca lit a cigar and jabbed its cherry at my eyes. "We want to know what you were doing in Sisterville."

"I was out with the girls, getting my hair done. What did I miss?"

I hadn't noticed it before because they were manhandling me, but now they all looked like a big happy family. They were united in grief and terror.

I excused myself and went to the head.

What? Just because this is the first time I mentioned it, it's hardly the first time in this case I had to drop some chocolate or water some lawns. I took a long, satisfying leak into the reflecting pool at Baptismal Park just before Sister Mildred picked me up to protest the crying lack of proper urinals; I dropped a deuce in the broken toilet in the ladies' room; and I peed incessantly, throughout, in coffee cartons, trash chutes, gutters, alleyways and the banana cream pie trays at the Sisterville automat.

But this time was different. I reached into my union suit, and I fumbled. I groped. I probed. I went and got a flashlight. I could not find my dingus.

With my foot propped against the door, I sat down to piss. When I came back, they were still trying to set each other on fire with their eyes. "Everybody's still here. Wonderful. Anyone care to guess why?"

Onionson said, "Warden Orkney was found dead this morning. We still haven't heard where you were."

"Since you fellows aren't plugging each other, I take it you've realized your common interests lie in keeping Boystown dry."

They eyed each other as if they'd only just realized they weren't alone. "Nobody's printing wedding invitations, dick," Onionson snarled. "But we know what's what, and like the Bible says: the enemy of my enemy—"

"Lemme guess... this morning, your righteous leader slipped on his boyfriend in the bathtub and got a baby rattle in his eye. I hope your second-in-command can cook his own food."

Onionson's pockmarked cheeks turned plutonium purple. Vince Cloaca said, "We're all just concerned citizens who agree that maybe it ain't such a good idea for booze to be legal."

I wondered what he'd say to a tall mug of milk-beer. "You think of that all by yourself? You're riding pretty tall in the saddle tonight, Vince. Maybe somebody clipped your boss, too."

He went a whiter shade of olive and spat his cigar butt at me. "I had nothing to do with the Boss getting clipped. Maybe I oughta ask you about it."

"Well, it's heartwarming you boys want to take up honest politics, but my office is a lousy locale for a campaign headquarters. I don't see what you clowns want with me. Or why you're not asking that guy all these questions. He makes an even uglier dame than me, but he knows his way around Sis-

terville." I pointed at Nimrod Cox, who practically jumped out of his shoes and down my throat.

"That's a damned lie!"

"What'd they offer you, Nimrod? The booze rackets are about to dry up, so an enterprising thug has to find a new revenue stream, and just like that, they tapped you and tendered an offer. I won't make you explain, I got a good idea. It was a cure for the Curse, wasn't it?"

The other roosters inhaled all the cigar smoke right out of the air. Nimrod was still fighting to get to me, but his partner got him in a hammerlock.

Cloaca smiled wearily and said, "Let him talk."

"Somebody tipped you off to expect me at the Terminal last night, so you could cross me out before Election Day, when you'd help pave the way for Sisterville to take over the booze distribution, in return for doses of the cure, and probably some sporting girls for your harem?"

Cloaca pulled out a revolver longer than my arm. "When were you going to share these exciting developments with me, Nimrod?"

Cox feinted like he was fainting, then lurched out and grabbed me by the throat.

Iggy moved pretty fast, for a boy with no bones. He darted out from under the couch and drove a fork into Nimrod Cox's boot, nailing his foot to the floor. Cox shrieked like a dogcatcher's claxon and swatted at my freakish offspring. Iggy sprang at Nimrod and tore up his shirtfront. Mother-of-pearl buttons flew like teeth in a slaughterhouse. Cloaca and Lummox and the screws all took turns gasping in horror.

Under his shirt, Nimrod Cox wore

a training bra. He'd taken the socks out of it, but hadn't had time to change after coming back from his errand in Sisterville.

Everybody drew their heaters, but before they cleared leather, Aloysius stooped and snapped up the only fruit of my loins and swallowed him whole.

I cocked back a leg to kick the dog. Cloaca bashed me in the mouth with his gun barrel, then shot Nimrod in the face. "I've had it up to here with all this double-crossing! Aloysius, put the bricks to him."

The dog stood upright and knocked me down with paws like clawed catcher's mitts. I tried to fend him off, but before I could cover my pooper, the dog was grinding his pipe against me.

Aloysius bit my neck and pinned me to the floor. Vince Cloaca hung over his dog's shoulder. "Who's behind this caper, flatfoot?"

"The dames!" I shouted again and again. "Playing all of us for saps! Babies–"

But nobody was listening. They were laughing too hard. And if I was watching some hump get sodomized by a Great Dane with a midget riding on his back, I probably would've joined right in. I felt something tear loose in my shorts, and something dropped down my trouser leg onto the floor. I took one look and hid my face. All my worst fears had come to pass.

Before anyone else saw it, Aloysius scarfed up my decaying dork and wolfed it down. I suppose that made us even, if you left out the canine rape I was still enduring. Cloaca was nose to nose with Onionson shouting while his dog raped me. I could only watch helplessly as a silhouette was cast against my frosted glass window… no mean

feat, since we were six stories up.

My frosted window said FLOYD MUNDY, PRIVATE INVESTIGATIONS.

Then it said FLO MU DY PR VAT IN EST GATOR. None of the guys in the room said anything. The gaping holes in their worsted wool tunics said plenty, but it was just busted plumbing talk.

On the fire escape, a tiny, adorable girl-baby held up something a lot bigger than a rattle.

Holy shit. Scissors.

It made a sound just like scissors snapping shut, which always struck me funny, because it was so much worse than a gun.

They clicked, and Inspector Onionson's head flew off like so much knockwurst. Click, and Aloysius was cloven neatly in half. A flurry of clicks, and Fufkin and Stencilton sluiced across the room in a pile nobody would ever be able to sort out. Lummox, neatly bisected from crown to crotch, hopped around until his two halves locked arms and grappled and tripped on my radiator and fell out the shattered window.

I lay prone on the floor under the Great Dane's hindquarters, which went on humping me for another couple minutes after everything else stopped breathing.

When I finally got up, the air was clear and still, but outside, I could hear the old familiar chorus of approaching sirens.

I rolled up Aloysius and Vince Cloaca in my office rug and stuffed Nimrod, Lummox and the screws into some old laundry bags. I changed into my dirtiest, sweatiest clothes from the hamper, with three pairs of soiled shorts to hide my secret shame.

I had an election to rig. But first, I had to dump a truckload of stiffs.

I found the Roosters' Studebaker parked behind my building. It took four trips to lug all the bodies downstairs, but I didn't have to worry about the law stopping me. Gunshots and sirens and tenement fires told me Boystown had its hands full.

I drove down to the canals and immediately tossed the rolled-up rug down the concrete embankment. It came open at once, splaying a yard sale of chopped chickenhawk parts to tumble into the sluggish green trickle below.

A longshoreman brayed at me from a passing tugboat. "Hey, blockhead, can't you smell the signs?"

They all said NO DUMPING in English and Odoranto, the language of coded urine. I could read them if pushed, but I dummied up and kept dumping.

I was kicking loose scraps down the slope into the canal when the flying squad roared in to surround me. A couple stooges grabbed me by the collar and dislocated my arms. "Hey Dogdick, I was just about to come around to see you guys about that job offer…"

Detective Doghart waded into the canal until his boots started to melt. He came back up spitting orders. "Awfulson, get a net and a meat truck for all these dead screws."

"I'm Offalsen, sir… he's Awfulson!"

"Nuts! And get this flatfoot a shower to get that whore-fish stink off him! He's got a date with the Main Man!"

7. GIRLS GO TO MARS

We're not savages.

We're a representative democracy; of the men, by the men and for the men. Anyone who's never been convicted of a crime and can pass a simple literacy test is eligible to vote in our elections. Out of about fifty thousand citizens, just over eight hundred are eligible to vote.

We have a robust two-party system. The Screws and the Bulls have each had their turns at the wheel, but from election to election, the Main Man is always the Main Man, until a bigger, badder model tosses him out of the ring and becomes the new Main Man.

The Main Man is too important to be chosen by the polls. He is the best of us: the finest specimen of manhood, selected at infancy and honed to perfection by Boystown's most ruthless trainers into an icon of our power. And he is our natural leader. He doesn't need to know how to read, or remember, or talk. When he is horny, we go to war. When he breaks his toys, we go to work to make new ones. When he makes a mess on the floor, we clean up the city. When he attacks his reflection in the mirror, we all go on a diet. The winning party takes charge of the Main Man's care, prepares the tests that divine his will, and interprets his actions before the public.

It's not a perfect system, but it works. He can't be corrupted. He'll never go mad with power. He gives us something to measure ourselves against, and always feel wanting.

We love him. He terrifies us. And it was only tonight, as I was hauled into his ring for the first time, that I wondered if it was really fate or dumb luck that left the pride of Boystown with nothing above his craggy eyebrows but thick, oily waves of autumnal auburn hair.

The bulls who picked me up had no use for the badge I flashed around. Doghart was too happy with all the stiffs in my wake to let me explain.

"If you yeggs turn this town wet, you'll all wind up sitting down to pee!"

"Brother, I know better than to argue with a killer, but you're wanted downtown."

Someone grabbed my legs and hoisted me out of the paddy wagon. I was carried on their shoulders like a football hero. "They're playing you like a fiddle, you saps! Don't drink the milk-beer—" They couldn't hear me.

I was carried down a long wood-paneled corridor lined with uniformed bulls. They were hell-bent on overturning Prohibition before Election Day started at midnight. That somebody had wiped out all their opposition only made them think God was on their side, too.

We passed through three separate cordons of guards, stooges and attack dogs. Boy-soldiers in horned kettle helmets gave me the raspberry and cracked me in the knees with their blunderbusses, but they threw wide the huge double doors to the innermost sanctum of the Hall of Justice.

Stuffed to the peanut galleries with lobbyists, solicitors, ambulance chasers, union goons, pimps, press gangs and police, city hall was about as decorous as a lion cage at feeding time. They stood on the desks and waved banners and sang fight songs, when they weren't just fighting. The cigar smoke was so thick you needed a shovel to cut it. My gracious escorts ushered me down an aisle to the apron in the center of the hall, and dropped me on my head.

I was still trying to turn myself around when Doghart and a sawed-off fireplug with mutton chops down to his elbows braced me and hustled me up the stairs to the open cage door.

"You're the pride of Boystown, Mundy! Sky's the limit, boy, if you can just get him to drink up…"

A big frosty mug was thrust into my hands and filled to the brim with creamy milk-beer. I grabbed it with my left and winced as my mangled fingers fumbled it.

The cage slammed shut behind me. The klieg lights blinded me. I blundered around the ring with the glass out in front of me. Something tripped me up—a barbell—and I fell to my knees to a roar of guffaws from the crowd. "Get up, you crumbum!"

He lay on a bench, pressing a bar with a V-12 engine at either end of it. His lats jutted out like bat wings from a chest the size of a dinner table. His handlebar moustache curled up like bedsprings when he took notice of his visitor. The smell took a while getting to his brain, but eventually, he sat up and cracked his knuckles.

I'd seen enough newsreels to know the standard procedure. The Main Man gets up and takes the proposal by the lapels and flings it around his cage like an empty food dish. If the guy survives a minute in the cage, the law is passed. Whatever idiot was supposed to go into the cage and try to offer the Main Man a beer, he wasn't stupid enough to go through with it, once they got their mitts on someone dumber.

I circled the Main Man with the beer outstretched, cooing, "Come on, boy, take a drink," but my heart wasn't in it. If Prohibition was rolled back, the city would be flooded with spinster-made milk-beer, and the male of the species would pass into the history books.

But if it didn't pass, I wouldn't get ten steps out of the cage before the bulls plugged me. I was double-damned either way.

The Main Man gave me a tentative love tap and knocked half my teeth out. I staggered into the bars and he caught me in a clinch. "Gotta make this look good," he rumbled into my chest, and shot himself a quick uppercut to the jaw, splitting his lip.

"You want this? You want it?"

The Main man's eyes were so clear, you could see the light pouring into his skull through his ears. They followed the beer like a hypnotist's rube locked on a cheap watch. He licked his lips and nodded.

I poured the beer out on the canvas. The Main Man roared and bent to lap it up. The crowd went wild. A brass band rode into the hall on a wagon.

I smashed the beer mug over the Main Man's head, and tore my shirt open. My budding C-cups runneth over.

"The beer supply's been poisoned, you dopes! Stay away from the milk-beer, if you don't want to end up like this!"

A few looked up at me. Their cat-calls and whistles made me glad I was in a cage. "Whoa, check out the zoomers on Mundy!" "Holy crap, he's a broad!"

The Main Man lunged at me and clapped his palms over my ears, and I couldn't hear anything but bells and tweeting birds. I dove, but he caught me by the ankles, slammed me into the canvas and dropped a piledriver across my throat.

He pressed in close enough for his moustache to poke me in the eye. His breath smelled like catmeat and cheap suds. "I don't want to hurt you," he growled in my ear.

"Could've fooled me," I whimpered.

"You've got to help me. You don't know what kind of a hell this is…"

"You've never been outside, have you?"

"All I ever wanted… was… to start over." the Main Man gasped and picked me up like he was going to body-slam me again, but then his lips latched onto my breast and began to suck.

Boos and howls of disgust split the room in half. Men climbed the walls of the cage, spitting and cursing. Something dropped from the roof of the cage to land on the Main Man's shoulders. Chubby little hamhock arms held an ice pick aloft to drive into the Main Man's spine. I tried to sock the baby assassin, but my depth perception wasn't up to it. Instead, I just shook my milk-makers at her, and whatever she was sent to do got washed away on a tide of Mundy-milk.

The Main Man and the greedy Barkdoll baby sucked me dry while the crowd went apeshit outside. I tried to want to try to stop them, but for the first time in my life, I felt the warm glow of doing something for somebody, of being useful. If this was what dames went around feeling all the time, no wonder they thought they were better than us. They were right.

I only wish I had enough to fill them up. The Main Man drained my left breast and gave a cheated basso yelp. He pried the baby off the other breast and cracked her overhead like a whip, flung her away to get at my other nipple. It was dry, too.

With the steroid fury of a giant, spoiled ankle-biter, he picked me up and threw me into the bars. Hands grabbed me and held me up. Drunken voices screamed, "Finish him!" in my ears. They sounded like a million miles of nowhere from where I was making out my will.

I looked into the crowd and saw a sea of howling, red-faced, self-destructive monkeys, and I thought, let them have a drink. The hell with them all. I'd done my bit before, to try to save these idiots from themselves. Better if it killed them all dead, but if they wake up tomorrow with no dicks, maybe they'd stop making so much trouble. And maybe me and the Main Man would get married and raise a family.

One of the faces in that sea of angry, drunken men wasn't screaming. Sardonic black eyebrows arched over sparkling violet eyes, but a shaggy black beard covered the rest of that face. A black kidskin glove came up holding my revolver.

The Main Man lowered his head, pawed the canvas and charged. I clung to the cage door and prayed.

The gun went off in my ear. The gate swung open on its busted lock. The Main Man leapt into the crowd.

The bulls tried to tear me limb from limb. The Main Man came out of the cage kicking bodies around like autumn leaves. I was dropped and forgotten when the news came down the hall. "Champagne! There's champagne coming out the terlets! Grab your hats and flasks, boys!"

The bearded stranger came up and saluted me with my revolver. "You stupid men have to turn everything into a war."

"You broads should talk. You got the valkyries and the nuns and babies killing their mothers—"

"Left to your own devices, you'd all kill each other, if we didn't provide a common enemy."

"There's gonna be a war. Boystown wants it. Aren't you worried?"

"Hell no. We outnumber you five to one."

"The hell you say."

"Why would I lie? We've outnumbered you for almost thirty years. We could've let the milk-beer go out and solved the problem overnight, but we liked this solution better."

"You were behind this, all along. You used me like an ashtray. You and your frigid sorority sisters cooked up those pint-sized slaughterhouses."

"Well, then, I suppose you'll have to arrest me, detective."

"Not me, sister. But I fully intend to turn you over to the first honest police officer we come across."

We walked arm in arm out onto a balcony overlooking the street. All the fire hydrants had been busted open and men and dogs lay in the gutters, drinking themselves sick.

"Ah, sweet democracy in action. Everybody's blind drunk for another Election Day. If they're hung over when they vote, they'll just vote to prohibit, again. But what about tomorrow?"

"Tomorrow, we'll knock down the Wall," she said. "And try to figure out how not to kill each other."

I grunted all the questions I couldn't fit into words at once.

"It's champagne, alright, but it's got more than bubbles in it. We cooked up a cure for the Curse from the blood of the murdered mutants." Her lovely eyes followed a bouncing ball. "At least their deaths weren't in vain."

"So, the Curse is lifted...?"

A pink trolley came barreling down the street. Some men panicked and ran, some threw rocks and bottles, but most cheered when a randy mob of women in long skirts jumped off to join the party.

"The Mother Superior's office is hotwired with cameras and microphones. After the film of you getting raped by Regina Barkdoll played on the daily newsreels, even the Spinsters were divided about whether to wipe out mankind...."

"Nobody's upset that I, uh... killed her?"

"The cameras were covered up when she tore off her dress... we thought she killed you!"

We strolled down to the garage and got into her cruiser. With Sister Horseface at the wheel, we rolled into streets carpeted in castoff hoopskirts and trousers. She fed me champagne, but it just dribbled down my shirt. I only had eyes for her, as she took off her beard.

Her mouth was wide, lips full and quirked into a hard heart shape. She slipped out of the judge's robe and began to undo the clasps and booby traps of her nun's habit.

"A woman's not just a man with his thing cut off, Floyd. A lock and a key may hate each other, but they still fit together."

"So, a woman's like a man, turned outside-in?"

She rolled her eyes. "Sure, Floyd. Or should I call you Flo?"

"Touché," I said, and looked away bashfully.

"I want to show you something, Floyd." She hiked up her skirts, revealing long, shapely legs sheathed in smoke-colored nylon stockings.

"I wish I could show you something, too, baby, but... I caught a dose of that milk-beer, and, my, uh... well, maybe it'll grow back, but, uh..."

The hem of her habit kept on going up like a theater curtain, until I saw the star of the show. There was no chastity belt in the way.

This is what remains burned into my brain: the swinging exclamation point of Sister Millie's manhood. "Holy smoking crow, Millie, all this time, how'd you hide that from the sisters?"

"I was another of the Mother Superior's experiments." She slid across the wide crushed velvet seat to thrust her eager cleaver against my thigh. "Come on, Floyd, it's not like you don't know your way around one."

True. The deepest mystery in my life was right between my own legs. "Well, I still want to lead, Mildred. Or should I call you Milton?"

The radio-telephone chirped. I ignored it, but Sister Mildred picked it up. I leaned in close enough for her stubble to tickle my cheek.

"Hey, Sister," Doc Livermint moaned, "God, I'm glad I caught you... that serum you gave me, they went and gave it to everybody... but the rabbits, they went and tore each other's throats out..."

"Do tell."

"Yeah, it works, but it's no cure-all! Maybe it's just a placebo, or maybe the virus is wired into our genes, but you gotta let 'em know it's only temporary..."

Mildred thanked him and tossed the phone out the window. I looked over at Sister Mildred and put my hand on her thigh, and started hiking north.

Only temporary...

Isn't it always?

CAMERON PIERCE

LOCATION:
Portland, OR

STYLE OF BIZARRO:
Bone Machine

BOOKS BY PIERCE:
Shark Hunting in Paradise Garden
Ass Goblins of Auschwitz
Lost in Cat Brain Land
The Pickled Apocalypse of
    Pancake Island
The Bright Lights Are Killing Me

"Pierce is one of the weirdest, most imaginative writers around." – Lloyd Kaufman

DESCRIPTION: Surreal nightmares that are funny, sad, sincere, and violent.

INTERESTS: Apocalyptic folk music, beer, bicycles, campy trash, cartoons, children's books, creation myths, Dada, death, depression, ethnobotany, existentialism, experimental cooking, fish, Italian horror films, minimalism, outsider music, pataphysics, post-punk, Romanticism, sea monsters, stop-motion animation, temporary autonomous art, toy stores, vegetarianism, walking down the street and thinking *I'm in a science fiction movie.*

INFLUENCES: Jan Svankmajer, Dr. Seuss, Russell Edson, Max Ernst, H.R. Giger, Alejandro Jodorowsky, Antonin Artaud, Charles Baudelaire, Samuel Beckett, Richard Brautigan, Brothers Quay, William S. Burroughs, Albert Camus, Kathy Acker, Hans Bellmer, Ingmar Bergman, Hieronymus Bosch, Raymond Carver, E.M. Cioran, Louis-Ferdinand Celine, Philip K. Dick, Daniel Johnston, Thomas Ligotti, H.P. Lovecraft, David Lynch, Terence McKenna, Arthur Rimbaud, Gertrude Stein, Franz Kafka, Lloyd Kaufman, and Harmony Korine.

WEBSITE:

meatmagick.wordpress.com

THE DESTROYED ROOM

I. SLOTH IN THE CITY

Simon and Celia are biking home from a dinner party on a smoky orange night in August.

A sloth falls out of a tree in front of Celia's bike. The brakes of Celia's bike have been worn down to nothing. Plus, she is drunk. She crashes into the sloth and flips over the handlebars. She rolls in a frenzy of limbs for several yards on the plastic grass that replaced streets and sidewalks last February.

Simon leaps off his bike. He kicks the sloth in the back. The animal screams. Its eyes are gone. It reaches a clawed hand toward Simon, mewling for help. Simon kicks the animal in the face, not because he wants to hurt it. It will die soon anyway.

The sloth's head splits away from its body and rolls in front of a cyclist on the green artificial speedway. The cyclist gives Simon the middle finger. Simon raises his hands in apology, then turns back to the sloth. Nose-shaped beetles are digging into its neck.

"What the fuck," Celia says. She stands beside him now. He meant to help her up, to kiss her wounds and make her feel better, but the sick animal prevented him from going to her.

"Are you okay?" he says. He puts a hand on her lower back.

"I'm fine." She crouches over the sloth, evading Simon's hand. Simon can tell by her tone that she is annoyed.

"Watch out for the beetles," he says.

"I know," she says.

"I'm sorry you crashed into a sloth."

"I used to like sloths. Now that they live in the city, I think they're pretty stupid. I wish they would send them back to the jungle. It's like we're living in a fucking zoo."

"I kind of like having exotic animals around," Simon says.

"Even the air we breathe is manufactured."

"It's better than living underwater. The oceans are dying and we couldn't ride bikes down there."

"I guess it's good that automobiles were banished to the ocean, but what does it matter if they replaced all the trees with fake plastic ones? We're living in a false city."

"At least we can ride bikes and not get hit by cars."

"No, you only crash into sloths now."

"You think you'd get used to it after six months."

"Get used to it? Get used to it? Fuck you, Simon. I will not buy into the apathy machine. Fuck you."

"You're drunk. You shouldn't have drank tonight. If our baby has fetal alcohol syndrome, I will never forgive you."

"I thought you wanted a freak."

"Can we go home?"

"Admit that the world is a cold dead place."

"The world is a cold dead place."

"You didn't say it with feeling."

"Because I'm so cold and dead that I feel nothing. Can we go home now?"

Celia crosses her arms across her chest. "Fine. Will you read me a bedtime story?"

"Yes. What do you want me to read to you?"

"Anything. I don't care."

Simon picks up his bike and stares at the decapitated sloth. The beetles move around inside its belly, making the sloth look pregnant.

"I'm sorry you crashed into a sloth."

"You said that already."

"What do you want me to read to you?"

"Gah, you decide."

"Penguin Island?"

"You decide," Celia says, as they pedal into the fractured bloom of a late summer night.

II.
TINY WHITE ELEPHANTS UNDERFOOT

Simon and Celia lock their bikes to a light post. They stand outside the door of their apartment, their fingers clasped loosely together. They hear the footfall and trumpeting of a miniature stampede within.

"Elephants again," Simon says.

"Impossible. I sprayed elephanticide this morning."

"The elephants are transcending our poisons. They are elementally evolving," Simon says in a monotone voice, but meaning it as a joke.

"This is serious, Simon," Celia says.

"It's just an infestation."

"They'll destroy everything we own."

Simon shrugs. "I don't like anything I own anyway."

"I think I'll kill them this time. I really think I'll kill them."

"We are beyond peaceful negotiations. We are beyond poison. We must squash the elephants beneath our shoes. We must boil their children in hot water spiced with cloves. We must be ruthless in the face of the intruder."

Celia unlocks the door and pushes it open. They stand side by side, staring into the darkness. Simon flips on a light. Tiny white elephants parade in a single-file line that spirals inward and outward like a vortex of pestilential cuteness.

Simon lets go of Celia's hand. He steps toward the parade of tiny elephants.

"Please don't kill them," Celia says.

"I thought you wanted them dead."

"I was just mad. I didn't mean it for real. They're only elephants. They don't know any better. Look how tiny they are."

"If we don't make a stand now, they'll never leave us alone. They'll run us out of our own fucking home."

Celia is crying now.

"There's got to be another solution," she says.

"We've tried everything. There's no other solution."

"Can't we wait until morning?"

"And let the elephants shit all over the floor and keep us up all night with their trunk music, just to kill them in the morning?"

Celia nods.

Simon looks at the tiny elephants. The tiny elephants are very cute. A while ago, Simon would have liked to keep one as a pet, but he hates them now. Celia hates them too. It makes them sad to hate tiny elephants because they used to love tiny elephants, before tiny elephants were imported to the city and infested their apartment. Simon hates the government for making him hate tiny elephants.

Simon looks away from the tiny elephants. He massages the right side of his face. He has a minor toothache. "Let's go to bed. The elephants have until morning to pack their bags."

"Do you hear that?" Celia says to the elephants. "You have until morning. Then your death bell rings."

Unlike rats, tiny elephants are not afraid of humans. They do not scramble for the dark when lights come on. They are festive creatures and might be pleasant to have around, if only they did not congregate by the hundreds or thousands and make noise all night, for tiny elephants are nocturnal.

"Still want a bedtime story?" Simon says.

Celia slips her arms around him, saying, "Yes please."

They hold each other close, and in holding each other dissolve the sandpaper feelings that rubbed them raw earlier in the day, when they argued about money. They say that money is shit, but they are in debt, accumulating more debt, and learned two weeks ago that Celia is pregnant.

"I love you," Simon says.

"I know."

"You shouldn't have drank tonight."

Celia buries her face in his chest and sighs. "Are you sure you still want to start a family with me?"

"Of course I'm sure. Are you sure?"

"Of course."

Simon kisses her forehead. She pulls away from him, kicks off her laceless red shoes, and tiptoes across the apartment, careful not to squash any elephants. She climbs into bed.

Simon unties his shoes and throws them across the room. He shuffles into the bathroom, where the elephants have unwound the entire roll of toilet paper.

Simon decides to leave the toilet paper alone. Celia usually wakes up before him. He wants her to see the toilet paper and get mad at the elephants for being messy and wasteful. Then they can kill the elephants together. Maybe they will eat one. He wonders what tiny elephants taste like. He thinks that maybe he should be more concerned about the baby and less concerned about the taste of tiny elephants.

He opens the medicine cabinet and picks up his toothbrush. He squeezes a cashew-sized glob of glittering blue paste onto the frayed bristles, closes the medicine cabinet, and sticks the brush into his mouth without wetting the bristles. He stands in the bathroom doorway. While brushing he says, "Will I make a good father?"

Celia lies facedown in the pillows. The sunflower-patterned sheet is pulled up to her waist. She has taken off her shirt. Her back is a pale honeydew rind, bereft of distinguishing marks, like a desert without cacti or rocks. Her breathing is slow and heavy. She has fallen asleep.

Simon spits toothpaste foam into the sink and rinses his mouth. He swallows two aspirin for the minor toothache.

He crawls into bed after turning off all the lights except the bedside lamp. He gets under the sheet and picks up the book on the nightstand. It is a copy of The Little Prince in the original French. Although he understands almost none of it, Simon begins reading aloud from the book.

After a while, he closes the book and turns off the lamp. He curls around Celia's sleeping form, wondering if fetuses get lonely, or if loneliness only comes on after the body grows larger than a crumb.

III.
FIRST LIGHT

Simon dreams that he and Celia are stapling bacon to the cardboard walls of a cathedral without doors or windows. They have coated the entire exterior of the cathedral in bacon when a yellow crow falls of out the sky and begs them, as its dying wish, to go inside the cathedral and sit very quietly. "But how can we go inside if there are no windows or doors?" Celia asks the yellow crow, who weeps profusely for it has been shot through the heart. "Ask forgiveness," the crow says, then Simon wakes up. It is an unsettling dream, not the least because he and Celia do not eat bacon, nor any other meat.

She has turned away from him in her sleep. They each take up one side of the bed, leaving the middle cold. They used to joke that they became one person as they slept. They used to sleep closer together. Now they sleep far apart, while tiny elephants cuddle on the floor around their bed.

He slides across the void of bed to spoon her. She stirs a little, pushing into him, murmuring, "Good morning." "Did you have good dreams?"

"A sad one. We were in a funeral home, trying to swallow green pills because we had died and one of us was being forced to go away. The green pills were supposed to make us inseparable, but the pills were as large as ostrich eggs. We couldn't choke them down. It made me sad. Did you have a good dream?"

"We were outside a cathedral,

doing something with bacon. I forget what."

He never remembers his dreams for long.

He moves his left hand over her hip, up the side of her body, across her chest, and down her belly.

Her belly, where the baby is.

"What the fuck," he says. "The blanket is squeezing my hand."

He throws the blankets off. Three powder blue strings protrude from Celia's bellybutton. They are as thin and transparent as fishing line.

The strings go taut.

He waves his hands back and forth. His hand passes through the strings without getting tangled or affecting them in any way, as if they possess no physical substance, like holograms. But when he makes to grab them, closing his hand into a fist, the strings feel solid in his grip. They feel cold and rubbery, like mozzarella cheese.

"What's wrong?" Celia says.

He looks at her face. The strings jutting from her belly are not the only strings. Strings come out of her hands, shoulders, feet, face, and other places.

"What's happened to you?" he says.

"Nothing," she says, wearing a panicked facial expression. "What's wrong with you?"

As she speaks, her strings move in sync with her words and gestures. Celia and the strings act in such accordance that Simon cannot tell whether she is controlling them or they are controlling her.

"There are strings coming out of you," he says. "Strings in your hands, feet, face . . . even strings coming from your belly. You must see them."

"What the fuck are you talking about? Is this a joke?"

Simon puts his hands on her shoulders and looks her straight in the eye so she knows he is serious. He speaks in a level voice. "This is not a joke. There are strings coming out of you. I don't know why you can't see them, but they're there."

She shakes her head and laughs. "I always knew you were a little crazy, but strings? Really, Simon?"

As she speaks, her body shifts like a marionette controlled by a trembling puppeteer. He imagines the strings weaving through her guts and muscles. He cannot touch her after thinking this. The strings repulse him. It is as if she is infected with a dangerous parasite. Despite his revulsion, he feels compelled to save her from these strings that are invisible to her.

"Let me cut your strings," he says, averting his eyes.

"I'm going back to bed." Celia turns her back to him and lays down. She pulls the blankets over her head. Her blue strings cut right through the blanket.

Simon tries to stay calm. He doesn't want to freak out. He feels irritated with Celia. He knows that it's irrational and that he had better stop before things escalate into a fight, but he cannot help thinking that it is her fault for not seeing the strings.

"Hold me," she says, in a half-asleep stupor.

Simon gets under the covers, but he cannot touch her.

"Let me cut your strings," he says.

"Go for it," she says.

"Do you want me to cut them with scissors, or just use my hands?"

"I don't care. Do what you feel like."

"Which do you prefer?"

"Dammit, Simon."

"Well which?"

"Hands. I don't know."

"OK, let me know if it hurts." He reaches for the belly strings first because they are the smallest, but Celia is lying at an angle where Simon cannot reach them.

"Can you move?" he says.

She rolls over, grumbling about what an asshole he is.

Simon grabs the three belly strings in his hand and jerks on all three at once. They go slack and slide out of her belly, unbloodied, damaging her in no discernible way.

"Did you pull out my strings?" Celia says.

"Be quiet. I'm waiting to see what happens."

Nothing happens for another minute, then the strings blacken and wither. They slip out of his hand and retract into the ceiling like vines.

"Do you feel any different?" he says.

"I feel exactly the same, which is annoyed and tired."

"Sorry. I'll be done soon."

"Can't you be done now?"

"Celia, there are strings coming out of your body. I don't give a fuck if you can't see them. I want them gone. Maybe they're a new breed of insect, or probes."

Simon collects all of Celia's remaining strings in one fist, thinking again of cheese. He will pull them out all at once.

"I'm going to pull all of your strings on three, OK?" He knows telling her this will annoy her, but since it is her body they are dealing with, he thinks he should at least keep her informed. "One . . . two . . . three."

He pulls the strings.

He slides a hand under the covers as the strings go slack and dark. He strokes her lower back. "All done," he says. "Thank you for being patient with me." Celia offers no response. Simon feels sick. "Celia? I'm sorry. Please say something."

Her deteriorating strings leave a sulfuric odor in the air.

She must be really pissed to ignore him like this. He knows it is better to leave her alone. After sleeping for a few more hours she will not be mad, but Simon cannot stand letting bad feelings simmer between them, even though Celia says bad feelings are sometimes necessary.

He tries tickling her. She remains still. "Celia." Frustrated by her unresponsiveness, but also growing concerned, Simon shakes her shoulder. "Celia." She does not move. "Celia!"

There is no question now. Celia is not breathing.

Pulling out her strings has rendered her unconscious.

And the baby, the baby. What about the baby?

Not knowing CPR, Simon leaps out of bed. He slips in elephant shit twice, banging his knees and elbows, before he reaches the phone on the wall.

Simon and Celia thought it would be charming to have an old-fashioned telephone. Now, as Simon struggles to pick up a dial tone on the antiquated machine, the receiver feels like a stone wheel in his hands.

Finally, the dial tone buzzes through and he punches in the emergency number. He wonders what he will say. That he has killed his wife and unborn child by ripping out the strings that tethered them to life?

"What is your emergency?"

"My pregnant wife is unconscious."

"How long has she been unconscious?"

"A few minutes I think."

"What is your location?"

"Seven-One-Seven Golden Oak Drive."

"An emergency dispatch will—"

"An emergency dispatch will what? Will be here shortly? Answer me!"

He looks at the phone, hesitant to hang up, but there is a blue string running out of his right hand, and he drops the phone.

IV.
AMBULANCE PEOPLE

Fifteen minutes later, an ambulance pulls to the curb outside the apartment. Simon opens the door. Two ambulance men dressed in gray uniforms and carrying a stretcher between them hop out of the ambulance and hurry into the apartment. One of the men has curly red hair and looks to be about Simon's age. The other man has a white handlebar mustache. The ambulance men have strings identical to Celia's strings, minus the belly strings. Simon decides to ignore the strings so the ambulance men can focus on Celia. He doesn't want to cause a scene.

The men place the stretcher next to Celia on the bed and set to work checking her vital signs.

"No pulse," the mustached one says.

"No temperature," says the one with red hair.

"Even if she's dead, she should

still have a temperature."

"Well it's obviously the temperature of a dead person, so it may as well be none at all."

"Standard procedure, Dan," says the mustached one. "Temperature is protocol." He turns to Simon. "Really sorry about the attitude. He's new to the ambulance squad."

The men roll Celia onto the stretcher.

"Is she OK?" Simon asks.

"For a dead woman," Dan says.

"Oh shut up," says the mustached one. "I'm sorry to report, sir, this woman here is beyond retrieval."

"Beyond retrieval?"

"It means there's nothing we can do to bring her back."

"She's gone, chap," Dan says. "Left you for a Mister Rigor Mortis."

"What did I just tell you?" the mustached one says.

"You said she's beyond retrieval."

"Of course she is, but no! I told you to shut up. Now shut up and lift." And to Simon: "Again, I'm terribly sorry for his behavior."

The men lift the stretcher and move toward the door.

"Hold on a minute." Simon hurries in front of them, blocking their exit. "Where are you taking her?"

"Trying to keep her around for some after-hours fun, eh?" Dan says.

"Idiot!" says the mustached one. "I'll be back in a moment to discuss the paperwork."

"Paperwork?" Simon says.

"Death papers, funeral forms, a load of bollocks if you ask me," Dan says.

"Nobody asked you," says the mustached one.

The ambulance men push past Simon, balancing the stretcher between them. They load Celia into the back of the ambulance and hop in after her.

The emergency siren howls.

Simon thinks they are about to drive off, having practically abducted Celia from the apartment, when the mustached one hops out of the ambulance, holding a thick stack of papers in his hands. The mustached one yells something to Simon, but his words are drowned by the siren.

They go inside and the mustached one says, "Take a seat."

Simon sits at the table. The mustached one lays the stack of papers in front of him. He puts a pen in Simon's hand and says, "Sign here, please."

"Sign where?" Simon says.

"Anywhere. I just meant sign the forms. It doesn't matter where you sign, or what order you sign them in, but all these forms do have to be signed."

"What are they for?"

"Records and Information. Tax men. Telemarketers. Local, state, and federal governments. The green forms contain information about the funeral. They certify that you trust the hospital to make all funeral arrangements. One of those forms is an Agreement of Notification. The hospital agrees to notify all immediate family members of the deceased. Were you her spouse?"

"Yes."

"The hospital will not contact your side of the family. They leave that up to you."

"OK."

"And friends. Should friends be attending the funeral, you will need to notify them in advance. Johnston Funeral Services handles all of our funeral affairs. Anyone who is not a member of the immediate family of the deceased must contact JFS and RSVP if they are to attend the funeral."

"Do I need to . . . RSVP?"

"No. Spouses are considered immediate family."

"Is there anything I can do? Anything I should be doing?"

"Sign these papers. Beyond that, you're off the hook. Call people, if you'd like. We have a grieving hotline, if you need. The hospital, or JFS on our behalf, will contact you soon with the date and time at which the funeral is to be held. I'm very sorry for your loss."

"Can I—"

"Can you hurry up signing the paperwork? Your wife is not the only person dead or dying today. We've got at least a dozen emergency stops after this one."

Simon signs the papers faster. His hand is beginning to cramp. Outside, the ambulance siren continues to wail. "I'm sorry. It's just—"

"I know. Hard. I'm sorry, again, for your loss."

After the final form is signed, the mustached one collects the stack of paperwork under his left arm. "The hospital will be in touch," he says. He salutes Simon and marches out of the apartment.

V.
SEVEN PIECES OF ELECTRICAL TAPE, PLUS ONE DEAD ARM

After the ambulance goes, Simon finds a pair of scissors. They are left-handed scissors because Celia was left-handed. The scissors feel awkward in his right hand, but he is right-handed and prefers the awkward feeling of using left-handed scissors with his right hand to the awkward feeling of using any scissors with his left hand.

He cuts the string attached to his left hand. It hurts very badly. He screams. His left arm falls limp at his side. He drops the scissors. He can no longer move his left arm.

Simon curls up in a little ball on the floor. He screams into the Persian rug. The rug is stained and smeared with elephant shit. He does not care. He is in severe pain. His left arm is immobile. He has killed Celia. He has killed their unborn child. He feels destroyed. Worse, he feels guilty.

Simon picks up the scissors in his right hand. He will kill himself.

He realizes that he cannot cut the string attached to his right hand if he is holding the scissors in his right hand. He can cut all the other strings if he wants, but he fears that if he cuts all the strings except the string attached to his right hand, his spirit or whatever will be absorbed by his right arm and he will live the rest of his days as a right arm. Simon does not want to live the rest of his days as a right arm.

Out of frustration and a sense that he has reached his grieving limit, he throws the scissors against the wall.

Unlike Celia's strings, his severed string does not disintegrate or retract into the ceiling. It floats about a foot above his head.

He gets up off the floor. He has resolved to make something work. He finds some thread and needle in a drawer. He will sew his broken string back to his left hand. No he won't. He cannot thread the needle with only one hand. He does not possess that skill.

In the same drawer where he found the thread and needle, he finds a roll of electrical tape. He peels the tape back and clenches it between his teeth. He holds the tape roll in his right hand, unwinding it in a slow and cautious manner. When his arm can reach no further, he drops the tape roll and unsticks the tape from his teeth and lips.

He sticks one tape end against the back of a chair, retrieves the scissors from where they landed, and cuts off the other end. Simon repeats this six more times. It is a tedious process but eventually he has seven pieces of electrical tape that are as long as his arm.

He grabs the severed end of his string and encounters another dilemma. He cannot hold the string in place and also tape the string with only his right hand, and no matter how he strains his neck, his mouth is too far away from his left hand to perform either task.

Simon feels doomed. Today's events have distorted his mind. In his sadness and confusion, he feels bad about wasting electrical tape. He does not want the seven pieces of electrical tape to go to waste, so he tapes his left arm to his side. At least then he can pretend that he is not using his left arm by choice. It is much better to choose what you do, even if you hate doing it.

Simon sits down on the rug, still indifferent to the elephant shit. Celia will never live here again. Her organs will be passed on to other people. Her body will be donated to science. Should I move out of the apartment or keep on by myself, he wonders. The news of her death will destroy everyone.

VI.
FIRST FEW
DESPERATE HOURS

On the morning of the funeral, Simon wakes up and puts on a pot of coffee. He lays two slices of whole wheat bread in the toaster oven.

He dresses in his grandfather's grey suit. He would wear something black, but he doesn't own anything black, nor any other suits. The left arm of the suit jacket hangs limp and hollow at his side.

In the bathroom, he brushes his teeth and combs his hair. He stares into the mirror above the sink while he does these things. He does not really see himself in the mirror. He only sees his strings.

The toast is burning. He can smell it. Celia's funeral is in three hours, but at the moment, burnt toast is his reality. I am expected to cry, he thinks.

In the kitchen, he turns off the toaster oven. He slides the charred toast onto a green plate, careful not to scorch his fingers. He pours a cup of coffee and sits down at the table with his black toast.

The toast crumbles like ashen logs in his mouth.

The coffee burns his tongue.

Company might be nice. He'd even welcome the tiny elephants, but the tiny elephants are gone. They sleep in the walls in the day.

He shuffles around the apartment, terrified that he will fail to occupy the hours remaining before the funeral. He wipes crumbs from the corners of his mouth and stares at the books on the shelves, anything to avoid looking at his strings.

He takes down Keats' Complete Poems.

Keats was Celia's favorite poet.

He sits down again and opens the book to a page marked by a coupon for dog food. The coupon must have been there since before Ferdinand and Fernando died. That was what? Three, four years ago?

The dogs were born of the same litter, and they died by the same rifle, fired by the same neighbor on the same day. Said the dogs threatened his goats. Simon and Celia loved their tent cabin, tucked away in the forest on the coast north of the city, but they decided to move after the death of Ferdinand and Fernando. Maybe they would have stayed on if only one of the dogs had died, or even both, if a mountain lion or bear killed them instead. Maybe, if they stayed, Simon would have never seen the strings. He folds the dog food coupon into his breast pocket and tells himself to forget the maybes.

The pages are blank because this is a talking book. In order to be read, the book must be wound like a music box.

After he winds the book, the pages melt, then rise and fold together in the shape of a human head. The visage is that of the dead poet. The paper Keats opens his mouth and begins reading from Part Two of Hyperion. Simon is not surprised that Celia kept this page marked for so long. Hyperion was her favorite poem. Face to face with the talking paper head, Simon has to turn away. Keats' breath smells of mildew and rust, probably due to water damage. The poet's croaking voice emanates from trembling, yellowed lips:

Just as the self-same beat of
Time's wide wings,
Hyperion slid into the rustled air
And Saturn gained with Thea

that sad place
Where Cybele and the bruised
Titans mourned.
It was a den where no insulting
light
Could glimmer on their tears;
where their own groans
They felt, but heard not, for the
solid roar
Of thunderous waterfalls and
torrents hoarse, torrents
hoarse—

The book spits up blood. A major problem with talking books is that as they get older, they assume the infirmities their human creators possessed in life. Celia's copy of Keats' Complete Poems has grown tubercular. Simon wipes the blood off the lips. It feels like blood, but when he looks at his fingers, he sees liquid words. He rubs his fingers together, smearing the words into a blob. He shakes the book. It sputters and fast-forwards through a few lines before continuing in its normal mechanical voice:

Forehead to forehead held their
monstrous horns;
And thus in thousand hugest
fantasies
Made a fit roofing to this nest
of woe.
Instead of thrones, hard flint they
sat upon,

The book spits up blood again.

Some chained in torture, and
some wandering.
Dungeoned in opaque element,
to keep
Their clenched teeth still
clenched, and all their limbs

Locked up like veins of metal,
 cramped and screwed;
Without a motion, save of their
 big hearts
Heaving in pain, and horribly
 convulsedconvulsedconv-
 ulsedconvulsedconvulse-
 dconvulsedconvulsed—

Simon rips Keats' paper head out of the book. He tears the head apart in his right hand. He wanted nothing more than to hear these words that filled Celia's heart and mind and spirit like balloon animals, but the book is a malfunctioning piece of shit.

As the words leak out of the destroyed paper head, tiny blue strings, so nearly invisible that he failed to notice them before, blacken and fall away from the book.

VII.
CATERPILLAR BUS

Simon prepares to leave the apartment for the funeral. He does not care that he will arrive early. He cannot remain where he is. He simply cannot stand his own company in this space of so many memories. He cannot stand knowing that the book was alive. It was Celia's favorite and he killed it. He loosens his tie. Maybe he's just anxious about the funeral.

On his way out, he slams the door on a hideous noise.

He spins around.

A tiny elephant's trunk has been crushed in the door.

He was not prepared for that.

Hands shaking, he fumbles with the door key. He finally manages to turn the key in the bottom lock. He opens the door.

The tiny elephant's trunk has been severed completely. The tiny elephant lies on its side, bleeding to death, choking.

Simon takes off his suit jacket and wraps the tiny elephant in it. He failed to notice the creature on his way out. It must have tried to follow or squeeze out behind him. He sits on the floor in the doorway, cradling the elephant in his right arm.

The elephant dies. Its strings dissolve, floating off in wispy flakes. Simon holds his breath so as not to breathe them in.

He shakes the elephant out of the jacket, onto the floor. Blood has seeped through the jacket. Blood stains his pants and shirt.

He moves the elephant's severed trunk with his foot until the elephant and the severed trunk lie side by side. They look like two sleeping creatures. If not for all the blood, they would look peaceful.

Feeling disgraceful, Simon puts on his jacket and leaves the apartment, careful not to smash any elephants on his way out.

He is concerned about riding a bicycle with only one arm. Even if he removes the electrical tape, his left arm will not function, so he leaves the arm taped, the left sleeve of the grey and bloody jacket unfilled.

When the hospital called with the date and time of the funeral, they also gave him directions and an address. He takes the piece of paper he'd written these things on out of his pocket. He looks it over. Although the funeral home is only three miles away, Simon has never visited the city sector where it is located.

He gets on his bike. He pedals down the street, right hand on the handlebars and then no hands. This is the first time he has left the apartment since Celia's death. He realizes how hard this is going to be.

He failed to consider how seeing strings might affect his getting around. Biking one-armed isn't even the hard part. There are so many things alive in the world, so many strings crossing other strings. He feels as if he is riding into a citywide spider web. The blue strings of people, birds, sloths, elephants, badgers, and other city dwellers thread the streets and sky, connecting the invisible dots of the psychogeographic landscape that maps every impulse, routine, pressure, and pleasure of the city's circuitry.

An eagle swoops down. It is tiger-eyed, its talons outstretched. A tiny elephant stumbles into Simon's path. The eagle's strings coil around the elephant's strings as the eagle swoops down. Unable to swerve out of the way, Simon crashes his bike out of fear that his strings will crisscross those of the predator and its prey.

He sits up, strawberry patches for elbows and knees, as the eagle lifts the elephant toward the sun.

He must hurry to the funeral. He is no longer due to arrive early. He picks up his bicycle and wheels it along beside him.

He steps in a gutter full of water and says, "Fucking hell."

He contemplates running into the street and pulling all his strings. Why wait to die. He figures he'd better wait until after the funeral. Touching Celia's coffin is the closest he'll ever get to holding her again, unless there's a Heaven and they both get to go there.

Maybe they'll reincarnate as slugs. They will rejoice, reliving the love and happiness of their human days, only slimier.

A caterpillar bus turns onto the street. Simon has always been afraid of caterpillar buses. He has never been good at riding with other people, let alone a few dozen strangers all at once.

The conductor of the caterpillar bus yells at the passengers to slow down. "Where you heading?" he calls to Simon.

"I'm going to the funeral home," Simon says.

A few people shout for him to go away. The conductor tells them to knock it off. He turns to Simon. "That's a steep climb. What are you willing to pay?"

Simon reaches into his pocket for his wallet. He removes a wad of bills from his wallet and hands the bills to the conductor, feeling glad that he always carries his money around despite the many times he has been called old-fashioned for doing so. Unfortunately, he is now totally broke. The conductor counts the money and nods. "Climb aboard," he says.

Climbing is not actually necessary to board the caterpillar bus. It is a huge metal caterpillar with bicycles instead of legs. The passengers pedal to operate a hydrogen engine located in the head. When the caterpillar bus moves fast enough, the hydrogen engine forms bubbles. The bubbles float out of a brass smoking pipe welded between the caterpillar's lips.

Simon secures his bike just behind the caterpillar's head, upon which the conductor sits behind an enormous steering wheel. The conductor shouts for everyone to pedal. Simon and the rest of the passengers begin to pedal. Since there are not many passengers, the caterpillar bus is very wobbly, like it is missing most of its legs.

As they pick up speed, bubbles float out of the caterpillar's brass pipe, but the momentum quickly dies. There are not enough passengers to propel the caterpillar bus to go any faster. At this slow pace, Simon would have almost been better off walking. Fortunately, the conductor does all the steering.

"We were moving along quite well before you came along," a person behind him shouts.

"That funeral better be for someone important," shouts another.

"It's for my wife," Simon shouts.

"He says it's for his wife!"

"His wife? He's riding a bicycle to his wife's funeral?"

"What a disgrace!"

"An imbecile."

"He's a slow rider too."

"Making us ride all the way up the damned mountain."

"And filthy. Take a look at his clothes."

"I'd looked forward to this ride."

"The funeral boy has ruined it for us all."

"A disgrace."

The passengers of the caterpillar bus continue to berate him as they teeter out of the city and through a forest of plastic trees. They ascend a narrow mountain road so steep that Simon must hook his chin over his handlebars to prevent from falling backwards.

When the caterpillar bus halts to let him off, Simon realizes that all the other passengers have tumbled off their bikes. The caterpillar bus must contain reserves of hydrogen or some other fuel source. Simon thinks this is illegal but says nothing. He could never have propelled the bus up the mountain by himself.

"It's not much further," the conductor says.

Simon detaches his bike from the caterpillar bus and thanks the man. He continues on foot, thankful that the road has leveled off, as the caterpillar bus turns around and begins its slow crawl down the mountain.

VIII.
THE FUNERAL

A sign on the side of the road proclaims WELCOME TO JOHNSTON FUNERAL SERVICES. An empty parking lot overtaken by plastic blackberry bushes comes into view. Beyond the field of bushes, a glass dome sparkles in the hot afternoon sun. Skinny blue strings protrude from the glass walls. The strings sway in a light breeze. Simon follows them with his eyes, but the sunlight obscures their endpoints. For all he knows, they continue into outer space, and perhaps even further.

Simon locks his bike to a FUNERAL PARKING ONLY sign and approaches the glass dome.

A path cut in the blackberry bushes leads up to the dome. The path is overgrown. He is cut by plastic thorns.

Simon remembers when he and Celia went to Newport Beach and the same jellyfish stung them both. At the memory, his mouth creases into a smile, sadness filling him like sand. That was their first vacation together. The weather was miserable, the motel had cockroaches and moldy sheets, and they got stung by a jellyfish, yet they had the most beautiful time together.

He approaches the doorway cut into the glass dome. The dome seems fancy for a funeral home. The strings rising through it belong to trees. Real trees.

Amidst the tree strings, there are smaller strings attached to the fruit that hangs from branches. Simon has not seen a fruit tree in almost a full year. He doesn't recognize the purplish fruit growing on the trees. He thinks they are plums.

He follows a cluster of larger strings down to the person they are attached to. She is a skeletal old woman swathed in vibrant greens, yellows, and reds. She is not frightening to look at, nor is she pretty.

"Excuse me," he says, rapping lightly on the glass.

The old woman looks up. Her lips have been eaten away by something black. Simon casts his eyes to his shoes. "I'm here for the funeral."

The pressure behind his face swells. He closes his eyes, afraid his eyeballs will pop out. His knees buckle. He steps inside the glass dome and leans against the wall for support.

The old woman limps toward him. She stops to pick some fruit off of a tree. When she gets close enough, she hands him a piece of fruit.

"What is it?" says Simon.

"Pluot."

"Thank you."

"It's good."

Simon looks at the smooth-fleshed, purple fruit. It fits perfectly in his right palm. As he holds the fruit, the blue string coiled around the stem disintegrates.

"Eat it," the old woman says. "It's good."

Simon takes a bite. He chews slowly. He doesn't know why he received this gift. He only accepted it to be kind. He has never tasted a sweeter, juicier pluot.

"The ceremony is about to begin," the old woman says. "You can follow me over there."

"Are you the groundskeeper?"

"I'm the accountant."

"The accountant?"

"I settle the books of the dead. These days I bury the bodies and keep JFS running, what with budget cuts and layoffs they've even released the gardener, but officially, I'm just the accountant."

"Is anyone else here . . . for Celia?" Simon asks.

"No one yet."

"Maybe they're running late," Simon says.

"Did you expect anyone?"

"No one in particular."

The accountant shakes her head sadly. "No one ever shows up late to these."

The mustached one said the hospital would send a notice of death to everyone in Celia's immediate family. However, Celia had been estranged from her family since before Simon met her. He has never even met her parents.

He intended to call his and Celia's friends, and also his family.

He failed to call anyone.

The accountant walks past him out of the glass dome and says, "Follow me."

"Where are we going?" Simon says.

He cannot feels his limbs. He thinks he must be going into shock. He's out of breath. He cannot breathe. He stares up at the glass dome pixilated by tears. A plane screams high above.

"We don't do funerals in the garden. Come around to the parlor."

"OK," Simon says.

The accountant bustles away. Although she is barefoot, she walks at a fast clip. The patchwork fabric of her dress billows around her like a carnival tilt-a-whirl. Simon has to jog to stay by her side.

The accountant's presence calms him a little bit, but uncertainty and shame gnaw at him. Uncertainty about the nature and regiment of funeral affairs. Shame over the absence of mourners, the absence of flowers. He failed to bring flowers.

"Do people still bring flowers to funerals?" he asks. "I know from reading articles that it used to be traditional, but what's the tradition now? I've never been to a funeral. I don't know what's expected. Are flowers normal? Am I doing something wrong?"

The accountant tilts her head and stares at him. Her eyes are cold and mean. Her blackened maw cracks into a smile.

They walk along a trail of stones that curves around the glass dome and zigzags through the fields beyond up to a trailer overtaken by flowering vines. The vines are blue and Simon initially mistakes them for strings.

"These vines are fake," he says. He knows this because the vines do not possess strings. He has learned that living things have strings attached.

"No, they're not," the accountant says.

The accountant pulls a set of keys from beneath her dress and unlocks the door of the trailer. They go inside.

The trailer is the standard classroom type. Cheap variegated carpet on the floors, burlap curtains over the windows, pastel butcher paper stapled to the walls to hide the structural cheerlessness, and a sputtering heating/cooling unit in the corner. Simon has not set foot in one of these since his school days. Rows of black foldout chairs fill most of the room. In front, a podium and a coffin rest on a plywood riser.

"Take a seat," the accountant says, approaching the podium.

"Is Celia in the coffin?" Simon says.

"It's her funeral, isn't it?" The accountant does not pause or turn around to respond.

"Can I look?"

"Look later."

Simon chooses a seat in the first row, center. He pictures every chair in the trailer occupied, except for those in the front row because the other funeral attendees, in awe of the depth of his grief, have left the front row empty. People stand in the back, but nobody dares sit in the front row with Simon. He can almost hear the people whisper, "That man loved her," and "She loved that man," and "True love found them," and "Even now, I long for what they had," and "It's always like this."

Simon turns in his seat, first caught in his daydream and then by the empty chairs. Family and friends are not here.

The accountant clears her throat.

He faces her.

"Celia Conk is survived by her husband, Simon Conk."

He clenches his right hand in his lap.

"The records of her birth and early life are contradictory and incomplete, and are therefore unworthy of repeating. In recent years, she graduated from

Gramercy College with a Bachelors of Science in Ornithology. She was employed by the St. George Free Zoo from the month of her graduation until April of this year. At the time of her death, Celia Conk was $1,916 in debt. She had not made a payment toward nullifying her debt since her termination from St. George. Her life was presumably a happy one, albeit short."

The accountant sighs. She looks bored.

"Is that all?" Simon asks.

"Unless you have something to add."

Simon rises and approaches the coffin. He kneels beside it, presses his right hand against the lacquered lid about where he estimates Celia's face to be, and bows his head. He has never been to a funeral so maybe this is how all of them go, but it feels wrong to him. There must be something he can say.

Nothing rises. Maybe silence is best. No reason to fill her coffin with words. Words don't help the dead.

"Do you have anything more to add?" the accountant says.

Simon opens his eyes and looks at the accountant. He realizes that his face is wet. "That is all," he says.

"Since it's only the two of us, do you mind if we discuss payment here," the accountant says.

"Payment?"

"Funerals aren't free, you know."

"Is there somewhere else we can go to discuss payment? I mean—" he gestures to the coffin.

"I'm afraid I shouldn't have suggested that we have another option. My office is all the way across the property and I've got to bury yours and prepare the next body before my three o'clock appointment arrives. There's really no time."

The next body. Three o'clock appointment. These are the terms of death. Simon hates this old woman who calls herself the accountant.

She takes a black binder from the podium and steps off the plywood riser, comes and sits next to him. She opens the binder across her lap and clicks her tongue against her teeth, like a teacher attempting to show a failing student what they're doing wrong.

"Total cost is $1,916."

"How can it be that much? You hardly did anything."

"The cost of a basic funeral is the debt owed by the deceased at the time of death. Had your wife owed nothing, her funeral would be free."

"Nobody said anything about payment."

"It's in the agreement that you signed. Ignorance does not absolve responsibility."

"Will Celia's debt be cleared, or is this additional?"

"It's additional."

"Can I pay in installments?"

"There's a monthly plan, but I warn you, the interest is steep."

"Fine."

"How much would you like to pay now?"

"Can you mail the bill? I'm afraid there's nothing I can do today."

The accountant studies his suit. She has a look on her face that says she's registering the blood and sweat and mud for the first time. She seems to spend a long time studying the flopping sleeve of his suit jacket.

"You've had a bad time of this," she says. She shuts the binder and looks at her wristwatch. "If we hurry, I suppose there's time to run over to my office."

"Is there more to discuss?"

"The monthly installment form is in my office. If you take it with you, it'll save me a stamp."

"If it means that much."

"It does."

The accountant springs up from the foldout chair, knocking it to the ground as she charges for the door.

Simon picks up the fallen chair and hurries after her. He has to sprint to keep up. He feels awkward and unbalanced, hustling down the stone path with one arm taped to his side.

About a hundred yards behind the trailer, they come upon another trailer. The accountant goes inside and Simon follows. Except for a white desk, three foldout chairs, and several rusting file cabinets, the trailer is bare.

"Sit down," the accountant says.

Simon collapses in a chair and rests his forehead on the edge of the desk. He is breathless. His side aches.

The accountant opens a file cabinet and removes a green document. She sits across the desk from him, studying the document. "You have twelve months from today to pay for all funeral expenses, including interest," she says, sliding the form across the desk.

Simon sits up. He creases the form down the middle and stuffs it into his inner breast pocket.

"Anything else?"

"Give me your hand," the accountant says.

Simon places his right hand palm-up on the desk.

"The other hand."

"I can't. I taped my left arm to my side."

"Why would you do such a thing?"

"It was acting up."

"Let me look at it. Maybe I can help."

"It won't move."

The accountant comes around the desk and stops behind Simon. She puts her hands on his shoulders. "Let me look."

Simon shrugs. He is too confused to resist. Plus, maybe if he lets the accountant look at his arm, she'll take pity and reduce the amount owed for the funeral.

She removes his jacket and rolls up the left sleeve of his shirt. She tears off a piece of electrical tape. Simon flinches. Hair and skin come away with the tape, but the pain does not alert his left arm into action.

The accountant lifts his left arm and lays Simon's hand palm-up on the desk. She reaches above him, grabs the withered string that used to be attached to his left hand, and returns to her side of the desk. She opens a drawer, comes up with a little sewing kit, and removes a needle and blue thread. Simon is too shocked to get up and run out of the trailer.

"Be still and don't speak," the accountant says.

"But how can you—"

"I said shut up."

Simon obeys.

The accountant grips his left hand string between her teeth while she threads the needle. After the needle is threaded, she loops it in and out of the severed end of his left hand string.

She lowers the string to the center of his left palm.

"This might hurt, but it won't take long," she says.

She weaves the needle in and out of his palm. Every time the needle enters his hand, it feels like a tattoo gun being pushed too deep. But she's right, it doesn't take long.

As soon as his string is sewn back to his hand, she bites and ties the thread, and returns the thread and needle to the sewing kit.

Simon digs his fingers into his palm.

He can move his left arm again.

Although the funeral just ended, he suddenly feels very excited.

He leaps out of his chair and says, "You see them too."

He has so many questions for her.

"Get out," she says. "I have much work left to do. Your business here is done. If you have any questions about the monthly payment plan, Johnston Funeral Services has an automated telephone system."

"What about the strings? I have questions about the strings."

The accountant points at the door and shouts, "Get out."

"But—"

"I'll call the police."

Simon throws on his jacket and walks out the door. As he walks down the stone path, he hears some keys jangle behind him. He looks back without losing stride. The accountant is locking the door to her office. She must be scared or worried that he'll return. He shrugs and sticks his hands in his pockets. At least he has his left arm back, and also confirmation that he's not the only one who sees the strings. Maybe someday he'll meet others. Maybe they'll talk about it. Maybe he will tell the truth about Celia. Maybe he will not.

It is his, this secret of the strings, of how he killed Celia and their unborn child. It is his secret.

IX.
THE DESTROYED ROOM

Simon unlocks his bike from the FUNERAL PARKING ONLY sign. A parade of mourners crosses the parking lot. Some of the people are wheezing and keeling over. As Simon walks past the mourners, an old man who looks like a walrus points at Simon's bicycle and says, "How vulgar. How dreadfully vulgar." None of the mourners have bikes with them. Biking to a funeral must be an improper thing to do. Simon lowers his head and continues on, ashamed.

He arrives at the main road and stops, allowing the last stragglers of the funeral march to pass before mounting his bike. The mountain is far steeper than it seemed on the way up. He feels nervous about riding down, so he takes a few minutes to admire the view, which he failed to notice during his ascent.

From the entrance of Johnston Funeral Services, he has a view of the entire city far below. It appears small and trapped, a pit of civilization surrounded by a plastic forest that swallows the horizon. The tinfoil bristling of the trees around him is ugly. He wishes the breeze would stop.

He has never biked down a mountain this steep. He might hurt himself. Maybe physical pain will distract him from the other pain. Considering the last few days, he'd welcome a broken bone. A smashed skull would be sublime. He'd lick gray matter from his lips and taste Celia.

He will not crash, although he likes to fantasize what would happen if he did. He just wants to go home. When he gets home, he will clean the apartment, take a hot shower and sleeping pills, and sleep for twelve hours. Then he can start making plans for the rest of his life.

He repositions his hands on the handlebars and kicks off. There's no reason to pedal. He gains speed in no time at all. Every bump in the road vibrates through his entire body, his skinny bike absorbing none of the shock. The wind is deafening, like swallowing an ocean in each ear. He's moving faster than he feels comfortable moving. The wind stings his eyes and pries his mouth into a flapping smile. He's crying, from the wind and from grief, but also from exhilaration.

A dark shape rolls into the road, directly into Simon's path.

Simon cannot use his brakes. He's going too fast.

The dark shape stands and raises its hands above its head, urging Simon to stop. He can see it clearly now. The dark shape is a sloth.

He swerves to his right to dodge around the sloth while the sloth also moves to the right in a miscalculated attempt to avoid his bicycle. He tries to correct his move, but too late and too sharply. This could be fatal, he thinks.

He collides with the sloth.

The sloth acts more like a ramp than a road block, launching Simon off the side of the road.

The bike falls away from him. He is weightless and almost floating, then he's falling after the bike, toward the bottom of a gulch so far fucking down it may as well be bottomless. Oh fuck stop falling, he thinks. Oh fuck stop falling, is all he can think.

He claws at the air out of desperation.

And he grabs onto something.

And he stops falling.

He's hanging over the gulch by two of his own strings, suspended in midair. He grabbed the strings because they were the only thing he could touch. He should be dead right now. Instead, he swings in midair, hundreds of feet over fake trees and sharp rocks. The road is thirty feet away and maybe a hundred feet up.

How fast was he going and how high was he launched to soar thirty feet? He tries doing the math, but the numbers ooze like broken yolks across his mind. How possible or impossible his arrival to this point in time and space is irrelevant because he is here now, and he'll die if he doesn't get elsewhere.

No matter how hard he tries to hold on, he's going to fall. His arms will lose the strength to hold him up. His death has only been delayed. He is still going to die in the gulch. He is still going to die today.

He starts to climb. His strings are taut, betraying no sign that they're about to fall out of the sky.

He climbs fast. His muscles ache and his breathing is ragged, but he keeps moving. He fears that if he pauses to rest, he might never get going again. A short break might kill him.

After climbing for a while, he comes level to the road. Now he has two options. He can climb a bit higher, swing from his strings, and hopefully land on the road, or he can forget about the road and survival, just say fuck everything and climb as high as the strings and his body will allow. Neither option guarantees survival.

His body decides for him. It moves upward faster and faster, eating up strings at an incredible pace. He has no idea what to expect, so he expects nothing. He should be lying dead in the gulch. Or he and Celia should have had a child, grown old together, died together. They had talked about that, how when they got to be a certain age they would meet in a dream and leave their bodies behind. They said that's how they'd live forever, by running away. Now Simon is running away. It is not a dream; he's doing it alone.

He climbs faster. His limbs feel like burning matchsticks, but he does not dare stop. The air grows thin, hard to breathe.

The blue sky assumes a feathery texture. A chartreuse trembling gnaws at the edges. The sky is molting.

Strings crisscross everywhere.

Simon shudders with anticipation and exhaustion as he reaches an altitude where he can no longer breathe. He cannot go on, but he must. He must be close to breaking into outer space. He goes on. After a while, a square of darkness forms above. The strings are now so thick around him that he cannot see the sky. There are only the strings and the darkness above. The square of darkness must be the source of the strings.

Simon's strings begin to merge with all the rest, forming one massive blue stalk.

I'm never coming down again, he thinks.

Closer, the darkness reveals its substance.

The darkness is made of wood.

The blue stalk hangs from the dark square like the cord of a household appliance.

Finally, Simon pulls himself up onto the dark wooden square that floats in the sky. He can see the charred re-mains of walls around three sides. This was once a room. His hands are bloody leaves. The dark square has scalded his hands, but when he screams, he does not scream out of pain.

A dead, half-eaten shark lies on the wooden platform. The tail of the shark is missing. Its blackened ribs jut out from rotting folds of skin like broken cast-iron fence posts. The stalk of tangled strings vanishes into the festering, cave-like hollow of the shark's head. The strings are sprouting from the shark's brain.

The shark's mouth is clamped shut, as if it died while grinding its teeth or smiling.

He is alive, alone with the shark head in the sky.

Bizarro books

CATALOG   SPRING 2010

Bizarro Books publishes under the following imprints:

www.rawdogscreamingpress.com

www.eraserheadpress.com

www.afterbirthbooks.com

www.swallowdownpress.com

For all your Bizarro needs visit:

WWW.BIZARROCENTRAL.COM

Introduce yourselves to the bizarro genre and all of its authors with the Bizarro Starter Kit series. Each volume features short novels and short stories by ten of the leading bizarro authors, designed to give you a perfect sampling of the genre for only $5 plus shipping.

BB-0X1
"The Bizarro Starter Kit"
(Orange)

Featuring D. Harlan Wilson, Carlton Mellick III, Jeremy Robert Johnson, Kevin L Donihe, Gina Ranalli, Andre Duza, Vincent W. Sakowski, Steve Beard, John Edward Lawson, and Bruce Taylor.

236 pages $5

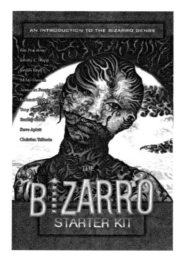

BB-0X2
"The Bizarro Starter Kit"
(Blue)

Featuring Ray Fracalossy, Jeremy C. Shipp, Jordan Krall, Mykle Hansen, Andersen Prunty, Eckhard Gerdes, Bradley Sands, Steve Aylett, Christian TeBordo, and Tony Rauch.

244 pages $5

BB-001"The Kafka Effekt" D. Harlan Wilson - A collection of forty-four irreal short stories loosely written in the vein of Franz Kafka, with more than a pinch of William S. Burroughs sprinkled on top. **211 pages $14**

BB-002 "Satan Burger" Carlton Mellick III - The cult novel that put Carlton Mellick III on the map ... Six punks get jobs at a fast food restaurant owned by the devil in a city violently overpopulated by surreal alien cultures. **236 pages $14**

BB-003 "Some Things Are Better Left Unplugged" Vincent Sakwoski - Join The Man and his Nemesis, the obese tabby, for a nightmare roller coaster ride into this postmodern fantasy. **152 pages $10**

BB-004 "Shall We Gather At the Garden?" Kevin L Donihe - Donihe's Debut novel. Midgets take over the world, The Church of Lionel Richie vs. The Church of the Byrds, plant porn and more! **244 pages $14**

BB-005 "Razor Wire Pubic Hair" Carlton Mellick III - A genderless humandildo is purchased by a razor dominatrix and brought into her nightmarish world of bizarre sex and mutilation. **176 pages $11**

BB-006 "Stranger on the Loose" D. Harlan Wilson - The fiction of Wilson's 2nd collection is planted in the soil of normalcy, but what grows out of that soil is a dark, witty, otherworldly jungle... **228 pages $14**

BB-007 "The Baby Jesus Butt Plug" Carlton Mellick III - Using clones of the Baby Jesus for anal sex will be the hip sex fetish of the future. **92 pages $10**

BB-008 "Fishyfleshed" Carlton Mellick III - The world of the past is an illogical flatland lacking in dimension and color, a sick-scape of crispy squid people wandering the desert for no apparent reason. **260 pages $14**

BB-009 **"Dead Bitch Army" Andre Duza** - Step into a world filled with racist teenagers, cannibals, 100 warped Uncle Sams, automobiles with razor-sharp teeth, living graffiti, and a pissed-off zombie bitch out for revenge. **344 pages $16**

BB-010 **"The Menstruating Mall" Carlton Mellick III** - "The Breakfast Club meets Chopping Mall as directed by David Lynch." - Brian Keene **212 pages $12**

BB-011 **"Angel Dust Apocalypse" Jeremy Robert Johnson** - Meth-heads, man-made monsters, and murderous Neo-Nazis. "Seriously amazing short stories..." - Chuck Palahniuk, author of Fight Club **184 pages $11**

BB-012 **"Ocean of Lard" Kevin L Donihe / Carlton Mellick III** - A parody of those old Choose Your Own Adventure kid's books about some very odd pirates sailing on a sea made of animal fat. **176 pages $12**

BB-013 **"Last Burn in Hell" John Edward Lawson** - From his lurid angst-affair with a lesbian music diva to his ascendance as unlikely pop icon the one constant for Kenrick Brimley, official state prison gigolo, is he's got no clue what he's doing. **172 pages $14**

BB-014 **"Tangerinephant" Kevin Dole 2** - TV-obsessed aliens have abducted Michael Tangerinephant in this bizarro combination of science fiction, satire, and surreal-ism. **164 pages $11**

BB-015 **"Foop!" Chris Genoa** - Strange happenings are going on at Dactyl, Inc, the world's first and only time travel tourism company.
"A surreal pie in the face!" - Christopher Moore **300 pages $14**

BB-016 **"Spider Pie" Alyssa Sturgill** - A one-way trip down a rabbit hole inhabited by sexual deviants and friendly monsters, fairytale beginnings and hideous endings. **104 pages $11**

BB-017 "The Unauthorized Woman" Efrem Emerson - Enter the world of the inner freak, a landscape populated by the pre-dead and morticioners, by cockroaches and 300-lb robots. **104 pages $11**

BB-018 "Fugue XXIX" Forrest Aguirre - Tales from the fringe of speculative literary fiction where innovative minds dream up the future's uncharted territories while mining forgotten treasures of the past. **220 pages $16**

BB-019 "Pocket Full of Loose Razorblades" John Edward Lawson - A collection of dark bizarro stories. From a giant rectum to a foot-fungus factory to a girl with a biforked tongue. **190 pages $13**

BB-020 "Punk Land" Carlton Mellick III - In the punk version of Heaven, the anarchist utopia is threatened by corporate fascism and only Goblin, Mortician's sperm, and a blue-mohawked female assassin named Shark Girl can stop them. **284 pages $15**

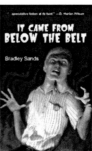

BB-021 "Pseudo-City" D. Harlan Wilson - Pseudo-City exposes what waits in the bathroom stall, under the manhole cover and in the corporate boardroom, all in a way that can only be described as mind-bogglingly irreal. **220 pages $16**

BB-022 "Kafka's Uncle and Other Strange Tales" Bruce Taylor - Anslenot and his giant tarantula (tormentor? fri-end?) wander a desecrated world in this novel and collection of stories from Mr. Magic Realism Himself. **348 pages $17**

BB-023 "Sex and Death In Television Town" Carlton Mellick III - In the old west, a gang of hermaphrodite gunslingers take refuge from a demon plague in Telos: a town where its citizens have televisions instead of heads. **184 pages $12**

BB-024 "It Came From Below The Belt" Bradley Sands - What can Grover Goldstein do when his severed, sentient penis forces him to return to high school and help it win the presidential election? **204 pages $13**

BB-025 **"Sick: An Anthology of Illness" John Lawson, editor** - These Sick stories are horrendous and hilarious dissections of creative minds on the scalpel's edge. **296 pages $16**

BB-026 **"Tempting Disaster" John Lawson, editor** - A shocking and alluring anthology from the fringe that examines our culture's obsession with taboos. **260 pages $16**

BB-027 **"Siren Promised" Jeremy Robert Johnson & Alan M Clark** - Nominated for the Bram Stoker Award. A potent mix of bad drugs, bad dreams, brutal bad guys, and surreal/incredible art by Alan M. Clark. **190 pages $13**

BB-028 **"Chemical Gardens" Gina Ranalli** - Ro and punk band Green is the Enemy find Kreepkins, a surfer-dude warlock, a vengeful demon, and a Metal Priestess in their way as they try to escape an underground nightmare. **188 pages $13**

BB-029 **"Jesus Freaks" Andre Duza** - For God so loved the world that he gave his only two begotten sons… and a few million zombies. **400 pages $16**

BB-030 **"Grape City" Kevin L. Donihe** - More Donihe-style comedic bizarro about a demon named Charles who is forced to work a minimum wage job on Earth after Hell goes out of business. **108 pages $10**

BB-031**"Sea of the Patchwork Cats" Carlton Mellick III** - A quiet dreamlike tale set in the ashes of the human race. For Mellick enthusiasts who also adore The Twilight Zone. **112 pages $10**

BB-032 **"Extinction Journals" Jeremy Robert Johnson** - An uncanny voyage across a newly nuclear America where one man must confront the problems associated with loneliness, insane dieties, radiation, love, and an ever-evolving cockroach suit with a mind of its own. **104 pages $10**

BB-033 **"Meat Puppet Cabaret" Steve Beard** - At last! The secret connection between Jack the Ripper and Princess Diana's death revealed! **240 pages $16 / $30**

BB-034 **"The Greatest Fucking Moment in Sports" Kevin L. Donihe** - In the tradition of the surreal anti-sitcom Get A Life comes a tale of triumph and agape love from the master of comedic bizarro. **108 pages $10**

BB-035 **"The Troublesome Amputee" John Edward Lawson** - Disturbing verse from a man who truly believes nothing is sacred and intends to prove it. **104 pages $9**

BB-036 **"Deity" Vic Mudd** - God (who doesn't like to be called "God") comes down to a typical, suburban, Ohio family for a little vacation—but it doesn't turn out to be as relaxing as He had hoped it would be... **168 pages $12**

BB-037 **"The Haunted Vagina" Carlton Mellick III** - It's difficult to love a woman whose vagina is a gateway to the world of the dead. **132 pages $10**

BB-038 **"Tales from the Vinegar Wasteland" Ray Fracalossy** - Witness: a man is slowly losing his face, a neighbor who periodically screams out for no apparent reason, and a house with a room that doesn't actually exist. **240 pages $14**

BB-039 **"Suicide Girls in the Afterlife" Gina Ranalli** - After Pogue commits suicide, she unexpectedly finds herself an unwilling "guest" at a hotel in the Afterlife, where she meets a group of bizarre characters, including a goth Satan, a hippie Jesus, and an alien-human hybrid. **100 pages $9**

BB-040 **"And Your Point Is?" Steve Aylett** - In this follow-up to LINT multiple authors provide critical commentary and essays about Jeff Lint's mind-bending literature. **104 pages $11**

BB-041 **"Not Quite One of the Boys" Vincent Sakowski** - While drug-dealer Maxi drinks with Dante in purgatory, God and Satan play a little tri-level chess and do a little bargaining over his business partner, Vinnie, who is still left on earth. **220 pages $14**

BB-042 **"Teeth and Tongue Landscape" Carlton Mellick III** - On a planet made out of meat, a socially-obsessive monophobic man tries to find his place amongst the strange creatures and communities that he comes across. **110 pages $10**

BB-043 **"War Slut" Carlton Mellick III** - Part "1984," part "Waiting for Godot," and part action horror video game adaptation of John Carpenter's "The Thing." **116 pages $10**

BB-044 **"All Encompassing Trip" Nicole Del Sesto** - In a world where coffee is no longer available, the only television shows are reality TV re-runs, and the animals are talking back, Nikki, Amber and a singing Coyote in a do-rag are out to restore the light **308 pages $15**

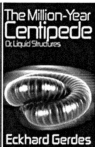

BB-045 **"Dr. Identity" D. Harlan Wilson** - Follow the Dystopian Duo on a killing spree of epic proportions through the irreal postcapitalist city of Bliptown where time ticks sideways, artificial Bug-Eyed Monsters punish citizens for consumer-capitalist lethargy, and ultraviolence is as essential as a daily multivitamin. **208 pages $15**

BB-046 **"The Million-Year Centipede" Eckhard Gerdes** - Wakelin, frontman for 'The Hinge,' wrote a poem so prophetic that to ignore it dooms a person to drown in blood. **130 pages $12**

BB-047 **"Sausagey Santa" Carlton Mellick III** - A bizarro Christmas tale featuring Santa as a piratey mutant with a body made of sausages. 124 pages $10

BB-048 **"Misadventures in a Thumbnail Universe" Vincent Sakowski** - Dive deep into the surreal and satirical realms of neo-classical Blender Fiction, filled with television shoes and flesh-filled skies. **120 pages $10**

BB-049 **"Vacation" Jeremy C. Shipp** - Blueblood Bernard Johnson leaved his boring life behind to go on The Vacation, a year-long corporate sponsored odyssey. But instead of seeing the world, Bernard is captured by terrorists, becomes a key figure in secret drug wars, and, worse, doesn't once miss his secure American Dream. **160 pages $14**

BB-051 **"13 Thorns" Gina Ranalli** - Thirteen tales of twisted, bizarro horror. **240 pages $13**

BB-050 **"Discouraging at Best" John Edward Lawson** - A collection where the absurdity of the mundane expands exponentially creating a tidal wave that sweeps reason away. For those who enjoy satire, bizarro, or a good old-fashioned slap to the senses. **208 pages $15**

BB-052 **"Better Ways of Being Dead" Christian TeBordo** - In this class, the students have to keep one palm down on the table at all times, and listen to lectures about a panda who speaks Chinese. **216 pages $14**

BB-053 **"Ballad of a Slow Poisoner" Andrew Goldfarb** Millford Mutterwurst sat down on a Tuesday to take his afternoon tea, and made the unpleasant discovery that his elbows were becoming flatter. **128 pages $10**

BB-054 **"Wall of Kiss" Gina Ranalli** - A woman... A wall... Sometimes love blooms in the strangest of places. **108 pages $9**

BB-055 **"HELP! A Bear is Eating Me" Mykle Hansen** - The bizarro, heartwarming, magical tale of poor planning, hubris and severe blood loss... **150 pages $11**

BB-056 **"Piecemeal June" Jordan Krall** - A man falls in love with a living sex doll, but with love comes danger when her creator comes after her with crab-squid assassins. **90 pages $9**

BB-057 **"Laredo" Tony Rauch** - Dreamlike, surreal stories by Tony Rauch. **180 pages $12**

BB-058 **"The Overwhelming Urge" Andersen Prunty** - A collection of bizarro tales by Andersen Prunty. **150 pages $11**

BB-059 **"Adolf in Wonderland" Carlton Mellick III** - A dreamlike adventure that takes a young descendant of Adolf Hitler's design and sends him down the rabbit hole into a world of imperfection and disorder. **180 pages $11**

BB-060 **"Super Cell Anemia" Duncan B. Barlow** - "Unrelentingly bizarre and mysterious, unsettling in all the right ways..." - Brian Evenson. **180 pages $12**

BB-061 **"Ultra Fuckers" Carlton Mellick III** - Absurdist suburban horror about a couple who enter an upper middle class gated community but can't find their way out. **108 pages $9**

BB-062 **"House of Houses" Kevin L. Donihe** - An odd man wants to marry his house. Unfortunately, all of the houses in the world collapse at the same time in the Great House Holocaust. Now he must travel to House Heaven to find his departed fiancee. **172 pages $11**

BB-063 **"Necro Sex Machine" Andre Duza** - The Dead Bitch returns in this follow-up to the bizarro zombie epic Dead Bitch Army. **400 pages $16**

BB-064 **"Squid Pulp Blues" Jordan Krall** - In these three bizarro-noir novellas, the reader is thrown into a world of murderers, drugs made from squid parts, deformed gun-toting veterans, and a mischievous apocalyptic donkey. **204 pages $12**

by Tom Bradley

BB-065 "Jack and Mr. Grin" Andersen Prunty - "When Mr. Grin calls you can hear a smile in his voice. Not a warm and friendly smile, but the kind that seizes your spine in fear. You don't need to pay your phone bill to hear it. That smile is in every line of Prunty's prose." - Tom Bradley. **208 pages $12**

BB-066 "Cybernetrix" Carlton Mellick III - What would you do if your normal everyday world was slowly mutating into the video game world from Tron? **212 pages $12**

BB-067 "Lemur" Tom Bradley - Spencer Sproul is a would-be serial-killing bus boy who can't manage to murder, injure, or even scare anybody. However, there are other ways to do damage to far more people and do it legally... **120 pages $12**

BB-068 "Cocoon of Terror" Jason Earls - Decapitated corpses...a sculpture of terror...Zelian's masterpiece, his Cocoon of Terror, will trigger a supernatural disaster for everyone on Earth. **196 pages $14**

BB-069 "Mother Puncher" Gina Ranalli - The world has become tragically over-populated and now the government strongly opposes procreation. Ed is employed by the government as a mother-puncher. He doesn't relish his job, but he knows it has to be done and he knows he's the best one to do it. **120 pages $9**

BB-070 "My Landlady the Lobotomist" Eckhard Gerdes - The brains of past tenants line the shelves of my boarding house, soaking in a mysterious elixir. One more slip-up and the landlady might just add my frontal lobe to her collection. **116 pages $12**

BB-071 "CPR for Dummies" Mickey Z. - This hilarious freakshow at the world's end is the fragmented, sobering debut novel by acclaimed nonfiction author Mickey Z. **216 pages $14**

BB-072 "Zerostrata" Andersen Prunty - Hansel Nothing lives in a tree house, suffers from memory loss, has a very eccentric family, and falls in love with a woman who runs naked through the woods every night. **144 pages $11**

BB-073 "The Egg Man" Carlton Mellick III - It is a world where humans reproduce like insects. Children are the property of corporations, and having an enormous ten-foot brain implanted into your skull is a grotesque sexual fetish. Mellick's industrial urban dystopia is one of his darkest and grittiest to date. **184 pages $11**

BB-074 "Shark Hunting in Paradise Garden" Cameron Pierce - A group of strange humanoid religious fanatics travel back in time to the Garden of Eden to discover it is invested with hundreds of giant flying maneating sharks. **150 pages $10**

BB-075 "Apeshit" Carlton Mellick III - Friday the 13th meets Visitor Q. Six hipster teens go to a cabin in the woods inhabited by a deformed killer. An incredibly fucked-up parody of B-horror movies with a bizarro slant. **192 pages $12**

BB-076 "Rampaging Fuckers of Everything on the Crazy Shitting Planet of the Vomit At smosphere" Mykle Hansen - 3 bizarro satires. Monster Cocks, Journey to the Center of Agnes Cuddlebottom, and Crazy Shitting Planet. **228 pages $12**

BB-077 "The Kissing Bug" Daniel Scott Buck - In the tradition of Roald Dahl, Tim Burton, and Edward Gorey, comes this bizarro anti-war children's story about a bohemian conenose kissing bug who falls in love with a human woman. **116 pages $10**

BB-078 "MachoPoni" Lotus Rose - It's My Little Pony... *Bizarro* style! A long time ago Poniworld was split in two. On one side of the Jagged Line is the Pastel Kingdom, a magical land of music, parties, and positivity. On the other side of the Jagged Line is Dark Kingdom inhabited by an army of undead ponies. **148 pages $11**

BB-079 "The Faggiest Vampire" Carlton Mellick III - A Roald Dahl-esque children's story about two faggy vampires who partake in a mustache competition to find out which one is truly the faggiest. **104 pages $10**

BB-080 "Sky Tongues" Gina Ranalli - The autobiography of Sky Tongues, the biracial hermaphrodite actress with tongues for fingers. Follow her strange life story as she rises from freak to fame. **204 pages $12**

BB-081 **"Washer Mouth" Kevin L. Donihe** - A washing machine becomes human and pursues his dream of meeting his favorite soap opera star. **244 pages $11**

BB-082 **"Shatnerquake" Jeff Burk** - All of the characters ever played by William Shatner are suddenly sucked into our world. Their mission: hunt down and destroy the real William Shatner. **100 pages $10**

BB-083 **"The Cannibals of Candyland" Carlton Mellick III** - There exists a race of cannibals that are made of candy. They live in an underground world made out of candy. One man has dedicated his life to killing them all. **170 pages $11**

BB-084 **"Slub Glub in the Weird World of the Weeping Willows"**
Andrew Goldfarb - The charming tale of a blue glob named Slub Glub who helps the weeping willows whose tears are flooding the earth. There are also hyenas, ghosts, and a voodoo priest **100 pages $10**

BB-085 **"Super Fetus" Adam Pepper** - Try to abort this fetus and he'll kick your ass! **104 pages $10**

BB-086 **"Fistful of Feet" Jordan Krall** - A bizarro tribute to spaghetti westerns, featuring Cthulhu-worshipping Indians, a woman with four feet, a crazed gunman who is obsessed with sucking on candy, Syphilis-ridden mutants, sexually transmitted tattoos, and a house devoted to the freakiest fetishes. **228 pages $12**

BB-087 **"Ass Goblins of Auschwitz" Cameron Pierce** - It's Monty Python meets Nazi exploitation in a surreal nightmare as can only be imagined by Bizarro author Cameron Pierce. **104 pages $10**

BB-088 **"Silent Weapons for Quiet Wars" Cody Goodfellow** - "This is high-end psychological surrealist horror meets bottom-feeding low-life crime in a techno-thrilling science fiction world full of Lovecraft and magic..." -John Skipp **212 pages $12**

BB-089 "Warrior Wolf Women of the Wasteland" Carlton Mellick III
Road Warrior Werewolves versus McDonaldland Mutants...post-apocalyptic fiction has never been quite like this. **316 pages $13**

BB-090 "Cursed" Jeremy C Shipp - The story of a group of characters who believe they are cursed and attempt to figure out who cursed them and why. A tale of stylish absurdism and suspenseful horror. **218 pages $15**

BB-091 "Super Giant Monster Time" Jeff Burk - A tribute to choose your own adventures and Godzilla movies. Will you escape the giant monsters that are rampaging the fuck out of your city and shit? Or will you join the mob of alien-controlled punk rockers causing chaos in the streets? What happens next depends on you. **188 pages $12**

BB-092 "Perfect Union" Cody Goodfellow - "Cronenberg's THE FLY on a grand scale: human/insect gene-spliced body horror, where the human hive politics are as shocking as the gore." -John Skipp. **272 pages $13**

BB-093 "Sunset with a Beard" Carlton Mellick III - 14 stories of surreal science fiction. **200 pages $12**

BB-094 "My Fake War" Andersen Prunty - The absurd tale of an unlikely soldier forced to fight a war that, quite possibly, does not exist. It's Rambo meets Waiting for Godot in this subversive satire of American values and the scope of the human imagination. **128 pages $11**

BB-095 "Lost in Cat Brain Land" Cameron Pierce - Sad stories from a surreal world. A fascist mustache, the ghost of Franz Kafka, a desert inside a dead cat. Primordial entities mourn the death of their child. The desperate serve tea to mysterious creatures. A hopeless romantic falls in love with a pterodactyl. And much more. **152 pages $11**

BB-096 "The Kobold Wizard's Dildo of Enlightenment +2" Carlton Mellick III - A Dungeons and Dragons parody about a group of people who learn they are only made up characters in an AD&D campaign and must find a way to resist their nerdy teenaged players and retarded dungeon master in order to survive. 232 **pages $12**

BB-097 "My Heart Said No, but the Camera Crew Said Yes!" Bradley Sands - A collection of short stories that are crammed with the delightfully odd and the scurrilously silly. **140 pages $13**

BB-098 "A Hundred Horrible Sorrows of Ogner Stump" Andrew Goldfarb - Goldfarb's acclaimed comic series. A magical and weird journey into the horrors of everyday life. **164 pages $11**

BB-099 "Pickled Apocalypse of Pancake Island" Cameron Pierce
A demented fairy tale about a pickle, a pancake, and the apocalypse. **102 pages $8**

BB-100 "Slag Attack" Andersen Prunty - Slag Attack features four visceral, noir stories about the living, crawling apocalypse.A slag is what survivors are calling the slug-like maggots raining from the sky, burrowing inside people, and hollowing out their flesh and their sanity. **148 pages $11**

BB-101 "Slaughterhouse High" Robert Devereaux - A place where schools are built with secret passageways, rebellious teens get zippers installed in their mouths and genitals, and once a year, on that special night, one couple is slaughtered and the bits of their bodies are kept as souvenirs. **304 pages $13**

BB-102 "The Emerald Burrito of Oz" John Skipp & Marc Levinthal
OZ IS REAL! Magic is real! The gate is really in Kansas! And America is finally allowing Earth tourists to visit this weird-ass, mysterious land. But when Gene of Los Angeles heads off for summer vacation in the Emerald City, little does he know that a war is brewing...a war that could destroy both worlds. **280 pages $13**

BB-103 "The Vegan Revolution... with Zombies" David Agranoff
When there's no more meat in hell, the vegans will walk the earth. **160 pages $11**

BB-104 "The Flappy Parts" Kevin L Donihe - Poems about bunnies, LSD, and police abuse. You know, things that matter. 132 **pages $11**

BB-105 **"Sorry I Ruined Your Orgy" Bradley Sands** - Bizarro humorist **Bradley Sands returns with one of the strangest, most hilarious collections of the year. 130 pages $11**

BB-106 **"Mr. Magic Realism" Bruce Taylor** - Like Golden Age science fiction comics written by Freud, *Mr. Magic Realism* is a strange, insightful adventure that spans the furthest reaches of the galaxy, exploring the hidden caverns in the hearts and minds of men, women, aliens, and biomechanical cats. **152 pages $11**

BB-107 **"Zombies and Shit" Carlton Mellick III** - "Battle Royale" meets "Return of the Living Dead." Mellick's bizarro tribute to the zombie genre. **308 pages $13**

BB-108 **"The Cannibal's Guide to Ethical Living" Mykle Hansen** - Over a five star French meal of fine wine, organic vegetables and human flesh, a lunatic delivers a witty, chilling, disturbingly sane argument in favor of eating the rich.. **184 pages $11**

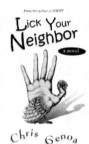
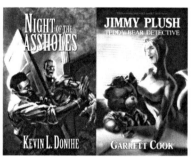

BB-109 **"Starfish Girl" Athena Villaverde** - In a post-apocalyptic underwater dome society, a girl with a starfish growing from her head and an assassin with sea anenome hair are on the run from a gang of mutant fish men. **160 pages $11**

BB-110 **"Lick Your Neighbor" Chris Genoa** - Mutant ninjas, a talking whale, kung fu masters, maniacal pilgrims, and an alcoholic clown populate Chris Genoa's surreal, darkly comical and unnerving reimagining of the first Thanksgiving. **303 pages $13**

BB-111 **"Night of the Assholes" Kevin L. Donihe** - A plague of assholes is infecting the countryside. Normal everyday people are transforming into jerks, snobs, dicks, and douchebags. And they all have only one purpose: to make your life a living hell.. **192 pages $11**

BB-112 **"Jimmy Plush, Teddy Bear Detective" Garrett Cook** - Hardboiled cases of a private detective trapped within a teddy bear body. **180 pages $11**

COMING SOON

"Homo Bomb" by Jeff burk
"Godzilla Girl" by Athena Villaverde
"Tentacle Death Trip" by Jordan Krall
"Christmas on Crack" edited by Carlton Mellick III

ORDER FORM

TITLES	QTY	PRICE	TOTAL

Please make checks and moneyorders payable to ROSE O'KEEFE / BIZARRO BOOKS in U.S. funds only. Please don't send bad checks! Allow 2-6 weeks for delivery. International orders may take longer. If you'd like to pay online via PAYPAL.COM, send payments to publisher@eraserheadpress.com.

SHIPPING: US ORDERS - $2 for the first book, $1 for each additional book. For priority shipping, add an additional $4. INT'L ORDERS - $5 for the first book, $3 for each additional book. Add an additional $5 per book for global priority shipping.

Send payment to:

BIZARRO BOOKS
  C/O Rose O'Keefe
  205 NE Bryant
  Portland, OR 97211

Address

City   State   Zip

Email   Phone

Lightning Source UK Ltd.
Milton Keynes UK
20 January 2011

166045UK00008B/119/P